BANANA
BUBBLEGUM

BANANA
BUBBLEGUM

BANANA
BUBBLEGUM

*The Second
Herman Grabfelder Mystery*

Melody Ortenburger Suppes

Library of Congress Control Number: 2016918367
ISBN: Hardcover   978-1-5245-5640-2
                   Softcover   978-1-5245-5639-6
                   eBook   978-1-5245-5638-9

Print information available on the last page.

Rev. date: 05/18/2017

To order additional copies of this book, contact:
Xlibris
1-888-795-4274
www.Xlibris.com
Orders@Xlibris.com
748798

Other Books By Melody M. Suppes

"WOMAN, DIVIDED"
A Herman Grabfelder Mystery

"THE SULTAN'S WOMAN"
A Victorian Novella

To all the Steinbauers, the Guettlers, the Ortenburgers, the Fausts, and the Suppeses, and especially Lydia Suppes

And to the man who was The Rose.

CHAPTER ONE

"Each becomes Both."

The Kama Sutra

"You don't remember me, do you?"

LAPD Homicide Detective Herman "Hermie" Grabfelder heard the man's soothing voice coming from behind him, turned to see a CHP officer who had a distinctively kind smile, starkly at odds with where they were standing, which was around a dead woman's blood-soaked body.

It was the Time of the Jacaranda, Hermie's favorite time of the year, when the brisk breath from far-off Alaska made purple-laden Jacaranda trees shiver and shed. Showers of trumpet-shaped, purple blossoms fell and skipped over the dust whorls around the polished leather boots of several other CHP officers setting up traffic control in anticipation of looky-loos, then tumbled past the worn shoes of LAPD Robbery-Homicide detectives, and finally twirled around the elaborate designs of colorful track shoes worn by the techies from the coroner's office. The trees were so heavy with blossoms, from a distance they appeared to drip purple foam. During these showy days, their scent was barely there, except to the infamous nose of Herman Grabfelder, called "the Old Bloodhound" out of his earshot.

Long before TV detectives began sniffing at corpses for clues, Hermie's nose was awed at from the time he was in Narcotics, where he bested beagles in sniffing out hidden stashes of pot, crack, ecstacy, meth-amphetamines, hashish, heroin, ganja, and various other mind-melting substances hidden inside walls, ceilings, floors, various appliances, car wheel wells, sprinkler tubes inside truck axles, shoes, boots, belt buckles, wigs and (definitely not his personal favorite) stretched-out rectums.

Old-timers still talk about the time Hermie smelled heroin on the breath of a very pregnant woman who was sober but getting sicker by the minute,

1

and it turned out that one of the condoms full of heroin her pimp made her swallow had broken and she and her unborn child were about to be poisoned. She never did get around to thanking him for saving her and her then newborn son's life, but so it goes; because she was in jail for gawd-knows how long and thus had other stuff on her addled mind.

After taking an aghast gander at her next of kin, they took her baby into protective custody and foster care, thank gawd, but from there who knows; a same-old-same-old story.

Weeks from now, when the Jacaranda blossoms rained down on sidewalks and streets and lucky lawns in a shower of purple and people complained about the "mess" and slippery sidewalks, their scent would rise from the bruised blooms and some people could smell it. But for now, only Hermie's nose could detect the scent of the Jacaranda blossoms, still elusive, like the memory of a beautiful, forever lost woman. Hermie had such a memory.

It began when he was transferred to Homicide as part of orders to quit drinking, or be fired, or die. There his nose continued to make news, most recently resulting in his arrest of the South Bay Serial Killer. Hermie was placed on that case because he'd had the FBI's serial killer training, and only he had caught that distinctive scent on the hands of Victim Number Six -— the scent of almonds made beautiful —- that would lead him to the crazed hermaphrodite who was killing the sons of the jurors who had condemned his/her serial killer father to death long ago.

What nobody knew until its own horrifying end was that at the same time Hermie was secretly trying to solve another murder case: The murder of a woman who turned out to have *three* husbands, all of whom had ripe motives for running her off that canyon road in Palos Verdes, mere hours after Hermie had fallen in love with her in the parking lot of his local saloon. But it was a *fourth* lover who had forced her car off that canyon road cliff in a fit of righteous rage; that lover was a charismatic preacher whose discovery of his secret passion's bigamy brought up cruel childhood memories that simply made him snap and do the first bad thing in his life. His horrifying suicide when Hermie came to arrest him -— he jumped through a stained glass window of the high belfry on his brand new church and was broken on the pavement below -— still caused newspaper articles to be written now and then. Although Hermie was mentioned as the one who had solved the case of who killed the female bigamist, so far no nosy reporter or anyone else around him had discovered that Hermie had solved the case because he had been secretly in love with Helen Bradford-Litton-Lawrence and nearly Turner.

There were only a few people who knew Hermie well -- and they kept this a secret from him, because "you know how he is" -- so even those few did not know that Hermie was capable of such a profound passion, a broken-hearted longing for a woman he met only once, but who so touched him with her wondrous eyes, her voice, her mystery, that discovering her secret life first disillusioned him, then became an obsession, and obsession became grim determination to get to the source of her pain as well as her murder. And all in secret because it was not his case and he was supposed to be concentrating on that South Bay Serial Killer matter.

Helen . . . she wore Joy Perfume . . . but even in the Time of the Jacaranda, her scented memory drifted by now and then, and Hermie's laser blue eyes would lift from whatever he was doing and stare off into that place where dreams go when they die.

Now, Hermie took in the tall frame, long muscles and golden tan of the CHP Officer, just as he got wind of a clean, citrus-y scent coming off him, mingling with the Jacaranda and the blood and the spoiler smell of a freshly lit cigarette from among the gathering of officers nearby. The CHP Officer's amber eyes were clearly amused as he looked at Hermie, and it was that amusement on that particular face that suddenly nudged Hermie's memory, but the nudge led to a blank.

"You're absolutely right, I don't remember you," said Hermie. "Well, not exactly." *Christ, where have I seen him before? Face, voice, smell, ringing a bell, but . . . damn!*

Hermie was beginning to have reasons to distrust his memory. He was now forty-six-and-then-some and was forgetting where he put things more often than usual, which pissed him off to the max; and when he didn't get enough sleep his eyes let him know it by blurring out in dim light.

Time was marching on in its cruel jackboots, stomping on him just like it stomped on everyone else, and Hermie resented the hell out of it, and this secret resentment had been known to feed his legendary temper. Last week, he lost his keys, found them locked inside Roberta, the retired patrol car he drove, kicked her left front tire in a fit of temper, and Roberta obliged him by exploding that tire, damned near putting his eye out with flying bits of rubber and soot. What added insult to injury was that this confrontation took place in the parking lot of his "stationette", the small police office jammed between a dry cleaners and a donut shop in a minuscule strip mall in Wilmington, so Nell Barlow, his secretary, and Claire Jennings, his Captain, saw the whole thing. And they *laughed*. Loud and long. *Dammit!*

What he kept from them were his passing thoughts that maybe this memory misfiring was a result of all those years of downing Stingers, and these couple years of being sober in clean, exercised living hadn't postponed dire things. So . . . *Was it too late?* . . . crossed his mind now and then, here and there.

"How sorry should I be?" he now asked, helpfully. And hopefully.

The CHP officer laughed easily, flashing the Los Angeles signature of remarkably white teeth, "Not sorry at all. We didn't even exchange names at the time. But I remember your sense of humor."

"Yeah, I get that all the time." It was well known by all that Hermie had an Olympic talent for sarcasm.

"Afterward, I read about you now and then. That serial killer coup -- colorful. And impressive."

"You don't know half. So, you gonna spill? I got a job to do here."

"Oh, sure, sorry for the interruption. We met at Gracie's about two years ago."

"Gracie's? That gay bar off of Overland?" In a flash of clarity and trepidation, Hermie realized the CHP was gay, they'd met during the years of his alcoholic blackouts, and Hermie wondered just how drunk and lonely he was that night. *Jeezus!*

As if he read Hermie's thoughts, the CHP's eyes crinkled up again with humor and he said, "No, you weren't *that* drunk. I wasn't your 'type'. You made that nicely clear up front. Pity. But instead, we had an interesting and memorable conversation, about love and life and the politics of fire. You're the only guy I'd every met who burned down his own house and tore up the insurance check. You don't forget a conversation like that." The CHP held out his hand. "Dane McGrady. Good to see you again. I'm off the sauce, too."

Hermie shook his warm hand and couldn't help wondering out loud, "How did you know?"

"Your eyes. You're not hiding anymore. Like me."

In a sudden rush, Hermie remembered the dim bar with the blue lights and the perfectly iced Stingers, Ella the Great singing from carefully placed speakers, and this good-looking man's gentle voice telling him about being thrown out of his family when he told them he couldn't possibly marry the girl he was dating, much to their approval, because he was gay. Mother, father, three brothers and one sister, all faithful Mormons, hadn't spoken to him since, except for Christmas cards wishing him well and assuring him that if he repented and became "normal" they'd be overjoyed to welcome him back to God and the family.

And Hermie had told him about his wife, Rachel, dead from an overdose while he was head of a Narcotics Squad, overworked, drinking, and so not paying attention. Hermie and Dane McGrady shared heartache, guilt, and a vast capacity for Stingers until the bar closed near dawn. On the sidewalk outside, they exchanged an awkward parting handshake, sincere and manly pats on the shoulders, all mercifully interrupted by a sudden rain shower, one of the few in the first years-long drought to strangle Los Angeles. Now, more years, more drought, and more experience later, they were shaking hands again and noticing how things were so different. Their handshake now lingered long enough to warm, then two smiles flashed below knowing eyes. "Good to see you're doing great." Hermie meant it.

"Thanks. I almost didn't recognize you -- what? -- thirty pounds or so?" Dane indicated Hermie's frame.

Hermie patted his slim front, "Oh, yeah. I did it the easy way -- through pain and suffering. You ever hear of the gott-dammerung going on at a place called Bud's Body Works?"

Dane laughed. "No, but apparently it works. You're a fox in your old age."

"Puhlease! I refer to these as my 'Interim Years'."

"You would. But, hey, you're about to be real busy. Good to see you and all that. By the way, I'm getting married in September."

"Married? Honest t'god?" Hermie didn't quite know what to say now.

"Yup. New civil rights run amok. He's a city attorney. Met him in the drunk tank."

"It attracts the nicest people. I oughtta know." *Married. Jeez, the times sure are a-changing.*

"If I sent you an invitation, would you come? Jason and I will be kinda lean on attendees. You know . . ."

So, the times haven't changed quite enough for this guy. "I'll be there with bells, and even a wedding present. Which should take some different kinda thought."

Dane laughed heartily, clapped him on the shoulder and turned to leave. "Thanks, Hermie. See you soon." He went to join the CHP traffic control guys, his fine, slim leather boots gleaming with each step.

Hermie felt himself sigh as he wondered again how many other people he had encountered during those boozy years would turn up with either interesting or appalling stories. He felt the worm stir, that sleeping craving deep inside that still made its presence known with its thirst, its longing for the icy, minty snap of a Stinger. He abruptly turned his attention to why he was here.

'Here' was the soft shoulder of a side street not too far from a Harbor Freeway off ramp. But it had a certain isolation, the Jacaranda-shaded neighborhood nearby did not begin for some blocks. Hermie noticed that a CHP officer was walking from the edge of the freeway and then down the off ramp with keen eyes on the littered terrain. He was carefully holding a pouched handkerchief in one hand.

This side street was flanked by a thick stand of Eucalyptus trees on the freeway side, planted long ago by Caltrans as a noise screen that half-worked: the roar of traffic rustled the trees, resulting in a confusing sound only slightly muffled and tinged with a scent like dusty Vicks Vaporub. Across the way were a couple of rare empty lots that had long ago lost the battle of litter: behind remnants of a rusted chain-link fence fluttered piles of paper trash, teetering mounds of discarded tires, and a scatter of broken bicycles, car batteries, shoes, shredded mattresses and parts of stained couches heaped here and there, like remnants of a party to end all parties.

Hermie looked around slowly, taking everything in. *Did the Perp know this was an ideal spot to kill? Or did he come here for a discussion and things got out of hand? Or was this just the dump-off place? Chances are, nobody in the neighborhood over there saw nuthin', unless someone was walking a dog.*

The breeze turned briefly and he got a whiff of dog-doo. He looked and saw dark piles here and there on dirt alongside the street and too nearby. *She must not have been here long, dog walkers would have seen her.* The yellow crime scene tape began a couple feet from the street edge, starting where the ground was soft dust. Hermie was standing at this edge and his gaze swept the length of the crime scene tape. He saw a variety of shoe prints in the dust, but no drag lines. He saw an irregular random path of holes and prints made by a woman's high heels, apparently the woman resisted walking in a straight line to her death. *She wasn't dumped, she walked. She did not go willingly but she also didn't struggle. Was she begging like mad right up to the end? Sex? Money? "Swear not to tell?" What did she offer for her life and lost?*

A man's smallish shoe prints followed hers. Mixed in were the prints of large track shoes, crisper as if the treads were new. *Three people at a killing? Odd.*

Hermie circled the tape to come in on the freeway side, climbing up and then down the dirt berm that flanked the freeway wall, enjoying the childhood memory of Vicks Vaporub as he went through that strong minty scent of the shivering Eucalyptus trees. Vicks Vaporub was everybody's staple during those icy-cold, virus-ridden and seemingly endless Michigan winters, which sometimes impulsively dumped hail and snow on a summery Fourth of July.

The CHP officer on the off-ramp noticed him and called out, "Hey, Hermie, I found something up here."

Hermie came closer but didn't go onto the off-ramp for fear of disturbing the 'something'. "Yeah?"

"Took a gander at the off-ramp and where it cut off from the freeway. A car might-a been forced off the freeway and onto this ramp. I found wavy tire tracks and glass from headlights, I'm pretty sure. We'd have to shut down the lane to photo and scoop for Ev."

"How can you be sure it's Evidence and not the usual crap on those freeway lanes?"

The CHP held up the handkerchief pouch, "Found this —- it's new glass, clean, sharp. From a headlight, probably."

"'Probably'?" Hermie said, teasing.

The CHP grinned, "Okay, 'soitainly'."

"What's your name?" *Hell, half of who I knew are gone onto better things. Like retirement.*

"Sandusky, Kyle. Pacific Station."

My old station, and I still don't know him. "Can you arrange to photo and bag that freeway lane and the ramp? Anybody give you crap, send 'em to me."

"Done and done, Hermie." And Sandusky whipped out his cell phone and punched buttons, delicately balancing the bundle within his handkerchief.

Hermie slowly came down the freeway's hill and onto the crime scene, eyes on the ground. The various people around the crime scene came to attention: *Quiet! The Old Bloodhound was zeroing in on the body.*

Hermie's sense of smell was the subject of many wagers won and lost, and the police photographers, forensic techs, CHP and a couple 'just-visiting' Robbery-Homicide detectives now stopped talking, focused on Hermie, waiting to see his nose go to work. Stories would be told over beers and swizzle sticks tonight, leaks of info would be phoned or texted to grateful and generous reporters who had yet to descend. And coroner's office forensics tech Andy Cho Hui wanted the best story to enjoy but never-ever tell, except to his Grandma because she had a weird obsession for crime as well as a fascination for Homicide Detective Grabfelder. So, he ambled forward until he was in Hermie's sightline, looking helpful.

Hermie spotted the forensic tech and recognized him because he was the tallest Asian guy he'd ever met, well over six feet of skinny, with flopping, black-satin-shiney hair constantly entangled with his futuristic-looking silver-framed glasses. "Andy, long time no etcetera." Hermie greeted him.

"Took a break for some college semesters. You go vegetarian or something?" After a hearty handshake was thought better of because he was wearing bloodied latex gloves, Andy waved at Hermie's slim frame.

"Yeah-yeah-yeah. I'm a shadow of my former self. Everybody really ought to get over it -— *I* have."

Then Andy noticed the solid muscles rounding out the shoulders and sleeves of Hermie's dark blue jacket, the hint of a six-pack lurking underneath his tucked-in pale blue shirt. *Hell, the man is buffed!* "But, Dude, you look great." *Wait'll Grandma hears this!*

"Ah, my fans . . ." sighed Hermie. "So, tell me a story. What the hell went on here? Pretend I'm your Grandma. How is she, by the way?"

"Still jogging at seventy-six. I can't keep up." Andy checked a complicated watch big as a radio strapped on his wrist, while Hermie swore internally that he would *not, NOT!* ask what the hell that was. "It's 10:15 AM, body found at 7 AM, give or take, by a gardener who was going to drop a load of clippings here –– he's a new hire, 'didn't know' he wasn't supposed to do that. Whatever. No I.D., but she's wearing a Medic Alert necklace, so we got a lead. From temp and tone, I'd say she was whacked last night, early, but don't quote me yet because morning sun's been full on her, it could have cooked her some."

"You're so picturesque."

"Oh," Andy held up a small plastic envelope, "Found some flower petals on her. Violets."

"Violets? Do they grow around here?"

"Nope. But it was Mother's Day, y'know."

"It *was*? Missed it. Why are you here instead of home with Grandma?"

"Crime never pauses. She understands. As for me, first word was that this was a doozy, so I got tempted, scrambled. Since I have no life, currently."

"Why should you be any different? Can I have the 'doozy'?"

"She was slashed with something humongously sharp and skilled."

"S'plain."

"One stab then one slice from neck to navel, getting all the blood paths. This kinda knife or machete I'd like to see."

"I'm sure we will. Crap."

Andy chuckled at the detective he enjoyed the most because you never knew with Hermie. What he'd say, what he'd do, what would make those scary laser-blue eyes flash hot enough to singe eyebrows on passers-by. You could never get up close –– nobody had the guts to get in close to this hulking brooder –– but he was still the most fascinating guy in LAPD Robbery-Homicide. Primarily because of what he was about to do: Examine a dead body with twice the perceptions, instinct and eerie horse sense of any other detective on the planet. *Like Grandma says, he's Sherlock Holmes, without the wardrobe.*

"The tape's good. Plaster and comb this entire area."

"Already mixing. Soon as you're done, we'll comb and paste before we bag her and then comb and paste where she landed."

"You know a Kyle Sandusky?"

"Very vague bell is ringing."

"CHP. Outta Pacific. He took a stroll up the ramp to the freeway, found evidence a car was forced off and down to here-by."

"No shit?"

"Shit. If he runs into miffed heads at the idea of shutting down the freeway to photo and scrape, can you or one of your warriors run interference for him?"

"Kyle Sandusky. We'll come to his rescue if miffed calls for warrants. Sharp eyes."

"And imagination. You should recruit him." Hermie turned and pointed to the street. "Perp and her came in from there, maybe out of 'that' car. A man's shoe prints, what looks like track shoes, and her heel-holes are all mixed up in that soft dirt, so pay attention, who went where."

"Already noted. Louboutin."

"Huh?"

"Her shoes. Christian Louboutin. Red soles."

"Should I be excited?"

"They can cost a thousand bucks. Maybe eight hundred at least for bare sandals like hers."

"You're kidding."

"Nope. Gotta cousin owns a shoe store, so I'm hip to this stuff. Of course, he isn't hip enough to stock Louboutins for the grocery store shoppers next door. He's discount, but I digress."

"Eight hundred. Red soles. If you stepped in gum you'd kill yourself." He turned to look at the victim's feet, to find both of them encased in plastic bags. He turned back to Andy. "You bagged 'em? Didn't want to get 'em scuffed?'

"Found something under her toes and jammed into where shoe meets sole."

"What?"

Andy grinned a challenge. "Guess."

The lasers flashed back the challenge, then Hermie walked to the feet of the body, taking care not to walk where she and possibly her perp had walked in the dirt. He pulled on latex gloves as he squatted down, knees cracking, and lifted one of the bagged feet. The shoe inside barely covered a slim, delicate foot, with maybe a four-inch heel making the foot arch prettily, hardly held by skinny straps of bright yellow leather, at odds with the bright red sole, dusty but still shining. A narrow strip of the same skinny leather barely encased toes and toenails painted a brilliant coral red. "Eight hundred bucks for four straps and a heel. Is this retail run amok or what?" Hermie muttered. Then he noticed the flecks: some were on the skinny straps, more were underneath the toes, others caught where the straps were tucked in and sewn to the sole of the shoe. He recognized them instantly. "Sawdust."

"We have a winner," Andy chuckled.

"My Grandpa owned a sawmill when I was a smooth-cheeked lad back in Bay City, Michigan." A fleeting memory of that wonderful smell of fresh wood being sliced with the shriek of the power saw, and Grandpa's pipe wafting the rich smell of Prince Albert's tobacco. *Do they still make Prince*

Albert's tobacco? Hermie's focus came back: "Of course, since then the only sawdust I see is on the floors of certain saloons."

"Exactly. There's a couple within little miles of here. Some are partly nice restaurants. Don't ask me how I know, but I've already made a list." He waved a sheet of paper, Hermie took it, tucked it into his jacket pocket.

"Good. Thanks." *So, they had drinks first. Maybe a Mother's Day dinner. Hope she was drunk enough to be numb.* Hermie turned for his first close look at the body.

Andy stilled, focused on Hermie. The whole area got quiet as *everyone* refocused on Hermie. The freeway traffic's roar became annoying, an unwanted intrusion as Homicide Detective Herman Grabfelder settled down alongside the body and went to work.

Though mute and utterly still, a dead body always spoke: *Look at the marks of outrage committed upon me. Look closer and see in those marks the signature of the monster who ended me.*

Hermie saw a woman who was not young but looked younger. Good skin in a golden olive tone sleekly covered the beautiful bones of her noble-looking face. Light lines hardly mattered around her eyes, across her forehead. Her lipstick was the exact match to the polish on her toenails, a coral red that gleamed with gloss. Her eyes were half open, their color a slate gray made darker by thick and long black eyelashes, mascaraed, casting shadows. Her shoulder-length hair was a rich ebony color, but Hermie saw the beginning: a few snow-white strands entangled within the shiny black silk.

Hermie had a fairly new habit of starting with the hands because of finding that distinctive scent on Victim Number Six's hands, the first fresh kill he'd encountered when put on the South Bay Serial Killer case. He turned these slender hands palm up and took a slow, deep sniff. All around him, elbows nudged torsos, leather holsters creaked as everyone leaned closer to watch the Old Bloodhound picking up the scent. Her hands smelled like flowery soap, so pure and alone, Hermie got the impression she'd washed her hands shortly before she died. *A fancy ladies' room in a saloon with sawdust on the floor? Weird.* He noticed two violet petals on one hand that Andy had left behind. He turned the hands over, the nails were also painted a bright coral red. They were undisturbed, clear underneath the tips — she had not clawed at her killer in a futile defense. *Why not?* She had beautiful hands, long, delicate fingers, the backs were only just revealing the age of veins underneath. She wore no rings to call attention to her beautiful hands, there were no tan lines where rings might have been. He carefully replaced the hands where they had been, alongside her hip line. A gold Medic Alert disk hung from a gold chain around her neck, in the open because the techs had spotted it and pulled it out in order to read it.

The knife wound was ghastly. It tore through her neck and down her slender frame, her simple, tasteful pale yellow suit sliced and soaked with bright blood turning darker from exposure to the breeze. The blood had spilled down both sides of her torso to pool in the dirt beneath her. A pool that held the prints of those track shoes coming alongside her. *Only the track shoe prints came that close to her, once she was down, bleeding out. Why not the other man's?* Dirt was on both legs, from knee to calf. *She was stabbed, sliced, sank to her knees, then fell over, her legs straightening as the rush of blood loss made her collapse. Her final rest was flat on her back as her body gave it up. She was so close to death when she went down, she didn't reach out her hands to break her fall. Or was she hanging onto the Perp, bleeding all over him as she fell? Track and shoe prints down by her feet, mixed in with her heel-holes. No way to tell who walked there first or after her, is there? Always complications . . . aggravations . . .*

Then Hermie saw it: The dirt around her shoulders had been disturbed, as if she'd been moved. The track shoe prints were also slightly disturbed in the pooled blood next to one of her shoulders. "Anyone around here move the body for any reason? I'm not pissed, just asking." He called out to the assembly.

Andy answered among the other "No's" coming from all around,

"No, Hermie, I was the only one who got close to her and I just took a cursory temp and tone, ballpark, to use with the neighborhood canvassing. And for questioning the gardener. Oh -- I did pull out her Medic Alert necklace. That's it."

"Did the gardener touch her? You know, maybe to see if she was still alive? What kinda shoes was he wearing?"

"Woven sandals on top of socks. And he didn't come near -- he saw her from the curb. Didn't even leave his truck, he used his cell to call 911 and just sat there, trying not to barf. Oh, he says he prayed for her till the cops came."

"Too late, but it's the thought."

"Wait a mo' -- I was too *on* her to take in the footprints, so let me gander," said Andy, and he went over to the curb to the soft dirt and its footprints. He eyeballed them, followed them toward the body, eyes took them in as they circled the ground where the body lay. "Interesting."

"Huh?"

"Three prints -- the vic's heels, obvious. A man's shoes, kinda small, actually, and I think it's the Perp's because there's lots of blood coming off 'em. Small feet, short Perp? And the track shoes, big feet, blood from the pool around her, and whoever was in 'em came close to her . . . Whoa!--knee prints! He kneeled next to her . . . maybe he moved her . . . then there he went -- jumped over her and ran away, back into the street," Andy gestured with his finger.

"How do you know he *ran* away?"

"Track shoes first stepped on the dirt, to the body, then scooped the dirt -- pushed on it from running -- *away* from the body."

"Before you make the casts, get some photos that show where all three of them walked, the directions."

"On it." Andy started texting on his giant watch.

Hermie shifted position, which didn't help his knees in the least, but it brought his gaze to her half-closed eyes looking up at him with an expression of profound sorrow. "Who did this to you, Baby?" he murmured, kindly. "Who was the Big Mistake you had drinks with on Mother's Day? And who was the other guy? Which one wore track shoes on a date with someone classy like you?" The sun moved in and out of a cloud, and a flash of brilliance shot through the dark hair covering her ears. He lifted the silky hair to discover substantial diamonds in her pierced ears.

Expensive shoes, expensive earrings. Expensive perfume? He bent to smell her neck and got a whiff of an exotic scent before her hair got in the way, bringing a lighter, flowery shampoo scent. He moved his nose to her lips and parted them and took a sniff of her mouth and got a pleasant whiff of tomato sauce and garlic. He was about to lift his nose from her face when the movement of a sun's ray set off a sparkle, and he noticed a slick, narrow sheen on her cheek, as though something had slimed her there, from just below her eye, then down her cheek, to the corner of her mouth. He took a long, slow inhale of the sheen and caught the faintest scent that was familiar but startling in this place: the smell of banana. Banana and not banana, because it was unnaturally sugary, synthetic. That scent had not been in her mouth or on her hands, but it was *there*, in a slick streak on her fine face. He rocked back on his heels and studied that face. "Before you tuck her in, I want her head in a sealed bag."

"You're kidding." Andy couldn't stop himself.

"Humor me. And tell Pierre I want to know what slimed her face on this side, here." He swept his large hand, indicating the left side of the woman's face. A twist of a breeze swept a lock of her hair onto that side, Hermie gently lifted it away and tucked it tightly behind her ear.

Andy bent down to peer closer, saw the gleam on her cheek. "Oh, yeah . . . I didn't see it before because the sun wasn't on it. That's my story and I'm sticking to it. What do you think it is?"

Hermie stood up, flexed his complaining knees, took his rubber gloves off, started to walk away. "Banana bubblegum," he answered.

As usual, he left everyone temporarily speechless.

But the lull didn't last. A patrol car roared up, siren screaming, tires smoking as the car slammed to a stop, avoiding but scattering fellow cops. The

CHP officer driving jumped out of the car nearly before it stopped rolling and he headed straight for Hermie. "Grabfelder! We got another one! *Really* bad!"

"A two-fer? You're kidding! Hermie quickly headed for the patrol car. "Can I hitch?"

"Sure!" The CHP officer dove back into the driver's side open door, un-punched the locks on the passenger side door just as Hermie yanked it open. Several of the CHP dashed to cars and cycles, gunned engines, sirens, to follow behind. Andy shouted to his tech assistants, "You heard Grabfelder, bag her head, tuck her in, start the plastering and combing. Call for another bus to head for the new scene, and somebody follow me!"

"Already rolling, Andy," one of his techs shouted out while he was hunched over his cell phone and joining two techs who were scooping up medical bags and following Andy at a run. Andy snatched up his own bag and trotted to a patrol car with its motor running and CHP driver waving him over, passenger side door already open for him.

Andy got in and recognized the driver because there was nobody like her: A tall, ebony woman with the breathtaking eyes and neck and skin and teeth of her gorgeous Watusi ancestors: Officer Cleopatra Padra. Delighted, Andy grinned over at her, "Ah, our first date." It was all a show, of course, because he was secretly glad he hadn't reverted to Korean which he tended to do when he was thunderstruck.

Cleopatra's dazzling teeth and spectacular cheekbones flashed at him for the instant it took before Andy's neck snapped backwards because she floored the accelerator and her black and white nearly set sail as she took off down the street. Andy had seconds to hang on as he realized the rumors were true: Cleopatra Padra drove like a veteran of the Indianapolis 500.

Nobody realizes how much blood is contained in the human body until they see it nearly bled out, Hermie thought as he leaned in the open driver's side door of the car to make sure. Yes, the man's head had nearly fallen off his neck after being stabbed and sliced by something sharp enough to do it neatly. *Same weapon, same slicing, same maniac.* And blood from the nearly severed neck had roared up and out with his last shocked heartbeats to bathe the inside of the new black Jaguar as though it had been squirted from a hose.

Red streamed across gleaming black leather seats, splattered upward on the black convertible top's ceiling, splashed forward to drip down the elegant dashboard with its gold-framed instruments set into burled wood below more black leather. Sticky red also dripped down the driver's side windshield, half-open side window, and inside the open door, and even splashed windows that were a car width or a car length away. As usual when beyond words, Hermie reverted to his ancestors: "Ach du lieber!" he breathed in astonishment.

A cloth tied one hand to the steering wheel, the other wrist also showed signs of resisting restraint. The man's legs were propped on the side of the driver's seat, his body thrown back. *He was tied to the steering wheel, got one hand free, got out of the car, and that's when he got it.* He looked down and saw a man's bloody shoe prints, coming and going, the same smallish size. *If this is where he got it, the Perp was standing right here, so why did he get out of the car? Hell, he could see what was coming. Why didn't he stay inside the car with everything rolled up and locked, phoning 911? Why didn't he just floor it and get the hell outta here? He knew who it was, didn't he? He knew the Perp and was going to try stalling, bargaining. Bad move. Bad, bad move.*

Andy arrived and also half-reverted: "Chidok'an, Man!"

"Puke if you must," Hermie said as he gingerly popped the latch on the driver's side door that opened all the door locks, but he noticed that the passenger side door locks were already open. He left Andy peering and calculating while he walked around to the passenger side doors, noticed that the car had rental car license plates. The Jaguar was parked curbside at an odd angle. In memory of Sandusky's search, he took a look at the exterior of the car, and saw one red and one clear rear lights smashed with that fender dented and scraped at the exact height of another car ramming into the Jaguar, *hard. Damage new — glass edges sharp and clean, body dents, chipped and scraped paint not rusted. This was the car forced off the freeway. Did Jaguar Man know who was trailing and smashing him? If he didn't, why didn't he just floor it — a Jaguar can outrun most other cars; if he did recognize the Smasher, again, why didn't he run?*

He came back around and looked in at the face on the head. It was very handsome. A neatly trimmed black mustache and goatee framed a mouth open, no doubt from a final scream through those perfect teeth. Above a noble nose, large dark eyes told him of terror and sorrow framed in thick, blacker-than-black eyelashes. Hair was thick and black, but here, too, white strands glinted here and there. Enough skin was visible in between blood splashes to reveal a deep olive color. *Mexican? Arab? Indian? South American? Samoan? Or, a tanning parlor junkie?*

Then Andy's fresh-latex-clad hands gingerly reached in and removed an expensive wallet from the victim's inside jacket pocket. "The jacket's Armani, cashmere and custom, we're talkin' about two thousand bucks . . ." He opened the wallet, ". . . wallet's a Hugo Boss, probably a hundred bucks and change . . ." He read the driver's license, ". . . Ah, a visitor from the East: Jordan Hashemi. Forty-two just recently. Hey, I know this address, it's the same as my ophthalmologist — it's a high rise in Century City. Odd, though, there aren't any apartments in that building, only offices." He searched, found a folded up yellow receipt, "Jag was a rental. Rental insurance sure ain't gonna cover this." He put the wallet, license and receipt in an evidence bag, wrote on the label, reached to hand it over to Hermie. "What are the odds of two slasher murders happening on the same night, a couple blocks apart?"

"Even. This *is* L.A., after all," Hermie answered. "The cloth binding his wrist –– DNA, hair, skin –– take it apart, it's significant."

"Significant?" asked Andy.

"Why not a rope? Or zip tie? Or designer handcuffs?"

Andy answered, "Why not, indeed, this being L.A. as you say."

Hermie opened the wallet and found five hundred dollars in fifties and twenties, the driver's license, the renter's receipt which indicated he paid cash, and nothing more –– no insurance card, no credit cards. *Lives on a cash basis and his address is an office building. This is not an ordinary guy. This might not even be a citizen.* He held up the license to the sun's strong light. It was a fake, the best he'd seen since those heady days in the Narcotics squad. *Drugs? Crap! Here we go again.*

"You gonna take a sniff?" Asked Andy, both helpfully and hopefully.

"Nah. Blood is all I'd get." Although a whiff of scent from a nice, clean cologne had wafted up from the wallet.

"Too right. We'll bag and send, then." Andy turned to find a couple techs scrambling out of squad cars and an ambulance heading toward them from down the street. He called out, "This one's messy, guys."

"Holy shit!" said the first tech who came up and got a look, and immediately turned aside and wretched, struggled manfully not to puke.

Hermie turned from the scene to find more officers unfurling crime scene tape, shooing away a couple citizens across the street who were intent on coming up to take a good look. He heard the buzz of approaching flies on a mission now that all the Jaguar's doors were open to the elements of nature. *Why no flies on the woman? Can't be out of respect. Maybe the scent of the Eucalyptus trees confused the issue. No purse, no wallet on her. Did the Perp take them? Hadda be –– she was dressed for a date, a purse would have matched those outrageous shoes, so women have said. If the shoes were eight hundred and change, what the hell would have been the price on that purse? The mind spins . . .*

When the annoying thrup-thrup-thrup of TV news helicopters approached overhead, he walked toward the officer who'd discovered this scene, didn't recognize him. "Grabfelder, here," he offered, holding out his hand.

"Yes, sir, I know."

Hermie braced himself, but the officer merely shook his hand normally. "Ewell, Roger. Good to meet ya." And Hermie was relieved that Roger wasn't a time-waster, didn't wait for the obvious questions: "I was coming off shift, heading home, when I heard the radios light up about that female body.

Thought I'd come by to help out, took a shortcut and came across this Jag. Colorful morning."

"I'll say. Oh, you're off shift? Well, can you find someone else to impound that car? Tell Joseph Esperanza at Impound to concentrate on the back seat area for prints and fibers and DNA-stuff. It's the only place the Perp could have been in, in order to avoid the bloodbath."

"I'll handle it, don't mind the time."

"Thanks." *This guy pulled an all-nighter and is no hurry to get home? Can't be married. At his age, must be divorced. Maybe more than once. 'Cops' Curse.'*

As Hermie walked away, Roger Ewell whipped out a cell phone, hit a button and spoke to an answering voice, "Hi, Nelson, it's Roger. I need a tow and a careful one, it's lousy with evidence. Yeah. A brand-new Jag. Your dream car no more, Buddy, wait'll you see this. A Grabfelder case. Yeah. Cool guy. And he says to make sure to tell Esperanza to pay attention to the back seat, prints, fibers, whole nine yards. Front seat you won't believe! I'll wait around for ya. Yeah . . ."

A couple officers alongside their squad cars, including the spectacular Cleopatra Padra, opened their passenger doors as an invitation to be his chauffeur back to his own car, but Hermie waved them off, walking back to the original crime scene in the direction the Jaguar most likely came from. *How did one guy gain so much control over two people? One of them -- both of them? Hadda have help. A driver? A big guy with a big gun for sure.*

Surprise was in his favor, considering Vic's size. Resistance came too late, ineffective against that lightning strike. I gotta meet this sonuvabitch!

He walked slowly, eyes scanning the street and curb, nose annoyed by the fumes coming from the nearby freeway. Jacaranda blossoms drifted along with bits of torn or crumbled paper and cigarette butts too numerous and too old to consider as candidates, all festooned the gutter. He came upon a storm drain entangled with some kind of vine but whose grid still had openings large enough to receive a weapon. He turned and let out a piercing whistle. Heads went up at the scene he just left and two officers broke ranks and trotted toward him. "Get a search going inside this storm drain," he asked when they got within earshot. "Look for anything bloody."

They both nodded. One officer whipped out his cell phone, the other kept going and was kneeling alongside and lifting the drain grid and tearing away vines as Hermie walked on.

He was nearly back at the first crime scene when his scanning gaze swept the middle of the street and he saw it: a bunch of dark purple crushed onto the pavement. He came near and bent down to see it was the remains of a nosegay of violets. *They used to call that a 'nosegay', didn't they? What you bought for the Prom when you couldn't afford an orchid wrist corsage?* Peering closer, he could see it was obvious that a car tire had rolled over it, crushing most of it. A flash of white made him carefully lift some of the bruised violets away, and he saw a torn card. One half of the card remnant had writing in ink in a strong hand: 'All things' . . . ; on the other half, 'thee'. A clear tire print rolled just short of 'thee', ripping and blackening the card into pieces. *This is where those violet petals came from. She's wearing diamond earrings and eight hundred dollar shoes and he gives her a nosegay of violets for Mother's Day. He's either a romantic or a bum.* Suddenly, Sinatra drifted into his thoughts, singing, *"I Brought You Violets for Your Furs"* . . . He carefully pulled the nosegay from the clutches of the dirty pavement and carried it away.

Back at the first crime scene in time to be annoyingly squinty from the already too-bright sun, and to see the ambulance pull away, silent, not in a hurry, the sign of a death on board. Techs were scooping up vials of that blood pool in the dirt, others removing plaster casts of multiple footprints. He called out to no one particular, "Anything?"

One very young-looking tech looked up, flashing a merry face full of orange freckles.

What is he? Twelve!? Aren't they supposed to be shave-able before they join the force? thought Hermie.

"The man's shoe size and depth of impressions –– if he's the Perp, he is not tall a-tall. Nor plump."

"Yeah, we got that. A short Perp. But with that kinda weapon, he's to size."

"I'll say! Never saw a cut like that. Sword? Ax? Even a machete don't cut like that."

"Mmmm-hmmm. I hate it when maniacs innovate."

"Track shoe is fairly new and pricey –– one of my guys recognized the print pattern as Flyaway's, the newest rage for teenaged basketball star groupies. They go for two hundred and change."

Hermie made an effort not to let his astonishment show. "Today I learned that I am completely out of touch, retail-wise. And the day is still young. You got an Ev envelope handy?" Hermie held up the mangled nosegay.

The Tech pulled out a bag from a bunch in his pocket. "Sure. Oh, I heard about Andy finding violet petals on that poor woman." He carefully took the nosegay from Hermie, gently slipped it into the Evidence bag, sealed it, wrote on it.

"What's your name?" asked Hermie.

"Ridgeway, Harry."

"Thanks, Ridgeway." Hermie didn't bother to introduce himself, since he could tell that the fuzzy-cheeked lad already knew.

CHAPTER TWO

"No human being can withstand close scrutiny."

Torgny Segerstedt,
Swedish Newspaper Editor, WWII

Hermie's retired patrol car, called "Roberta" by him and a select few, with its light rack empty and the bullet holes rusting and whistling on its flanks, smoked her way through the neighborhood ahead of the crime scenes. It was the usual jumble of well-cared for older, wood-framed houses being crowded out by super-sized, pseudo-Spanish stucco monstrosities looming above their too-small lots, crowded with landscaping hoping to disguise this environmental disgrace. There were frequent sad sights of drought-caused brown lawns, but there were also lawns of defiant green, some of them manufactured green plastic.

There were no kids playing in this first street, no bicycles resting in yards. An adult neighborhood, a rarity in the family-oriented community of Torrance. After two blocks he turned onto another street and there found an after-school's mob of kids of all ages, shapes, races, playing ball, bicycling, skate boarding, boom-boxes blaring hip-hop, voices yelling in various languages, with the f-word always in English albeit rich with accents.

Several small, grubby boys' faces turned to look as he smoked by, and he heard one with a felonious future yell, "Hey, what's with the air pollution, asshole?!" in Roberta's stinking wake. *Kids are here and not surrounding the crime scene yet. Word hasn't gone out. Nobody seen nuthin', for sure, otherwise this whole neighborhood would have been an audience at the scenes before even we got wind, especially that blood-soaked Jaguar with the motor running,* Hermie mused. *The times being what they are, I wouldn't put it past some enterprising young lad to shove the body out, put a towel down on the seat, snap a Selfie, and drive it off like a prize.*

He drove on down to Pacific Coast Highway, heading toward Wilmington and his "stationette", manned by his Captain Claire Jennings, the rare, uppity black female who could crucify him with That Look, who had been the one who ordered him to quit drinking and get healthy or she would see him fired or retired before his liver actually died. He adored her and secretly treasured the fact that she loved him, too, so he had shown up at Bud's Body Works as she had ordered, met the storm trooper Bud Vance, real name Boris Vanderhausen, and submitted to a completely foreign diet and a daily workout that had him praying for death -- Bud's -- but which had saved his life.

As usual, the partitions in the place shook with his presence as he came in the door and yelled, "Honeys, I'm home!" And Nell Barlow's secret heart did its usual lift and glow. Nell had been walking wounded from a painful divorce when she'd answered the ad for a Temp at this small police station over a year ago. Captain Claire Jennings, the boss of the joint, had thoroughly warned her about Herman Grabfelder before offering her the job, and then commanded her to feed Hermie a tuna salad when he'd ordered her out for a burger and fries and shake on her very first hour on the job. The subsequent explosion on Hermie's part was colorful and telling, but also instantly defined their relationship. Herman Grabfelder terrified her, fascinated her, exasperated her; but he also insisted that she tell him what she thought about his cases because he actually wanted to know, he sought a woman's take on things because he appreciated their unique insight. He *appreciated* her, even more so when she inadvertently gave him an important clue that helped him solve that serial killer case, and then saved his life when she walked in on a confrontation between Hermie and the hermaphrodite serial killer, Victoria Keyes, right in his office. Thanks to Nell throwing a stack of file folders in an automatic response to Hermie's yelled order "THROW SOMETHING!", when Keyes stabbed Hermie, she/he had missed his heart by an inch or so and Hermie lived to fight another day.

After recuperating --- a process somewhat shortened because the irascible, impatient Hermie had been tossed out of the hospital for cause, the cause being he was completely and nastily uncooperative --- he'd asked Nell out to dinner. But they didn't get a chance to go because Hermie had spotted a shocking clue on her TV that solved the murder of female bigamist Helen Bradford Litton Lawrence: Helen in the adoring crowd listening to the famous and charismatic Reverend Arthur Turner with a look on her face that revealed *everything* only to Hermie, because he'd fallen in love with that face at that chance meeting the night she'd been murdered.

Since then, Hermie and Nell had settled into a not-at-all easy working relationship, subject to the upheavals of Hermie's temper and sarcasm, always followed by darling, awkward efforts to make amends. Long ago, she realized that if she didn't see him naked before she died, she'd die twice.

Hermie, ironically a clueless male, hadn't realized a damn thing in spite of the fact that he had learned the sound of her distinctive footsteps because he figured out that she hit the ball of her foot harder than her heel (click-CLICK); and he had a compulsion to check the color of her eyes every morning because their moss green changed with the color of her blouses or shirts, and he waited for the rare days when they changed to the startling 7-UP bottle green remembered from his youth, and he now knew by heart what clothing colors brought about this wondrous phenomenon.

He'd also gotten so aware of her face that he knew when she'd had dinner with her son, Matthew, by the signs of a sleepless night under her eyes. He had a feeling Matthew was taking on his father-the-Shithead's ego quirks as he got older, and Nell couldn't stop it and hated it because he was going farther and farther away from her.

He also knew there was indeed a God when the economy tanked and so did her ex's Phillip Barlow's law firm. Gone with the wind went his house and his fairly new wife -- Tiffany was it? -- who apparently hadn't taken seriously the vows "In good times and bad", and had scatted. Another justice was she was expecting alimony and there waren't-none to be had.

Claire had taken the jubilant Nell out for a celebratory dinner on that occasion, and just for fun wangled the powers over them all to get Nell a nice raise. Claire had expected Nell would waste the money on Matthew, but she surprised them all by using it on computer and yoga classes. Nell had learned -- the hard way -- to think of herself for a change. So, the Matthew-caused sleepless nights didn't do the damage they'd once done, and Hermie began to wonder what would happen if he asked her out again.

But a lot of time and neglect had gone under the bridge of the obvious affection and patience she had for him and his ways. Everything was good now. Why screw it up with an actual relationship?

Knowing all too well how Hermie's mind worked, the entire frustrating, time-wasting situation had Claire in teeth-grinding angst which amused her husband no end when she came home and vented about the lagging love story going on between her two favorite dorks. He took to calling her the world's first Black Yenta. He urged her to invite them both over for dinner, which would get them on a "date"; but Claire knew that would scare them both off to know she was matchmaking, even though it would be a relief to have her in charge, which meant they didn't have to make a move that would end badly, their lack of confidence and experience playing a constant mental scenario of disaster: "And then what?" Having to see him/her, work with him/her every day after embarrassing disaster? Hoo-boy. Or in Hermie's case, "Ach du lieber!"

So, Claire had to wait, all smiles, all patience, not giving the slightest hint, wait for the day one of them asks her advice. And then she'd whomp some sense into them!

Instead of stomping past Nell's desk, his mind elsewhere, Hermie had taken to politely stopping at her desk when he came in, ostensibly to pick up his messages and get his cellphone charged. But he was secretly checking the color of her eyes as well as inhaling her unique scent: cut grass and clean laundry. He still said the wrong things most of the time, he knew, but what had been a shy, tentative, dumped wife over a year ago had grown into someone who could give as good as she got whenever he was snotty, which pissed him off even as it endeared her to him.

The two other officers that shared these small quarters spent their days on patrol and waiting for retirement, so they were mere uniforms that went in and out with "Good morning" or "Have a good evening", and wrote their reports, so neither bothered Hermie much. Unless they failed to replenish the coffee in the pot after they'd drained it into their thermoses before going on patrol. Which they had been warned not to do *"Or else!"*

Coffee... He really wanted an iced tea, but coffee was all they had back on the shelf and sink that was all the kitchen they had. *Why didn't I pick up some iced tea on the way in? Because I forgot. Again. 'The lights are really dimming on the old marquee.' Where'd I hear that one?* He sighed deeply as he shuffled his phone messages, startling Nell with its wistfulness. She surreptitiously started to check him out. But his dangerous eyes turned away and twinkled toward Claire as she came out of her office. He didn't notice that she scanned him inch by inch, looking for pain as she'd begun to do after seeing him topple from being stabbed by Victoria Keyes. She exchanged a quick glance with Nell, who'd done the same secret scan, both communicating that all was still well with their Beloved Bastard.

Just above the LAPD's height requirement, Claire Jennings' muscular frame glowed with ebony and energy. Having assured herself of Hermie's physical well-being, she now kicked in her habit of judging his mood. Not that she ever adjusted her own mood to his, but rather because she wanted to know what she was dealing with at any given time.

"What?" Claire asked him.

"Female, white, late thirties or very early forties, wearing would you believe eight-hundred-dollar shoes -- according to Andy -- plus real diamond earrings and no I.D. A Medic Alert tag he's checking. A stab and slice with great skill, down her whole self, damn near drained her. About two blocks away, male, Mideast somewheres, early forties recently, sitting in a new rental Jag with his head nearly lopped off in the same efficient manner, *completely* drained *him*. Fake driver's license says he was 'Jordan Hashemi'. Fake address says his apartment shouldn't be there because it's an office building in Century City, also according to Andy."

"And?"

"Banana bubblegum. That's all I got. From her."

She cocked her head with a straight face, but amusement danced in her large, dark, and warm eyes. "Banana bubblegum. It's never ordinary with you, is it, Grabfelder?"

"It's part of my charm. You always liked my charm. Now, don't deny it, you *know* you liked it."

Look at him -- smile as sweet as Jackie Robinson's on a giant, buffed white guy with the spooky nose. Now it's banana bubblegum? "I want to ask you something."

"My Queen is asking my opinion? Should I shower and shave first?"

"Shut up. Come on in." She turned back into her office.

Hermie followed, overwhelmed the only guest chair in the small room, looked around at the neat-as-a-pin desk, file cabinet, small table that held "Isidore, the Ivy What Was Taking Over Cleveland". It had been a mere sprig when she'd bought it over a year ago at the 99 Cent Store and put it here, her first station command. Now the ivy was a robust, burgeoning vine, having out-grown three pots, and was climbing from a fourth pot and up the wall, heading for the file cabinet, supported by helpful lines of string Claire had thumb tacked into the wall to give it a leg up.

Claire sat on the edge of her desk in front of him, the light from her office window lit up Hermie's hot blue eyes and she noted the whites were clean, his skin gleamed with golden and rosy health, and she inwardly reacted with relief. "You know Cruz and Trenton are looking at retirement in six months," she said, referring to their two in-and-out patrolmen.

"'Looking'? They're *drooling*. Lucky bastards."

"Your time will come. Sooner, if you don't behave." She was referring to the time Hermie had failed to inform her of a crucial procedure he'd undertaken during his serial killer investigation, not to mention hiding from her the fact he was secretly investigating the death of Helen Bradford Litton Lawrence. Even though it was the Lomita Sheriff Station's case and even though it was on the watch of their friend Gordie Norris, who ended up lying to his own Captain to cover up Hermie's investigation.

"You're never gonna forget that, are ya?"

"Hell, no. And you know why, Grabfelder."

"Because I'm lower than dirt, a sexist pig, not fit to shine your boots, I am snail spit, I am —"

"Oh! Shut! Up!" But her eyes were twinkling as she tried to scowl her professional scowl.

So Hermie relaxed and tried -- failed -- not to appear too pleased. "Okay, my Captain, 's'up?"

"When Cruz and Trenton decamp, we're shorthanded. I'm thinking of closing patrol duties, making us homicide investigation exclusively."

"Won't that piss off Robbery-Homicide? Territorial shits that they are?"

"Undoubtedly. I'm going to try to convince them we lust after being a part of their department, just want to start a southern branch."

"Good luck. I mean that sincerely." Hermie did snide almost as well as sarcasm.

"I got budget cuts on my side. They don't have enough shekels like everyone else, so they are chronically short of bodies. Live ones, that is. We'd add bodies at less cost and also mileage. I think I can finesse this."

"If anyone can . . ."

"Now, if this happens I can't ask you to take on all the cases we're handed. I could pitch in here and there, but I couldn't be consistent because of all the meetings I have to go to, paperwork crap I have to do."

"Yeah, all that butt-kissing over croissants and cappuccinos over at the spanking-new LAPD digs does cut into your poe-leece work."

"Don't complain, the butt-patting -- patting, no kissing, you know the quality of butts I have to deal with --"

"I hear ya, Girl. Well, at least the new headquarters offers you better atmosphere. So we're told. I've only seen picures so far."

"Oh, yeah, we once lived in hope. However, the new center was designed by a man, need I say more? No offense. Anyhoo, with enough patting of butts I think I can persuade Long Beach to extend their patrols a couple of miles to include our territory. They patrol, we investigate any homicides."

"'Any homicides'? In Long Beach? We're talking double digit bodies. I know, I used to work over there, remember? Yeegods."

"We can pawn a percentage off on Robbery Homicide -- the gang-banger stuff they live for because they make headlines and photos in the Breeze and the Times -- so they'll be able to keep on feeling important. Save the juicy cases for us. Also, I have an idea I want to hoist over those dippety-do's at Command Central and I want your opinion and support beforehand."

"My gun is at your service. Soon as I find it."

"What do you think about having Gordie over here?"

"I won't have him here! He's too damn good looking. He'd dim my star."

Claire couldn't help it --— she laughed out loud, took a playful swipe at him as he ducked and grinned that sly fox grin of his. "Be serious! And think of the political logistics -— he'd be quitting the sheriff's turf and joining the enemy. At least that's how his Captain would look at it. Maybe he'd screw up his pension or fire him with a bad note on his record, you know what kind of a backstabbing sneak he is."

"Mmmhmmm, and that was *before* the hemorrhoid operation. I heard they grew back, by the way."

"Couldn't happen to a nicer guy."

"He'll fight you all the way and make Gordie's life a living hell while he does it." Hermie declared.

"Is there any way around that?"

"Gordie should shoot himself in the foot, retire on disability, and we could hire him because you'll take *anybody*, present company as proof."

To Claire's surprise, those laser blues were grinning at her with a heartfelt gratitude. *He knew. And he was grateful.* "Oh, pish-tosh, even as a drunk you were irresistible and clearing cases like Attila the Hun. I wanted the star power in this backwater joint. And you did not disappoint. More or less."

He laughed, raked his raggedy hair with strong, laborer's fingers and tried to smooth it down. She saw shots of silver hairs now obvious among the wild gold. *He's going from a golden fox to a silver fox, right in front of my eyes.* "So, what's your advice, Hermie?"

"Let me talk to Gordie. He'll have more firsthand poop about his Captain and how to deal. That is, if he's interested."

"Do you think he will be?"

"Don't know. He may be planning on being Captain one day over there. And have you seen that station? Flower boxes, real tile floors, central air, silent flush in the toilets . . ."

"I know this place is a dump, Hermie, but we -- *you* --— keep clearing cases like you do and I'm going to parley our record into a two story office building with covered parking and windows in every room and a full-sized kitchen and *four* bathrooms -- two on each floor, with six stalls per."

"Stop -- I'll swoon!"

"I think Gordie can help us get there sooner. Don't you? You know him best."

"He's got a calm, analytical mind and a lot of patience, the making of a first class investigator. His choices of movies to see lacks understanding, but nobody's perfect."

"He doesn't like foreign films or silent films, like you? What? He doesn't do subtitles?"

"That's not half. Have you seen those giant robot movies? And don't get me started about the *"Sharknado"* on TV. It's the end of civilization as we know it. Why do I laugh?"

Claire laughed. "Oh, Hermie, you do remain *so-o* unhip. Well, do dinner ASAP, test the waters. Put it on your expense account and I will pay."

"You will actually *pay*? I hear and I obey, before you change your mind." Hermie got up, loomed over her five feet and almost nothing. "Did you tell your Mama I hand-waxed my floors last week?"

"I did. She said she'd have to see it to believe it. Expect a visit any day and a white glove inspection."

Claire's mother, Maya, and her crew of architecture students from UCLA were the ones who had saved Hermie's inheritance -- his precious 1929 house passed on to him from his Crazy Aunt Fern, hand-built by one of her husbands. Third? Fourth? Everyone forgets.

Maya and her students had rescued it from the ruin of Hermie's years of drunken neglect by scrubbing, stripping, waxing, painting, polishing every inch of it during long weekends over months. Since then, acting on Maya's threat of bodily harm, he had taken upon himself the Care and Feeding of his home, including the waxing away of every mark and dust speck he saw on the wood floors, door frames, hand-carved furniture.

"Really? She'll come over? I better clean the leftovers out of my fridge, put in fresh baking soda. Oh, my, my, so much ta-do-o-o." He left the room with a comical bustle that made her chuckle.

Seven-Up bottle green was flashing at him when he came out, because Nell was wearing an olive green sweater over a gray blouse and slacks that had subtle olive and grey stripes, and because she was looking directly at him while she was on the telephone and waving him over, indicating he should wait. She had the phone receiver tucked in the crook of her neck and she was listening intently and writing rapidly on a yellow pad.

Without realizing it once again, Hermie was mesmerized by her fingers as they did stuff. She rarely wore nail polish, much to his relief, but her modest fingernails were always pink and shiny, with immaculate white tips.

"Well, thank you anyway, Mrs. Burnside. I'll let you know what I can. Bye-bye." And she hung up, ripped off the top two sheets from the pad with a flourish, handed them to him. "You're not gonna believe this," she said.

He secretly loved it when she got this shiny look of eagerness on her face. "Don't you say, 'Hi, Hermie', anymore? Have I become just another worker bee to you?"

To his instant pleasure, a pink flush flashed on her round cheeks. "Hardly. But I got interested. 'Hi, Hermie, how you been, have I got news for you.'"

"Enough of this chit chat. What?"

"Remember Andy told you about the Medic Alert medallion around your female victim's neck?"

"Yeah, I saw it. How do you know about it already? Was he wired?" He teased.

She ignored the tease. "Well, he called Medic Alert and got next to nowhere, so he gave me the phone number and I called. And got *really* next to nowhere, just now."

"Huh?"

"Like the medallion, Medic Alert records say, 'allergic to penicillin, anaphylactic: bee stings, asthma, saline IV only'."

"This is news?"

"Oh, hell, no –"

He laughed at her rare profanity, she blushed more.

"Sorry, you've corrupted me. Anyway, what's news is that her medal was purchased over 20 years ago, her information was never updated, renewed. Mrs. Burnside at Medic Alert had to go back to the days before computer records to find her info. Last address was in New York City for a 'Lila Miller'."

"Ah, good."

"Ah, no, not so good."

"I'm losing the thread here . . ."

"I tried to find a current address for Lila Miller. There is none. There is nothing, I mean *no-thing*. So I called Hank O'Dell out of desperation. Thank God he took it as a challenge. He began a computer search, you know how he does."

"Legal or illegal?"

"Like I was going to ask."

"Smart girl. And?"

"The address in New York City? Fake. No birth certificate, no social security number, no job history, no tax records, no bank records, no credit cards, no record of residences, no driver's license, no voter registration. No police record. He even tried searching under anaphylactic shock, in case she had an ambulance or hospital record, or went back to Medic Alert or some other such organization. No medical records. Zip. Lila Miller does not exist."

"She did until earlier today, believe me. In this day and computer-crazy age, how can there be no records? No birth certificate? She wasn't born in a field, for crying out loud."

"Hank tried one last thing –– real estate records."

"Real estate? What's that got to do with --"

"Buying, selling, estate transfers, renting, land, houses, apartments, condos. Even evictions and foreclosures."

"Her name was on a transaction?"

She gestured at the paper in Hermie's hand: "Just one: Lila Miller's name was listed as the owner of a condo in Manhattan Beach: 27034 Dillard Street, Unit 4-C. I said 'was'."

"'Was'?"

"Here's the weirdest — Hank was just about to write down the address when his computer screen went blank — Lila Miller and her condo disappeared. And he couldn't get the site back. Luckily, he has a photographic memory so he wrote this info down."

"What the hell was going on with Lila Miller?"

"According to Hank, someone, somewhere was making 'damn-fucking sure', quote, that Lila Miller was not and will not ever-never be found. 'Bye."

* * * *

Following the coastline's curve, there nestles a parade of condo and apartment buildings marching along the edge of a street, flanked by a bike and pedestrian and skateboard path known as the Strand, until it becomes known as the Esplanade. This path linked three seaside cities south of Los Angeles: Redondo Beach, Hermosa Beach, and Manhattan Beach. Identical to the other beach cities nudging its shoulder, Manhattan Beach is a jumble of bulky condo and apartment buildings, small, old and charming houses being eyed for demolition by obsessive developers, oversized and tasteless new houses, and a variety of small vintage and boutique clothing shops, mom-and-pop deli's, candy and ice cream parlors, quaint restaurants, and lots of singles bars.

The ambiance is beach-casual, friendly, neighbor-knows-neighbor, so crime is low, until the nightly singles bar decampments get rowdy and singles start puking or peeing in the bushes or onto the curbsides, staggering on their way to their cars, where more puking is usually done in parking lots. Local police struggle to do an efficient and thankless job of clapping the cuffs on most of them before -- gawd-forbid! -- they get behind the wheel of a car. If it weren't for the stinking fumes of lumbering SUV's and RV's crowding the streets made even narrower by endless lines of parked cars, the air would be rich with the smell of the sea.

Roberta belched and quit and Hermie got out of the car to get a good look at the condo building on Dillard Street. It was fake French, but had a certain elegance in its tall windows, rounded on top, and spacious balconies made to look quaint with stone railings instead of the usual painted wrought iron. The walkway to the entrance was uneven flagstones made to look antique, flanked by a colorful riot of Impatiens flowering in reds, pinks, whites. To Hermie's pleasure, two tall Jacaranda trees flanked the walkway, dipping branches heavy with large clusters of pale purple blooms, casting cool, dappled shade on the walkway and bushes.

Hermie had lifted his nose to take a hopeful sniff when the dark, carved wood and sparkling beveled glass of the heavy front door opened and a tiny, elderly woman bustled out. Her white hair was cut in a pixie bob that suited her apple-cheeked face. She was wearing a hot pink velour track suit with matching running shoes on a tiny, trim figure. A large straw purse graced with a pink organza rose hung from one arm and she was about to put on pink plastic sunglasses when she spotted Hermie flashing his badge.

Her bright, brown-berry eyes were wreathed in shiny lines as they twinkled from a pink lipsticked smile that revealed perfect teeth that should be whiter, which meant they were not dentures. She teasingly raised her freckled hands that flashed long, pink fingernails. "I surrender, Dear," she said.

Hermie chuckled, already enjoying this dynamo. A flash of memory of his own indomitable Crazy Aunt Fern passed through his mind as he looked down on maybe sixty inches of suntanned energy, knowing those bright eyes were evaluating everything from his haircut to his shoe size. "I'm LAPD Detective Grabfelder, and --"

"Grabfelder? Go on! The one who caught that nutso serial killer?"

"Well, I had a lot of help, Ma'am," said he, hoping modesty would end this line of discussion. After he'd apprehended Victoria Keyes, the media and public attention had been overwhelming. He'd spent months dodging reporters and "fans", in a couple of instances throwing them off his lawn or out of his office or off his car.

Luckily -— or unluckily —- home-grown pseudo-terrorist-wannabe's school shootings, a series of police shootings, drought-sparked fires, and another round of astonishing city government corruption finally edged him off the local media's attention span. But he still got recognized, sometimes at the oddest moments, like standing at a urinal in the men's room at Home Depot when a woman who'd gone into the wrong door while pursuing the ladies room had recognized him. And like now.

The familiar gush was more pronounced in women, and this one patted his arm as if to make sure he was really standing there. "Ooh, wait'll I tell the girls at Curves. Can I have your autograph?" She began rummaging in the depths of that large straw purse, came up with a small, ratty-looking spiral pad of paper and a blue Magic Marker, handed them over.

His first impulse was to refuse, then, *what the hell*, he needed to get into that building without a warrant and she just came out of that building, so . . . He signed his name with a fake flourish that in no way resembled his actual signature.

"Ma'am, I'm here on police business, and maybe you can help me. Can I have your name?"

"Only if you add it to that autograph."

He paused, Magic Marker hovering as he questioned her with a look.

"It's Pepsi Potter. Honest t'God. My high school years were hell."

He swallowed back laughter, saying "Grabfelder wasn't a cake walk for me, either," as he added 'To Pepsi' above his name, handed it over. "Miz Potter, I take it you live here?"

"Sure do. I'm the President of the Homeowners Association. It's a condo building."

What luck! "Then you'd know a tenant by the name of Lila Miller."

"Four-C. Best corner unit in the building, on account of its distant view of the ocean on both sides. She paid a pretty penny for it, I can tell you. Don't know where her money comes from since she doesn't work. But I have my ideas."

"Do you? Care to share?"

"A *man*, my dear. Lovely creature like that, with no job? It's always a man. Sad, really, because she's the nicest woman. Elegant, very well-spoken. A real lady. But I have to say the man is a prince, treats her very respectfully and even dotes on her boy."

"'Boy?'"

"Her son. Maybe he's twelve? Thirteen? Hard to tell because he's scrawny. Odd kid. Always kinda bouncing when he walks, like he's listening to some kinda music. Reminds me of those black kids at the mall, with the earphones stuck in their heads. I swear, twenty years from now, a whole generation of deaf idiots will be trying to run this country. I won't be around to see it, thank God."

"Oh, I don't know. From the looks of you, I think you'll be around." He meant it, admiring the glow of health and energy radiating from her tiny, taught frame. "You remind me of my Aunt Fern. Family always called her 'Crazy Aunt Fern'. Never walked when she could run, awesome energy, interested in everything and anything, outlived all four husbands. She was ninety-seven when she passed away and the only reason that was possible was because she was asleep at the switch -- died in bed."

"Well, bless her heart. I'm seventy-eight at the moment. Hope I get lucky like her."

"I'm sure you will. Now, back to Lila Miller --"

"She's not in yet."

"'Yet'?"

"I saw her go out yesterday. I assumed for a Mother's Day dinner. A fancy black Jaguar picked her up this time. Always a different car, but same man.

The boy was in the car already, like most times. They were all so dressed up for the occasion. Reason I know she isn't back yet is her newspaper is still at her door."

"Black Jaguar?" *Christ, the boy was in the car?! Her son saw her killed?! Saw them both killed?!* "Can you describe her guy?"

"He's not white, but very handsome. Black hair, black eyes, eyelashes to die for. Some kinda black mustache. Reminded me of Omar Sharif, only handsomer, and he's much taller, bigger."

Yeah, even without his head, the guy was big, tall. "Did you ever meet this guy?"

"Only in passing, in the hallway, going in and out of the door. Always a friendly greeting, always a polite little bow of respect to me. He had a darling accent. But he didn't pause or linger long enough to strike up a conversation, know what I mean? He was never rude, just . . . passing."

"He had a key to the front door?"

"Yes, he did. And a key to Lila's unit. Of course, he would, under the circumstances."

"The circumstances being . . . ?"

"They were a couple. Almost like a family, with her boy included. Only difference is she went to him more oftener than he came here to stay with her. And her boy rarely stayed with her. I thought that was all very odd, but . . ."

"Always a different car and all his cars had rental license plates, right?"

"How can you tell?" Then Pepsi Potter suddenly caught the gist. "Yes . . . every time he came, he was in a different car, so I assumed . . . Hey, is there something wrong? About Lila? Her boy?"

"Is there any way I can get into her apartment? And, no, I don't have a warrant."

"Well, no. A condo is like a house, only the owners and kin have keys to their units. You could contact the property management, but good luck with that. Why? Say, I am the President of the Association, so if something illegal is going on, I have the right to know."

He took a chance: "I'm sorry to tell you, but Lila Miller was found this morning, murdered."

The tanned apple cheeks went suddenly yellow, then white. "Oh, no! *No.* Not her. Dear God! Was it *him*?"

"Her 'date'? No. He's dead, too."

"What the *hell* --? I gotta sit down." She turned and headed for the beautiful door, rummaging and retrieving her keys from deep inside her purse. She opened the door, called over her shoulder, "Come with."

Pepsi Potter's apartment was a shock because it looked so unlike her. A pale jade green was the dominant color and set off the deep, glossy brown woods of Japanese furniture. Delicate soji screens made of wood and rice paper divided kitchen from dining room, dining room from living room. Silk brocade pillows in Japanese florals or flying crane patterns warmed austere chairs and couches. More pillows flanked a low, beautifully carved mahogany table in the middle of the living room. A pale pink jade tea service rested on the table, so delicate it was nearly transparent. An Asian movie fan, Hermie recognized the set as priceless as well as perfection.

Two large portraits dominated one wall: A Japanese emperor in one, an empress in the other, both dressed in costumes made of satin and brocade glued onto their portraits; the emperor in gold, the empress in scarlet, with real gold and green jade earrings hanging from her painted lobes. A nearly full-sized sword in a golden scabbard hung from the emperor's deep blue, floral-embroidered silk belt. A large, red jade ring was set onto one of his painted fingers. Other smaller prints on walls were delicate water colors of lotus blossoms, cranes in flight, and misty views of Mount Fuji. Cool serenity was everywhere.

Hermie smelled a faint memory of morning toast, but the predominant fragrance in the rooms was a delicate, greenish scent like bruised leaves of an unknown plant. It was clean and fresh and alive. *Tea leaves?*

"Miz Potter, your home is very impressive. Beautiful."

"Thank you. My late husband and I lived in Japan for many years. We just loved the culture, the people, the artwork, the food. He was in import-export –– Japanese cars -- he was one of the first to bring them over here. Knew they'd be a game-changer in the auto business."

"He sure got that right."

"Until manufacturing was set up in the states and his job changed to a lot of pencil pushing. He took early retirement, we were planning to stay over there, but lung cancer cut that short. Cigarettes."

"Oh, I'm so sorry."

"Me, too. What a waste. He was a doll. White women on their own without family don't fare too well in Japan. We didn't have children, you see. So, I came home." She gestured at the rooms, "But I brought our Japan with me. I need a drink." She abruptly went into the kitchen, opened blonde wood cupboard doors, took out two tall, green glasses.

Since he was a holding-his-own reformed alcoholic, Hermie automatically piped up, "Not for me, Ma'am."

"Not even lemonade?"

Relieved, Hermie answered, "Lemonade would be terrific. Thank you."

"My own lemons. See that tree on my balcony?"

Hermie walked over to the ceiling-to-floor sliding glass doors, framed by more soji screens, these hand-painted with cherry trees in full pink bloom. Outside, on a large balcony an enormous blue and white porcelain Japanese urn sat, holding a lemon tree, branches dipping with the weight of bright yellow fruit. Smaller porcelain urns in green and red with golden dragon patterns held scarlet geraniums, orange lilies, and two camellia bushes crowded with palest pink blooms.

He heard ice tinkling and turned to find Pepsi Potter holding two large and very green glasses brimming with ice floating in a rosy liquid. She held out one to him. The fresh zing of lemons wafted up, joined by a sweetness that wasn't sugar. She gulped, he sipped, testing. Lemon and another fruit, sweet and calming.

"Fruit-sweetened cranberry juice instead of sugar," she said, "I find it more interesting. And healthier."

"It's delicious," he meant it and took a long, chilly swig.

"Oh, my manners! Detective Grabfelder, won't you please *sit*, anywhere you like."

She sank into the nearest chair, put her glass on the table alongside, grabbed the chair's brocade pillow, clutched its flying cranes to her chest. Hermie perched on the edge of one of the austere couches. There wasn't enough padding for a man his size, he felt the wood slats of the frame through the sigh of the silken yellow cushions.

"Murdered," she said, and sipped her lemonade. "*Both* of them? I can't believe it. How?"

He told a polite, less grizzly lie. "We won't know exactly until the coroner makes his report."

"Autopsy." She shivered, ice tinkling merrily in her glass. "They were so beautiful. And now . . ." She gulped lemonade, blinking tears, then abruptly stopped, "Ohmygod! What about her boy!?"

"He wasn't found with them." *He ran, that's what his footprints in the blood and dirt said.* "At this point, that's good news." *Gotta get a BOLO out for that poor kid.*

"Thank God. But where is he?"

"You're sure he went with them yesterday?"

"Yes, I saw them. He nearly always did go with. He was already in the car when her man picked her up. Other times, he was here and got into the car when Lila did. The man would get out of the car and hold the doors open for both of them. And I often heard him say to them, 'Remember, buckle up.' Always, so gallant. And like always . . ."

"What?"

"You know those wrist phones they have nowadays?"

"Frankly, I can't keep up. I have a cell phone and I've been ordered to use it. The man had a 'wrist phone', or whatever?"

"Whatever, exactly. Well, every time he and Lila and the boy went out, I mean *every time*, he'd tuck them into the car, then he'd stop and check the street, up and down, up and down, and then speak into that wrist phone. Then he'd wait a second, for an answer I assumed, then he'd sign off, and into the car he'd get and they'd go."

This guy acted like he assumed he was being stalked. Or was it Lila who was being stalked — Lila, who didn't exist?

"What can you tell me about her?"

"Well . . ." Pepsi leaned back, took a swipe at her streaming eyes while collecting her thoughts, stroked the flying cranes. "She bought the unit about a year ago, maybe more. For *cash*, can you believe it? Three bedrooms, three and a half baths, from the original owner, Mister Roger Tilden. Widower. His daughter had to put him into assisted living. Alzheimer's, poor dear. Nice as pie, he was. Before he got helpless, we went out to dinner now and then, just as friends. We both had had the best, you see, so we weren't looking for replacements. But we enjoyed each other's company. We liked to try out new restaurants. We took turns treating. There's always new ones popping up in the beach cities. They come, they go . . . Until the economy went into the toilet, that slowed things down considerable." A wistful expression as her thoughts drifted.

Just as Hermie was about to ask something, she looked at him, smiled, and returned to the matter at hand. "A little over a year ago, yes. I thought it was odd that a single woman bought such a large unit, for such a large price. Then the man started coming by. He was never introduced, never told me his name. Although he'd say "Hello" to me when we came across each other, on the way in or out, always polite, always that wonderful, movie star smile. Then . . ."

"'Then'?"

"This is odd — one day soon after Lila moved in, her man appeared to inspect the entire building. Walked the whole property, went in and out of all the access doors, toured the garage. He was like a building inspector or something. When I made it known that I had been watching him, he couldn't have been more friendly when he explained he was buying earthquake insurance for the Lila Miller unit and wanted to inspect the integrity of the building."

"Makes sense."

"Oh, sure. Except no insurance agent ever came by to verify anything. And believe me, I've had insurance inspectors come by and know how they work."

"When did the boy turn up?"

"Lila had been moved in for less than a month when he came by. That's when I noticed the relationship between the boy and Lila's man. The man looked at him like he was Christmas. The boy would just turn up, stay a couple days, go out with Lila and her man, and then be gone for days. I assumed Lila was divorced and the boy was living part-time with his father or in some kinda boarding school."

"Could Lila's man have been his father?"

"No, I doubt it. Absolutely no resemblance. For one thing, the man was not white. Lila appeared to be, except she had an accent —- come to think of it, her accent was similar to her man's, so maybe she wasn't all that white. But the boy was Lila's through and through, same eyes, nose, and that shy smile. So, I'm sure he had a previous father, if that's the word."

Hermie now took out his own pad of paper and pen. He used to buy such supplies at the now gone Pic 'N Save. When they all became Big Lots they just weren't the same, so he'd switched to the 99 Cent Stores, so the pad's cover celebrated Harry Potter's long-gone last episode with a studio shot. But his plastic pen was an homage to *Sponge Bob Square Pants*. "Can you describe this kid for me?" He clicked the pen and began writing.

"As I said, I think he's about thirteen, light blue-gray eyes, light freckles, dark hair. He's always popping and snapping gum. He's much too thin."

"Did he and his mother go anywhere together, that you know of?"

"Funny you should ask. That's another thing, they *never* left that apartment together. Never went out to eat or shopping. He walked here and stayed with her, inside the apartment. They only went out and about when her man was with them."

"Did she have a car?"

Pepsi bolted up. "Yes! And it's still in the parking garage."

"I'll need a wire hanger and a warrant."

"Phooey! I'll get you the hanger and never mind the warrant. I am the President of the Association and I give you my permission. Anything to find out who could do that to that poor girl and her sweet mystery man."

The underground parking garage had that familiar cement block chill and damp smell, mixed with carbon monoxide fumes, gasoline fumes, and the sweet scent of pink Oleander bushes that were outside but pushing through the iron bars of the various wall openings all around. Daylight pouring through these openings sufficed now, when the overhead lights were off for the day. Parked cars were few, this being a work day. Her car was a four-door Honda Civic sedan, in a dark blue. It was not new but the gleam on the paint showed care. Wearing latex gloves now and using the crook of the wire hanger, Hermie slid it down the passenger side glass and popped the lock.

"I don't believe it," Pepsi said, admiringly.

"The things they teach you at the Academy," joked Hermie. When he opened the car door, a rush of perfume reached out to him. It was an exotic mix of spices and strange, musky tones that was decidedly sexy but wasn't Hermie's taste; it demanded attention instead of seducing it. He remembered this scent from the trace of it on her neck. The car was immaculate, the only clutter a stash of small slips of paper in a tiny, square shopping bag hung from the shaft of the gear shift. He examined the slips of paper, they were store receipts of cash payments: groceries, dry cleaners, a gas station, a dress shop and a sporting goods store. It dawned: *All cash receipts, no credit cards. What kinda woman has no credit cards?*

The glove compartment contained the car's manual still in its original plastic sleeve, and various road maps of the Los Angeles basin, and the state of California, and very good forgeries of an insurance card and a driver's registration. *Forgeries, so her name, address wouldn't show up in the records. How did she avoid getting her name on then off the deed to the condo? Of course, 'he' bought it for her. Jordan Hashemi. Lila Miller does not exist.*

There were a few CD's in their cases: one was *"Patsy Cline's Greatest Hits"*, another had Arabic writing listing songs, two others were the soundtrack from *"The Phantom of the Opera"*, the original Michael Crawford version. And one appeared to be blank, had no label and it was not in a case. He pocketed that one. *To Nell: Here's your latest project: listen to this CD to see what's actually on it.*

A neat box of tissues sat on the passenger seat, with a daisy print on a blue that matched the car's interior. A pair of sunglasses was stuck in an elastic band on the driver's side visor. Hermie waved them toward Pepsi, with the a questioning eyebrow, cautioning: "Look, but don't touch."

She looked them over keenly, pronounced, "Expensive, Italian, non-prescription, fairly new because the lenses aren't scratched at all yet."

"How do women keep track of these things?" Hermie wondered, aloud and with admiration. And then he noticed an almost invisible lump in the passenger side floor mat. Hardly noticeable because it was against the usual center hump. He lifted the floor mat and discovered a set of keys. One Honda key, a house key and a safety deposit box key. It was her spare set. "Thank you, Beautiful," he said to the exotic scented ghost that still lingered in the car.

And then he noticed a delicate hanky wrapped around something too heavy for it. He looked inside and found a small pistol. Loaded. Serial numbers completely gone. He jumped to a conclusion that made sense: *So, <u>she</u> was being stalked, too. Her man never let her out of his sight, but a gal has to* *go shopping. She went shopping loaded for defense. And there would be no record of her purchasing and/or owning this gun. Because Lila Miller did not -- yada-yadoo.* He re-wrapped the pistol, replaced it where it had been. *Let Forensics deal with it.*

Like all doors in the complex, her apartment door was the same beautifully carved wood and beveled glass. The door key fit roughly, as if it had rarely been used. When the door opened, that same exotic scent wafted into his face like a ghostly kiss. Pepsi Potter stood behind him, peering around his shoulder, fascinated. "Jeez!" she said. "She never even changed the furniture."

"What?"

"It's all Roger's -— Mr. Tilden's -— stuff, just like he left it. It doesn't go with her at all, so why didn't she buy new after all this time?"

"Maybe she couldn't afford it after paying for the condo. You said it was a pretty penny."

"But she was with a man of means. He would have bought her anything and everything she wanted."

"True." *But buying furniture and stuff would require her name on a receipt, her address for delivery. Or maybe she assumed she'd be on the run sooner rather than later, so why bother decorating?*

They entered the beige tiled foyer and he pulled plastic booties out of his pocket and over his shoes. He didn't have a spare pair. "Ms. Potter, this place could be connected to the crime scene. I'm going to have to ask you to stay put here."

"Oh, of course, I understand."

"I'm just going to take a quick look around, the forensics techs will really vet the place later. But stay there in case I need to ask you something."

"Sure." She seemed content to eye the surroundings from her post.

He entered a large livingroom that did not go with the feminine murder victim he'd recently viewed. The furniture was pseudo-South Seas in flavor, blonde rattan and colorful floral prints. The walls were a yellow that was too lemony, the carpeting a dull flax weave, somewhat worn in the traffic patterns. Pictures on the walls were lively florals or Gauguin native prints. The kitchen had black lacquer cupboards and black refrigerator, stove, dishwasher. The walls and floor stark white tile.

The master bedroom had dark green carpeting and too-pink walls. The exotic scent was heaviest in here, insistent, almost like a tap on his shoulder. Plantation shutters were closet doors. Hermie slid them open and saw fewer clothes than he expected, half the closets were empty. What clothing hung inside was expensive -- Hermie felt cashmere and silk, and linen light as gossamer. From this morning's education from techie Andy Cho Hui, the few shoes that were in a neat, colorful row on the floor probably added up to a down payment on a beach house in Cabo San Lucas, or a first class round trip ticket to Paris.

He pulled open a drawer in a night-stand alongside the bed, admired the satins, silks, and snowy lace of a collection of delicate underwear neatly folded inside. When he closed the drawer he would later not recall what made him run his fingers underneath the edge of the night-stand. But he did, and he found it: a listening device, no larger than a pencil eraser, stuck under the edge. He examined it, *They sure make these things teeny-tiny these days.* And confident that he'd find more throughout the apartment and they'd lead him to their source, *As if I don't know!* He first stepped on it to disable it, then pocketed it. Then he checked the walls, the lamps, everything he could think of, looking for a camera, but found none.

The bathroom was also pink, this time the fixtures were in a delicate seashell color that clashed with the too-pink bedroom walls nearby. Purple soap was set in white porcelain soap dishes alongside the sink, tub and shower. He sniffed -— her exotic scent was more delicate, nicer in the soap. A perfume bottle was also purple, with a tall, pewter floral top to the stopper. He smelled the stopper and his nose tingled with the overwhelming scent. The gold label on the bottle had Arabic writing. The listening device was tucked underneath the little, mirrored wall cabinet. No camera in here, either. *No one looking to get a thrill from the sight of her naked in the tub or shower? Odd.*

One of the other bedrooms had been used as a home office. Its beige tones matched a blonde wood desk and bookcases and file cabinets. A computer sat on the desk. *Another job for the flying fingers and brain power of Hank O'Dell,* mused Hermie, recalling the skinny computer geek from Computer Whammy who Nell felt free to call because Hank had dragged him kicking and screaming into the computer age at his office. He ran his hand underneath the edge of the desk. Another bug. He glanced at the computer, but didn't bother, thinking, *They can track from <u>inside</u> the hard drive these days. A special treat for our O'Dell.*

He went into another bedroom. He instantly picked up the strong hormonal scent of an adolescent boy, although the room looked little used, no teenaged clutter anywhere, not even an elaborate music component set, just a small TV on a stand. *No stack of music CD's? No giant TV on the wall? What kinda teenager is this?*

He picked up the TV remote and up wafted the scent of banana bubblegum. *It's the same kid, orphaned now.* A listening device was tucked underneath the TV stand.

A red plaid covered the walls and color-matched the red carpeting and red drapes on a single large window. Navy blue corduroy bed covering and upholstery on a couple comfy chairs contrasted the red nicely. The furniture was vaguely colonial in style, in a dark wood. Dark wood plantation shutters were closet doors. He opened them to find a couple of t-shirts printed with messages, including *"I'D TURN BACK IF I WERE YOU", "PEACE IS PATRIOTIC", and "PARDON ME, I WAS RAISED BY WOLVES"*. Some plaid flannel shirts, well-worn jeans neatly hung. On the floor below, a pair of worn-looking Flyaway track shoes. He picked them up, noted that the soles were really worn but they were the same. *These track shoes . . . must be his original pair. He was <u>there</u>, wearing new shoes, stepping in her blood . . . that boy witnessed his own mother being killed! Jeezus H —- did he see Hashemi's slaughter? Did a teenaged boy see such horror?* His hands were shaking when he opened the drawer in the next cabinet to discover a boy's white briefs and socks, little worn, as if recently purchased.

This was a boy who stopped in but did not really live here. With his own mother. Why? And whose idea was it? His? Or hers? Hashemi's? And where the hell else did he live?! Hashemi's non-existent residence in that Century City high-rise?

He went back, into the kitchen. The cupboards contained little else but cereal, pasta and a few jars of organic sauce. The double-door refrigerator was also nearly bare -- a large jug of organic orange juice, three bubble-shaped bottles of pomegranate juice, what was left of a dozen organic brown eggs, a tub of Danish sweet butter, a few slices left of a loaf of organic raisin walnut bread, a jar of French black cherry preserves, a quart of organic nonfat milk, and a bowl of the ordinary green grapes that probably came from Chili because it was not yet the season for the giant California Thompson green grapes. In a specialized plastic dispenser were a variety of soft drinks -— Coke, and juice-type carbonated waters: black cherry, blueberry, mandarin orange and strawberry.

In the freezer were two loaves of the kind of bread Hermie had discovered when he began dieting: dark and heavy with grains and seeds. But these had Arabic writing on their labels. He opened a last cabinet and found stacks of envelopes of micro-wave-able popcorn in a variety of flavors: caramel, cheese, jalapeno cheese and kettle. Totaling up the scant amount of food in this kitchen, Hermie concluded: *This gal ate out a lot! And her kid rarely ate here. Was she that bad of a cook?* He found two listening devices in the kitchen.

As he once again went through the livingroom, he found two more listening devices, one tucked under the couch, the other in a lamp filial. On a hunch, he went to the one wall that flanked the entire livingroom and held a large print of a South Seas scene. He looked closely, zeroed in on a coconut hanging from a palm tree —- the camera lens fit invisibly within the coconut.

Jeezus H. — somebody's surveillance budget got shot to pieces with this job. What the hell were they after?

He came back to the foyer to find Pepsi on tenterhooks, but rooted to her spot as ordered. "Did you find anything?"

He lied with a straight face: "Zip. She not only didn't bother to change the furniture, she barely filled the closets or the cupboards. You say she lived here for over a year?"

"Yeah. Weird isn't it? I mean a man might be that blase' about his digs, but a woman? Long past the messy college age? *Way* weird. Especially her — I mean, she was elegant, classy, it was obvious she had taste in things."

"Some things, maybe. I deal in weird, but this is new. In a few hours, the place will be crawling with forensics techs. Sorry for the hullabaloo that will entail." *Not to mention the conniption-fits in the LAPD when they discover this surveillance operation and nobody told them nuthin' beforehand. Especially the Chief. This kinda budget marks it an outside job. Wa-ay outside, like Quantico.*

He ushered her out, closed the door behind him, and was about to put the keys under the mat when he noticed the safe deposit key. "Do you know where she banked?"

"Yes. Her condo maintenance was paid by that bank just down the street."

"You're my witness: I swear to gawd almighty that I will get this key to forensics immediately, if not sooner."

"I believe you."

Hermie removed the key, pocketed it, put the rest of the keys under the mat. The mat was a thick raffia-type with a charming print of deep blue and pink Hydrangeas. "I'll leave the these keys here so the Techs won't have to disturb you. If you could leave the front door open for a time, until they get here?"

"Sure, no problem."

"Great. And I'm trusting you to make sure nobody goes in that apartment until they clear it. Not even her boy, should he turn up. You'll know when because they will take down the police tape."

"You have my word of honor," she said dutifully.

He pulled out one of his business cards from a jacket pocket, straightened the bent corners, handed it to her. "If you see the boy come around, make sure he stays here and call me. Also, if you think of anything else, even if it's something trivial, I'll want to hear it. It's been my experience that a woman's 'trivial' can be a cop's best clue."

"Certainly, Mister — Detective Grabfelder."

"'Hermie' will do." He gave her a grin that all women thought cheerily flirtatious, were it not for those dangerous eyes, then turned to go. "Thanks for the lemonade and double thanks for your help. Oh --" he turned back with the grin still there, "I have-ta ask, as I'm sure everyone does . . . 'Pepsi'?"

"You're right, everyone does. A high school addiction saved me from my real name, thanks to my best friend at the time."

His eyebrows arched up with the question.

"Would you believe 'Prudence'?"

He chuckled. "Oh, yeah, I believe it. After all, I'm a 'Herman'."

She chuckled back and this time he really left.

When his beat-up squad car smoked away down the street, Pepsi Potter practically galloped the three blocks to Curves, arriving breathless with both exertion and excitement and the thrill of telling the "girls" *All*, including the fact she had to hot-foot it back to her condo building to wait for the police, trilling "Homicide, my dears. Forensics!"

Later, Hermie went to Lila's bank with a "Look But Don't Touch" kinda warrant to persuade the bank to allow him to look inside Lila Miller's safe deposit box. He needn't have bothered. The bank manager, Paul Nickerson, assured him, with emphasis, that there was no account, no safety deposit box, no bank issue of any kind under the name of Lila Miller. However, Paulie got a downright flummoxed expression but no explanation as to why Lila had this bank's key to said box, or as to how the bank paid Lila Miller's condo maintenance if Lila and her account didn't exist. Hermie could only conclude that Jordan Hashemi paid Paul Nickerson very, *very* well for this anonymity. He could-a hauled Paulie's ass in for some snotty interrogation, threatened arrest for obstruction of a murder investigation, but why bother? He'd lawyer up out the whazoo and a lot of time would be wasted, a lot of futile aggravation spent with no return. And it was early days . . .

CHAPTER THREE

*"It is forbidden to kill and, therefore, all murderers are punished. Unless
they kill in large numbers and to the sound of trumpets."*

Voltaire

"Anything quirky?" Hermie asked while the elegant green malachite Mount
Blanc ink pen wielded by Coroner Pierre Bonay dipped and swayed with
his exquisite handwriting on official forms. Pierre did not type. It follows
that he did not compute, unless for research. But since his handwriting was
perfection in deep navy ink, and he wrote English less colorfully than he spoke
it, allowances were made. A Temp would later transform his elegant reports to
the mundane computer records and printouts required for court and LAPD
Robbery Homicide records.

The bodies of Lila Miller and Jordan Hashemi lay nearly side by side,
both tucked inside sheets. Ordinarily, Hermie would have lifted the sheets
and taken a look, seeking information. But he didn't need to see those horrible
wounds again, cleaned up though they were by now, thanks to the respectful
Pierre.

"Bien sur, 'erman, zere ees always somezing, as you say 'quirky',
regarding ze murdaire. Death ees nevaire seemple, no? How-evaire, zis one
ees historical." With a flourish, "Bon," he finished writing with his famous
signature, recapped the exquisite pen, put down the forms on a silvery steel
table. "Ze time eet ees what?" Pierre craned his long neck around to view the
plain, round clock on the wall. The second hand swept up to click at 6:55
PM. "Voila -- queeting time. Dinnaire, mon Ami?"

One never refused "dinnaire" with Pierre Bonay because to do so would
mean missing a sublime experience, which Hermie was addicted to. Pierre was
relentlessly French, therefore food was sacred. The restaurant of choice was
always the Madame de Lis, where the staff revered his exquisite taste and Old

World manners, and his unspoiled-by-English-slang-French. They also had a great respect for Pierre's frequent guest, the LAPD Homicide Detective with the 'formidable' eyes, who obviously had a mother who taught him correct table manners. Thus proprietor Charlemagne Junot would always instruct Chef Henri Chabot to create something special for "Le Grande Monsieur Bonay and ze Grabfeldaire." Pierre never read a menu at Madame de Lis; he merely *arrived*, was seated at the best table --— in back, next to a window open to a bright fuchsia Bougainvillea vine that took a turn up and around this window before it spread out over the Country French tiled roof of the tiny treasure that was the Madame de Lis restaurant. It was tucked deeply into the narrow space between a small toy store called Clickety-Clak Toys that only sold electric train sets and the robots that became teenagers' obsessions after the latest hit movies, and a used book store and lending library called Linger Books that had entire walls stuffed with books but had room for only two ancient couches and accompanying lamps, in case you wished to take up the offer to linger over a well-worn copy of anything by Jane Austen, or the complete collection of Vince Flynn's paperbacks, or an interesting collection of books by Middle Eastern writers, translated, or you were the last person on earth to begin a Harry Potter addiction.

This kind of store could not possibly be making its rent since it did not carry anything electronic or the plastic hand-held reading devices that were the current depressing rage, so rumors floated around: The owner, Malcolm Knickerbocker, was either an eccentric millionaire with a reverence for *real* books who used the store to keep his retirement interesting; or he was laundering money for a drug cartel; take your pick. It was dreaded by the entire neighborhood that whoever, whatever Malcolm Knickerbocker was or what his motives were, when he passed away (or got arrested), the bulldozers would appear and would not linger over "Linger". Bets were placed as to what would replace the tiny store. Yet another Starbucks was the chief dread, followed closely by a 7-11, a bank, or a dark horse: a dry cleaners.

Pierre was always served the same first course while his special dishes were being created: a clear, beef consomme brimming with sweet Peruvian onions, and a wine so deeply burgundy it was nearly black. The combination warmed and relaxed the stomach, softened the mind, erasing the irritations of a day spent slicing up and peering inside the dead, and preparing the senses for the fragrances and textures and tastes to come. It had become noticed some time ago that the detective friend of Pierre's now barely sipped this wine when before he had drained several glasses.

This is not alcohol, Hermie's mind insisted as he guiltily sipped the fragrant, deeply fruity wine, *this is therapy.* Since wine was not his drink of choice during his drinking years when only a Stinger would do, he had grown confident that he could confine this drinking to these meals.

As usual, already, he felt his newly healed gut, the back of his neck, his shoulders, his knees all relax; even his feet got so pleasantly flabby he had to restrain himself from kicking off his shoes. As he neatly spooned up the rich consomme and sweet onions and sipped the wine, his nose celebrated the fragrances. He took a deep, relaxed breath just as Pierre did.

"Zis ees pairfect, no?" Pierre asked, smiling languidly, his large, mournful eyes shadowy from the thick eyelashes above, once black now turning gray.

"Zis ees," answered Hermie.

It was an unspoken rule that had long ago been decided when Hermie had first become speechless over the exquisite food Pierre had introduced him to: No talking business until dessert. So it was a nearly silent, sensual pleasure while they ate: a cold, crisp endive and grape tomato salad drizzled with olive oil mixed with garlic chunks and the snap of dark mustard and lemon; tender pork chops drenched in mushrooms caramelized by a plum sauce zingy from a dash of lime; an asparagus souffle that was mere foam on the plate; tiny yellow potatoes that tasted like buttermilk.

And later, dessert was a delicate ice cream made palest pink from the flavor of crushed red rose petals. It came with a hot cookie made from pie dough topped with cinnamon and sugar, just like Hermie's mother used to make. Except hers weren't so light and flaky they threatened to float off the plate, like these did now.

"If anyone ever wept over a meal, I'm about to bawl out loud," Hermie said around a spoonful of the light-as-a-cloud ice cream. He could actually smell as well as taste roses.

"Ah, I may make a Frenchman out of you yet, mon Ami," Pierre grinned, his long teeth biting into the hot pastry cookie, which he had just dipped into the roses. "But, eet ees ze business zat ees on your mind, so --?"

Permission given, Hermie asked, "'Historical'?"

"Both were kill-ed by someone who knew how to do eet."

"Yeah, I saw that. First a stab, then one slice through everything important."

"Oui. Eet was a weapon I 'ave not seen since my Army days in ze Middle East."

"Columbians, Arabs, Asians, Latinos, I can take my pick. Hey, wait -- 'Middle East'? The 'Army'? Pierre, I suspect you have hidden depths. Spill."

"Zis murdaire was Ismailian Hassan-I Sabbah."

"Wha-at?! You *know* this maniac? Where do I find the sonuvabitch?"

"In Persia. In ze Eleventh Century."

Hermie sat back, stunned, gaping, roses and cookie forgotten. "You're gonna explain that, ri-i-ght?"

"Ismailian Hassan-I Sabbah is ze man who invented ze Assassin. Ze stealth, ze method, even ze daggaire. In ze time of ze sword and ze curved scimitar, zis daggaire was small enough to conceal in a sleeve, sharp enough to kill wiz ze two blows you saw: ze stab, zen ze slice. Eet is unmistakable."

Hermie was dumbfounded. "So . . . I'm looking for an Arab. A 'Persian'. That's Iran now, right? An 'Assassin' . . ."

"Oui. One who *plans* before ze kill. Zis man knows every- s'ing, *all* s'ings about zese victims before he kills. Zis man is ze most dangerous."

Hermie could barely contain himself: "In 'Persia' . . . Eleventh' . . . What the hell, Pierre!"

"In ze Eleventh Century, eet was ze very beginning of ze religious wars within Islam, Sunni against Shiite. Ze Sunni were more in numbaires because zey joined ze community, zey made neighbors, created political influence. Ze Shiite claimed zey were cousins, direct descendants of Mohammed, so zey demanded ze authority, ze influence on ze laws."

"This has been going on since the Eleventh Century? What's the goddamn point?!"

"Ze point is always ze same in all ze religions: Power."

"No, no, this all doesn't make sense in *this* case. Jordan Hashemi was a fake and Lila Miller didn't exist. Literally."

"So . . . both were hiding . . ."

Hermie perked up. "Well, yeah. *Really* hiding, as much as they could. They were being stalked. And they knew it. He must-a paid large for a ginormous surveillance camera set-up."

"Zen zey knew ze Assassin was coming for z'em. Perhaps even knew who he was."

Hashemi got out of the car right in front of him. He did know him! "From the evidence at the crime scene, you're right. At least concerning Hashemi. But the woman?"

"Ah, oui. Ze woman does not fit — Islam forbids ze killing of women and children, ze innocents."

"But she was a witness. She had to be stopped, poor thing."

"She was a moth-aire. She had at least one child at an early age."

"Yeah. Her son was there when she was killed."

"Oh, no, mon Dieu! Oh, no! He saw eet? Such a horror?"

"Yeah, his shoe prints were at the scene. Landlady told me her son came around on a really odd schedule, but she saw him in the car with his mother and Hashemi, going out for Mother's Day. And he wasn't Hashemi's son. She mighta been on the game. She had lots of money with no job."

"I found no evidence of ill-use on ze madame. No abrasions, no scar tissue one expects to see if she lived such a low life. Zere was semen wiz-in madame, but it was not fresh. Ze DNA will match Monsieur Hashemi, I am certain. As usual, we await and await ze tests."

"Maybe their habit was getting it on *after* some good eats."

"Ze 'eats' –- zey both had eet. Ravioli wiz ze lobstaire, spinach salad wiz ze cheap olive oil and ze wrong vinegar, not too much wine, and ze spumoni."

"A nice last meal for Mother's Day. Cheap olive oil and wrong vinegar excepted." Hermie teased. *How the hell does he know the difference? I gotta ask one day: 'Wrong' vinegar?*

Pierre nearly sniffed with a sneer, "Eef you prefer ze careless Italian, zat ees."

Cold roses slid over Hermie's happy tongue as his thoughts slipped in.

Pierre sat back and studied this hulking man whose thoughts occupied his blazing eyes while he ate with the manners and grace of a European. *Sacre bleu*, Pierre thought, *zat nose of hees, what a wondaire to pick up ze scent of zat tiny, invisible trail . . .* "Eet was *your* idea to put ze plastique on Madame's lovely head, was eet not?" Pierre asked, knowing the answer. *It could only be you, 'erman.*

"What?" Hermie saw Pierre had stopped eating and was studying him. "I got ice cream on my chin or something?" He dabbed a fine pink linen napkin here and there on his strong chin, without crumpling the napkin.

"Not at all, Mon Ami. I was merely saluting your nose een my mind. So to speak. Once again."

"Huh?"

"S'anks to you and ze nose, ze shiney trail on Madame's cheek was not disturb-ed. I was able to make ze scrapings and ze analysis."

"Banana bubblegum must-a been, right?"

"Indeed. Saliva wiz ze sugar and ze chemicals of ze banana booblegum. Ah, me, anozaire sign of ze decline of civilization d'Americaine."

"Can't argue." Hermie suddenly became thoughtful. Then he continued: "Poor boy. He kissed his mother goodbye after seeing her slaughtered, banana bubblegum stuffed in his cheek."

"Ah, oui, you will be correct. Ze DNA will match, it is certainement. Zat explains ze salty moisture alongside ze saliva. He was weeping wiz zat kiss. Ah . . . merde," Pierre swore with soft delicacy and sympathy.

"Luckily, he ran like hell."

"Oui, very luckily, eet saved his life."

Hermie looked up into those sad eyes. "I'm up a brand new creek, aren't I? A goddamn creek in Persia, for crying out loud."

"So sorry, Cher Ami. But you will not find zis killaire. Zey are nev-aire found. But you must find zis poor boy. He will not escape zis assassin for very long."

"That's what I'm afraid of. But you're wrong on one point."

"What eez ––?"

"I'll find that sonuvabitch. Eleventh Century my ass!" Hermie chomped on the remains of a last cookie.

Pierre thought that this was not the time nor the place to inform Herman that the Assassins were also experts at killing their pursuers.

* * * *

As usual, Eleanor climbed up his right pant-leg, up his suit jacket and settled on his right shoulder to sniff his face and lips in order to ascertain what he'd been up to. *Porkchops! And cream!* She let out a rumbling, feline growl that was decidedly annoyed at having been left out.

"And I didn't bring you a doggy bag, so to speak. A thousand apologies. But there was nothing left ––– I damn near licked the plates," Hermie answered, dodging hatpin-like whiskers that jousted too near his eye.

Eleanor was a bossy witch disguised as a black-as-sin cat, with a bright pink nose and lime green eyes that missed nothing.

An injured and hungry stray who had taken refuge atop his car a few years ago, Hermie had taken her in and suffered the consequences. At the tail end of his drunken years, she had brought unwanted order to his life with her demands for food, water ––– she would allow only bottled distilled water to pass her fuzzy black lips –– and attention that began the re-focusing on Life that was the first step to saving Hermie's.

Like always, Hermie slipped off his shoes, and in stocking feet walked over the gleaming wood floors and antique rugs of his little house. Into the kitchen, with its white wooden cupboards made charming by beveled glass in the doors that neatly marched above sunny yellow tile counter-tops. Like always, Eleanor made a silken leap from his shoulder onto the counter, and like always he growled, "You should not be on the counter, you've got germs. And probably bugs. But I give your form a Ten." And, like always, her green eyes went into slits as she snorted with the insult of that idea: *Germs? Bugs? Really! An Empress does not have germs, much less bugs, and when are you going to get that, you silly but somehow winsome human?* This was all clearly apparent in her attitude.

Hermie opened the pale yellow refrigerator that had been humming contentedly since 1959, with only two motor replacements in the Seventies and the Nineties. Since he had learned to cook as part of the diet and exercise program he'd been forced to take up over a year ago in order to ward off forced retirement due to drink and decrepitude, gone were the days when the fridge contained only mold-covered remnants from Taco Bell or McDonald's. Now there were containers of organic yogurt, organic apples and grapes, and in the high summer, peaches, below the shelf that held a hefty jug of brewed green tea, another jug of Cranberry Juice, a smaller quart held fresh-squeezed organic orange juice, and there were also leftovers from a couple of home-cooked meals: A jar of chicken noodle soup, a plate of stir-fried turkey strips and assorted colorful veggies. And two loaves of dark and grainy bread that were due to be partnered with the butcher paper wrapped sliced low sodium ham or the sliced low sodium chicken breast, both to be accompanied by "stinky cheese" from Denmark, organic tomatoes from the farmers' market, and sprouts. His first encounter with alfalfa sprouts had been, "Don't these belong in an Easter basket?" But now he was addicted.

The one concession his antique kitchen made to this century was a microwave oven, and into this Hermie placed a small bowl of chicken and noodles and a little broth, as Eleanor danced the Anticipation Dance on the counter top. Seconds later, as Hermie was carrying the warm bowl to her special place in the boot room near the back screened door, the phone rang. Startling him so he jumped, the bowl jumped and a noodle jumped and draped itself over his thumb. Muttering curses cops were famous for, he checked his kitchen's glossy linoleum floor for splatters of broth with a socked foot, found none, then set the bowl down at Eleanor's "table" -– a solid silver-footed tray, circa 1929, set on a fluffy, colorful placemat made from woven t-shirt strips, circa 2010, alongside her cut glass water bowl, circa 1935.

The phone was ringing for the tenth time when a throughly annoyed Hermie snatched it from the wall. "WHAT?!"

Normally, Gordie's greeting was a hearty, "How's it hangin', Hermie?" But this time six-foot-six of black man what don't take crap from nobody was reduced to a drunken whisper: "Hey, Hermie. Sorry to call so late, Man. I woke you up?"

Hermie glanced up at the sunflower wall clock, it was way after midnight. And something was *wrong-wrong-wrong*. "It's okay. I just got in. Had a long dinner with Pierre Bonay."

"Oh, one of *those* dinners. How many courses?"

"I lost consciousness after the salad."

A soft chuckle from Gordie that sounded heavy with effort. Gordon Norris was still occasionally called "Magnum" by his Lomita Sheriff's station buddies because of his uncanny resemblance to Tom Selleck in his heyday, right down to the dimples and mustache, albeit in his own deep mahogany skin. The size of him ordinarily made that soft chuckle of his sound like soothing cello music; now it sounded off-key.

Hermie's instincts were overwhelmed with alarm. "Where are you?"

"Was on my bike." 'Bike' was a humongous silver and red Harley, which he raced over jumps now and then just to shock the natives.

"*Where* are you?"

"Alongside Manhattan Beach Pier. Or is that the Hermosa Pier? Redondo Pier? Naw, Manhattan. For sure? Sure."

"I'll be right there."

"Hey, no, you don't have to. I only called to --"

"I'll be right there!"

Hermie was about to hang up when he heard Gordie's voice crack with pain. "Thanks. Thanks, Herms."

Hermie was out of his house and into his car in thirty seconds flat and knew he'd catch hell from the Neighborhood Watch President Maybelle Comstock in the AM when a window-rattling backfire from Roberta exploded the sleeping stillness of the cul-de-sac he lived in. Maybelle would also no doubt complain about the smoke Roberta belched and the stones she sprayed as she took off down the gravel road -- circa sometime during the Great War -- and raced to Pacific Coast Highway.

As Hermie weaved in and out of sparse traffic, his clenched hands on the steering wheel betrayed his thoughts and began to throb. *What the hell happened?* Gordie was not the kind of guy to get upset. Massive, strong, steady, with a humor disarming and wry, Gordie did not go down from life's blows; he winced and carried on with business. This strength came from being a young boy who watched his six-foot-four, 300-pound father shrink to a 100 pound shell as he died from cirrhosis of the liver caused by alcoholism. After that, *nothing* made him waiver.

Did he break up with Sweet-As-Sugar-Sharon again? Gordie and his girlfriend had broken up once before, when her city councilman father convinced his Harvard graduate daughter that a cop wasn't good enough for her, because he had his own designs on her future: in politics.

But for the first time in her life, she had defied her father and come back to Gordie, with a heartfelt apology to boot. *Since then, everything was hunky-dory. Wait -- if they had broken up again, he'd get mad now, morose later. Can't be the girl. On the other hand, if he's got a major crisis, why call me and not her? What the hell --?*

Roberta did a squealing turn left through a red light and onto Manhattan Beach Boulevard, heading west. It was seen by CHP Patrolman Lyle Tennison from his watching post in the parking lot of a real estate office nearby, but just as he was about to kick-start his motorcycle, he recognized Roberta. Didn't realize he was talking out loud: "Grabfelder. In a hurry. At this hour?" To make sure, he checked his radio, but all was quiet for a change. "Something's down, but it's not a body." He knew better than to intrude unless invited, Hermie being the way he was. Still, he got on his cell and called a fellow CHP, Hector "Heck" Juarez, who was at his post in the parking lot of Fry's Electronics where Pacific Coast Highway changed its name to Sepulveda, and gave him a heads up. In ten minutes, cops' cellphones all over the South Bay were crackling with the news: Grabfelder was out and about, just blew through a red light ("Aw, hell, is he on the sauce again?") in a whacking-great hurry, but there wasn't a dead body in the direction he was headed. At least nobody had heard of one tonight. So far. The dread of another slice and dice like the last one was vivid in everyone's minds and talk.

The last sighting was as Hermie headed toward the Manhattan Beach Pier, where a Sheriff's station CHP had spotted Gordie Norris's Harley, "unattended", around three hours ago, and a debate had been going on as to if it should be "attended", since Gordie was oddly draped over the handlebars. Tennison and Juarez decided to hover, since they were near the end of their shifts, and headed for the Pier, where they nested not close enough to be spotted but close enough to hear and observe, just in case. Tennison let it be known to all who listened that they were now "attending".

He was drunk. But Gordie, being the son of an alcoholic with all the horrible memories that entailed, didn't drink to drunkenness as a rule. He was also drunk aboard his Harley, which Gordie *NEVER* did. In profile, his massive spine was curled downward, as if unable to support the broad shoulders, enormous arms that were now draped over the chrome handlebars. His huge hands dangled, as if their strength had gone, looking strangely young, like when he was a boy. He heard something, turned to see Hermie standing there, laser-blue eyes glowing even in this dim light. And seeing *ALL*.

Cold, bleached moonlight fell on Gordie's black Tom Selleck face, making the large eyes and deep dimples cavernous with shadows. "Hey, Herms. How's it goin'?" He swung long, powerful legs off the Harley and came nearer, his outstretched hand expecting a handshake.

It was Gordie's eyes that did it. Bottomless pools of . . . *fear*. Hermie was so startled at the sight, his impulse ignored Gordie's hand and sent his own arms round his massive friend in a brief, manly embrace, during which he smelled Scotch, remnants of a lime cologne, and fear sweat. He pulled back gruffly, "Don't get me wrong –– you sound like hell, you look like hell, you smell like hell, so you're not my type."

To Hermie's great relief, the familiar chuckle rumbled strong and clear in Gordie's huge chest and a flash of a smile gleamed beneath the mustache. "Yeah, you're still pretty resistible, too." But up close, Hermie was seeing so much, Gordie had to turn aside. His large hand with its poetic fingers smoothed his mustache as if holding something in.

Hermie saw the struggle. "Any place to sit down around here? Since ya don't have a sidecar and all."

They walked down alongside the pier to the sand, sat, knees up, arms propped on top. The indigo sky above was dotted with pinpoint stars, and Someone had neatly cut a thin slice out of the whiter-than-white nearly full moon on one side, but it didn't affect the brilliant cascade that flowed down to light up the black waves sparkling below.

The ocean's breath swept in chilly but soft, and Hermie's nose filled with smells: the green scent of kelp beds, heavy salt smells from schools of fish passing nearby, the ugly stench of diesel oil from tankers, jet fuel from planes murmuring past above, a flower or two, and only he could smell the faintest hint of sulphur in the air from minor volcanic activity in far off Hawaii.

After a brief pause of both of them just looking and breathing, Hermie said, "It weighs less if you get it out."

"I know." Gordie's voice cracked. He grabbed a handful of sand, let it trickle out of his fingers, silver grains flowing through ebony. "It also makes it *real* if you say it out loud."

"You called."

Gordie nodded, scooped some more sand. Hermie did the same, was surprised to find it still warm underneath. *The sun sleeps under the sand . . .*

"I . . . Uh . . ." A deep breath in his massive chest. "I had the physical a couple days . . . yesterday? . . . ago."

Aw, no, God, please no.

"They found . . . found a lump. Did the biop. It's . . . cancer. And it's not sure if it's the usual slow-growing kind. They *think*. Yet."

Hermie had to swallow hard to remain calm. "Where?"

"Prostate. Seems it's a common thing with us younger 'black folks'. Lucky bastards that we are."

A glimmer of hope. "But they can do things for that these days. Prostate. It's curable. Isn't it?"

"Sure, sure, that's what they tell me. But in my case, it's surgery. Lucky me."

"They can operate? Isn't that good news?"

"Oh, sure. Surgery. Some radiation. And I'll be cured of cancer. They say. But chances are I'll be turned into a dribbling old man who can't get it up no more."

"Aw, how do you know that? I don't believe that."

Gordie turned to look at him with large eyes as hard and glittering as obsidian. "That's what can happen, Hermie. I checked. Nerves get cut. Radiation finishes them off. Snip-snip, I'm done. And Sharon . . ." His voice stopped dead, obsidian melted into tears, he turned away. One more smoothing of his mustache, this time to keep it from trembling with his lips.

Hermie's first impulse was to argue on the side of the positive, but knew it would be bullshit. "I'm not gonna bullshit ya. This sucks, big time."

Gordie could only nod.

"But first things first — get rid of the cancer. After that, anything can happen, including *good* things."

"No way, Herms."

"Huh?"

"No way am I letting 'em cut me."

"But the surgery will —"

"The surgery will destroy my fucking life. Literally!"

"You don't know that for sure!"

"If I know it for sure, it'll be too late to go back and undo it."

"If you don't have the surgery it will be too late for *anything*! It's *cancer*, for chrissakes, Man! You gotta cut that out or die!"

"And what kinda life would I be fighting for? Huh?"

"Are you telling me your whole damn life is in your dick? Jeezus, who knew!"

Gordie turned just long enough to give him a dirty look.

Hermie suddenly heard that the shallow, nearly flat waves onshore sounded like a series of rifle shots as they slapped on the shore in the distance, then advanced nearer and nearer, to finally smack in front of them, then move on down the shore in crack-crack-crack-sounds echoing in the blackness. Suddenly, it came to him: "First things first. Get a second opinion."

Now Gordie's look was hopeful. "A second opinion?"

"Yes, dumb-ass! You don't take this kinda thing without asking around — other doctors in the same field, scrape the Internet, that's your favorite thing for info."

"Yeah . . . a second opinion . . . Maybe it's not — maybe there's something else —"

"Maybe, yes! Get your doctor to send you to the biggest, baddest cancer center on the planet, or at least the state — City of Hope? Mount Sinai? Whatever. Get every test known to science. Then you'll know where you really are."

"Yeah, yeah . . ."

"Then you and Sharon talk it over and —"

Gordie's head snapped back around. "Are you nuts? No way am I telling her! Not anything about this! *And don't you dare, goddammit! Swear!*"

Hermie shrugged. "That's your choice. But that's cheating, you know."

"'Cheating'? Where the hell do you get that?"

Hermie stood up, brushed sand off his pants, stared out at the moon-splashed ocean clinging then disappearing into a vast, black horizon. Far off to the right, the curve of the coastline showed off its colorful lights, Malibu showing off her jewels. He took a breath, glad of the scented distractions on the breeze because a dark memory intruded as he spoke from bitter experience: "You cheat when you withhold vital information from someone you are important to. You disrespect them. In the end, you starve them. Love dies from that kinda hunger. People die from that kinda hunger."

Gordie knew what memories Hermie was seeing in that vast, silvered ocean: Rachel, dead on the kitchen floor from an overdose, when Hermie was too wrapped up in his job in Narcotics and his drinking to pay attention to the hunger of his own wife.

Gordie got up from the sand, swayed a little when the Scotch danced in his head, didn't bother brushing off the sand. "I know what you're sayin', Herm. But this is different."

Hermies eyes looked icy when they nailed him. "So you say. So far, I've only met the lady on the phone and through how you've been since you've been with her. But just from that, I can still warn you: She's too important to neglect like that. And to get through something like this, she's *essential.*" He could see Gordie was not buying it, deliberately. But it was early days, so Hermie moved on. "But, get a second opinion. Maybe even a third. And fast."

"Yeah. I'll make some calls tomorrow. Get on the Net. It's something I can *do.*"

They began walking back up to the walkway by the pier and then to Gordie's Harley. "No way you're driving that thing home while you're drunk as a skunk." Hermie said.

"I drove it here, didn't I?"

"Dumb luck. Think of it this way, if you get fired for driving drunk, you lose your health insurance."

"Low blow."

But it was a measure of the seriousness of the situation and the straight-shooter nature of the man himself that Gordie went quietly and let Hermie tuck him into Roberta. "Keys," Hermie gestured.

"What are ya goin' t'do with 'em?" Gordie clumsily fished them out of his pocket.

"How quick you forget. Eyes and ears, Buddy, there's always eyes and ears in the Family."

Hermie took Gordie's keys, walked over to a pool of light under a street light, let out a loud whistle and then a wave as if gesturing someone over. Immediately, from down the street two choppers coughed into life and rumbled, carrying two CHP patrolmen over, where they circled Hermie and stopped. Hermie had a vague recollection of the darker rider and took a shot, "Heck, is that you?"

Hector Juarez's pearly teeth flashed in the light. "Been a while, Grabfelder. You lookin' buff, Man, lose 'bout thirty?"

"Clean living."

"Yeah, right." Juarez chuckled, knowing all about Herman Grabfelder's astonishing sign-up at Bud's Bodyworks. Bets were made as to how long the Old Bloodhound would last before the stroke, but here he was, buffed and toned -- *And, for crissakes, still sober! Who would have dreamed?*

"Man needs his Harley babysat this evening. Can you guys get it over to Silver Sail Avenue? Number's 2435, a condo building. There's a button on this key chain that opens the gate of the parking."

"It's handled," said Heck Juarez.

"No problem for Family," said the other CHP, who Hermie now saw was one of those bleached blonde surfer dudes. "Lyle Tennison, good to meet ya." Hermie shook a hand thick with muscles and tough with calluses.

"I owe you one, guys. Scratch that -- *he* owes you one. Gordie Norris out of Lomita Sheriff's station."

Juarez shut off his purring motor, kicked the stand out. He took the keys from Hermie and began walking toward Gordie's Harley. Tennison swung his chopper around slowly, parking alongside Juarez's chopper, shut off his motor.

When Hermie started up Roberta, Gordie's Harley was roaring off into the night. Tennison was talking into his mobile, "Franklin? You about heading home? I need a babysitter for Juarez's bike for maybe an hour. It's right here at the Pier, can't miss it. I'll wait for ya, then I gotta go pick him up, he's making a delivery. It's a Grabfelder request. Yeah, I just met him. Now I know what all the shittin' was about -- even in this light, spooky eyes, man. Yeah."

Gordie stirred at the sound of rumbling Harley's "What's goin' on?" But exhaustion shut down his lights and sleep compelled him. The seat back wasn't high enough to support his neck, so he sagged against the door window as his eyelids slid down and stayed put. And the rumble of his breathing was as great as a lion's.

Mercifully "alone", Hermie allowed himself to let go. He gulped air and fought the rush of fear he'd been holding back ever since Gordie had said the word "cancer". He felt a sudden chill and realized his whole body had been sweating and now the night air was cooling him abruptly all over and he was shivering. Mentally, he offered his soul for a bucket of Stingers and a straw.

Roberta coughed and belched into the night air and chugged up the hill toward Pacific Coast Highway. By the time they got to Gordie's condo building, Juarez and Tennison were waiting, doubled up on Tennison's chopper. Hermie retrieved Gordie's keys, thanked them again, and they purred slowly away, in deference to the sleeping neighborhood, and so as not to startle the young driver of a small truck making his early morning delivery of the Los Angeles Times. Although he did do a double take at the sight of two CHP's on one chopper, and flashed the thought as to how cool it was that gay date-nights had come to the LAPD.

Hermie knocked on the passenger side window where Gordie's head rested inside. He stirred, opened his eyes, clearly didn't know where he was or how he got here. Another rap of knuckles and he looked out at Hermie, focused, opened the door. Six foot six of black muscles and heavy bones unfolded out of the car, Roberta bobbing with relief on what was left of her shocks as his weight left her. "Where are we?" He coughed and gulped air.

"Home," Hermie answered.

"Hell, what a night. Got gravel in my brains." Gordie rubbed his head, trying to clear it. "Where's my bike?"

"In its place. Remember who you owe: Tennison, Juarez, CHP."

"Tennison? Juarez? Yeah, yeah."

Gordie's condo was two corners in the back, where a screen of Pepper trees dappled the sunlight on his patio during the daytime. Now it dappled ivory moonlight and high beam security lights. Hermie still had the keys, so he opened the door, turned on a wall light switch, while Gordie was still polling his pockets. Hermie suddenly realized he'd never been inside Gordie's digs and took the opportunity to check it out, following behind the lurching figure of Gordie, who headed for the kitchen to open a wooden door the size of a double garage door, revealing a giant fridge, reach inside to grab a half gallon of milk and start chugging.

Hermie hadn't known what to expect, but he was not surprised to find comfort everywhere. Large, soft chairs and a vast couch filled with huge, "come, sit-sit, relax" pillows. The colors were muted, tans and ivories and pale aqua contrasted with oyster walls and immaculate, pale cocoa carpeting. Neat stacks of magazines on blonde wood coffee tables, one whole wall of books in the living room, another wall taken up by the biggest TV screen Hermie had ever seen, alongside the most complicated audio and video equipment he'd ever seen. He joined Gordie in the kitchen. Blonde wood cabinets matched the fridge door and gleamed above olive green granite counter tops. Gordie was still gulping milk. "Want something, Herms?"

"Nah, I gotta get going. Besides --"

And suddenly she *appeared*, at the interior hall entryway to the kitchen. She looked tinier than she actually was because of her delicate slenderness. Hermie immediately thought of a fawn, with her long legs and arms and neck, and her enormous black and tilted eyes that looked as if drawn by Disney. Thick, black mascaraed eyelashes quivered as all she saw was Gordie. Her blouse and skirt were rumpled, as if she'd been sleeping in them for the time she waited.

She froze. Gordie froze. Hermie froze. And nobody said a word. But three different kinds of breathing was heard.

Then Hermie recognized the voice he'd heard on the phone on one occasion, warm and sweet as caramel, with a strong touch of the South: "Ya didn't answer yer phone all day and all night. I got scared. Yer job . . ." And then she saw that he was drunk.

To the rescue, Hermie stepped forward with his best smile and an outstretched hand. "Totally my fault. Gordie was tied up, helping me on a case. We were kinda celebrating tonight. A load too much, in fact. Hi, I'm Grabfelder. Hermie. 'Bout time we met in person."

He wasn't that tall, compared to Gordie, but he still loomed large into her space, so she was compelled to look way up and focus on him. The intense laser blue eyes made her catch her breath -- *He could see ever-thing!* -- even now, when those eyes were glowing with a kind smile. Her hand was swallowed up in his huge, warm mitt and then she felt a reassuring pat with his other hand. *He's tellin' me not to worry. Somethin' awful's happenin', but he's takin' care of it. He's tellin' me to let it go for now.* She forced a smile at him. "Mr. Grabfeldah, I'm Sharon Menloe, and it sure is good to meet ya at last. I guess Gordie -- and you -- just lost track of the time."

"Exactly. This case was a brain-burner. But it's done and done now."

I bet when he lies for real, nobody -- but NOBODY -- can catch him out. But he only lies when it's important. Like now. "Oh, well then, ever-thing's all right." She turned to Gordie and saw he wanted to be alone. *Bad.* "I'll just go on home then, now that I know ever-thing's . . ." She glided across the floor and had to stand on tiptoe to kiss the bottom of Gordie's chin. His free hand went around her and he hugged her with one giant arm and with a desperation in his eyes that she couldn't see because her own desperate eyes were hidden in the curve of his neck. He let go first, turning to replace the milk in the fridge. "I'll call you tomorrow," he said, lying.

"That'll be fine, Honey." she said, knowing he was lying and turned away, so she missed the guilty look on Gordie's face and he missed the fear on her face. As she passed by Hermie, her enormous dark eyes flashed helpless messages at him and she said, "Hope t'see ya again soon, Mistah Grabfeldah."

"Hermie, please," he smiled comfort.

"Thank ya kindly. For lookin' after mah man." And she glided out the door, leaving the scent of lilies in her wake. The door quietly clicked shut behind her.

They both stood there, transfixed. Then Hermie sighed, "Now *that*, Son, is what we-all's been fightin' for."

He spent another half an hour with Gordie, making sure he was tired enough to just pee and go to bed and stay there, snoring, instead of wandering the streets some more.

Good thing, since it was long enough to miss the poignant sight of Sharon in the darkest shadow of the building's court-yard, hanging on to a sympathetic ficus tree as she sobbed the pain of the heartbroken and afraid with barely a sound, before she ran to her small, yellow sports-car and drove off as if pursued.

CHAPTER FOUR

"It is accepted that a man's first truth is what he hides."

Andre Malraux

The second last thing that ever happens is to be woken up from a deep, dreamless sleep by a sharp knock on his front door. No one dared except Neighborhood Watcher Maybelle Comstock, bringing yet another complaint. The first last thing that ever happens is to yank open the front door with the usual "WHAT?!" and find it's *not* Maybelle Comstock. It was the FBI.

Alan "Trots" Trotsky was a pal from the days when Hermie took Quantico's serial murder course. Trots looked him up and down, took in the rumpled, still-golden hair and older-than-dirt Brooklyn Dodgers t-shirt and said, "Hip as ever, I see."

After a round of manly-man hugs, back-slapping and guffaws, Trots came in and Hermie led him into the kitchen where the automatic timer of his coffee pot had just gone off and a dark and fragrant stream was dutifully flowing into the glass carafe. Hermie got dressed, grabbed two cups from the cupboard and gave Trots the one from Knotts Berry Farm, 1996, while he kept his usual, the Green Hornet cup he'd had since who remembers. Both liked their coffee black and harsh, so after a pour, a blow, a sip and a sigh, the preliminaries were over and kitchen chairs got pulled out, sat on, and the catching up began.

"How goes it, Snoopy?" Trots used a nickname for Hermie known only in certain FBI archives.

Hermie indicated his now svelte frame, "Can't you guess? And what happened to the flame-haired scamp I once annoyed? Can't call you "Red" anymore, wouldn't make sense."

Trots sheepishly brushed his hand over one of the world's last crew-cuts, now silvery-gray instead of rusty-red. "Don't it make me look distinguished? Sort of a PFC Cary Grant?"

Hermie nearly sprayed a noseful of coffee, laughing. "You realize the ever-lovely Brenda will come calling again, once she hears I am now svelte-ly sexy and remain crowned with a surfer's locks." and his strong fingers raked back the still blonde, still thick, still unruly hair from his forehead, with barely a silver strand here and there.

"You make me sick."

"It's what I live for."

Eleanor finally appeared, having dashed into the nearest closet upon hearing the knock on the door, because it was the second to the last thing, etc. She slipped into the kitchen and quickly checked out her personal food court in the boot room by the back door, to find nothing missing or disturbed. She relaxed enough to allow her slim-line self to sidle over to the kitchen table and test the air -- the smell of the stranger slid into her nose, just as a new face turned down to her and she saw non-threatening eyes and heard a gentle voice say, "Well, hello, kitty-kitty. Who are you?"

"Eleanor. She's my boss," answered Hermie. "Took over some time ago. P.S."

"'P.S.'?"

"Pre-Sober. She did the initiation period."

Then Trots realized what was really different about Hermie: he was not hung over. He recalled a prodigious capacity for Stingers that made Hermie come to class looking like a remnant from a New Year's Eve. It never affected that steel trap intellect of his, but even back then Trots had wondered when Life would lower the boom. Especially after his wife Rachel had O.D.'d. But now, even at this ungodly hour, the sly-fox lasers were clear and bright, there were no grey circles below his eyes, and his new trimness was rock solid with muscles.

"You look good, Man, really. I'm putting Brenda in leg irons and locking her in the basement."

"Hell, I've broken into better than your basement. She shall be mine. Aside from that, what the hell are you doing here? Don't tell me -- Jordan Hashemi, that fine Irish lad? And the oh-so-unlucky Lila Miller?"

Trots sat back, rubbed his stomach. "You got any breakfast? Would you believe they served just a granola bar and coffee or booze on that plane? You hadda pay extra if you wanted a goddamned muffin. Or a pillow. Mark my words: there'll coin meters for the johns next."

"Ah, yes. Remember when they said de-regulation would be a 'good thang'?"

To Trots' astonishment, in minutes Hermie had whipped up scrambled egg whites —- *The man actually had a jar of organic egg whites in his fridge!* -— toasted slices of a bread studded with whole grains, walnuts and raisins, pulp-rich orange juice from a gallon jug labeled "Organic, fresh squeezed", and half a cantaloupe each, stuffed with Greek yoghurt topped with fresh strawberry slices —- organic, too, no doubt, from the taste that spoke of real, dark-dirt fields, hot sun, and Time.

Trots waved his hand grandly over the food, "What, you got Rachel Ray on speed dial or something?" *Jeez, the guy's blushing!*

"Who?"

"Never mind. Just tell me the source of all this domestic hoo-hah."

"Oh, this? Met a couple gals in a supermarket who shaped me up, food shopping and eats-wise. Now I'm stuck in the habit. I am entirely organic."

"You're picking up women at the supermarket? Home Economics teachers? Suntanned divorcees in botox and tennis duds?"

"Not exactly. Jasmine and Carmen are my black and tan Moms . . . it's a long story."

"And that ain't half, I'm sure." Trots dug into the fluffy egg whites that were speckled and flavored with bits of fresh mushrooms and sweet onions, and fresh parsley. "Egg whites. They taste like actual eggs. Who knew?"

Hertmie answered through bites of his own, "It's the yoke what's got the cholesterol and fat. Who needs it?"

"Oh, hell, yeah, who?" Trots teased. After moments of good eating and the astonishment of Hermie leaning down like a doting retiree to coo and treat his cat with a bit of egg and toast, they sipped fresh coffee fragrant with hazelnuts.

And then Hermie's familiar laser blues peering over his own cup told Trots that he'd find everything he left out, but go ahead anyway. "Spill," Hermie said, "Unless you want to discuss the ups and downs of your crime lab. Or is that old news? Anymore incompetent ding-dongs looking at them slides?"

"Ancient news. Heads rolled. Brooms swept. Money descended. National DNA database now pristine, but some yahoos still challenge it on Constitutional grounds."

"Do they got grounds?"

"This is DNA from felons. What grounds do they got?"

"Too true."

"Your own 'old news': I hear your new headquarters and crime lab debuted with mucho fanfare. Cold drinks and cookies to all who attended. Love the artwork on the patio —- 'cow splats' still being bandied about?" Trots grinned.

"Do you know how much those things cost?"

"Didn't someone see a sketch beforehand? Ask a question? Laugh heartily?"

"This is 'art'. The emperor has no clothes."

"Always. Money don't buy taste."

"Always."

A pause for mutual coffee sipping.

Hermie said, "S'okay, spill it. You wouldn't be here unless ya got a load in your pants."

"Ah, colorful as always."

"And before you decide to lay on some clever little lies . . ." Hermie reached into a pocket, removed the bug he took from Lila's apartment and put it on the table in front of Trots' plate. "They sure are 'compact' these days. I'm so-o-o impressed. Thus the stomping on it."

"Up yours."

"And the horse you rode in on. Lila Miller was worth all those efforts toward a documentary? Yes, I found the camera, too."

"Actually, Lila isn't the issue. Regrettably, she was --"

Hermie blew, "If you *dare* use the words 'collateral damage', I'll throw you outta my kitchen!"

"Sorry. Bad habit." But Trots bit his lips like he always did when he was feeling guilty.

"You didn't see the wounds. She was slaughtered. With Eleventh Century skill."

"What? *Eleventh* --? What the hell, we heard she and Hashemi were *stabbed*, by the same guy."

"They were. Short guy, by the way. Small feet. One stab, then a slice down and all the way through. It's a technique and a weapon -- a dagger -- used by Shiite Muslims in the Eleventh Century. The word 'assassin' was invented because of them."

Trots sits back, stunned and staring at him. Then gets a little annoyed: "Why weren't we told about this? Our people called your people and made a very firm request for *all* forensics information. *Very* firm."

"Don't blame anybody. This can't get out, because forensics-wise is *SO-O* politics-wise. And according to the usual habit -- let's make that plural shall we? -- the FBI has been known to leak. Now and then, here and there."

"Oh, and the LAPD hasn't?! Do not get me started!"

"Point made over and over, I know. That's why only one person knows about the murder details. One plus me. That's two. Three, if you count yourself. And that's where it's gotta stay, Red. Till *I, me, myself* tell you different. So if it gets out beforehand, I will know it was from *your* happy campers, and you and I will have to get a divorce. I will get full custody of Brenda the Beauty. Support payments will whittle your paycheck to a nub."

"Okay, consider me warned and onboard." Trots sat back, still stunned, sipping coffee carefully.

"Horse of a different color, huh?" Hermie said, pointedly.

"I don't know where to start."

"Anywhere will do."

"It didn't start with Lila, by any means. It started with Hashemi. We were already on to him when she came along. Well, we were *trying* to get onto him."

"Start with Lila. I got my reasons for asking. Yes, I will share."

"Lila is — *was* an 'employee' of a particularly high class organization in New York City that supplied elegant, educated, 'escorts' to those of the Middle Eastern persuasion."

"And who runs this little sorority?"

"It's a joint operation."

"You and the CIA are playing nice together? Mom and Dad must be *so*-o proud. Or did hell freeze over?"

"Nine-eleven made us all grow up and cooperate. I'm not saying the pissing contest is over between us, but everybody's got everybody's phone numbers, e-mail, and they use them. Most of the time. Now and then."

"But in this case — *women*? How did you expect them to get inside an Arab network? They hate women."

"Only the tribal-type fanatics do. But there's another wing that's not the cliche' wing-nuts: Western-educated, super-successful businessmen, some with close, secret connections to their governments. Wealthy, social, they don't even look Arab, you'd take them for rich South Americans or Italians, except for the accent. They play polo, gamble, have country club memberships and elaborate wine cellars with beaucoup rare wines, since they have the scratch to pay for them and the egos that sidestep all those pesky, outdated restrictions in the Koran. They own banks, stock portfolios in the largest American businesses, usually fronted by other oh-so-American companies. These guys all have wives, from arranged marriages usually, and their job is to have kids. Sons a priority, of course. So, on the side they like classy call girls that make them look good — not only beautiful, but educated, discrete, personable, able to carry on an interesting conversation, able to behave in high society, blend in at charity functions, business dinners. These 'ladies' even send thank-you notes when appropriate, on elegant stationary."

"Emily Post is turning in her grave. In order to throw up."

"This operation fills a necessary purpose, Snoops. Some of these kings of capitalism also finance terrorist networks."

"And you don't arrest these assholes as soon as their expensive shoes touch down on our tarmac?!"

"Better to keep track of them until their plots thicken and we can catch them red-handed and knee-deep in evidence, along with their associates and underlings. Not only what their targets are, but who's giving them a helping hand *here* –- their cells."

"Cells. I'm getting nauseous at the thought. Are all those 'ladies' as wired up as Lila was?"

"All are wired or tracked in some form or other. Some know about it, some don't. The ones who know are our or the CIA's special agents, who know the drill and the risk. Their 'employer' also owns a lot of expensive suites in certain expensive and discrete hotels and apartment buildings. All those are wired."

"So . . . Poor Lila was an agent?"

"Lila was unique. Not only beautiful, classy, but highly educated. Had Masters degrees in both international law and economics, plus a Minor in Medieval history -– who does that? She was Jordanian on her mother's side, father was Iranian. She spoke, wrote, read Arabic like a native, in *all* the dialects. Everyone salivated over the chance to recruit her, but . . ."

"'But', got there too late, did ya?"

"Not exactly. Lila had some baggage that could cause a problem, psychology-wise."

"What the hell do you mean by that?"

"Lila's parents, Alvaro and Deah Begum came here from Iran. They were among that country's elite –- educated, successful, very wealthy, only casually religious, enough for show. But the Ayatollah and cohorts were and still are a constant threat, spies everywhere, looking for people who aren't Islamic enough, so to speak, rat on them for money. Somebody ratted them out –- a business rival, most likely, as it usually is. They had to run for their lives with only what they could stuff into their pockets. After a long shlep through European countries, some friends sponsored them, got them into the U.S. Once here, her father became a classic American success story –- changed their names to Albert and Dinah Bennet, started import-export in cosmetics."

"Cosmetics?"

"Exporting American cosmetics to the Middle East. He was one of the first to convince American companies there was a market over there for that stuff. Lipsticks, makeups, face creams, hair stuff –- it was well-known in those countries that American cosmetics are pure and keep innovating, with more colors, more skin treatments. You'd be surprised at the buying habits of ladies who aren't allowed to show their faces in public."

"The mind staggers . . ."

"Anyhoo, dear old dad got rich all over again, first in that business then branching out to soda pops, candy, fabrics, tennis shoes. Nobody played tennis over there at that time, but everybody loved those shoes because they were comfy, didn't cost the earth, and wore like iron. Made millions. Go figure. So, their only child, real name 'Ashwari', got all the best: Private schools, fully paid stints at Cornell and Yale. She was a top student, with honors."

"With all her brains, why didn't she end up working for a bank or the stock market or even our guv'ment -- the *other* branch?"

"Her doting Dad had other ideas. He couldn't leave his fortune to a daughter, even one as unique as Ashwari. Tribal prejudice against women, it's ingrained and unyielding, at least to the *first* generation of "Americanized" fathers, especially fathers whose *only* child is a female. He wasn't about to lose a large chunk of his fortune because of American alimony laws, so he didn't take the classic tribal route of divorce and marrying a fertile young thang who would give him sons. He also didn't take a mistress because mistresses in America are not like mistresses in the Middle East -- they can demand, they can *sue.*"

"Poor Lila -- 'Ashwari' was it? All her gifts and hard work, and not a friend in the room."

"Yeah. A marriage was 'arranged'. A cousin of Dad, who was still back in the old country -- Iran -- and he was working for the government, which made him well paid. But stifled ambitions and always looking over his shoulder for informers with jealous grudges and outsized religious credentials made him antsy. He already had a wife, but she was expendable, for large money. Paid to her father, of course, she got a pittance but enough to keep her quiet and cooperative."

"Another poor gal without a friend in the room." Hermie's disgust was obvious.

"So, Dad arranged for Shahawar Azzawi, known as "Shah" among his friends -- of whom there must be a few, a *very* few -- to come over here and marry Ashwari, eventually take charge of the family business and her fortune."

"But she was educated, had a future of her own, yet she went along with this crap?"

"Oh, no, she had rights under Islam, so she refused and threatened and even arranged to run away from home. But our boy Shah laid on the charm. He was a handsome guy, so he was a practiced charmer. He made sure she heard him telling her Dad that he was shocked -- *shocked!* -- that in this day and age Daddy was forcing his daughter to marry against her will. Quoted the Koran, quoted American law, quoted state law -- how he got his hands on *that* is certainly grist for someone's mill -- and assured Ashwari he would not be a party to this 'backward, illegal and sexist conspiracy'. And he let it slip, when it counted, that any wife of his would be free to use her education to pursue a career and would have his full support. Even if it meant putting off having children for a few years."

"She *didn't*."

"Oh, yeah, she fell for it. The main thing, she did not know about the wife left behind in Iran. Neither Daddy nor Shah shared that with her, or *anyone*, of course. The other thing, well, Ashwari knew she owed her father a lot, all that money and opportunity for education. And her mother had the usual longing for grandchildren and only one child to bring them to her."

"Aw, Lila-Ashwari, all that book learning did not prepare you for the workings of the Guilt Trip."

"Nope. The marriage was just two months old when Shah took his first swing at her. Cracked one of her cheekbones. His complaint was that she was not yet pregnant. And she had dared to object to the regular rapes."

"Aw, hell."

"Hell is a picnic compared to . . . what came after. 'Nuff said. He 'paused', shall we say, when she finally got pregnant. After a boy was born, to the great relief of one and all, he took up punching and assaulting her again. Not long after, she ended up in the hospital unconscious, with a broken jaw and cracked ribs. Police were notified by the hospital staff, hubby was arrested, bail was high enough to make a point, and only then did Mom and Dad realize what was going on. Lila hadn't told them up to that point. Pride, maybe. More guilt."

"God save women who keep hanging in when they should be buying a gun. And using it."

"Amen to that. But I give Dipstick Dad credit, he went to court, paid the fine and swore on his honor to the judge that it would never happen again, he'd be responsible for his son-in-law's future conduct, and he'd personally call the cops on him if Shah so much as frowned at his daughter again. Notice he never mentioned being responsible for his *daughter*. But he warned Shah that his fortune would vanish with the stroke of a pen on a new Will if he ever raised a hand to Ashwari again. Shah was allowed by Dad to get an accommodating mistress for his 'workouts', but soon Shah began swatting his little boy for 'disrespecting your father'. The boy was just four years old."

"Sonuvabitch."

"Yeah. But apparently there *is* a god: Lila's husband was driving home from his favorite casino in New Jersey when someone shot out his tires and then did the world a favor and shot out his brains. We're pretty sure it was 'arranged' by Lila's father, or maybe even her mother, but nobody could prove it then, nobody ever will."

"And who would much care to? He was Iranian. And an asshole."

"Mmmhmm. Unfortunately, Lila's problems didn't get killed off with him."

"Because . . . ?"

"Her son."

"*Because* . . . ?"

"He was the only male heir. Her father couldn't wait to get his hands on him, once the boy came of age. Which to Daddy, six years old was soon enough. And if his Mom interfered, precious daughter, genius daughter though she was, she was expendable if she was a problem. She had a dead husband as an example."

"Jeez!"

"Culture again. They never erase the village from their genes. Lila took her boy, some jewelry to sell, and *ran*." Trots got up, poured some more coffee in both their cups.

"Dad searched?"

"Oh, yeah. He hired dozens, spent thousands, but he looked in all the wrong places. And for the wrong woman. 'Ashwari' no longer existed. And 'Lila Miller' didn't turn up in any professions she was educated for, or in any other 'normal' job. In his wildest revenge dreams, Dad could never guess his daughter became a well-paid courtesan who could speak fluent Farsi or Urdu or the rest of them over cocktails."

"So, she was a hit at the 'Gotham Social Club'. Daddy certainly would have had a cow over that. Some kinda justice."

"Better justice: dementia did Dad in. Ironic, when you think of it, all that brain exercise in plotting, scheming, business wheeling and dealing, and –– pffft! It must have done a number on her Mom as well, because she went back to Iran, of all places. But she still had some family there, so that was the draw, since Ashwari and grandson never came back. And never will, she figured."

"Where-all did Lila go? Before becoming the most popular girl in class, I mean."

"Haven't a clue. Some time later, we heard about her language skills and education from the head of that New York City organization. We risked a lot by calling her in for a recruitment interview."

"I'll say you did. But more important to all should have been why she became a call girl when she was free of marriage and presumably Daddy, and had all that untapped education."

"That was the psychological baggage I mentioned. We never got the answer for that. But aside from that, our offer intrigued her because it was an opportunity to use her education and language skills in a dangerous environment for a good cause: keeping America safe."

"Did you put that on a recruitment poster? You really should put that on a wall somewhere. Or the side of a bus."

"I know, I know. But these days, we need all the help we can get. You have no idea what's out there."

"And not so out there. They're *here*."

"Exactly. That's what keeps us awake nights."

"I'd sympathize but I've got nightmares of my own. Change of subject, almost — what about Lila's son?"

"I'm embarrassed to say we don't know. She hid him very, very well."

Hermie decided to give an inch: "I just found out about his Mom being your Lila Miller, and he occasionally dropped in to visit her and sometimes stay the night. Pre- and post-Hashemi."

Trots' brow suddenly smoothed over. "So *that's* why she did that."

"'That'?"

"Every once in a while, the recordings went blank. For some hours, a couple days. Lila claimed ignorance, 'power failures' in the building, yada-yadoo. We checked. There weren't. So, *he* was there. Her son. I'll be damned."

"If it wasn't her, it was Hashemi. They both weren't about to give *anyone* a line on that boy. Even the spooks she worked for."

"She was more unique than we knew. Good for you, Ashwari-Lila," Trots saluted her memory with the last of his coffee.

"Here's the problem, Sport," Hermie ventured.

"Oh, hell, 'the problem'?" Trots groaned.

"It's certain Lila's son was at the murder scene. He saw *everything*."

"Aw, Jeez! The poor kid! Where is he? Is he all right?"

"Damned if I know. He ran."

"Then how do you know he was there?"

"Footprints. Forensics. Banana bubblegum. And Pepsi Potter."

For a second or two, Trots was speechless, gaping. Then, "Oh, I just give the hell up!"

"Pepsi Potter is the HOA president of Lila's condo building. She keeps an eye out on *evv-erything*, especially concerning Lila, Hashemi and the boy, because she was fond of them. Lila and Hashemi were obviously close, and Hashemi doted on Lila's son, they were like a family those three. But Hashemi was always on guard, like he knew they were being stalked. Clever ducks, huh?"

"Okay, okay, don't rub it in anymore than you're going to."

"I'd venture to say that your bugs and camera were yanked and replaced by Hashemi, not Lila, putting in place his own security system in order to keep a guard on Lila and the boy."

"I'm not gonna share that information with anyone."

"I don't blame you. Embarrassing. Pepsi caught Hashemi scoping out the entire building and property, claiming it was for earthquake insurance — no doubt he was doing wiring already. He then came by regularly, as did her boy. Knowing Lila, as you've told me, Hashemi must have been someone special, because I can't see Lila trusting *any* man, particularly a Middle Eastern one. You'd told her Hashemi was a terrorist?"

"No, we didn't. Because, frankly, we didn't exactly *know* he was a terrorist. We just knew for sure that he was an arms dealer. Well, we didn't know *for sure*, but . . ."

"Yeah, I get it. But that afternoon her son went with them to a Mother's Day dinner. And, according to Pepsi, Lila's boy was almost always included in their 'outings'. But this time, their car was forced off the freeway and down to the murder scenes. Did the killer know the boy was with them? Good question."

Trots got back on track: "'Forensics?' 'Scenes?' Wasn't everyone killed together?"

"Three footprints at the first crime scene — Lila was killed first — Lila's shoes, the killer's shoes, and the kid's track shoes."

"Only three? What about Hashemi's?"

"He was at the second scene. He was tied up in the car when Lila was killed. At the second scene, he'd managed to free one hand and barely got out of the car when he got it. Stab and slice."

The most astonishing thing for last: "Banana bubblegum?"

"Apparently, the boy was addicted to it. Left traces on Lila, and I smelled it in his hardly-used bedroom at her condo. When he stayed, it wasn't for long. And where he went afterwards or in between visits, who the hell knows." For some reason, he didn't want to betray the boy's kiss on Lila's cheek, so he didn't mention it, even to someone he trusted not to denigrate it. "How did Lila meet Hashemi? I assume your eager beavers played matchmaker. 'Terrorist Mingle Dot Com'?"

"How very, very amusing. Look, Lila's first gig was an embassy party, a 'go see' escorted by one of ours, supposedly an oil man from Yemen who showed her off to the salivating sons of the desert. One of them she was introduced to was Rashid Rasfani, who was with his 'associate', Jordan Hashemi. Frankly, we were surprised that the likes of Hashemi would associate with Rasfani. Hashemi was sane, undoubtedly a genius; Rasfani was a certifiable loon. Prior to this, we had been trying — and pretty much failing — to track Hashemi because he was literally taking over the arms sales for Iran, Pakistan, Yemen, Nigeria, etcetera-and-beyond. Not selling to their governments, but directly to the bands of shitheads who are killing and kidnaping their way through cities and villages in their zeal to create a religious caliphate. You know the type, they behead the innocent while quoting the Koran. Not Hashemi's type at all."

"And yet Hashemi was arming these assholes?"

"In those days, Hashemi was arming everyone and anyone who had the money to pay. Hell, he nearly sold high-capacity rifles to white supremacists in Texas before we stepped in, and got flack from those god-fearing Texans for denying them their gun rights."

"Ain't they a peach, though?"

"We still don't know how Hashemi got certain Russian rockets sold, on paper, to some sons of Yemen. They'd just left the factory, were destined for the Russian troops who were not — *NOT!* — fighting the locals in the Crimea. Well, they simply vanished. Pfft! Until someone of ours spotted them being unloaded off a Russian aircraft in Nigeria. Nigeria, yeegods!"

"How the hell did they get there instead of Yemen?"

"Who the hell knows? So far. Internet traffic was lit up like Christmas between Yemen and Hashemi, 'We don't got the rockets and you got the money'. Didn't know Farsi had that many swear words. Colorful. But at least those particular rockets went kaput."

"'Kaput'? How kaput?"

"Tsk-tsk-tsk, such a terrible accident on the tarmac. All those fumes, a careless cigarette . . ."

"Kaboom?"

"Humongous Kaput-y-Kaboom. However, there was no mention of it in any news media. Russia is so good at that, especially when it's embarrassing. They're still sending official denials, usually misspelling 'Nigeria'. But think: Russian rockets sold to Yemen end up in Nigeria? Why for? Tell me that. How the hell did Hashemi do that? *Why* did he do it? Other than making millions in the deal."

"And you still let this Hashemi clown into the country."

Trots' long-time frustration blew: "We *didn't* let him in! He simply . . . *appeared*! And to this day we don't know how he did it! That's the genius part."

"He doesn't have to be a genius when you and the CIA are so lousy!"

"Hermie, we've had computers and our several kinds of geniuses and agents trying to track Hashemi. FBI, CIA, Scotland Yard, Mossad, Germany, France, Switzerland, *all* the good guys out there, even some bad guys we bribed with *large* money, *everybody* focusing on Jordan Hashemi. Nada. Zip-eroo. There is not a single record in Europe, in Asia, or in any Middle Eastern country of any existence. No birth record, family records, school records, no passport, no tax returns, no property records. Where the hell did he come from? How the hell did he get here? *Why* did he come here? We don't even know if this is the first time he's been here — he could have come here before and we didn't know about it. *There's* a nightmare worth having! Especially since this time he turned up with Rasfani."

"What kinda nutcase is he?"

"Rasfani went to college on the Internet under a false name/identity, got an engineering degree. Then his specialty became making an ordinary bomb smaller but deadlier. We're talking small as a deck of cards that could basically disintegrate an aircraft. Rasfani never stayed in one place long, visiting cities in Iran, Yemen, Nigeria. Over here, Detroit, Miami, Dallas, San Francisco. We know they are his cells and he's rallying his troops, making sure they're still longing for martyrdom."

"'Cells', for chrissakes?! What are these loons up to?"

"Best info thus far: amusement parks. Coordinated attacks."

"I think I'm gonna puke breakfast."

"But we've got that covered."

"I'll just bet you do!"

"We do, as good as it gets. Or did. It was Lila who gave us this early information. Rasfani was a dangerous psychopath and we had warned her and even given her an Out if it got too dangerous. But Lila was not only brave, but oh, so clever."

"How so?"

"When she was first introduced to Rasfani, he spit on her."

"He did *what!*? In public?"

"Yup. Because her arms were bare."

"I just can't stand it."

"Wait for it. She thanked him for reminding her of her duty and place. Rasfani was flattered to the max. Hashemi was dumbfounded, this was his first encounter with Lila, before he dragged Rasfani away for being out of line."

"'Out of line', he says!"

"But then Lila kept appearing with Rasfani's admired cohorts, more modestly dressed than the other women. And she made quite a lot of news when she excused herself now and then, because, quote, It was time to pray, end quote. The other men didn't cotton to a woman raining on their parade with modesty and the reminder of religion so they drifted away, with the exception of Hashemi, who remained a bystander. We had to use our own operatives to replace the scattering, annoyed zillionaires. But Rasfani still turned up, of course, always in search of financing, and there was Lila: modest, religious, and always oh, so fascinated by this distinguished, pious gentleman. She was admiring, sympathetic, docile, and above all of service to that sexually repressed sadist. We don't know what she endured, but she was urged to get out of the situation if she wanted to. She stuck it out for some months, long enough to find out about Rasfani's baby food plans."

"Baby food? If I'm going to be sick, I'm gonna need air."

Hermie's back yard became like an enchanted garden when he neglected the landscaping. A gigantic weeping willow, an even taller Ficus, and a purpled-up Jacaranda tree grown wild as nature intended dappled shade all around. A brisk breeze had swirled in ahead of the usual 2 PM ocean winds that blew most of the stench of car exhaust off to the east as far as it could get. The trees were gossiping in whispers, branches creaking, leaves smacking leaves, and purple blossoms twirling as they fell to their fate on the roof and ground.

Rose bushes on the edges of the lawn were nodding splashes of red, pink, yellow, and the lawn's only-occasionally-cut grass had decided to grow four inches tall and no higher. And everywhere, to Hermie's constant pleasure, was the scent of growing things.

Trots looked around, inhaled, said, "You got Paradise back here, Snoops."

"Yeah. Although Maybelle Comstock is constantly after me to trim, mow."

"Who's Maybelle Comstock?"

"Neighborhood Watch. A hundred pounds, maybe, of radar. She's the one responsible for the street into here still being gravel. Newbies complain, want pavement, but to Maybelle Comstock that gravel road is history. Been there since the first house was built smack in the middle of what used to be farms and fields. Hers and her Bobster's."

"'Bobster'?"

"Her hubby. Bob Comstock, everybody called him 'Bobster'. He built their house, just as Crazy Aunt Fern's husband built this. Husband Two? Three? He was a 'Harry', but Fern had two 'Harry's', so nobody is really sure. The Bobster passed on fairly young, as did Fern's Harry-whichever. In between Fern's serial marriages she and Maybelle were close friends. Same kinda bustling energy. They don't make 'em like that anymore. Maybelle can tell whose car was driving in, just by the sound of the tires on the stones. Your car put her on the alert. She knows it's a rental, and if you don't leave at a decent hour, she will be paying me yet another visit to make sure all is well."

A rioting chorus of birdsong was undoubtedly designed to taunt Eleanor, but she pretended to ignore them by sitting in the exact center of a patch of sunlight to do her ablutions, licking paws and washing face. Soon she would gracefully head for the shade-dappled grass, nestle in deep in a pose that recalled her grand-papa the sphinx in Egypt, her lime-green eyes half-closed and her purr close to snoring.

Hermie and Trots were seated in the antique glider that was tucked inside the swaying, cool fronds of the weeping willow. The fronds were so thick, they were completely hidden from view, the world outside was barely glimpsed now and then when the breeze swayed and briefly parted rustling curtains of brilliant green leaves. A few red-headed Finches dropped inside now and then, to tweet a greeting and take a look-see before flapping out.

"I can still smell those roses inside here."

"Yeah. Fern had a magic touch with roses. Too bad Rachel never saw this. She'd have surrounded this whole yard with white peony bushes. Peonies and roses, that would have been a sight."

At the mention of his dead wife, Trots did a quick check of Hermie's eyes and was glad to see that the guilty rage was gone; there was now a calm peace. *So . . . finally . . . he's gone past it. Rachel has left him at last.* A sudden piercing blast of loud birdsong startled him: "Twitter-twitter-twitter-twee-ee-EEE!". "Jeezus! What *is* that?"

"Finches. Courting. Sometimes they sing so loud, they go up on their tippy-toes and damn near fall over."

Trots would have gone into the wonder of Herman Grabfelder knowing such things as the courting songs of Finches, but there were more important things at hand. So, he picked up the thread: "Black market baby food appealed to Rasfani much more than a bombing here and there in amusement parks."

"Black market baby food. Now I've heard everything."

"We're talking $35 billion bucks stolen every year. They snatch it from supermarket warehouses, re-package it, re-label it as more expensive brands, re-do the expiration dates, then re-sell it to supermarket wholesalers here and abroad, and it's soon on the shelves. Sometimes it's contaminated. This gave Rasfani his favorite idea, way better than briefcase-sized poison gas bombs left inside amusement parks: Toxic contamination of baby food on a massive scale. 'Kill the sinful spawn of the infidels and send them to hell, to please God.'"

"Ach du lieber!"

"It was Lila who got us this information. At what cost she never told."

"And I hope you made her efforts worth her while by locking up Rasfani where the sun don't shine and asking the powers that be to re-instate hanging."

"Didn't have to. Rasfani was found sliced and diced in a palatial hotel suite in Miami."

"How sliced and diced?"

"With the ax that was in the hotel's fire extinguisher box in the hallway."

"Any idea who?"

"Hadda be Hashemi, but we have no evidence. Because he leaves none. We can't even place him in Miami. He's just too damn good."

"Now, now, y'all don't be too hard on yerself," Hermie teased. And he got up and went back into the house, dogged by Trots. They went back into the kitchen, now dazzling with sunshine pouring in the window over the sink.

"When he arrived here, we figured, satellite tracking on his car, 24-hour surveillance eyes on him, bug his office, bug his house, you know, the usual."

"Uh-huh." Hermie started the sink's faucet pouring water into the sink, hot enough to steam, preparing to wash the dishes.

"Every day he rents a different car. So, no trackers."

"Awww . . ." Hermie melded sarcasm with sympathy. "I got his nice fake driver's license."

"I'm sure you did. But the address is an office building, right?" Trots located the neat stack of dish towels in a drawer, lifted one out carefully so as not to tumble the stack.

"Yeah."

"There are no living quarters in that building. It's all offices. 'Swear, according to the building's owner. And no office is even remotely connected to Jordan Hashemi, again 'Swear. We checked homeowner and business property records for all of LA county first, then checked records for the state, then the entire country –- there is no record of any house or other property bought or leased by Jordan Hashemi. And before you ask the obvious, there is no record of Hashemi connected to Lila's condo. There aren't even records of *her* owning that condo. It's like they both didn't exist even though we knew they were here."

"I saw their bodies. They do exist. Or did. 'Till that dagger. From the Eleventh Century. Crap!"

"Who does that?! Who did that?!" Trots nearly bellowed.

"That's why they pay me the big bucks."

"Look, let me get to the point."

"Ah . . . the point. I *live* for your points," Hermie cooed.

"Snoopy, pay attention! I came here to ask you to let the case grow cold until we pick up the pieces and drift away soundlessly in the night."

"Yeah, right."

Trots handled the hot porcelain gingerly. "Jeezus, how can you stand water this hot?"

"I am a manly man. And we Germans wash everything in hotter than hot."

"Why don't-ya have a dishwasher?"

"Crazy Aunt Fern thought they were the devil's underpants. Uses too much water and would ruin her precious silverware."

Trots had wondered about the elegant real silver, heavy and ornate with carved flowers, that they had used to spear and scoop up breakfast. He now dried an elegant knife that weighed as much as the plate he'd just finished. "I wondered about these. Real silver through and through, you don't see much of this these days. 'Crazy Aunt Fern'?"

"Family joke. Her silverware, this house, furniture, she willed it all to me a while ago."

"Lucky you. Let it go cold, Snoopy. I wouldn't ask if it weren't important, national security and all that crap."

"Convince me. Start with why you didn't arrest Hashemi's ass along with Rasfani when Lila went through hell to get that baby food horror to your attention."

"We were obsessed to, after the ax fell. So to speak. But Hashemi didn't exist, remember? At the same time, the CIA tipped us off that they'd received info from Tehran — some yellow cake had gone missing and rumor had it that it was 'in the mail' with Rasfani's name on the shipping label."

"Good night, Nurse! Since Rasfani wasn't alive to receive it, where is that cake?"

"Good question. We were spelling 'Hashemi', until current events. That's also part of why I'm here. Me and my persuasive powers."

Later, they were sprawled on Aunt Fern's comfy chairs in the livingroom, sipping tinkling iced tea from her heavy, ruby-red Depression-era glasses. Hermie had opened every window in the house, so cross ventilation of the outside breeze made all the curtains dance and the scent of roses waft in.

Eleanor was at her usual post, atop Hermie's shoulder. Every once in a while, when Hermie raised his glass, she stepped down from his shoulder just far enough to take a few licks off an ice cube floating in his glass.

Trots indicated one of these exchanges, "You, a cat person. Astonishing."

"I am totally embarrassed, and often pissed off, but I have no choice — she *owns* me."

Trots took a deep drink of the fruit-wisped tea and asked, "So, what do you say, Hermie? Can you give me a couple weeks, maybe a month? Let us find out what the hell's going on. Was Hashemi the target alone and Lila was just in the wrong place at the super-wrong time? Or did someone know about Lila's FBI connections and decided to get rid of her and Hashemi for being too nosy. Or, did someone take revenge for Rasfani by killing Hashemi? And where the hell is that goddamn yellow cake? If we can't get to the bottom of this in a month, or more, be generous, huh? I'll throw in some scorched earth searching for Lila's son. Protection, too. Uber lots. After, you get your homicide case back and we will share all our info and not interfere. Because, frankly, you might be the only way to get to the bottom of it all, if we blow it. *All.*"

"You mean, blow it more than you have already?"

"Ouch. Point taken, on my last nerve. You're the best I've got, Snoopy."

"Flattery will get you a month."

"You're lying aren't ya?"

"Only a little."

But then both Hermie's cell phone and his home phone rang simultaneously, and a two-handed, two-eared answering revealed Claire on his cell phone and a Torrance police officer on his home phone, both telling him that a young woman had been found, horribly slashed, just outside a local high school campus.

It was at this moment that both Hermie and Trots realized that Hashemi and Lila and Rasfani were not the be-all and end-all of this case.

CHAPTER FIVE

"The facts are always less than what really happened."

Nadine Gordimer
South African Nobel Prize-winning Author

Her wallet, found in her book bag, contained a student I.D. for Amira Farsadi, nineteen years old, and five bucks in cash, all ones, no credit cards.

She's a teenager and all she has on her is five bucks? Hermie wondered. There were also two photographs of Amira alongside what was surely her mother; both she and the mother wore chadors and constraining headscarves, the mother's black, hers pearl grey, both shared the same large, dark and sad eyes above barely smiles. The second photo was tucked behind this one, and was more candid: both their headscarves were loosened considerably, showing off dark, shining hair; both of them smiled unrestrained, eyes dancing, faces rounded.

The books in the bag were on engineering, chemistry and physics.

Hermie went through the bag after he'd gone over the tiny frame that lay so violated and bloody, crushing a bed of bright pink Rosea ice-plant. One slim hand was raised up and caught in her long, dark hair, the other hand rested calmly on her midriff, alongside that same bloody slash from neck to waist he'd seen before.

He saw there was something unusually modest about her. Her simple blouse buttoned to the neck, with long sleeves to the wrists. Her dark skirt was down to her mid-calves, she wore dark, somewhat thick stockings, everything so uncharacteristic for a California coed. And she wore no makeup at all. She didn't need it; her eyelashes were thick and long, her skin flawless with the blush of good health tinting her round, ivory cheeks, and the full lips were naturally rosy. There was no slick, moist trail glistening on her face, so Hermie moved closer and began that slow, deep intake through his nose, searching,

77

taking in messages, looking for the specific one, the scent, *the* scent . . . from someone evil.

Her hair smelled like a musky, exotic shampoo, the hand resting in it had a faint scent of a harsh soap -- probably from the nearby campus bathroom. Her neck smelled slightly buttery, her blouse flowery from fabric softener and bitter from so much blood. *It's the same sonuvabitch. Two women. Well, one woman and one innocent girl, here. But if it was women this killer was after, why was Hashemi slaughtered? Just for show?*

And then he realized something: her hair, and that hand. Her hair was somewhat pressed down on top of her head, and it dawned: *Her headscarf. This kind of modesty, she'd surely be wearing a headscarf, like in the wallet photos; and it's gone. Her delicate hand -- it was raised onto her hair like she had maybe grabbed at her headscarf, trying to keep it on? But the sonuvabitch took it. Trophy, covered in blood for an extra goddamn thrill. I'll hate you till you die!*

Hermie stood up, shook off the protest in his knees. The Torrance breeze fluffed through his hair and the fumes from the traffic passing nearby harassed his nose. "She looks older than a high school kid," he said out loud to no one particular.

"Adult Classes," Andy Cho Hui answered, hardly pausing from typing his notes into his Palm Pilot. "She's been here overnight. She was enrolled in a computer drafting class that let out at 9 PM. From temp and tone, I'd say he got her not long after class."

"And nobody saw nuthin'."

"Everyone else was headed in a different direction, to their cars in the parking lots. She was headed toward the bus stop. It's just some yards past this landscaping."

"And nobody from her class offered her a ride home? Why?"

"Good question. In the dark shadows from these bushes nobody saw she was lying here. School gardener came by early A.M. to rake some leaves, saw her. The puke over there is his, poor amigo. Breakfast burrito with all the fixings."

Hermie had wondered at the growing fainter smell of vomit in the air. He took a look around at the groups of Oleander bushes all around, their branches heavy with blooms in cotton-candy pink. He checked the position of the body, did some mental calculation, then slowly backed away from her until Oleander pressed against his back. Andy noticed and got ready.

Then Hermie turned and pulled apart the two bushes he'd backed into, looked at the ground. "Here . . . here's where he waited." The soft ground was moist from the usual nighttime fog and the moisture had made the footprints settle into the dirt. In a few hours the sun and the breeze would have dried the dirt into its former dust and these footprints would be gone. But now, "Get some plaster casts of these, quick before they dry."

In seconds, Andy and four techs were carefully pulling aside Oleander branches and exposing the prints, measuring rulers were placed, photos taken, and plaster was being stirred. Both Andy and Hermie got a good look at the footprints. "It's him," said Andy.

"Same short, lightweight ass-wipe?"

"Same wipe. We'll know for sure by the end of the day. Any word from Bonay about what kinda weapon did these bloody deeds?"

"This goes no further. *No* further. Not even to Grandma."

"'Word."

"It was a dagger kill. From the Eleventh Century."

"Aw, shit." said Andy.

"What particular shit?"

"It's a Muslim problem."

"You don't know half."

* * * *

Roberta did her usual belch and smoke as Hermie turned her onto Pacific Coast Highway and headed for his stationette. He looked at his watch, realized he'd missed his morning workout time at Bud's Body Works. *Hope that Nazi doesn't get his spandex in a knot with disappointment.* Actually, on the few times work made him miss his workout, his body objected in a way he could actually *feel*, as if it went into a kind of suspended animation as it waited for that movement and sweat that was now a habit. The daily exercise had started out as a supremely aggravating way to save his job and possibly his life; but the aggravation had become a habit as the weight came off, his veins and arteries opened up and relaxed, and muscles appeared all over that changed his walk, his posture, and his stamina.

Maybe I'll go in after work and throw some iron around, he promised himself. His stomach gurgled a warning and he realized that breakfast with Trots had been too many hours before, and food was demanded by his hypoglycemic system. He checked around to see where he was, did a quick map scan in his mind and turned off Pacific Coast Hightway to find Rosa's Ranchero on Narbonne, where he had the specialty of the house: A steaming burrito stuffed with lean steak, mushrooms, spinach and a snappy salsa, washed down with strong iced tea that had a dash of lime in it. He ate slowly so he'd have time to think.

A dagger, for chrissakes. Eleventh Century Assassin, for chrissakes. Two women, well, one woman, one girl, and one man. What's the point? He knew the killer had a point, they all did. A point, a message, a revenge, a cause, or simply pissed-off issues. The point *was* the Perp. But now the point was *off.* The murder of Lila and Hashemi belonged to an entirely different world than this slaughter of a young girl. But the weapon, the method, the footprints, the necessary stalking --- all the same. *What the hell was the link? What's the point of a dagger? Why not a gun? Didn't he know how easy it is to buy a gun? Hell, these days you can get one on sale if you gotta coupon. Or maybe he's a lousy shot. He didn't strangle, so it's not personal. Or did he maybe not strangle because he's a little guy, not strong enough? What he did was strike them down, literally. One man, but two females. Was he pissed off at all women because he was not able to impress them with his manifest charm? Did he want to impress Hashemi with his skill? WHAT?!*

Maybe this all started with Hashemi. After all, he's worth killing, by enemies as well as maybe jealous subordinates. Don't forget Rasfani. But Rasfani was killed first. Why? By who? Whom? Trots assumes it was Hashemi. Did Hashemi kill Rasfani because he was a nut out of control? Or was it someone out of the shadows, striking for his own reasons. Dirty bombs in baby food for chrissakes! Would be nice to trump the FBI on this one. Only one way to do that. With help.

And so he finished his meal, tipped uber generously as always, and aimed Roberta toward some memories and a secret friend, someone who always knew what was going on in the criminal underworld. And why.

* * * *

He thought he'd be able to just scoot on by without this compulsive ritual, but he chalked it up to Roberta having a mind of her own and he had nothing to do with her coming to belching rest alongside the familiar curb. But he kept her motor running while he looked at the overgrown lot where his home once stood. He couldn't tell if any charred remains were still there after another --- *What was it? Two more years of time has passed?* Because a riot of lemon yellow mustard weed bushes were waving in a dense five-foot-tall wall. He'd be getting another terse letter from Public Works soon, ordering him to mow the weeds on his property or else they'd do it and fine him. *Large.* So he'll call a guy and the weeds would be mowed, and they'd fall upon remnants of his long-ago life: a house with a large, curved window in front, framed by a cluster of white Peony bushes. *Were there any traces left of the Peony bushes?* Peonies weren't supposed to flourish this far south, where the ground never froze like they required. But they grew here, for Rachel, his wife. They grew and flowered with dozens of dazzling white blooms, as delicate as silk, with their secret fragrance deep within their pale pink hearts.

Once more he recalled those white Peonies disappearing inside yellow and red flames and roiling black smoke, and the diamond glint of shards of glass cascading after that front window exploded, blowing up Peonies and dreams and firing up guilt.

He found out how many friends he had in all the right places when he wasn't jailed for arson, maybe because it was known he tore up the insurance check; maybe because it was also known that Detective Herman Grabfelder was deep in drunken grief, so secret allowances were made in those right places, although he spent another night in the neighborhood drunk tank and was removed from the Narcotics department. Hadda be. Transfer to another department was not forthcoming until he cleaned up his act; or better yet opt for retirement from the force with the reason kept confidential. *Do one or the other,* he was warned, *or you're publicly <u>done</u>.* And then Captain Claire came into power to seal the deal.

He shook the memory off and was relieved that he didn't have to throw up like the last time he was here, when he again had that compulsion to stop by on his way to a secret source of information. This time his gut was tight, tense, but burrito was in control. Maybe enough time had finally passed so it all didn't feel like yesterday anymore. Rachel had finally passed away. Away from him. He took a deep breath of gratitude.

He nudged a toe on Roberta's accelerator and for once she moved on without an accompanying belch and pop, as though out of respect.

In an older part of Pico Boulevard, where there were still a few houses instead of stacks of giant condos and office buildings, the pawnshop was small and innocuous, a wooden charmer built in the Forties, its front window still strung with wires holding pawned golden wedding bands. Some shelves under those held a variety of cast-off goods: a couple electric guitars and their speakers, four elaborately decorated accordions, sets of real porcelain dinnerware, ornate silverware, expensive watches, sets of designer luggage, and a few odds and ends that had been pawned and forgotten. A fine layer of dust coated these items, because this was a pawnshop that saw little activity, since its owner did not depend upon it for making a living. His living was made selling information, with an occasional arms deal thrown in if he thought he'd be supporting the nobler side.

Years ago, Narcotics Detective Herman Grabfelder had gotten a tip from a smarmy gentleman caught red-handed with a Toyota flatbed loaded with cocaine under an innocent-looking pallet of bales of hay purportedly heading to the fine, hungry horses boarded at what was once the historic Hollywood Park Racetrack, not yet eyed by could-care-less developers and their moneyed bulldozers. Desperate for a deal, the gentleman braved the scary eyes of the hulking detective he knew on sight because everyone in the drug business knew LAPD Narcotics Detective Herman Grafelder, whose infamous nose had taken one whiff of the bales of hay and had them dumped on the street to reveal —- ta-da! —- enough coke to keep half the state nuts for some considerable time. In exchange for a deal, the gentleman gave Herman a name that had nothing to do with narcotics, since this name refused to deal in that poison; but the name had everything to do with information about arms sales.

Of course, Hermie was not at all interested in arms sales, although he could certainly place a call to Quantico and let them know that a gentleman had given out a hot tip. But this same gentleman told Hermie that this source had other information, concerning every player, every shipment, quantity, source, political support and reliable gossip about every drug cartel and arms dealer on the planet. Not to mention information about what was then the new and baffling problem of home-grown terrorists. "He knows every rag-head yahoo with a grudge," was how the gentlemen put it, "cuz they're his people. He's one of them Ay-rabs, see?"

And thus, out of sheer curiosity Detective Herman Grabfelder had entered this pawnshop for the first time that long ago, struck up a conversation and an odd but absolutely faithful friendship with the man who knew "every damn thing": Farouz Selah.

It was Selah who had once told him who had bugged his house when he was tracking the South Bay Serial Killer; and why.

Now Hermie entered the shop to the familiar tinkle of the ancient brass bell above the door, the soft, endearing creak of worn wooden floorboards beneath his shoes, and to find, as always, Farouz Selah waiting for him with a smile that was not of surprise, but with the certain knowledge of why he was here, so there was no need of the usual small talk of greeting. How Selah always knew Hermie was about to cross his threshold was never discussed and had long since stopped being spooky.

"It is a secret wish of mine that you will one day pay me a strictly social call, Detective." His voice was low, warm, the accent British-educated Egyptian.

"It's my not-so-secret wish that one day I will have time for a social life. How are ya, Selah?"

They shook hands warmly, Selah's large, dark eyes the only inviting aspect of his impassive, dark face. He was once a handsome man, and there were still glimpses of that in his face, but Time and too many pounds and cigarettes had rounded and lined what where once pronounced cheekbones and a fine jaw and beautiful lips that were now hidden in a carelessly trimmed mustache, black turning to white.

"Do you have the time at present for a coffee?" Selah asked.

"Always." Selah's invitations for coffee were rare, usually made when information was just as rare, so Hermie's interest piqued already. Besides, he had a vivid memory of the dark, bitter Turkish coffee Selah preferred, and how he made it mellow and fragrant with plenty of real cream and slivers of black chocolate.

Pleased, Selah nodded and pressed a hidden button beneath the worn counter-top upon which he'd been leaning. Instantly and almost soundlessly, heavy drapes dropped down to seal off the shop's windows, and the door clicked with a bolt lock. From the outside, the shop looked *very* closed.

Hermie followed him deeper into the shop. Selah's sandaled feet were small, and neatly manicured, but they set the old polished floorboards to creaking as he led Hermie to the back of the shop, where he had only a few times before seen the hidden revelation: A compact apartment furnished like a tent in the Middle East. Deceptively homey, Hermie had once been given the privilege of seeing how this part of the building had been fortified with steel panels and girders to make it strong enough to give an armored tank or a rocket pause if intent on blasting into this lair. Not to mention the secret escape route that opened up smack into the obscuring crowds of a nearby mall.

Two small, low couches were piled with colorfully embroidered pillows, a few of which had tiny pieces of mirror trapped and twinkling within golden threads. The rich, nutty tobacco smell of countless non-filtered cigarettes smoked through the years lingered throughout the room, permeating the wormwood paneling and silken drapes. Hermie waited for it, and it soon drifted into his nose above all the other scents, familiar and tantalizing: the mysterious cologne of Farouz Selah, the scent of sandalwood and secrets.

An open sliding glass door overlooked the small back yard surrounded by a tall and tightly woven bamboo fence. Hidden motion detectors and silent alarms were everywhere, Hermie knew, but all were invisible. Selah's secret affections showed here in the number and variety of birds calling his yard home: Hummingbirds buzzed, perched and drank from several hanging feeders. Orange-capped male and cap-less female Finches fed from several seed feeders. California Scrub Jays squawked and flitted azure wings around feeders holding unsalted peanuts, stuffing their beaks with a perfect row of the nuts before flying off. The shock of brilliant yellow and black feathers showed off Grossbeaks dashing from feeder to feeder, seeking opportunity. Gray wings with snowy bars flashed as Mockingbirds swooped in to take notes on the various bird calls before heading back to Florida.

A few words of no consequence were exchanged while Selah brewed Turkish coffee in a French glass brewer, and Hermie tried not to get too comfortable against the sumptuous pillows on one of the silken couches that obviously encouraged dozing.

Selah pulled near a low, wooden table glowing with mother of pearl floral carvings, and placed on it pale green glass cups cradled with silver handles, matching creamer and a sugar bowl piled with large chunks of dark sugar, and lastly three gold-rimmed plates containing a display of dates, almond cookies, and tiny, golden cakes.

Alongside where the coffee was steeping, Selah placed an ornate silver coffeepot, into which he put slivers of black chocolate shaved from a chilled block with a silver blade. Then he poured the coffee into the silver pot. The spout steamed, the fragrance of daunting coffee and seductive chocolate filled the air. He brought the pot over to the table, poured black and thick coffee into the two green glass cups, set the pot aside but handy.

"Lethal, as always, I see," Hermie said, pleased.

Selah chuckled, added a dollop of heavy cream to each glass cup, handed one to Hermie. "You do not prefer the sugar, as I recall."

Selah slowly descended his bulk onto the opposite couch, put a chunk of dark sugar between his large, and remarkably white teeth, considering, and sipped coffee through it.

Hermie took a tentative sip through the steam of his own cup and got a blast of caffeine hardly tempered by the mellow cream and the chocolate. After a few more sips, his heart did a jumpstart and blood began to pound through his veins, rushing up to his scalp and all the way down to his feet. He felt the familiar combination of being warm and relaxed and yet compelled to pole vault.

Selah took another sip of his coffee, crunched the sugar and quietly said, "Jordan Hashemi, yes?"

"Ear to the ground, like always. And you probably know he was awesomely clever at escaping the FBI's radar. Was this a hit?"

"No. Several times 'hits' as you say have often been contemplated, even arranged, large money changed hands. But of course there was always the problem."

"'The problem'?"

"No one knew who he was or where he was. Jordan Hashemi did not exist."

"Yeah. That was the guv'ment's problem, too. Been driving those dorks nuts for alotta years, apparently. All they could find was clever transactions for arms sales to those wild and crazy guys in all those vacation spots in the Middle East."

Selah was smiling That Smile before he took his next sip, so Hermie got the 'message'.

"*What?*" asked Hermie with emphasis, intrigued, preparing for a surprise.

"They were misinformed. Hashemi was not an arms source. That was his disguise."

"You gotta be kidding! The FBI, CIA, Homeland-so-called- Security, they all managed to get that much in their expensive date nights, surveillance, cyber-searching. Hashemi buying, selling . . . Oh, you mean the toxic baby food gig. I still can't quite stomach that idea."

"That was Rasfani. Not Hashemi. It was Hashemi himself who put an end to that. And to Rasfani."

"I'm sorry Hashemi's dead. I'd like to pin a medal on him."

"I would not go that far. He was very much ahead of his time and place. He was a very dangerous man. Still is. Because of his death. It is a mystery. Was it done by someone even more dangerous?"

"Are you going to 'spill'?"

"With whom will you share this 'spill'?"

"My priority is a murder case. Three. Three bodies, two of them women. Plus Hashemi. The FBI and I were guessing that Hashemi was a hit, traveling in the circles he does. Did. But that doesn't explain the two women, one of which is a young, innocent girl."

"You may share all of this, but you won't be believed at the moment. And there is a missing element, which even *I* do not know."

"But you're my teenage idol! If *you* don't know, hell! What 'element'? Should I be glad I'm sitting down?"

Selah's smile was warm with affection. "Let us begin. At *his* beginning. Jordan Hashemi began this life as Winston Delano Safir. He was named after his father's personal heroes, Churchill and Roosevelt. He was born somewhere in England, where his father, Farbod Safir, was a renowned Professor of music of the violin and the cello. His mother, Hannah, was also a teacher and a gifted pianist. They were famous for giving concerts at which they played together. They were an unusually loving man and wife, their son adored them, and also his younger sister. It was with a reluctance felt by the family that the son went away for his classic British education. Boarding schools were the place for very elite education, but being away from his family home was a sacrifice. This all was interrupted when both parents and sister died in the crash of a small plane, on their way home from a concert. Winston buried them and then *vanished. Ceased to exist.*"

"But why didn't the FBI or the CIA or any of their brother and sister spooks find this information?"

"What do you know about cyberspace?"

"They installed computers in my office some time ago. It took me a while, but I found the On/Off key. Or is it the 'switch'? 'Button'?"

Selah laughed heartily. "Somehow, my friend, I knew this would be the case with you. In a way, I am glad. Your mind still works without the aid of machines. You are rare, even as you are behind the times."

"If you say so." He took an embarrassed swig of his coffee.

"Do you know about the war being fought with computers? Cyber terrorists stealing information, records, confidential sources of governments, corporations, and the like? Have you heard of 'Red October', 'Stuxnet', 'The Viper', 'Flame' or the NSA disclosures by Snowden, and other such computer data threats and break-ins, by China, Russia, North Korea, and other very secretive and dangerous governments?"

"Yeah. I read the papers. Doesn't help. Can't keep track."

"No, indeed. And what makes the news is not the whole story, is not even a hint of the story. What makes the news is what is chosen to be discovered, released. By politicians of governments who call themselves our 'guardians', our 'patriots'."

"You don't have to name names, tempting though that is."

"No. What is important is that these stories do not and cannot mention Hashemi. He is *there*, indeed. But he is not. The story of him being a secret arms dealer, that was skillfully planted and carried on for years by Hashemi himself. He created a reputation as an arms dealer with resources of all things lethal at a fair price and -- what is that phrase? -- 'No charge for shipping'."

"But he *wasn't*?"

"He made . . . *'particular'* sales. *Large* sales. The terrorists in Country A bought millions of arms from Hashemi who said they would be shipped from Port B as soon as Country A's check arrived. So . . . the check was sent by electronic means -- Internet."

"And?"

"Their check was received by Hashemi, but when he went to deposit it -- tsk-tsk-tsk, oh, dear, oh, dear, the check bounced. 'Insufficient funds'. Shock! He e-mailed and asked for an explanation from Country A, whom he 'trusted' and went to oh, so much trouble on their behalf. Horrified, embarrassed, Country A profusely apologized, and investigated. To find their entire account had vanished. Poof! There was no money. And no evidence of what or how vanished those funds. Hashemi sympathized sincerely: 'Who would do such a thing, tsk-tsk.' Naturally suspicious, Country A made attempts to investigate him. But he had vanished. Gone. So no one anywhere found any bank account for Jordan Hashemi to discover that all those millions were now his. Hashemi did not and does not exist."

"I'm not only losing the thread here, I never got it to begin with. Help me out. Again."

"Do you know how he got into this country without a trace?"

"No. And neither does the FBI, CIA, NSA, yada-yadoo. He just *appeared*. How?"

"By doing what his genius does best: Manipulate cyberspace. You can assume –– as did Hashemi –– that every government computer data collector, every terrorist group who is looking to buy or has bought weapons, is looking for him, world-wide. Searching birth records, family records, immigration, passports, diplomatic corps, government enemies' lists, airline tickets records, cruise ship rosters, cargo planes, cargo ships, train tickets, immigrant smugglers boats, trucks, vans, passenger cars, any and all border crossings, driver's licenses, home addresses, tax returns. I need not go on, surely."

"So, *how?*"

"By telling all those computers that he does not exist. That he is not there, nor here, nor *anywhere*. *How* does he do this? Fingers dancing on computer keys. Simple. But in Hashemi's case, brilliance beyond belief. He designed computer systems that did it all, without a trace."

"So . . . he's a thief. A cyber Robin Hood, he robs from the terrorists and gives to his own bank account."

"Presumably."

"Oh, crap! 'Presumably'?"

"Because there is no evidence, world-wide, that Hashemi has or ever did have a bank account."

"Okay, he's so–o-o smart and he's so-o-o careful. So, how did he allow himself to get mixed up with a Call Girl, Lila Miller?"

"Especially since she worked for the FBI."

"*You* know? *He* knew?"

"Of course. From the moment they met."

"Wasn't he risking everything? Lila was that good. Rasfani told her about the baby food plans. And *he* didn't trust *any* woman as far as he could throw them. Or spit at them. What made Hashemi take up with her after she'd been with that maniac?"

"Perhaps . . . loneliness?"

"Aw, c'mon! With his money he could buy any woman he wanted. Hell, he bought Lila! Didn't he? *Didn't he?* You're giving me That Look. What the hell was going on?"

"An empty man met an empty woman. Both of them had been playing their parts for years. Empty parts. Fake parts. Lying parts. Dangerous parts. It is exhausting, my friend. It is nerve-shredding. Heart burning. It is living within . . . famine. They recognized each other. And, Lila had a son."

"Are you telling me there was a love story going on here? They were a happy, little family? I don't believe it!"

"Someone did. And ended them."

Hermie sat back, sipped more of the chocolate-flavored rocket fuel. "You may be right. They were killed on Mother's Day. And I found a bouquet of flowers near the scene. The killer had tossed it, took the time to drive over it."

"Ah . . . that means very much of hate."

"Her son saw her murder. He ran."

Selah perked up, face twisting with sharp concern. "Oh, the poor boy. Oh, my . . . If so, you *must* find him, protect him."

"Do you know where the boy is? I mean, you know *everything*, no offense."

"I knew he has vanished. I didn't know why, till this terrible moment. Oh, that poor boy . . ."

"Any ideas as to who killed Hashemi and Lila?"

"Not at this time. Hashemi did not exist, so how was he found, killed? Lila had the FBI's deepest cover -- so, again, how was she found, killed? As to the young girl, this is a puzzlement to all. She was an innocent. Why was she chosen for such slaughter? I am still listening. I *will* discover."

"I know. That's why I'm here. Where else would I go? But, please, let me be the one who tells the FBI they have spent all this time and money on Hashemi and they got nuthin' *real*. He's been scamming them all for years. Let me have my fun."

"You might also tell them not to assume that Rasfani is truly gone. He was a leader of lunatics. Much admired. They may carry out what he had devised."

"'Much admired'!?" Hermie's disgust was obvious.

"Rasfani once saw an American woman in a bathing suit getting into her car near the beach in Santa Monica. He had to be restrained from cutting her throat. It made him famous in certain circles. Like most of that kind of deranged religious fanatic, he was obsessed with sex. And death. Lila Miller is to be honored for being able to penetrate that madness. Her life was very much in danger from that man."

"So Hashemi off'd him. Since True Love Had Found Andy Hardy?"

"In the truth, yes. But I believe it was also done to announce his 'ghost' presence, to tell the fanatics who followed Rasfani that he was watching and that kind of thinking was not acceptable. At the moment, they are subdued because of being without a leader. But only for the moment. A few bent sermons from a blasphemous fanatic and they will once again contemplate and act upon plans of blood against those who they think offend Islam and refuse to rein in Israel. They are easily inspired when someone deranged calls it a religious duty. And thus, it will never end. Hashemi saw this very clearly. And it was yet another opportunity for his unique skills."

"How so?"

"We may never know, now. Hashemi's end was truly a loss. For so many sides to the present terror."

"It's sickening -- do they honestly think they will accomplish their goals by slaughter?"

"Of course they do! Because the world is not stopping them! Think of the rise of the Nazi's. Same kind of propaganda and depravity: the feeding of religious hatred on a government scale. The only reason they failed was because most of the world got together, cooperated in the war to eliminate them. Until the world unites again, declares these fanatics are committing 'crimes against humanity' and must be stopped by *all*, these monsters will go on, killing and conquering, village by village, city by city, country by country. Hashemi knew this. His skills in cyberspace would have been invaluable to America, Europe, and the parts of the Middle East who find this kind of killing appalling as well as shaming Islam. Hashemi could have saved the world. Truly."

"Then who the hell damned near chopped the head off our Winston?"

"Unknown. At the present time."

"Again there's something you don't know? Selah, if you start slipping, I'm up a creek."

Selah chuckled, popped a date in his mouth and washed it down with coffee. "It is not a matter of my not knowing, I assure you. It is a matter of an Unknown. Hashemi was a ghost, he did not exist anywhere. How did someone find him?"

"The FBI found him. Sort of. Tried like hell for surveillance -- more bugs in Lila's apartment than a Mayfly orgy. But outside surveillance -- he rented a different car every day or every night. His fake driver's license has an address that is an office building that has no living quarters, no apartments, and no Jordan Hashemi on the tenants' list. So, how did a killer know where he'd be to kill? And why bother with the woman, Lila? And why the hell slaughter a young girl going to night school?"

"This is what makes a certainty -- a hit -- a mystery. This young woman has no connection. Her tribe is not a rival to Hashemi's, nor Rasfani's, not a rival clan or sect. She is a stranger. An innocent. Killed by the same assassin."

"The same? Yeah. How do you know?"

"The same as you: the dagger. The stab and stroke. This is a message. We must discern it. We must know who this man is, and quickly."

"He's 'different', isn't he?"

"Yes. That training, that weapon. But there is confusion: The Assassins do not kill innocent women and children. It is forbidden by Allah, forbidden by Islam. That is why it is urgent that he must be *stopped*. Not caught and punished, but *stopped*. He is an Assassin without honor."

Hermie looked into the dark and shining face, looking at another culture, another race, another agenda, won over to Hermie's side long years ago with a felon's bit of blackmail over drug running. It was his honesty and trustworthiness that made him a repository for information from all over the world, and information became another specialty of his, which he gave to Hermie back then and now because each instinctively knew the other could be trusted. There was no doubt between them, ever. Hermie finished his coffee, now feeling the caffeine was actually lifting his hair at the roots. "It wasn't a hit. Crap. That leaves me clueless, so to speak."

"I will make inquiries. Especially about her boy."

"That kid totally escaped the FBI's ever-thorough vetting. I had to laugh."

"He is a key. Not the only key, but the first. And now . . . he is alone."

"Where?"

"Lila and Hashemi would have taught him well. He is in the deepest cover."

"Where will you look?"

"Where you cannot go."

"Oh. *There.*"

Selah grinned, gestured to inquire whether Hermie wanted more coffee. "No, thanks. I still have some fillings left." He struggled to get his large frame up and off of the too-comfortable pillows and couch.

Selah followed him up, with even more effort. "If this Assassin is a rogue like Rasfani, he already has too much power because of his deeds. At the moment, in those circles there is astonishment. Everyone knows the dagger's significance; so, there is fear. Everyone knows Hashemi was invincible; so, there is also panic. Someone will emerge, of course, claiming credit. But he will be a lie."

"So, he's a lying sack of cow shit but not a serial killer. Whatta reactionary."

Selah smiled, "I love the American Language. No one has so many phrases that suit so many situations so very well."

Hermie stopped to look at him, wondering not for the first time why this particular Muslim had not succumbed to the call for fanatical religion, "Jihad for Allah", the romance of martyrdom. By the returning look in Selah's eyes, he knew Selah knew what he was thinking, so he said it out loud: "It can't be just the money. Or the power. Or even the free pass to Paradise."

Selah answered him with his kind voice: "Of course not. I believe it is jealousy by people who feel . . . 'powerless'. This country has too much freedom, that angers the fanatics because freedom puts everyone out of control, free to think for themselves, free to expose and resist power they don't believe in. Someone who feels powerless does not know how to live with such freedom. They are obsessed with achieving control. And, of course, the notoriety. Above it all, it's the notoriety."

"These days, a little control in this country might not be a bad thing."

Selah smiled that wise smile. "With all its faults –– and they are *many* –– to the open minds and willing hearts, this country is a promise that can be kept by one's own efforts. Since I came here, I have found that promise quite endearing."

Hermie offered his hand to this strange and interesting man. Selah answered it with his own, then led Hermie back into his shop. A quick glance out the shade dropped over the front window and Selah stopped Hermie. "It is best not to return this way." And he led him back through the building, out into another garden, this one neglected, weedy, where no birds came, only bees buzzing among the flowering weeds. Sunlight dappled with squinting intensity.

"Sharks circling already? Or still?" Hermie asked.

"Information is wanted by more than you. Or the FBI, or the CIA. Much more urgently, for reasons we just spoke of. You remember the back way?"

"Yeah. From our long-lost youth."

Before Hermie could turn away, Selah grabbed his shoulders with an affectionate squeeze. "As always, Detective Grabfelder, it was enjoyable to see you and talk again. 'Do not a stranger be', is that the expression?"

Hermie grinned, patting Selah's warm hands. "Close enough. You know, one day when we both retire, we'll hang out, go surfing, play poker, jog in the mall." He left Selah laughing heartily.

He picked his way through Selah's overgrown garden to a door in the bamboo fence, entirely hidden by a thick hedge of Bougainvillea running riot in crimson and royal purple blooms and obscured thorns. The door creaked a protest from little use, and opened into a garage full of rusting gardening tools. A side door in the wall opened onto an alley that led into a little used door of a gigantic indoor mall. After quite a shlep through smells of a food court and perfumed shops, and truly awful and too loud musak, he emerged from the noisy mall and walked through the quiet upscale neighborhood of mature but well-kept houses to arrive at his car. Before he got in, Hermie scanned the neighborhood carefully, as Selah had. No cars, no joggers, the silence of a neighborhood whose residents were all away at work. A burglar's wet dream.

He got into Roberta, fired up her engine and took the long way to the freeway, further distancing himself from obvious routes to and from Selah's place. Just in case.

Later, sitting in the bumper-to-bumper parking lot that was the San Diego Freeway at any hour, any day, Hermie turned to thoughts: *Who the hell do I look for first: An Assassin or a serial killer? What if they're one and the same? Of course they're one and the same! That's what makes me crazy!*

Finally arriving at the stationette, throughly annoyed now that the Turkish coffee buzz had drifted away or was gone into hiding inside some vital organ to rouse itself later, no doubt when he'd try to sleep tonight, Hermie scanned the phone messages and saw nothing important -- the usual gaggle of reporters and city councilmen and council women that came out of the woodwork, looking officially busy, whenever the body count went up. He pulled open a desk drawer, took out a new, five-subject spiral notebook, the kind kids used in school in the days before laptops, I-pads, and sundry, this one with a cover announcing the crime-fighting prowess of Vin Diesel. The large ceramic beer stein on the center of his desk, filled with novelty pens, yielded one that had an empty Pez dispenser on top, a homage to Shrek II.

Nell came to the doorway to find it was not the time to interrupt -- Hermie was writing up the cases with the absolute concentration and intensity that awed her. Later, she'd get to read these spiral notebooks as she typed up the notes into the official computer case record, and she'd admire the fine handwriting, the astute and often poetic thoughts that took a case and analyzed it with all the precision of a scientist working out a theory of quantum physics.

As she turned to go, his voice stopped her. "One was an FBI agent posing as a call girl with her John, and the other, the John, being a badass Middle Eastern computer hacker who basically didn't exist. The third a downright virginal girl, with no sign of rape, thank God. What the hell's the connection?"

She loved this, when he picked her brains because he was actually interested in her take on things. Of course, working *with* him as well as *for* him required an ever-more strenuous effort on her part to avoid letting on that she absolutely adored him. When she wasn't scared to death of him, that is. So far, he hadn't a clue, which was amazing, since those laser blues looked at her with a knowing intensity that saw *everything*, she feared, like now, as he looked up at her. "Was the second girl Middle Eastern?" She asked.

"Yeah. He stole her headscarf. Why?"

"That makes two. Middle Eastern Muslims, that is. Is that a coincidence?"

"Oh, hell, I hope so. Times being what they be." He sat back, lifted his massive arms and shoulders to stretch. Nell's knees fluttered so she looked away and made something up: "I was going to make some iced tea, want some?"

"Oh, Baby, I just had enough caffeine to drop a moose. Turkish coffee, Egyptian-style. I may not sleep for weeks. I better pass." And then suddenly his eyes drifted away, to a thought an idea, and the Pez pen began traveling across the lines of the spiral notebook sheet, quickly but still neatly. He was gone again.

She quietly left the doorway, went back to her desk, iced tea forgotten.

He re-focused, looked up to find she'd gone, the doorway looming with emptiness. *Hell, I've got to watch it. I'm a sexual harassment lawsuit waiting to happen. Thank God she doesn't have a clue.*

She never brought up the date they almost had last year, when he had to run out of her condo after getting a revelation by a program on her TV that led him to the Reverend Arthur Turner, the tortured, revered man who had killed Helen in a rage of disillusionment when she'd confessed to him about her secret life with three husbands and one lover: him, Arthur Turner. The familiar wistfulness at the memory of Helen drifted in, the regret he'd not kept her lingering in that parking lot of his local saloon where he'd fallen in love at first sight with the lovely woman who reminded him of the actress Jennifer Jones, in all those Turner Classic movies he loved. Had he kept her there after she dented his already dented fender, she wouldn't have kept her date with the Reverend Arthur Turner, and she'd still be alive, and perhaps still his, if he could have ever gotten past all her secrets, all those husbands.

He remembered Nell's neat-as-a-pin condo, and her spooky, shaggy gray mutt, Daisy, who had hopped up on the couch alongside him to give him an intense once-over with her amber eyes and black, quivering nose. He remembered trying to fit into one of her ex-husband's expensive suits, his weight loss having made his own clothes flap around his new muscles, and she'd volunteered the suit as a way of helping him avoid the Fate Worse Than Death:

Shopping.

Did she wonder why he hadn't asked her out again? Did she notice he had to hide boners at least once a day when a certain light bounced down into her dark hair, or a childlike curl wandered inward to encircle one of her smooth, apple cheeks with such a . . . He swallowed, throat tight and dry. *Did she say she was making iced tea?*

The phone startled him, it was his private line, not the station's. "Yeah?" He said into it.

Pierre Bonay's voice drifted in, relentlessly French, as always: "A'llo, 'erman. I have ze call from ze parents of Numbaire S'ree. Ze Farsadi's. Zey are coming in to make ze identification. Perhaps in ze hour."

"I'm there." He hung up and put his jacket back on, checked his breath *Ga-a-ah!* Chocolate and caffeine had turned toxic. He went into the tiny bathroom at the back of the stationette and sloshed red cinnamon mouthwash throughly until it burned his tongue and made his eyes water. Washed his hands, splashed and dried his face, and was leaving when he realized he also had to wiz. Annoyed, he wizzed and then washed his hands all over again, his long-ago-lost mother's instructions inescapable.

He passed by Nell's desk, answered her questioning look with, "Morgue. Parents are coming in to identify Vic Three."

"Uh-oh, parents?"

"Yeah."

"Poor them. Good luck."

And then he was gone, and like always it was like suddenly going deaf — all sound, all energy simply *left*. The world stopped turning, and the waiting began. Waiting until he came back: his noise, his scent, his definite presence on the floor boards.

CHAPTER SIX

"In the English language, we have words: 'widow' and 'widower', to describe the loss of a spouse; 'orphan' to describe somebody who's lost their parents. But there is no language anywhere on earth to describe the loss of a child. Because it is without words."

"Fear Thy Neighbor", ID Network;
spoken by the father of a murdered daughter.

Although he had assumed Amira Farsadi's parents were Middle Eastern, Hermie was startled by the appearance of those parents. The father was small and wiry, the dark skin of his face half-obscured by a scraggly black beard streaked with gray. He wore a simple, collar-less, nearly white shirt that was untucked, extending down almost to the knees of his worn, barely black pants. Black socks poked through the brown straps of comfortable-looking sandals. He might have had beautiful black eyes, but those eyes had a look of anger, suspicion, quite at odds with the occasion. He was a mean man, and it showed.

But it was the wife who drew Hermie's attention. In all his years of experience, it was *this* that made the job a heartbreaking calling: the bottomless sorrow on the faces of those whose loved ones have been snatched away, not by Nature or God and their powers, but by random, awful violence committed by a monster.

She was behind her husband, her face barely visible inside the pulled-tight headscarf of her black chador, but what was visible was terrible. Grief had pulled the outer corners of her eyes down, her extremely pale lips turned down, even her cheekbones looked as though sorrow had yanked them down, making her face hollow, lifeless. Hermie noticed part of a bruise showing beneath the left edge of her headscarf. Her shimmering amber eyes flickered up from the floor to take the briefest glance to see Hermie, then dropped down again. Her black gloved hands were clenched together so tightly, Hermie wondered that the fabric seams didn't split, that the bones didn't break.

Recalling his days in Narcotics at Pacific Station, he remembered a fellow Cop named Shaikh Mohammed, known as "Shakey", who taught the squad some cultural courtesies when they began dealing with witnesses and vics and perps within the recent influx of Muslim immigrants. Hoping his recall was correct, he put his right hand over his heart, bowed slightly as soon as he caught Mr. Farsadi's eye, deliberately ignoring the presence of his wife. "Mr. Farsadi, I'm Detective Grabfelder. I'm investigating what happened to your daughter. Please accept my sympathy for your terrible loss."

Behind her husband's shoulder, the mother glanced up at him again, just long enough for Hermie to see that all her hope was lost; she had hoped it was a mistake up until this very moment. Her eyes dropped and spilled tears and Hermie heard the softest moan of pain. Her husband snapped a look back at her that was a command. Hermie was glad she hadn't seen it, but then he knew she had *felt* it; her shoulders and spine slumped as she withdrew into herself.

"What is it we do now?" Mr. Farsadi asked, without any curiosity whatsoever. His accent would have made his perfect English interesting, in another type of man. Not this one.

"We require that you make an identification. I'm sorry, I know this will be painful."

Mr. Farsadi merely waited, so Hermie began to lead the way. "This way, please."

Both of them began to follow him, but once again Mr. Farsadi turned to give her that commanding look. This time she saw it, Hermie saw the briefest pleading look before the spilling eyes dropped back down, defeated. She stopped, sagged against the wall. Her husband moved on. Hermie led him through doors and hallways.

"I identify my daughter. Now what?" Farsadi said, after the briefest look at the face of his daughter, her plainness now lovely in the serenity of death.

Hermie exchanged a look with Pierre, who was politely standing nearby, and the classic Gallic and Midwestern-German word for "asshole" was mentally passed between them. Then Hermie hoped they were still in tune when he said to Pierre, "Pierre, would you take Mr. Farsadi to the conference room, help him with the forms . . . should take like -- what? -- ten minutes? *Fifteen*?"

Pierre's eyebrow questioned why he wanted him to take the man halfway across the building to fill out forms that were waiting on a shelf in this very room. "*Fifteen*?"

Hermie's laser blues glowered and Pierre got it. He scooped up the forms, graciously indicated to Farsadi that he should follow his lead. "Meestair Farsadi, if you please to come zis way." They swept out, Hermie followed to the door and watched until they went down the hall and turned the far corner. Then he quickly walked the opposite way through doors until he reached where Mrs. Farsadi was now turned into the wall, her face pressed against it.

"'Ukh-tee?" He gentled his voice with the flash of memory of Shakey's teaching that made him call her "my sister". He hoped it was the right word because he could not stomach calling this broken woman "Mrs. Farsadi".

She jerked, startled, and turned her tragic eyes to him, took a step back.

"Do you understand English?"

She nodded, "Little English. From my –– my daughter." A wince of pain at that last precious word.

"I've come to take you to see your daughter."

Hope leaped in her eyes, then she dropped them to the floor again. "My husband . . ."

"He will not know. *Never*. We have fifteen minutes. Come with me."

Her eyes leaped up to him again and she took a step toward him, her gloved hands unclenched for an instant as they reached toward him, then stopped short. He nodded, turned and led her away.

He fervently hoped she wouldn't disturb the sheet that covered her daughter from the neck down, the sheet that hid the hideous wounds and the stitched autopsy incisions. Her soft keening echoed off steel bins and ceramic tiles as she covered her daughter's face with tears and kisses and the caresses of her bare hands. He had picked up the black fabric gloves she had yanked off her hands and dropped onto the floor when she rushed forward at the first sight of her daughter's body. Arabic words were sobbed that needed no translation, and Hermie noticed one phrase over and over and filled with longing. Overwhelmed, her hands tore at her chador and the delicate fabric ripped, then her hands returned to her daughter's face, with a touch that was like memorizing, smoothing the forehead, the cheeks, the eyes and arranging the hair to frame that precious face, for minutes not long enough.

He checked his watch, then quietly slipped into her view, holding out her gloves.

Her eyes were empty of all but tears. "No, no, no . . ." she keened, her face pressed to her daughter's cheek.

"Your husband," he said softly.

Her body went rigid, she lifted herself up, she took deep breaths to calm herself, but failed. Her headscarf had slipped back, exposing shining dark hair, and the bruise on her face in detail. It was a large, nearly perfect handprint.

"She will be returned to you, for burial."

"Why –– why return?" She gasped, "She still be gone." And a last sob tore what was left of her as she gave her daughter final kisses on both cheeks, both hands, with a tenderness that closed up Hermie's throat with shared pain.

She stepped back, Hermie came up alongside her, her eyes were to the floor when she took her gloves, and jerked them onto her trembling hands. But she looked up and watched as Hermie gently pulled up the sheet and re-covered her daughter's face, as if tucking her in for the night.

He led her to the door, opened it and checked the empty hallway to be sure, and then was stopped by the question he was asked so often by so many, in countless accents, all with the same demand that was justified by the same grief: "You will . . . *stop* . . . who did this?"

Sorrow met resolve as amber eyes lifted up and met his intense blue gaze. "I will find him, I will stop him, and I will try to get the law to execute –– kill him –– for what he has done to Amira."

Something startled her. "You know my daughter's name."

"Yes. I will never forget her name."

And Hermie knew that she went against her religion, her culture and her fear when she reached out one gloved hand to touch his arm as she whispered, "Thank you." Then the gloved hands clenched together again, and again she hunched over, withdrawing into herself, as Hermie led her back the way they had come.

When her husband returned seconds later, he found her alone and silent, standing in the exact same place against the wall where he had left her. He walked past her on his way out, assuming she would follow behind. Which, of course, she did, holding in her secret, holding with her arms the tears on her torn chador.

* * * *

One of the annoying aspects of getting older was that his photographic memory for phone numbers sometimes pooped out. So now, sitting in Roberta in the morgue's parking lot, he racked his brain for Shakey's cellphone number. He remembered the main number of Pacific Station, remembered his old desk number, remembered the cell numbers of, so far, three guys in his squad, but Shakey's number eluded him for a good five minutes of temper and curses until it suddenly flashed vividly into his mind. He dialed and was startled when Shakey picked up after only a single ring. "Jeezus, Shakey, after only one ring? You that lonely?"

"Who is this?" The familiar voice and its elegant Middle Eastern accent demanded.

"Grabfelder. How the hell are ya?"

"Well, by the beards of all the prophets, it's my favorite infidel! How the hell are *you*? I have been hearing a lot about you, you old fart --- good clear on that serial killer gig. We all were so-o-o proud," he teased.

"Up yours. How are things at the Pit of the Pacific?"

"Haven't you heard? We got renovations. Windows, carpet, toilets that flush, there's an actual tree planted. I have seen it. Birds are moving in, making music and deposits."

"And you thought that Christmas list was a waste of time. Where are you?"

"I'm on a stakeout at a location what will remain nameless, eavesdropping being so sophisticated these days."

"'If only they'd use their genius for good instead of ee-vill'." Hermie cracked a favorite saying the squad used whenever they came up against the increasingly technically ingenious ways drug lords and their runners were using in order to evade the law --- eavesdropping on cellphone calls being the most annoying. "Why they don't get off the street and join Homeland Security is beyond me."

"What, and give up shew bidness?"

He laughed at the familiar comeback. "Hey, I know you're busy, but you're the only Muslim whose phone number I can remember."

"Ah, the Grabfelder tact. How I've missed it. What do you need?"

"I'm trying to do some cultural homework here. Or maybe it's religious, who the hell knows? Anyway, I've just gotten a Muslim murder Vic, a sweet young girl, she'd break your heart. Barely twenty, killed on a high school campus. She was going to night classes, college classes, there. The parents showed up for the I.D. and the father acted like the whole damn thing was annoying. First class shithead."

"Describe the parents."

"He had a beard and did not bother to dress up for the occasion, she was wearing a chador head to foot, plus gloves, and her headscarf did not hide the bruise on her face. And he treated her like crap, in public."

"Oh. Fifth Century Redux."

"Huh?"

"They're *very* traditional, conservative. They think like the fundamentalist Christian or Jewish mind-set: literal and usually inaccurate interpretation of the Bible --- or in this case the Koran --- and absolutely no empathy or tolerance. That kind of thinking is getting rare these days, the USA culture wearing it down whether they like it or not, 'Thank you, Allah'. But it's still going on here and there, only more in secret."

"Okay."

"Your vic –- daughters aren't significant until offered for marriage. You said she was near-by twenty and single?"

"Far as I know."

"Marriage arrangements must-a fell through. And she's going to college classes? Brave girl. But to her father, she was dead before she was killed. Does she have brothers? It could be an honor killing."

"Don't know about brothers. But even if she had 'em I doubt they were to blame. Forensics, history, weapon too unique and used previous."

"'Previous'? Is this a repeat?"

"This is Number Three."

"Crap! You poor guy. Still, check for sons, check if daddy has brothers living over here or in the old country. He could hire them to do the deed."

"Are you serious? They'd kill her because she was going to college?"

"Not exactly. She could be killed for disobedience, shaming the family. She should have been married to Daddy's financially generous choice of man while still a teen and had kids immediately, sons preferred, of course. She's not, so that means she disobeyed. And going to school, a *coed* school? That makes her no better than a whore, to dear old righteous Dad."

"In this day and age? In this country?"

"Fundamentalism –- in *any* religion –- it's all the same. Men have total control and women hardly matter. Unfortunately, they breed."

"Her mother . . . I had to get rid of the husband so she could spend just fifteen minutes with her girl."

"You did that?"

"Had to. Like I said, he was a first class shithead -– in any religion. And she . . . well you've seen that look before, you know what I'm talking about. Uh, I called her 'ukh-tee' on impulse –- that means 'my sister', right? Hope to gawd."

"It's right. You called her your sister? That was a kindness she really needed. Made her know she wasn't alone. Uh, you should be prepared. You will be talked about."

"Oh, that'll be a change!"

Shakey laughed, "No, this is something different. The 'shitheads' have got their women locked away and silent, they *think*. Shows how dumb they are. Within twenty-four hours, your name will be pronounced among women you will never meet, because of their male 'guardians'. You will be prayed for, and you will be trusted. It will make your investigation a lot more fruitful, not to mention very interesting."

"Just what I need. Well, thanks for the class. I appreciate the info. Hey, is it hard to learn Arabic?"

Shakey laughed heartily. "Don't tell me you're willing to go that far! Dear Allah, let me live long enough to hear Farsi spoken with that mid-western twang!"

"Well, no . . . well, whatever it takes. This is a bad one, Shakey. Three Vics. Killed with a goddamn dagger. Do not share that — with *anyone*."

"A dagger?! Holy shit! The Assassins?! We only heard stabbings."

"We're keeping the assassin thing out of the news and out of anyone's scuttlebutt. For obvious reasons. 'Swear?'"

"'Swear, hand to God. Aw, hell, more backlash against Muslims, sure to come."

"Not if I can help it. Besides, the first Vics were supposed arms dealer Jordan Hashemi and a Call Girl who was working for the FBI. Hardly a poster boy/girl for Islam."

"Hashemi we know about. Even though he doesn't exist. The 'invisible genius'. Assuming the Call Girl was in the wrong place at the wrong time, what connection could they have to a brave little Muslim girl with aspirations?"

"I'm reading the tea leaves day and night."

"Hey, Hermie, if you need help, culture-wise, an interpreter or a go-between, call me. I got after-hours time or I could call some Muslim buddies in your area, even an Imam or two if you need it."

"'ppreciate it."

"In the meantime, any bookstore has Berlitz English/Arabic language books so you can learn an appropriate phrase or two, and some cultural things to ease the way."

"Good idea."

"Just remember: Don't touch nobody, man or woman, unless they touch you first. Don't look a woman in the face, unless it is permitted — you'll know. And if you go to their homes, be prepared to be fed — Arab hospitality is a tradition and a pleasure."

"Even if I'm in their house because of the worst news?"

"Even then. I've seen you interview Koreans, Japanese, Malaysians, Filipinos, and I think I recall an Aborigine. Nobody ever got insulted on your watch. Your Momma raised you right, Grabfelder, you'll be cool."

"Thanks for your vote."

Shakey chuckled. "Blessings upon you, Hermie. 'Later." And he clicked off with the only obvious indication of his Muslim faith: "Blessings upon you." He was the kind of Muslim who did pray five times a day, but rarely on a prayer rug or in a mosque. Hermie had seen him pause in the squad room, in a parked patrol car, in a restaurant, or even on a sidewalk, eyes closed, hands with palms up, lips moving, and that was the end of it. A couple times, some yahoos in the squad would tease him about not facing Mecca or not being face down on his "flying carpet." But Shakey would merely smile that calm smile of his and assure them that since God was everywhere, he didn't much care about the format or location of the conversation, so long as the conversation took place.

Hermie started up Roberta and instead of heading back to the stationette, he decided to drive to Century City to check out the address Jordan Hashemi had on his fake driver's license, the office building that had no apartments to live in.

CHAPTER SEVEN

"The secret of a great success for which you are at a loss to account is a crime that has never been found out, because it was properly executed."

Honore de Balzac

Hermie hated Century City. He thought of it as New York City West because of the endless parade of towering office buildings, streets jammed with traffic, and the stench of carbon monoxide unrelieved by the occasional whiff of expensive perfumes coming from invisible, expensive shops tucked into the feet of some of these towers. The only difference was, in contrast to New York City traffic, a car horn was rarely heard here. Music blasting from custom-designed sound systems in custom-designed cars, yes, but car horns not so much; because L.A. was that laid back, even in traffic aggravation. Hear a car horn, see an out-of-state license plate, nearly always.

The unhelpful directional signs failed to ease the traffic crunch on the streets, where there was little or no parking, and Hermie had a phobia about parking in the underground garages, earthquakes being the ever-promised threat; particularly in these buildings where the parking frequently required driving down, down, down for half a dozen or more levels, where little outside ventilation appeared to feed the ineffective blasting of fans that failed to ease the stench of exhaust fumes belching from cars, SUV's, RV's, trucks, vans, and motorcycles the size of jeeps, festooned with buckled carry-alls.

So Hermie drove Roberta down a residential street that branched off of what was called Big Santa Monica Boulevard, by the locals, which paralleled Little Santa Monica Boulevard. The march of "One Hour" parking signs hoisted by neighborhood associations in their futile battle to keep Century City workers and shoppers from turning their streets into parking lots apparently worked, because there were a few empty spaces of temptation. He pulled into a space in front of a gigantic and pristine Colonial, circa the 1940's for sure, as this was once the community where movie stars dwelled when they worked on the studio lots that were now obliterated by the relentlessly ugly cuboids of Century City.

He propped a *"Police Business"* card against his windshield and then started to walk back to Century City, instantly regretting it when the traffic fumes assaulted his nose and scraped his throat, and the blast of intense sunshine soon had him sweating. In the South Bay, where he lived and worked, it was still a cool, breezy Spring; here the heat was already full-on summer and would get even worse within weeks. By the time he reached the black granite and glass square tower that was Hashemi's address, he was thoroughly annoyed and a headache had begun to ascend from his complaining nose up into his eyes.

It was a relief to step through whirling black glass revolving doors and go from hot-heat into the sweater-weather of a cavernous lobby where super-chilly air conditioning swept the air clean. Tall, shiny black granite walls rose up two stories to a ceiling aglow from wall to wall lighting, the lights designed to look like futuristic stars. The gleaming black floor had iridescent chips imbedded in it that flashed specks of silver and gold. A smoky glass reception desk was in front of a bank of six elevators, their doors burnished bronze, a whooshing hum coming from within as the cars rose and fell in answer to calls. He looked around among the few walls that had no gigantic windows, but couldn't find a Directory. So he went to the reception desk in the center of this floor.

A guard manned the reception desk, dressed in an immaculate wine-red uniform with tasteful gold braid on the sleeve cuffs. Perhaps in his late fifties, a designer haircut showed off his white hair, his face was tanned, his grey eyes did not smile when he did because they were evaluating who he was looking at: a hulking man who moved with grace, taking deep breaths of the air conditioning, looking him over with astonishing, hot-blue eyes that were slightly reddened, he hoped from smog and not from cocaine, times being what they are. The eyes focused beneath a scatter of choppy blonde hair that was discretely shot with silver here and there. He was surprised when the man pulled out a badge -- he didn't look the type at-tall.

"Hi. Where's the Directory?" Hermie asked.

"There is no Directory. You gotta be directed. Through here. Nobody gets into the building unless they get here first, for clearance."

Hermie was too curious to get annoyed. Yet. "What happens if they use the elevator in the garage?"

"All tenants and their employees have key cards that run the elevators. The card sends you and only you to your floor, or here, or the garage. Guests who use the garage elevator without a key card are sent to here, where they are given access to the elevators and the floor they are visiting. The computer here makes sure they only go to the floor they are visiting, and a return flight. Uh, ride, down. Our security level is one-of-a-kind, and a big attraction to prospective tenants."

Hermie waved his badge for emphasis "Detective Grabfelder. I'm looking for the offices of Jordan Hashemi. H-A-S-H-E-M-I."

"Hashemi? Let me check, but —" His gaze dropped down to the hidden computers tucked under the counter top and a keyboard clicked as he typed, paused, typed again. "Thought it wasn't familiar. Sorry, Detective, I don't have that name here. Are you sure he's at this address?"

"Positive."

"Maybe his listing is under a company name?"

"Smart thought. Hell."

The guard watched the man's annoyed thoughts stir his dangerous eyes. "Can you print out a list of the building's tenants? Maybe I could recognize something."

"Uh, I'm not allowed to do that."

"Of course not. Which means I gotta slap a Warrant onto your boss, and nothing aggravates a boss like a Warrant, and it all takes up so-o much of my time, especially when I have to spend another half day driving through the Traffic From Hell, and walking through the Air Pollution From Deeper Hell, and I really hate the whole goddamn thing. What's your name?"

Startled at the sudden switch in subject, the guard didn't censor himself: "Barsamian. Howard."

"Look, this is a murder investigation. So far, I got three bodies and it all started with Hashemi. Can you help me out here, Howie?"

Hermie watched the guard weigh committing a firing offense against helping out a scary cop who was oddly polite and honest about the whole thing. *Three bodies? Sheesh!*

It had always been Howie's opinion, drilled into him his whole life by his pig-headed father who hadda come up with a plausible explanation for all those speeding tickets and "Failure to Yield" citations, that all cops were first class "sonsabitches" with guns, so his first impulse was not to cooperate. But *this* guy . . .

Howie yielded: "Look, this could only come from one source. So you can't show it around, it's my ass, pension and health insurance."

"I hear ya. You have my word it won't leave my hands and I shred it when I'm done with it."

After a last evaluating look, Howie hit a couple computer keys and a printer somewhere inside the desk tweaked and buzzed. Then he had second thoughts. "Aw, shit, I forgot — there are surveillance cameras watching me do this!"

"Seriously? Where are they? Try for subtle."

Indicating with a nod of his head instead of pointing, with Hermie looking without appearing to look, four surveillance cameras were located. Two aimed at the doors, another covered the bank of elevator doors, and one was above those doors and aimed right at the back of the reception desk, looking over Howie's shoulder, no doubt taking in not only the computer but Hermie as well.

"Crap!" said Hermie.

"Sorry."

The printer went quiet, the guard was reaching for the printout when an elevator door opened up behind him and four men in expensive suits and carrying designer briefcases got out, crossing directly behind the reception desk. Hermie did a quick sight-line check from the surveillance camera above and behind the guard's desk. "Hold it!" he snapped.

The Howie froze. "What!?"

"Fold up the printout as small as you can get it. Keep it under that counter. Now."

His hands staying under the counter top, back blocking the view of the camera, Howie dutifully folded the thick printout down to nearly envelope size. "Okay."

"When I step behind you to get to the elevators, don't turn around. Just hand the printout back toward me."

"Okay."

Hermie went from the reception desk to stand in front of the elevators, his back turned to the desk and Howie. Another elevator door opened and a small group of both men and women dressed in similar suits and briefcases scattered out, split up, some walking closely past the reception desk, others making a wider route as all sought the wall of revolving doors to the street. As if helpfully getting out of the way, Hermie stepped back, coming close to the guard, one hand dropped down and reached back. "Now –– pass it."

The guard handed the printout back, Hermie grabbed for it, missed and it fell to the floor.

"Shit!"

"Shit! Sorry." Embarrassment from Howie, even though he wasn't sure who dropped what.

"Don't turn around," Hermie hissed and bent to pick up the printout, jamming it into a jacket pocket while his back was still turned up toward the surveillance camera above. "Got it. I need a chair, anything in the building?"

Howie surreptitiously handed a key card to Hermie. "This gives you universal access for a couple hours, but you are in the system as to where you go in the building and what offices you access and how long you are there. If you don't return the key card to me by 5 PM, you won't be able to get out of the building by any door and Security will be all over you."

The situation begged for sarcasm, Hermie obliged: "I've never felt so important."

"Punch R in the elevator. It's the restaurant floor."

"Thanks.

Hermie moved to the elevators, Howie leaned on his counter to just *breathe*.

Another gleaming set of bronzed doors sighed open and Hermie headed for them, sidestepping people getting off, wondering if they all shopped at the same store since they were all wearing virtually the same expensive suits, carrying similar designer briefcases. He stepped inside the elevator to be surrounded by ethereal piped-in music heavy on the violins, and brass walls that had been polished with an abrasive that left subtle whorls shimmering in the brass. The elevator buttons were set into a panel of burled wood, the buttons black onyx with pearly numbers alongside the bumps of braille information. Hermie found the button marked "R: RESTAURANTS", punched it. He tried not to feel claustrophobic as he felt the car descend into the bowels of the earth.

Then the elevator bumped gently to a stop and the doors opened onto the bizarre: A fake Parisian city sidewalk with fake cobblestones flanked by fake gaslights meandered its way past a row of storefronts dressed up to resemble a French bistro, a patisserie, a post office/Federal Express, an ice cream parlor, and a unisex hair stylist called Cut-Ups. He was overwhelmed by smells of flavored coffees brewing, yeasty bread and sugary pastries baking, savory meats broiling, and here and there a whiff of hair tonic and shampoo. Also in the air was the blast of air conditioning and the warble-y voice of a French chanteuse.

Aghast, Hermie backed up and let the elevator doors shut him inside the car again, and felt sweat starting to leak from panicked glands. He checked the elevator buttons, found "PH: PENTHOUSE", and punched it. The car rose slowly, then accelerated to what felt like warp speed as it soared upward and Hermie watched the floor indicator count past ten floors, then twenty floors, finally shuddering to a stop on the thirtieth floor "PENTHOUSE". The doors whooshed open, and to Hermie's relief he stepped into a blast of chilly air conditioning in a hallway lined with large windows looking over Century City and eastern miles beyond, swimming in light beige smog. *Sunlight, space, air, ahhh . . .*

Royal blue carpeting led to huge, ornately carved double doors that closed off one end of the long hallway. A brass plaque was on one of the doors, reading: "Private. Admittance by Appointment only."

But no chairs in this vast hallway. Annoyed, Hermie dropped down onto the plush carpet, made himself comfortable leaning his back against the wall, rummaged in his pockets and pulled out the printout and a forgotten pencil from Home Depot, relieved to find a thick, long point on it. He separated the papers, splayed them out on the carpet, scanned the long lists of company names, not really knowing what to look for. He hoped to find something that was a play on Hashemi's name or ancestral country or an Arabic company — *something*.

To his surprise and then exasperation, there were over a dozen Arabic-sounding companies in the building, along with twenty Chinese, five Indian, four British, nine French, a few that might be African, and a bunch of companies that at least *sounded* American. He envisioned himself going from floor to floor, office to office, in a nightmare of endless interviews and snooping until he found the right place. He recalled Trots saying the FBI had already started this tedium, looking for Hashemi's lair.

He sighed his annoyance, wondered what were Claire's chances of getting him some extra manpower out of the stretched-thin Robbery-Homicide Division budget, especially since this would be routine shoe-leather duty instead of the flashy stuff.

A passing thought reminded him he was now in the computer age, property records were accessible, so he could find the owner of the building, wave Warrants, and find out which office in this behemoth belonged to Jordan Hashemi. However, the FBI had no doubt done this already, to nada. Because Hashemi rented the office under a false name with phony references, fake backgrounds, and then all records disappeared, which was likely, given who he was and what he was, existence-wise.

Irritation began pricking at his stomach, then he thought of handing the whole thing over to Hank O'Dell, the computer whiz who once hooked up the computers at the stationette and then went on to give him invaluable if slightly illegal computer hacking that helped him track down who would have been future victims of the South Bay Serial Killer. Surely O'Dell could track down which was Hashemi's office using the wonderfulness of cyberspace. *He wouldn't have a problem with the fact that Hashemi didn't exist. Doesn't exist. Hadn't existed. Would he?*

He began to gather up the papers when something caught his eye: toward the bottom of the last page was listed "Winston Violins". He recalled Farouz Selah telling him that Hashemi's real name was Winston Safir and his father was a violin and cello performer and teacher in England. Winston Violins was located in an office on the floor below the Penthouse. He lurched up, flexed his knees, gathered up and folded the lists, and headed back to the elevator, not in the mood to spend time locating the internal fire stairs, since he doubted they'd share the hallways' air-conditioning. He had to wait several minutes before the elevator returned to him, but in seconds he was bumped down to one floor below.

This hallway was carpeted in a deep emerald green, and several blonde wood doors marked a variety of offices, with shiny brass plaques announcing company names for a corporate realtor, an investment consultant, six lawyers in a variety of nationalities were packed behind one door, and at the far end, Winston Violins. He tried the ornate brass handle and to his surprise the door opened onto an office reception area.

This emerald green carpet was embellished with curved, golden palm fronds in the weave. Comfortable beige suede couches lined the walls. A closed blonde wood door probably led to inside offices, as its brass plaque stated: "PRIVATE. NO ADMITTANCE."

The walls were blonde wood, decorated with a couple tasteful landscapes of lush countryside scenes that could only be England, as well as dramatic photos of violinists and their glowing instruments: Itzhak Perlman, Yehudi Menuhin, and a photo of a man who looked like an older version of Jordan Hashemi, obviously his father. He was standing, holding his violin. Alongside him a cello was propped against a piano, and at the piano sat a lovely dark-haired woman that was probably Hashemi's mother. Her smile was what anyone would call "welcoming".

Not so the smile pulled onto the face of a young Middle Eastern man who sat at a receptionist desk in the exact center of this pleasant room. His slender frame betrayed the slight bulge at the left side of his suit jacket that Hermie knew was a gun holster and its gun. And here *he* was, a cop, unarmed, and all alone in this labyrinth of a building. A passing thought: *If I don't come back down would Howard Barsamian notice, and more importantly would Howie give a rat's patoot?*

He was taken aback when the young man stood up, but his hands stayed down, relaxed, and he gave a slight bow. *Good manners, what a relief. Or he's pegged me for a cop.* He pulled out his badge and the young man looked at it courteously, but Hermie doubted he read it. "Detective Grabfelder. I'm in charge of investigating Jordan Hashemi's death."

"And who is Jordan Hashemi?" He spoke English with a crisp British accent layered over the melodious Middle Eastern.

"Nice try. He's the son of that violinist over there." Hermie thumbed in the direction of the photo on the wall. "And that's his Mum, I'm sure."

"I see."

"Good. Then we'll save time. This office was listed as the home address of Mr. Hashemi. Did he actually live here?"

"I am not at liberty to say." The black eyes were like two still stones.

"Would you feel more 'at liberty' if I took you down to the police station to answer questions?" Hermie snapped, to establish the pecking order here.

"As you wish." The young man's face was perfectly passive, although a sudden yellowish cast on his dusky skin was an indication that some blood had drained.

"Ah. The people you work for would not be happy about that, would they?"

From face to feet, not a muscle moved in the man's thin frame.

Hermie whipped out the folded tenants' listing sheets and his Home Depot pencil. "Okay, give me your name."

"Hari Ibn Saud."

"Can I see your driver's license, please."

"I have none."

"In L.A.? Okay, your green card, then."

The man reached inside his jacket, on the side opposite of the gun, pulled out a plastic laminated green card. Hermie started writing down name, address numbers, even though he recognized the card as fake and the address numbers were the same as this building. "I see you live here, too." He handed the card back. "Can I see your license to carry a concealed firearm? And the firearm?"

The young man took a single step back.

Oh, shit! Hermie had mere seconds to lament the absence of his own weapon, the fact that he hadn't called in to let Nell, Claire, *anyone* know where he was headed before coming here, and to wonder whether there was a fancy trash chute in this fancy building big enough to dump and slide his body down to wherever. Thirty-odd floors would be quite a trip, and him being too dead to enjoy it.

Then all his muscles tensed, ready to drop to the floor in an instant, which was his only defense until he figured out how to get some sort of advantage here, like rising up from that floor with the bottom edge of the desk in both hands to shove into what may turn out to be a shooter who could not miss at this range. He tried bullshit: "You wanna hand over that weapon peacefully, or do I signal my SWAT team outside? Their AK-forty-sevens will make such a mess. Of this office. And you."

Laser blues and black stones met and held while things were decided. Then the stones flinched and the man's thin hands slowly opened his jacket and moved toward the holster.

"Hold it!" Hermie ordered, and he reached across the desk, flipped aside the man's jacket lapel, and yanked the gun out of the holster, checked to see if was loaded, it was, *Jeezus H.!*, and waved the gun at the man, indicating the closed door. "I'll need the keys to that office. Or should I shoot out the lock? Noise, wood chips, gunsmoke."

"On the desk, by the calendar," the man pointed.

Hermie found several keys hooked onto a large, black metal ring. "Who else has these keys?"

"Mr. Hashemi."

"Not anymore. Who else is in that office?"

"No one. Only I am here, as security in daytime."

"And doing a helluva job."

Now, logistics and protocol intruded, as always, requiring present elements of the situation to be juggled. "Please sit down there." Hermie indicated the couch farthest from the front door. "And don't move. I am known for my bad temper. And I won sharpshooting medals at the police academy. Don't get me wrong — I won't kill ya. I'll just wound ya. You'll live for years, wearing diapers." *Jeezus, he bought it!*

The young man indeed heeded the warning, doing as he was told, body language indicating years of doing exactly as he was told. Hermie went to the desk, picked up the phone, and was pleased he instantly remembered the phone number of the Century City Station. Then he called a judge who owed him a favor — back in his Narcotics days he had persuaded his teenaged son of the error of his ways by using off-duty hours to pick him up for Possession and put the fear of God into him by giving him a tour of the slimiest part of the Men's Central Jail to show him the night's collection of junkies, which he'd be joining if he did not mend his ways, which he did, being a basically good kid who hadn't learned the Law of Consequences yet. So Judge Mackey Davenport did not hesitate to grant him an instant Search Warrant, faxing it to the small machine that sat on the corner of the reception disk, its FAX number pasted on its face. Within half an hour, in answer to his other call, two Century City cops showed up with handcuffs and arrest warrant for carrying a concealed weapon and without a permit, besides. *Who does that?!* And another one for carrying a counterfeit green card. As they were cuffing the docile Hari Ibn Saud, Hermie arranged with them to keep Saud away from the general population until he could be subject to some serious interrogation by the FBI. Since they had heard of the grisly offing of Jordan Hashemi and the two young women, the cops were easily cooperative since they wanted to get all the poop on the resolution to this bizarre case, and perhaps a little reflected glory. So they sealed the scene and left a couple officers on guard for when the FBI showed up, to show how cooperative they were to outside investigators who often did not appreciate them. After all, it was Grabfelder.

Hermie had to search among the keys on the black ring until one worked to open the inner door, which opened onto spectacular views.

It was a curved, corner office, two walls were ceiling to floor curved windows facing west and north, toward neighborhoods where there were still trees greening up the streets and houses with yards where movie stars used to barbecue and play croquet. Through the light layer of smog, the ocean sparkled deep blue in the far west side distance.

Over-chilled air moved through the large room, smelling faintly of maleness, pine needles, and some kind of flower: *Lily of the Valley?* Virtually every foot of the other walls was taken up with electronic equipment atop various desks: several computers, printers, scanners, telephones, FAX machines, and dozens of monitors across which flowed Arabic writing and numerical symbols; other monitors showed a few television stations: American, British and Al Jazeera. The sound was off but SAP scrolled at the bottom of the frame, in English and in Arabic, wherever appropriate. There were other unrecognizable, silvery machines that were humming at their work, but he hadn't a clue what they were or what their work was, the designer being Hashemi. *Hank O'Dell would positively drool over these things!* He went to the desk that squatted in the middle of the floor. More blonde wood with a caramel leather chair permanently dented by the body that had sat in it for some time. It was a large chair, with a large dent, just Hashemi's size as Hermie could recall. Two matching smaller leather guest chairs were in front of the desk. On top of the desk were several papers and files, all looking like they were embroidered with the delicacy of Arab writing. Set aside was an appointment book with more Arabic writing inside its red leather cover. A familiar whiff of a man's cologne mingled with the richness of the scarlet leather drifted up, reminding him of the Hugo Boss wallet found in Hashemi's pocket.

With hanky-clad fingertips, he tried the center desk drawer. To his surprise it slid open. *Not locked? Must not be important stuff in here.* Underneath a few papers graced with flowing Arabic writing, by hand or from a computer, was a heavy, elaborate silver picture frame. The color photo inside was undoubtedly Mom, Dad and Sis. This time his mother was wearing a chador in a lilac color, its headscarf very loosely draped around her dark, glossy hair and welcoming face; it was for show, not piety. The sister wore a dark blue chador, its headscarf pulled tight around the face barely exposed. *Probably to show the marriage market that you were a good, GOOD, girl, huh?* Her face was more dramatic than pretty: high cheekbones, straight nose, lush unadorned lips, black wings of eyebrows above deep blue eyes tilted up at their outer corners, long eyelashes following that curve up. Her eyes *dared* the observer. *What a face. I bet Sis was a Pip. Why tucked away in a drawer? Probably the sight of it reminded Hashemi of what he lost in that plane crash. Left him completely alone. Sad. Might explain a lot about our guy. Like, maybe after that he didn't want to exist. So he didn't.* He tried other drawers in the desk, all were locked with key locks, the deepest bottom drawers locked with combination locks. *Oh, they'll be just swell to crack, Hashemi being a numbers kinda guy and all. Ah, the Overtime on Trots' watch.*

A red phone was centered near the outer edge of the desk. Several lines were noted by Arabic names and their numbers. Using his hanky to protect fingerprints, Hermie gingerly picked up the red handset and punched one of the line buttons with the tip of one fingernail. The line rang an odd br-r-r-ing sound that Hermie recognized, being a foreign film buff. *It's a foreign phone, betchya.* It was picked up and a man's voice shouted out a greeting in Arabic. Hermie could hear the unmistakable sounds of this being a long distance call. A *VERY* long distance call. He hung up, decided against punching all the other buttons. *Don't want to spook or alert the people the FBI or CIA would be descending upon in the uber near future. Like tomorrow. Or even this afternoon -- 'day', 'young', yada-yadooo . . .*

Then Hermie punched in a cellphone number he knew. Trots picked up on the second ring.

"I'll bet ya haven't made much headway, have ya, Red? Er, 'Grey'?"

"Snoopy! I take it from the snide tone in your voice, that you have?"

"Still canvassing for his residence, Hashemi-wise, are we?"

"Well, this is not news. You know Hashemi would give fake information on lease agreements then have those agreements vanish, so it's going to take us some time to find . . ." The pause was so-o-o pregnant. "Uh-oh, what have you done, Grabfelder?"

"Well, I was in the neighborhood . . ."

"Aw jeez!"

"When's your birthday? No matter, this is a gift for your birthday, Thanksgiving, Christmas, Father's Day, Flag Day, and your wedding anniversary, a black day though that was. Those vows she made? A tiss-ew of lies. It was always me she lusted after."

"What? WHAT!?"

"I'm calling from Hashemi's office. Using his phone, in fact, remember to tell the techs it was just me calling you when they find this call in his records."

"His office? How did you find --?"

"You're going to have a field day in here."

"Goddammit, Snoopy, if you broke in there without a damn Warrant --!

"I got Warrant-sss. I got keys-sss. I got a receptionist-slash-security guard in custody at the Century City Station, waiting for your visit. His green card's phony and he's carrying, unlicensed and concealed. He will talk, because he lives to do as he's told. But don't drool, I doubt he'll give you much, he's definitely low-level, circling the loop but not ever invited in."

Trots' slow, deliberate comeback dripped with envy, irony and grudging gratitude, "I. Hate. You."

Hermie laughed, "Oh, don't be so hard on yourself. I'd have never found his office either. The whole damn building is a United Nations of corporations. We shared nightmares of going door to door until retirement set in. I just had a lead that paid off."

"Where was he?"

"Winston Violins."

"How did you come up with that?"

"Ah. You didn't know his real name was Winston Safir, son of a prominent violinist in England? Mom was a famous piano-player, too. Well, your excuse is that you didn't find any such records, because they were killed in a plane crash just before Winston vanished. Into Hashemi. Who doesn't exist."

There was silence on Trots' end.

"Maybe if you sat down, put your head between your knees and just, you know, *breathe*."

"Up yours, Grabfelder! Where's the office –– I got a couple agents inside the building today, doing door to door."

"Gee, we coulda passed each other in the halls."

Only a moan of annoyance this time.

Hermie tried not to laugh. "And how did they get past Howie, the Key Card King?"

"Who the hell's 'Howie'?"

"Howard Barsamian."

"Who the hell's Howard Barsamian?!"

"Lobby guard. I had to threaten Warrants to get a tenant list outta old Howie."

"We dealt with the building owner directly. He had no record of Jordan Hashemi being a tenant, of course. But he gave us the tenants' list and passes to get past the guard, under cover of being ordinary businessmen with meetings to go to. We didn't want word to get out to Hashemi's staff that we were in the building, looking for him."

"Gee, I didn't even get a pass."

"Grabfelder, I swear –!"

"Okay, okay, wouldn't want to hurt yer 'fillin's' and all. His office is one floor below the penthouse. Couple-a great guys from Century City have it locked down. Be grateful and let them know it. I'll wait here for the kids. But then I got places to go, people to see . . ."

"Hold it! You didn't take anything from that office did you? You know why I have-ta ask."

"Now, you know I am sometimes faithful to the rools of ev-ee-dance and all. No, I didn't take anything. First, because most of his stuff is on computers. Second because everything's in Arabic. But I have some info up top, to steer you through all that Arabic."

"Aw, hell, *what*?"

"Hashemi was *not* an arms dealer. Not never, not now. That was his cover. He was the world's best computer hacker. Cleaned out bank accounts on an international scale from those terrorist creeps who were buying weapons he pretended to sell. Don't know if he was a bad guy or a good guy in that business, but no computer was safe from his genius. In short, he was everyone's worst nightmare in this hyper-cyber age. And he didn't exist. Clever ducks."

Trots barely got the words out. "Good . . . God . . ."

"I once told everyone that these computer machines would be up to no good, I did, you should have heard me. Should have heeded me. But no-o-o . . ."

"I think I'm gonna be sick. This means we gotta share with others. CIA, Homeland Security, warring government committees, ours and everyone else's, both domestic and all those foreigners. Not to mention our president. *Everybody* will have a cow."

"Should keep you busy. Off the streets and all."

"Why is retirement so far away?" Trots said wistfully.

"Well, while you're translating and sharing, you will share if something smells like the Assassin, right? Maybe somewhere in Hashemi's vast Computer Land is something from someone about Assassins. Eleventh Century or current, I'm not picky. There was no reason to do that to an innocent girl, and I just can't stand it."

"Yeah, we heard the details about that outrage. I really sympathize, Snoopy. God . . . glad I don't have your job. I'll give that info search a priority. I do owe you large."

"Then let's get off the phone and get busy."

"Done." And Trots hung up.

A few minutes later, Hermie was handing the office keys to two FBI agents who were still young enough to look eager. And when Hermie left, he heard an astonished voice as one of the agents entered the computer room, saying that universal epithet used by one and all when thoroughly flummoxed: "HO-LEE SHEE-IT!"

He dutifully stopped by Howie's desk and gave him back the purloined list of building tenants, just to ease his mind. He told him that soon the building would be swarming with FBI agents and sundry, some of them rude because of the daunting task at hand. And he also made a point of thanking him for his help, telling him he'd soon be hearing how it was worth risking pension and health insurance. And Howard Barsamian shook his hand and fairly beamed, because he was thinking that for the first time in his life he'd be able to one-up his cop-hating father when he showed him what excitement happened because he helped a cop.

Hermie was sweating when he arrived back at Roberta, grateful she was still parked in the shade because the day had turned even more hot and steamy, the kind of weather that turns a closed car into an oven. While he cranked down windows, his cellphone rang and he snatched it up. "Yeah?"

"Uh, Hermie?"

"O'Dell? What the hell —?! I was just thinking about you. Came across a computer set-up just now that you'd think was damn near orgasmic. You don't speak Arabic by any chance?"

"Huh? Uh, no, I don't. Uh . . . that's . . ."

The usually cheery voice was octaves lower than normal and nearly trembling. *Something was more than wrong.*

"O'Dell? What's going on?"

"'Kevin's' been arrested. They think he killed somebody!"

CHAPTER EIGHT

*"Not everything that is faced can be changed, but
nothing can be changed until it is faced."*

James Baldwin

They had taken his clothes for evidence, since a Hawthorne police patrolman found him standing in a daze on El Segundo Blvd. with his shirt and pants and socks and new-ish track shoes splattered and smeared with blood, dried though it was. Juvenile Hall-issue shirt and trousers overwhelmed his thin frame. The now about-thirteen-year-old boy who had insisted on calling himself "Kevin Costner" when Hermie met him in Computer Whammy about a year ago hadn't changed a bit, except for his eyes. The pale face was still spattered with either freckles or dirt, but instead of the eyes of a budding felon like before, dancing with mischief and snotty fearlessness, now their clear blue-gray stared out at nothing, without a sign of either the life or soul within. He sat on the far edge of a bottom bunk bed with his knees up, arms wrapped around his legs as though clutching a shield. And he was shivering.

Hermie came in quietly and instantly recognized the signs of severe mental trauma. He turned to the escorting guard, who he didn't know but who had recognized Hermie and got him in here with no questions asked. "Not a word since he was picked up," said Bill Corey, the guard. "Blood on his clothes was human, but not his. There's not a scratch on him. We're doing DNA to see if it's in the system, but it'll take a while, you know the back-up situation."

"Yeah. Save some time –- compare his DNA to a recent homicide: Lila Miller."

"Lila Miller? Hey, I read about that. Aw, not this kid --"

"No. She was his mother."

"His –? Aw, hell, he was *there*?"

117

"Yeah."

"Aw, hell . . ." Bill Corey went quietly back down the hall, forgetting for the moment the ache in his back and throb in his feet as he thought about telling the wife he'd met the Detective with the infamous nose, and a kid who'd seen too much to bear.

Hermie went to sit alongside the boy, close enough to read him, but not close enough to disturb him. He dropped his voice down to a near whisper, the level used to talk to a frightened animal. "Hi. Remember me? Grabfelder. Hank O'Dell called me, said you were in a jam."

Nothing moved in the boy's face to indicate he heard.

"I know something really bad has happened to you. You don't have to talk about it now, not until you *can* talk about it. But you're safe now. *Safe.* I want you to remember that: *You are safe now.*"

He recalled the first time he met this boy in Hank O'Dell's workplace, Computer Whammy in the vast Del Amo shopping mall in Torrance. He'd gone there to get superficially educated on computers and ended up watching O'Dell delve into the vast network of information in cyberspace, skirting legalities as he called up clues for Hermie to use in the South Bay Serial Killer case, predicting and thus being able to protect future victims. O'Dell worked with a youngster's group in Gardena and the boy had bopped into that community center one afternoon, full of sass and intelligence, but a fingerprint check, computer check and a constant surveillance by some curious cop friends of O'Dell had failed to discover either his real identity, where he'd come from, or even where he lived. Hermie now realized that even back then Jordan Hashemi must have had a hand in wiping out any record of this boy, including his real name. He doesn't exist. Just like Hashemi. *That kind of protection must have eased his Mom's mind.*

Hermie recalled thinking that this kid's smart mouth and sense of invincibility could put him in danger, but when Hermie had laid a hand on his shoulder to emphasize this point, the boy had flinched like someone who had been hit in his past, and that flinch had touched Hermie's heart. Trots had just given him the origin of that fear: his brutal father. He'd come across many damaged children while raiding crack houses and drug selling and cooking dens in his past, and it never failed to pain him to see the emptiness in their eyes, and to feel or just see that same flinch when they were gently touched, because their entire lives had been spent associating touch with a blow, and with longing. Now Hermie felt so torn by the sight of this traumatized boy, maybe thirteen but already broken, it was an effort not to reach out and hug him forever.

Though he appeared to be still as stone, Hermie suddenly became aware that the boy was shivering. *From cold? From fear?* From deep within that skinny frame he shivered, Hermie could hear that even his breathing shook. On impulse, Hermie grabbed the blanket that was neatly folded on the opposite end of the bunk, unfurled it, and gently wrapped it around the boy's shoulders. He couldn't help resting his arm lightly on the fragile shoulders, and he felt the trembling radiating upwards into his arm. He gently patted the bones shivering underneath his palm.

Suddenly, the boy collapsed, caving into Hermie's side, the blank stare was shut off as the eyelids closed, tears spilled through trembling eyelashes, but not a sound came from him. Hermie scooped him up, the slender body feeling nearly weightless, then turned and laid him down comfortably on the bunk, unfolding his long, coltish legs, wrapping the blanket around him. He grabbed another blanket from the bunk above and unfurled it over the boy, tucking him in. He couldn't tell whether the boy had fallen into an exhausted sleep or a coma. The shivering breathing continued, whistling through his nose. A shock of hair that had long-since needed a good cut fell onto his forehead all the way down to the bridge of his nose. Hermie smoothed it back and the boy's head dropped to the side, his lips parted and the shivering breathing began to puff out from his cracked lips. And with it came that scent . . . banana bubblegum.

* * * *

For once Hermie was glad he was recognized, because when he asked for a phone—his phone left in his car like always—he was immediately ushered to an empty office, a phone pointed out, "dial nine", a chair pulled up, and a variety of beverages offered. A blitzkrieg of phone calls followed: a call to Babs Matthews in Social Services to make certain she was the one to bulldog the case of "Kevin Costner", his murder witness, in particular getting the services of a child psychologist specializing in hardcore emotional trauma. Then a call to an attorney he knew from his narcotics days, Alice Franco, who specialized in child advocacy, taking up the defense of children left behind like so many discarded crack pipes when their parents were busted. Babs and Alice knew each other and could be counted on to work as a team to make sure "Kevin Costner" was protected, treated, and isolated until he pulled out of the trauma that silenced him.

Then a call to Andy Cho Hui to ask him to personally handle Bill Corey's request regarding "Kevin Costner's" bloodstained clothes, so the timetable of DNA testing in the overwhelmed system could be bettered, days instead of weeks. Hermie astonished Andy when he said specifically to test if there was a match between the blood on the boy's clothes, the blood in the boy's veins, and that of Lila Miller, the lady Vic who wore eight hundred collar shoes.

And then he explained, "Remember those track shoe prints at the first scene? They were his. He saw it all. He saw his own mother . . ."

"Kkumtchik'an!" When horrified, Andy also reverted.

Hermie ended all these phone calls with a statement that startled everyone: If there was any problem about financing all this, or getting official sanctions, bills and angst should be sent to him personally. He had a final word with Bill Corey, asking him to keep the boy isolated and as undisturbed as possible, calls of nature and meals being the only exceptions. Only himself, social services and their psychological or medical personnel, and Hank O'Dell were to be allowed to visit him. And most importantly, no one was to *touch* the boy, ever.

Bill Corey doted on three pre-teens of his own, so he knew kids and had sympathy for this silent, damaged boy. He volunteered to step up and stay on guard until further notice.

Then Hermie went to meet Hank O'Dell, who was pacing the parking lot outside of juvenile hall, with every bone in his tall, skinny frame rigid with tension, even his copper-colored hair looked upset. Hermie took his arm and led him over to Roberta, leaned him on top of some rusted bullet holes. "Deep breaths, O'Dell, even your hair is tense."

O'Dell pushed up his glasses, nodded, they slid back down, and he attempted to just breathe. "What's — what's going on?"

"Damned if I know, O'Dell. How'd you know he'd been picked up?"

"Jim Wiggens, Hawthorne cop I know. He's a coach on our kids' baseball team. He spotted him standing curbside near El Segundo Blvd., in Hawthorne. Recognized him as our "Kevin Costner", picked him up. Lucky he drives a patrol car and not a bike."

"'Standing'?"

"Yeah. Just *standing* there, in a daze, covered with blood. He booked him into Juvie, called me. I called you."

"Hawthorne isn't my territory, O'Dell."

"I know. But —"

"But you did me a favor. I think "Kevin" witnessed the killing of his own mother. Lila Miller."

"His —?! Jeezus! How do you know that?"

"Banana bubblegum."

"What?!" O'Dell gaped at him.

"Long story, for later. But I think that's what's freaked him out. This is a real maniac we're dealing with, O'Dell. If "Kevin" saw it all and this nutz-oh saw "Kevin" —"

"Oh, no! We gotta *do* something!"

"Calm, calm. I've got him a lot of protection watching out for him while he's in Juvie. He'll be safer here than anywhere else, until I can figure out what the hell's going on. If he can I.D. the killer, great, but from the looks of him, it's going to be some time before he pulls out of this trauma and can talk about it. Even then, he may not remember anything or what he remembers is distorted. I might not get a useable I.D. to give a sketch artist, much less a court. We just have to wait him out."

"Yeah."

"Can you visit him a lot?"

"Absolutely."

"Good. I've cleared it with them to allow you unlimited visits. Anyone gives you crap, ask for Officer Corey, he's on it. It'll help if a familiar face keeps turning up. Don't ask him questions, just be there, talk to him about ordinary stuff. Don't freak out if it seems like he doesn't hear or see you."

"Jeez!"

"If he starts talking about anything he saw, get a-hold of me right away."

"Yeah, yeah."

"I've given your name and numbers to a couple people, someone in Social Services, a lawyer who defends kids, here --" Hermie handed him a sheet of paper where he'd written down names, phone numbers. "I can't tell you why, but the FBI may come sniffing around "Kevin"."

"The FBI?! Jeezus God!"

"Don't panic, I'm only telling you this because if the FBI does come around, don't let them intimidate you, and don't let them anywhere near "Kevin". Call me first and then that lawyer's number."

At the end of it all, O'Dell was breathing somewhat normally and his bones had bent a little, signaling an encouraging release of tension.

"He was either sleeping or still out of it when I left him. It would be good if he saw a familiar face when he woke up, if you can manage it."

O'Dell lifted himself off of Roberta, nodding, "Yeah, yeah. I'll go on in." He turned to go, then turned back with his hand out. "Thanks, Hermie."

"Nada." Hermie shook the cold bones of O'Dell's slender hand. "I take it, no luck finding out his real name, his history?"

"Nope. I've done enough computer searches to shake a stick at, so have other cops I know. He's not in any system. So there's no way --"

"No way, for sure. Someone made sure of that some time ago. Someone who loved him and his mother a lot."

"Jeez!" O'Dell slumped a little at that, tried to smile and failed, then turned to walk back into the shabby strangeness of Juvenile Hall.

When Hermie opened Roberta's door, his cellphone was ringing.

* * * *

She'd been hidden behind a dumpster, her blood smeared the way she was dragged. *Why bother to hide her but leave the blood trail to point the way? Idiot as well as nuts.* A late-working lawyer, her boss, had come into the underground parking lot and noticed two things as he approached his car: His paralegal's car was still parked alongside his, even though she'd left the office hours before he had; and the blood splashes on the driver's side of her car and the drag path of blood led him to the dumpster, and its hidden horror.

She was so beautiful, thought Hermie as he crouched alongside the body of a tall, slender young woman with a nearly perfect face. Sunidhi Askar was only twenty-two, and was the best paralegal the lawyer Amitabh Khan had ever worked with, and as dear as a daughter. He was now leaning on his car and sobbing aloud, in between answering patient questions from one of the several police officers assembled in this underground parking lot, who'd be turning all their notes over to Hermie.

Sunidhi Askar's slenderness was accented by the black caftan that fit her snugly in places, with flared sleeves and hem decorated with floral embroidery in pink silk. The embroidery also circled the neck of the garment, and Hermie saw her hair bore the pressure marks of having been wrapped in a headscarf. *He takes their headscarfs. Trophies decorated with blood. Asshole!* Her light brown hair was splattered with blood and the elegant caftan was nearly sliced in two from that familiar dagger's stab and slash that bled out from neck to waist. Her right hand had also been sliced nearly in two, a sign that she had raised it in a futile effort to fend off that terrible blow. Her face was a delicate oval, shining with health beneath the flecks of blood. No makeup at all, but she didn't need it — her eyes were a startling teal blue within long eyelashes, neatly trimmed eyebrows framed them. Her nose was slightly long, flanked by wondrous cheekbones, the shape of her lips like something from a carving in marble by an ancient artist who had dreams of love.

Mingled with the coppery smell of blood, Hermie got a whiff of the clean, soapy scent of her perfume. Her undamaged hand had a golden ring on the first finger, holding an oval stone in the exact teal blue of her eyes. A gold bracelet was also on this wrist, a wide cuff that was imbedded with a variety of small, glittering colored stones. *A pile of expensive jewelry, but he only took her headscarf. This means something. What the hell, I haven't got a goddamn clue, but —.* Her fingernails were perfect ovals, clean and unpolished. The skin on her undamaged palm as soft as rose petals. Rage pushed against the sorrow within Hermie. "Who the hell . . . who the fucking hell . . . !" Luckily, he was then distracted.

Andy Cho Hui took a step back when Hermie's enraged blues glared up at him in answer to his merely saying his name. "Sorry, Hermie — I —"

The heat in his eyes turned down somewhat. "No, no glad you spoke up. Distracted me. I was gonna start throwing things. Cars, maybe."

"Yeah. She — she — who could do this to someone like her? Or *any* girl?"

"Info?"

"I'd say about three hours ago, according to temp and tone. Which makes it just when she got into the garage, according to the timeline of her boss, there. She left the office three hours and change before he did."

"And nobody down here to see nuthin'." Hermie rose up, knees cracking. He rubbed his face, hair, neck, as though to wipe out the scene. "Why the hell . . . that fucking dagger . . . how did he know she was here? The others were outside, this was inside an enclosed garage. How did he know she worked here? He stalked her? Why her? This is an office building, must be full of women. Why *her?* Did he know her? Did he know the others? Shit-shit-shit!"

"We're dusting everywhere — her car, her boss's car, elevator inside and out."

"You won't get lucky. This sonuvabitch is too good and too bold."

The squeal of tires shattered the tension, and a large, tan Mercedes barreled past the waiting ambulance and shrieked to a stop in one of the empty spaces not cordoned off by yellow police tape. Four cops headed toward it, hands on guns.

"Uh-oh," said Andy.

"What?" answered Hermie.

"This is what I came to tell you. After her boss called 911, he called her parents. They're close friends."

"Aw, hell! Get her covered up. And cover the blood path, too." Hermie hurried toward the Mercedes, the cops that were closing in on it gave way for him and stopped. "It's okay, guys, it's the parents."

One of the nearby cops moaned in sympathy, "Aw, no . . . aw . . ." and turned aside, yanking a hanky out of his back pocket, jamming it against his suddenly streaming eyes. The other three turned aside, swallowing hard, clearing their throats.

Andy gestured to two nearby techs who were waiting with sheets and a body bag. But before they could cover her, Andy spotted something on the sleeve of the elegant caftan the girl wore. "Hold it!" he demanded. He dove to his knees alongside the girl's arm, pulled tweezers out of his breast pocket and a paper envelope from another pocket, and set about picking, pulling something off that pink-embroidered sleeve. Something so nearly invisible, the Techs nearby couldn't see it even as Andy tucked it into the envelope. A single, long, thick, white hair.

Both car doors opened before the motor cut off. An elegant man and woman got out, both red-eyed and distraught. The man went around the car to her, putting an arm around her, just as Hermie came up in front of them, effectively stopping them in their tracks as he pulled out his badge.

"Hello, I'm Detective Grabfelder. You are Mr. and Mrs. Askar?"

"Yes, we — what has happened? What has happened?! Sunny!?" Her voice was just short of a shriek. The woman's face echoed her daughter's, except hers was softer around the edges. Her hair was cut short and flattering, gold earrings flashed, perfect blushing pearls descended from her slender neck, onto a white silk blouse tucked inside the jacket of her suit, which was a deep, navy blue with blue and white enameled buttons. A perfect manicure in pale pink polish; large, heavy rings with expensive stones. She shook with dread, her beautiful eyes running with tears.

Her husband pulled her closer into his sheltering arm, he was tall against her and she tucked herself inside this shelter as if she'd been there often, for many years. His daughter was in his long bones and slenderness. It was starting to recede in front, but a lot of thick, black hair remained on his fine head. His face was poetic, large, dark blue eyes turned down at the corners, a nose just missed being too large, a neat black mustache did not obscure the flash of large, white teeth. "Yes, we are the parents. Mr. Amitabh Khan, he is a friend. He said . . . he said —" Terror cut into his voice.

"I am so very sorry to tell you. Your daughter . . . she has been killed."

A cry of anguish from her, a helpless moan from him. Both of them cried out, "Sunny! Oh, our Sunny!"

They pressed their faces together and hung on, each seeming to breathe for the other. Then he kissed her face and said something in Arabic, softly, gently. She nodded and she let him put her back into the car, where she sobbed the raw tears every mother in the world would recognize. He pulled out an immaculate hanky from an inner pocket of his expensive charcoal grey suit. He mopped his eyes, uselessly, wiped his nose, tried his voice, "May I see her?"

"Oh, no, Sir. You don't want that memory. Trust me. She was positively identified by Mr. Khan. It'll take a while for the coroner to release her, but then you can send a funeral home to the coroner's to pick her up. They will . . . *restore* her." *Why the hell did I think of that word?*

It seemed to work. He changed the subject: "We were in the restaurant, waiting for . . . her. Our weekly dinner out with Sunny."

"'Sunny', is it?"

"Yes. Everyone called Sunidhi that because —" He needn't go on, Hermie had seen her luminous face.

"She had her own place?"

"Oh, no, she was more traditional than we are. Didn't think it right for an unmarried girl to live . . . live apart from her patents. Until she got . . . got married."

"Was she seeing anyone?"

"No. She was waiting for us . . . for us to find her someone . . . suitable. Who has such a daughter in this day and age, in this country? Sorry, no offense."

"None taken. I could tell by the modesty of her dress that she was special."

"Special. Yes. Oh, Sunny . . ." He sobbed, breathed, unfolded the hanky, folded it to make a dry place, then mopped his eyes again, his chest jerking with silent sobs.

"Your daughter was very traditional as you said, yet she worked outside the home?"

"Mr. Amitabh Khan is a friend from our school days –– university. Sunidhi had such a brilliant mind, we encouraged her education from when she was young. She acquired a great love for the law, the *American* law, how she *loved* --. So she went to school and Amitabh heard about her good grades –– yes, from me, I bragged all the time --" His breath caught again with his almost-smile. "And Amitabh offered her this part-time job, while she continued her studies." He suddenly gasped with utter misery, "Did we kill my daughter for this job?!" Sobs punched at his slumped shoulders.

"Oh, no, no, Mr. Askar. This was not your fault, nor your friend's, and certainly not your daughter's fault. She is the fourth victim of a --"

He raised his head, eyes horrified above his hanky. "*Four*? God have mercy!"

"Amen," said Hermie impulsively. "By the way, did Sunidhi wear a headscarf?"

For an instant, he nearly smiled, "Oh, yes, Sunny had quite a collection, each more beautiful –– why do you ask?"

He skipped over it deliberately, "Not important. I'm going to have some more questions for you and your wife, but they can wait for another time. You need to go home now."

His anguish nearly strangled him, "But home is now without her . . ."

Someone brushed past Hermie and Mr. Askar was overwhelmingly embraced by Mr. Khan. The two men kissed each other's cheeks and clung to each other, both sobbing, "Our Sunny, our dear daughter."

Hermie turned away, motioned over an officer he didn't recognize.

"Barry Scala, Detective. What do you need?"

"Thanks. Get the three of them driven home –– nobody should get behind the wheel in their state. If somebody could volunteer, get their cars home, too?"

"I think more than a few would sign on. Jeezus, beautiful girl like that, who the fucking hell --?"

"Someone who needs killing off. Slowly, painfully."

"I'll volunteer."

"Yeah. Thanks again, Scala." Hermie walked slowly back to where he'd left Roberta. There he stopped, looked around at the enclosed parking garage. There were only about twenty parking slots, since it was below a small office building that was only three stories. Outside, he had noticed plenty of metered street parking, so he doubted that many visitors bothered to drive down here in the semi-dark and fumes rather than park on the street. He walked over to the elevators to find an office directory set into the wall alongside. The law office took one whole top floor, a real estate office and a dentist shared the second floor, the ground floor had a tax consultant, a nail salon and a florist. *How did he know she'd come into this garage at just that time? How did he know she'd be alone and he'd have the time? Nobody heard a scream. Nobody ever heard a scream. Why? Did he look so ordinary, so harmless? Nobody ran from him. How did he hide that dagger so nobody ran at the sight of it? How was he able to do this so goddamn easily? She was the only one who raised her hand against the blow. Why didn't the others? Did he blindfold them with their headscarves? Then why didn't he just leave the scarves where they were?* With a sigh of weary frustration, Hermie walked back to Roberta and drove slowly up and out of the underground garage, surprised to see it was nightfall outside. And found the gathering darkness both comforting and threatening.

CHAPTER NINE

"A well-adjusted person is one who makes
the same mistake twice without getting nervous."

Alexander Hamilton

Nell always knew when he hadn't slept well: he looked angry, a scowl furled beneath the shock of tousled old-gold hair. The faint lemon scent from the gym filled his office as usual, which was a good sign. It meant he actually *went* like he should, but she had visions of him stomping the belts out of a treadmill or ripping the oars out of a rowing machine in his fury. His towering temper used to scare her. The office partitions trembled, desks moved, windows shuddered, birds outside scattered. But eventually she realized he never blew without a good reason, the explosion was humongous but brief, and when he should, and rarely when he shouldn't, he apologized. Neither of them were aware that these days he apologized less and less because he knew she understood.

Now, having arrived on time to discover he'd already been here for a while and had made coffee and drank half the pot, Nell silently peeked into his doorway, inhaled the lemons and the fury. He had done some wall work, clearing a space among the National Geographic pages that festooned his walls with baby baboons and polar bear cubs cuddled by their mothers, leopards draped on tree branches doing game surveys, a circle of zebras, shoulder to shoulder, with their mouths open, teeth bared, as though laughing like hell, and closeups of elephants showing off their dark gold eyes and vast eyelashes. Hermie had lined up crime scene photos and brief notes on one cleared wall. His official Murder Books were open and stacked on his desk. He was staring at the wall display with an angry concentration, stopped to write a note on one of the pages below the photo of the mutilated Sunidhi Askar. "You got any ideas?" he asked without turning around to her.

How did he know I was here?! I never even breathed! "They're all Muslim, except one."

"That's obvious. What's not?"

"Why the dagger? Why not a gun? Or an ordinary knife?"

"It's an Eleventh Century murder weapon used by Shiite Assassins. Didn't I say that somewhere, sometime?"

"Shiite against Sunni, like always?"

"Not in this case, I checked. None of the victims or their kin were that tribal. And certainly not Lila. Begum. Azzawi. Miller."

"That ghastly wound –- perfectly the same on everyone."

"Hadda take training. Hadda be a particular kinda dagger. If you got time, ask around, antique shops, weapons shops, anyone sell or buy a dagger like that? Persian history –- any museum or fine arts store have stuff from the Eleventh Century, dagger-wise? If you got time, that is, check with Claire."

"Will do."

His gaze turned to her, lasers went suddenly on high, startling, trapping her.

"What!?" she asked, making a furtive check of buttons and zippers, as she always did when that hot blue look hit her, seeing everything and then some.

For the first time that he could recall, she was wearing a deep purple blouse and it changed her eyes to a glittering lime green. *Christ, she's got Eleanor's eyes!* Having to say something because she had that spooked look she got whenever she knew he was about to do or just did say something crappy, he managed, "Nice blouse."

"Oh. Thanks. Got it at Ross," she quipped, relieved.

The joke didn't register with him and she saw it was an effort for him to pull his gaze away from her. *What the hell is he looking at? I knew this purple was too much!*

"A Muslim assassin killing young Muslim girls. No way can we let that idea get out into the news. Our 'stabbing' line has to stay solid. *Anybody* can stab." He dropped down into his desk chair, the springs made their usual protest. "But then there's Hashemi."

"Maybe *he* was the one in the wrong place at the wrong time, the woman was the target."

"But she wasn't a Muslim. Why the ritual on *her*?"

"Her parents were, right? And that husband?"

"Yeah, but nobody but the FBI knew that. So, think: 'Lila Miller abandoned Islam, shame on her and she should pay, I will assassinate her like they did in the good old days'. Naw, it doesn't fly because nobody but another FBI agent would know her history. And they aren't Muslim fanatics. At least not *yet*."

"Okay, then what does Lila Miller, an FBI agent, have in common with these two innocent girls? Especially—" she started, then thought better of it. And, of course, as always she didn't get away with *that*.

"*What?*" he demanded.

"Well, you once said, 'There's random and there's planned. Which is which tells you a lot.'"

He was trying not to smile, but he was pleased. "You been taking notes?"

She had long ago learned about his back-handed compliments, and this was one and she blushed. "No, no, just remembering. Learning."

"Okay, what about random and planned?"

"*None* were random. They were *all* targets that took some doing to get to them and kill unseen. He had to have stalked them first."

"Dammit."

"I'm — sorry?"

"No, no, you're absolutely right and I was hoping we were wrong."

"I don't understand." With everyone else in her past life, particularly her egomaniac ex-husband and often her egotistical son, she could never say such a thing without being made to feel like a clueless and patronized fool. But with this man, her lack was always met with understanding, curiosity, patience.

"If they were all planned — and you're right, they were, goddammit! — that could mean he's not through yet. Not to mention we're back to square one: What the hell do they all have in common that pisses this perp off?"

"They were all . . . successful?"

"Good one. They all could have been envied — they were good looking, or rich, or smart, they all had great futures ahead of them in life. So, the killer was a loser? Aren't they all?"

"No, I meant they were all successful *women* — a strict Muslim man would hate that. They were not in their place, where he thinks they belong, Islam-wise."

"Better one. We're looking for a fanatic, and these days, in this town, fanatic Muslims are noticed. Because they mouth off."

"But . . ."

"Oh, hell, what 'but'?

"The worst nightmare: What if it's a non-Muslim killing Muslims? Belated 9-11 revenge or something."

"Using a dagger?"

"Turning their own weapon against them?"

"How would a white guy know about Eleventh Century Assassins, much less get that kinda training, dagger-wise?"

"Maybe a white guy who spent time in the Middle East kinda recently? One of those losers who saw the radicals' philosophy and cause on the Internet, fell for that bullshi– uh, propaganda? He wouldn't be unique, these days."

"Yeah, one of those lone-wolf terrorists who decided he'd come back home and be a good little Assassin For Islam? There's a nauseating thought. But it *is* a thought, and a good one. As for me . . ." He got up and stretched his massive frame, his pale blue shirt pulling up from his dark blue pants waist. And it was all Nell could do to refrain from grabbing the door frame for support, since the sight of the size of him, the power lurking within him, always rocked her knees, not to mention various female parts that hadn't been rocked in –– well, it was no good thinking about it.

". . . the legwork continues. Hashemi, the FBI already did most of the legwork on him. All that legwork getting everything *wrong*, but any port in-a storm." He tucked his shirt back in, grabbed his matching dark blue jacket from the back of his chair. He tucked a small spiral notebook into one pocket, Nell glimpsed "Dagger" written neatly across its yellow cover. He grabbed a couple souvenir pens from the beer stein on his desk, tucked them into another pocket. He put on his jacket, buttoned it, smoothed it down, uselessly smoothed his rebellious hair and presented himself to her with a teasing grin, "What do you think? Ready for Sunday school?"

She laughed and went to her desk. His cellphone was in the charger on her desk. "Wow, you remembered," she teased as she handed the phone to him and instantly knew he'd forgotten the phone was charging and would have walked out without it.

"I still think these damn things are the devil's underpants," he growled as he walked out. "Don't call me, I'll call you, unless disaster," before the door shut behind him.

She was startled when he did an abrupt U-ee outside and came back in, heading for the bathroom. "Coffee overload," he growled.

Nell laughed, turned to switch on her computer, contemplated her desk, none of the usual paperwork waiting was the least bit interesting. "Shopping for daggers," she mused with an eager interest, and clicked the keys that sent her to Google.

Moments later, he sailed past her again, saying, "This time I'm serious." and he was out the door and gone.

Nell sank into her desk chair in the familiar silence, and breathed in the memory of lemons and the quiet of waiting. Then she shook off the reverie and turned to her computer keys, muttering, "Work-work-work." So that when Claire came in about ten minutes later, Nell was clickety-clicking keyboard keys as though it was just the beginning of another ordinary work day. Only with Eleventh Century daggers in the mix.

* * * *

"I understand not wasting the taxpayers' money and all, but this is ridiculous," Hermie referred to the austere office in the impressive Los Angeles FBI building. With the exception of a nice-sized window that looked onto Ficus trees dressed in sprightly Spring green leaves and foamy white blossoms, Trots' office was eggshell white walls, utilitarian grey carpet, an Ikea-plain desk, chairs and filing cabinets. Trots' desk was shoulder to shoulder with an industrial strength shredder, cluttered with computer hard drive and monitor, keyboard, bulging file folders, stacks of DVD-R discs, pens, empty and full Styrofoam coffee cups, and down below was a large, dented metal wastebasket, overflowing with trashed bounty. "Your paper shredder probably cost more than your furniture. Oh, how the standards continue to fall . . ." Hermie moaned, dramatically.

"I am, after all, a mere Temp here. At least we got six stalls, I hear yours is a unisex share kinda thing. Can you get Air Freshener of the Month? You know, like Fruit of the Month?"

"I don't wanna know how the FBI investigated my station's bathroom. I especially don't wanna know why."

Trots chuckled. "Sit it," he said, indicating the only upholstered chair in the room, in front of his desk. "I hear now you have four down. And the last two young. I'm so sorry. That's what people say, isn't it? Don't know why, it doesn't help, at all, at all."

"And he's still using that goddamn dagger."

"Hell."

"Yeah."

"What can I —— *we* —— do for you, Snoopy? I am volunteering, with sincerity. Make note of the date."

"I'd be happy if you'd just *share*. Play nicely with others. That sort of thing."

"What?"

"I'm starting at the beginning. I'd like to see all the files the FBI's got on Hashemi and Lila Miller. For comparison. As inaccurate as we all know they are."

"Bastard."

"You know I hadda take at least *one* shot."

"Okay, okay. Some I *can't* share, accurate or not."

"Understand. I don't need your secret stuff, 'national security' and all that kinda crap —— I can get better than you got from another source. An *accurate* source."

"Are you serious?"

"Yup."

"I'd be wasting my time asking?"

"Oh, my yup. But I did pass on all the poop and genius on Winston Delano Safir, AKA Jordan Hashemi, you gotta give me credit for that."

"I suppose I gotta. But it don't solve the mystery of who the hell off'd our boy. And his Lady."

"My source says it was not a hit, so it was not a hit. But *I'm* sayin' Hashemi *knew* his killer — he got out of the car when faced with the doer of the deed. If it was a stranger, I don't think he'd dare. Why make it easier for him? However . . ."

"Oh, crap — 'however' what?"

"We-all assumed this started with Hashemi. I don't think it did. At least, not in the way we think. Thought. Our Invisible Man Winston Delano just might-a been in the wrong place at the wrong time."

"I swear to God, Grabfelder . . ."

"Don't get your fruits in the loom, this is all irrelevant."

"It is?"

"As sure as I can get, at this point. If I hear any different, I will gossip. You know that."

"Really? Then what about the gossip of you visiting a young lad in Juvie that was picked up for being bloody? Is that 'irrelevant'?"

Since Hermie expected this, the FBI being as anal as they are, he wasn't shocked nor annoyed. He calmly said, "It is. For now. And I'm asking you not to interfere. Until further notice. It's important to someone's life. And sanity."

Trots and Hermie exchanged looks that were like handshakes, exchanging the history of a friendship, the depth of their trust, and a dollop of one-upmanship.

"Deal. Hashemi-wise, I've got background files in computers, on DVD-R discs, and on plain-old hard copies. Which do you want?"

"Which do you think?"

* * * *

Hours later, Hermie was still at one end of a vast but cheaply made conference table in a windowless conference room, surrounded by dozens of folders containing printouts, DVD-R discs, and a loaded laptop of background information on Jordan Hashemi and Lila Miller. He was amused by what the FBI hadn't known about Hashemi: there was a fresh sheet listing his real name, hometown, education and parental and family information, all "relevant" information having recently come from Hermie, courtesy of Farouz

Selah. There was assigned tasking regarding Hashemi's phony arm sales, highway robbery on a cyber genius scale. There was also an angry memo from Trots to a variety of agents demanding to know why and how they failed to track Lila Miller's son. A fresher sheet ordered that the search for the son be suspended until further notice.

There was no information about what was found in Hashemi's office. But Hermie had expected that information was being kept uber-Classified until someone, somewhere could figure out how to get into those computers. The FBI no doubt managed to find enough Arabic-speaking and Arabic-writing agents to go on Overtime delving through all those machines and all that data, but language wasn't the problem. Hashemi's genius was the uber-UBER problem. His computers were ingenious bastions against everyone and anyone except him. And he never existed.

There was a collection of photos, some original copies, some photocopies, some obvious surveillance photos. Photos of Lila Miller, taken by the FBI when she was recruited, her face fresh and sleek, even if her eyes had the haunted look of her history. There was also a vast collection of surveillance photos of Lila on her "dates", all with Middle Eastern men whose Western suits shouted "money", all with faces, eyes you wouldn't trust to take out your trash much less take out this exceptional, brave woman. He'd also realized that there were absolutely no records of Lila's past, Hashemi had seen to having all her background vanish from every cyber-record ever made of her. She didn't exist, either, soon after meeting him.

However, there was one photo carelessly jammed among the others that brought Hermie up short. It was a surveillance photo, to be sure, taken at what looked like an expensive restaurant in a hotel. At a table sparkling with crystal glasses, shining silverware and gleaming porcelain plates, Lila and Hashemi sat side by side. They'd obviously been talking, their faces turned toward each other. And there it was, so obvious, so glowing: that look of Discovery, of arriving at a safe place after a long and lonely journey, that Look of Love very new, but very *there. They were both gone, so what the hell. Besides, "Kevin" should have this.* So Hermie slipped the photo into an inside pocket of his jacket. A thought that there might be hidden surveillance cameras blanketing this room gave him pause, but didn't change his mind.

There was the color photo he'd noticed in Hashemi's Century City desk: mother, father, sister. Someone had written on the back, "Safir family. Mother, Father, Sister?" *Why the question mark?* There was a color photo-copy of Hashemi's fake driver's license, enlarged to better show the details of his face, that face revealing nothing of his exceptional intellect, his history, or even of his calm nature. This dangerous, ingenious man who didn't exist had managed to grow the confidence and affection of a damaged, spying woman and her damaged, elusive son, in spite of considerable risk to himself and his cyber plans. *Whatever the hell those plans are. Were. Was Selah right — they were empty people who recognized each other, recognized that they had become empty in self-defense; their secret natures had been broken yet longing, seeking, so capable of loving. Oh, for chrissakes, why don't you set that to music, Grabfelder?!*

But something made him gather up the fake driver's license of Hashemi's, and the photograph of the "Safir family", and some printouts of the Safir family's history in England that he'd shared from Selah. He carried all out of the room, walked down the hallway and approached the first desk he thought looked like it was manned by a secretary rather than a low-level agent who hadn't yet been promoted into an office with its required picky-ness protocol.

Along with twenty extra pounds and glasses too small for her large but impishly-cute face, the secretary was wearing dictaphone headphones so didn't hear his approach, but paused in her frantic typing on her computer keyboard when her peripheral vision indicated something *large* had loomed up alongside her desk. She looked up to see Hermie, felt the usual flutter women felt when getting a full-on look at the sly fox blues and the tousled dark gold hair and naturally white teeth flashing a sincere smile. She had seen agent Trotsky take someone large into the conference room earlier, but was taking notes while on the phone, so was too distracted to notice what the huge man had looked like. Now, here he was. And *Wow.* "Yes, Sir? Can I help you?"

"Sorry to bother you. Is there a copy machine nearby? I'd like to make a copy of these," he held up the photo, printouts he'd gathered. "I'm Detective Grabfelder, working on a case with Trots. Uh, Agent Trotsky. I'm sure he wouldn't let me take these out of the files, you know how picky he is, so I'd like to have copies." Dazzling smile. *Hope to gawd it would not get it into her head that she should ask Trots first if I had permission to have the copies at all.*

"Sure. I'll do it for you." She got up from the desk, forgetting the dictaphone headphones until their cord yanked at her ears, snapping her head back. Hoping he hadn't seen that, she untethered herself.

"Oh, you don't have to —" he insisted, apologetically.

"Yeah, I do. Ya have to type in a permission code first. I'll use mine."

"*Oh.*" *Oh, crap, will she get into trouble if they find her code took the copies?* "Well, if there's any problem, you just say it's all Grabfelder's fault. People will believe you." *Please God!*

She laughed and led him around the corner to a massive copying machine that radiated heat.

"I'll cover my eyes so I don't see your code," he teased, covering his eyes but peaking underneath.

"Stupid, isn't? But people were copying their screenplays and what-all, so copying costs got over the top. So, now you have to identify yourself before making any copies. Do you just need one copy?"

"Better give me two. I lose things."

"Just like a man." She typed in a code, punched buttons, and the machine belched into life. She barely looked at the photo or printouts when she arranged them onto the glass. Almost instantly, she handed him the perfect copies, in color and everything. "Here, I made you four of each, just in case."

He twinkled at her. "Ya read my mind. I hate that. But thanks a lot."

She watched him walk back down the hall to the conference room, was sure the floor shook and relaxed, smelled lemons in his wake, and then it hit her because she was an avid reader of the LA Times: *Oh, my gawd, that's* **THE** *Detective Grabfelder!* And she hurried back to her desk and yanked up the phone to make the one personal call she'd have time to do all day. But it was a beaut.

* * * *

There was a soft knock and then the conference room door opened, revealing Trots carrying several restaurant bags bulging with take-away boxes and tall cups. "Since you're still in Reformation, I made sure the sandwiches were low-fat turkey with sprouts and grains and stuff."

Hermie laughed and got up, stretched. "At this point, I'll eat anything. But you got someplace with a window? This room is a hole."

"I got even better. Come on . . ."

Trots led the way, so he didn't see Hermie making sure the photo copies were folded just so, enough to be invisibly tucked into the inner pockets of his jacket.

Had not the surrounding traffic stench been spoiling things for Hermie's nose, the patio would have been pleasant, surrounded as it was by tall, leafy trees rustling with hollering birds and low bushes thick with tiny pink blooms that Hermie once heard called "Pink Ladies". The sandwiches were *real* -- actual turkey sliced off an actual doomed bird's breast instead of a press, crisp and cold dark green lettuce, red tomatoes that almost had flavor, pitilessly judged by the Michigan Man that was Hermie, and a sauce that was creamy and also tangy with sweet pickles.

Trots had also brought Paradise iced tea, with its familiar whiff of fruit, and two large chocolate chip cookies, lumpy with pecans. "I know, the cookies will send us straight to hell," Trots quipped, "but without chocolate chips, Life has little meaning."

"I'm hip. But you know they now have sugarless chocolate chip cookies at Ralph's that are dee-vine."

Trots slowly shook his head in astonishment. "Ya think ya know a guy."

They munched and sipped in companionable silence, squinting at the sunny, breezy day, listening to the bird riot that sounded like it was getting closer as well as more musical than mere chatter. Sure enough, a red-headed finch dropped down and hopped in front of them, looking hopeful.

"We are going to eat it all up, our own selves," Hermie said to the bird. Who got it, and flew off.

The breeze ruffled Hermie's hair, but left no trace in Trots' crewcut.

"Was it helpful? The files?" Trots asked, between bites and sips.

"Once I weeded out the inaccuracies, yeah."

"Don't remind me."

They munched for a moment, then Trots threw caution to the wind: "Hashemi. Your source. Dish."

"Dash your hopes, Big Fellah. He will not be recruited, he will not be bought, he will not be known. Ever."

"Whose side is he on? Whose side are *you* on?"

"Truth, justice and the American way. When it suits."

"Just one: Was he in any way connected to Hashemi?"

"No. He does not connect. With anyone."

"Except you."

"He adopted me."

Trots chuckled. "One more?"

"Oh, go ahead, if you must."

"The kid you got in Juvie."

"I want an absolute guarantee of non-interference. Hands off, and I mean *really* hands off, until and *if* I say different. This is non-negotiable, Trots."

Trots was somewhat startled by the sudden seriousness in Hermie's tone and eyes. "Non-. You have my word."

"He's Lila's son."

"Holy –!" Trots sprayed some cookie in shock. "The Juvie?! That's *him*?!"

"Yeah. He was found, covered in his Mom's blood, standing alongside El Segundo Blvd. And he's completely catatonic. I mean, he is *gone*, gone far away in his mind."

"Jeezus! For real? That poor kid."

"This is why you can't interfere."

"'Word, Snoopy."

Hermie took a bite of a cookie, but not being used to sugar these days, it was too sweet. He passed it over to Trots, who took it without hesitation, and it was the second cookie he munched on with his thoughts. "That blood?"

"I've got a Korean Tech guy sneaking blood tests for me -- the blood on "Kevin's" clothes compared to Lila Miller's. But we both know now."

"His own mother's blood . . ." Trots slowly shook his head in sympathy. Then: "'Korean'? Is that significant?"

"Hell, no. But Andy knows his shoes."

"'Shoes'?"

"Andy noticed Lila was wearing shoes that cost eight hundred dollars. Did she put that on her expense account? Hmmmm?"

"Up yours. Hey, wait – 'Kevin'?"

"I met that kid before, through a friend of mine. Some time ago, the boy turned up at a youth group he and some cops are involved with. Baseball. Kid called himself 'Kevin Costner'. My friend and every cop he knew checked every data base and never got a line on him. Next thing I know, he's Lila's son. Surprise, surprise. And he's the witness to her murder." Hermie checked his watch. *He's had plenty of time he can steal. Hopefully.* "Can I use your cellphone?"

"Where's yours?"

"In my car. It's better that way."

Trots handed over his cellphone.

Hermie thought for a moment, exasperation about to appear.

"What?"

"Trying to remember the goddamn number."

"Slowing down, are we?"

"My gray is less than your gray."

Trots sheepishly brushed his gray-white crewcut.

"Ah -- got it." Hermie dialed confidently.

Then Trots listened to a conversation between Hermie and an overworked Korean technician in LAPD Forensics and marveled at how smoothly Hermie was able to get a DNA result that should have taken weeks, caseloads being what they were in Murder Capital West.

"Andy, I owe ya all over the place. Yeah. Love to Grandma, too. Later." Hermie hung up, handed back the phone. "They're a match."

"You knew from the start, huh?"

"Oh, yeah."

"How? Just askin'."

"The banana bubblegum," answered Hermie. And when he finally told about the banana-scented kiss he'd smelled on Lila Miller's cheek, Trots nearly inhaled an ice cube.

* * * *

The next day blew apart all the best laid plans. Someone in Juvenile Hall blabbed to Tommy Velasco of the LA Times because he, or she –- Hermie couldn't find out who, other than it wasn't Bill Corey, who was so furious he burst into tears over the phone -- thought it would make a fun headline: ""KEVIN COSTNER" (NOT REALLY) ARRESTED, LOCKED IN JUVENILE HALL."

Fortunately, Hermie had picked the right person at Social Services and Babs had her own mole at the LA Times. So, when Tommy Velasco descended upon Juvenile Hall with minicams and groupies, they discovered that "Kevin Costner" was missing, having been sprung by unknown child advocates (secretly aided and abetted by the valiant Bill Corey), and his and the Advocate's whereabouts were unknown.

Social Services feigned ignorance, in a manner that conveyed how pissed off they were yet again at the lax security measures in Juvenile Hall. Thus the people's right to know was thwarted and Velasco was infuriated. Couldn't happen to a nicer guy.

The Police Chief was apoplectic, and the D.A. was beyond profane, and the whole damn bunch made the expected phone calls to LAPD Homicide Detective Herman Grabfelder. Since Detective Grabfelder was "out in the field", with a "dead cellphone battery", according to his sweet-as-pie secretary, Nell Barlow, and his sincere and gracious Captain, Claire Jennings, messages were taken down with little hope of being answered in anyone's lifetime.

And, since the DNA results on "Kevin Costner's" clothes were "still pending", as believably lied by overworked and complaining Andy Cho Hui, no one was informed of what Hermie knew, so there was no link to the murder of an undercover FBI agent and her mark, thus a grateful Trots was spared pithy phone calls from his own Quantico superiors who had a habit of reading the LA Times.

Luckily, or unluckily depending on your loyalties, in the midst of all this tsouris, the Social Services union went on strike for some very good reasons, to everyone's shock-SHOCK! So this major-MAJOR! turmoil turned all attention aside. For the time being.

Claire, whose main goal in life was being the Los Angeles Police Chief some day, was the type of Captain who knew exactly what everyone on her watch was doing hour to hour and day to day, and exactly why. So, she did call Hermie on that "dead battery" cellphone and ask the question he knew she would ask. "Hermie, is this trip necessary?"

"You know me." he answered.

And that was enough for her. For now.

CHAPTER TEN

"He who will not reason is a bigot;
he, who cannot, is a fool;
and he, who dares not, is a slave."

William Drummond, Scottish Writer

Amira Farsadi's family lived in an apartment building on Normandie that had absolutely no character. A square block with six stories, painted off-white, the only design touch being the rust-colored, fan-like stains on the outer walls from sprinklers that tended the few hedges and scraggly Bird of Paradise plants that passed for landscaping. The outer door opened into a plain lobby, walls more off-white, festooned with too-few prints of beach scenes not even interesting enough to be postcards; a floor of wine-colored linoleum three-fourths covered with a deep gray outdoor carpet that had various nearly-black stains. An elevator was in a foyer beyond, reached only if you were buzzed through a sturdy-looking metal door. Apparently, a breach had been tried — there were dents in the metal around the huge steel lock plate.

Hermie wondered if the breach had been successful as he pressed the button marked, "FARSADI 3C". He had called ahead to make this appointment, had gotten Attitude from Mister Charm, who finally consented to this in-home interview after he was threatened with "official warrants from the District Attorney" that would lead to a "trip downtown, escorted by Officers" for "police questioning that could take hours, you'll miss a day of work, Mr. Farsadi, maybe two". Now when he announced himself to the male voice that yelled out of the microphone plate, he was not acknowledged. The voice merely hung up, and a loud BUZZ sounded around the door, so Hermie pushed it in.

The door opened to reveal the elevator. The elevator doors were open between floors, revealing two dusty workmen who were servicing it. They looked up and nodded, one of them said, "How you doin' man?" and pointed a hammer helpfully to direct Hermie to the stairwell in the corner of the foyer.

"Thanks," acknowledged Hermie. "That's some job you got there."

"Can't be picky nowadays." answered the other workman.

"I hear ya. Have a good one," Hermie sympathized and walked to the stairwell.

The smell of grease, dirt and years of dust had wafted out from the elevator shaft. Now, the stairwell smelled of old air, dust and mold. Dust bunnies held their ground amongst stains of unknown and best not contemplated liquids of various colors.

The smell of people was strong in the hallways of the third floor -- cooking oil, laundry detergent, boiled greens, body odor and a savory whiff of fried meat. Hermie pressed a black button below the rusted metal that announced "3C" and heard an unpleasant CLANK-CLANK instead of the usual musical doorbell sound. Feet stomped to the door inside, locks clicked, and the door was yanked open to reveal a Middle Eastern male in his late teens or early twenties, small, dark and wiry, with the same arrogant eyes of the father Hermie had already met. He wreaked of cigarette smoke. Hermie showed his badge and tried on affable, "Hi. I'm expected. Detective Grabfelder."

He snatched the badge from Hermie's hand and examined it with contempt. Then he handed it back with a shove.

"And you are?" Hermie asked, holding his ground.

The male suddenly got a good look at the dangerous blues glowing at him from this hulking presence. A step back before he said, "I am Izzat Farsadi. My father waits."

Hermie yanked out the small spiral notebook and a pen that announced "The Green Hornet" and made a show of writing. "Izzat Farsadi . . . I'll write that down. So I don't forget it." It worked: the boy's arrogance evaporated, uneasiness took over. He stepped aside, letting Hermie in, but then took a last stand-- he slammed the door and walked off, expecting Hermie to follow.

The small foyer opened onto a large livingroom. Hermie sensed another hallway to the left, no doubt leading to bedrooms and bathrooms, a shorter hall on the right led to a kitchen. Hermie caught a glimpse of a shadow on the kitchen wall just inside the open door: someone wearing a chador was standing there, very still.

Mr. Farsadi was seated in the exact center of a deep green corduroy-covered couch that ran almost the length of one wall in the livingroom. The room was simply decorated, with comfy chairs upholstered in red and blue, dark wood end tables that held tall lamps with white silk shades and ceramic

vase bases in pastel colors of blue, yellow and red. A separate end table held
an elaborate silver and crystal water pipe, the silver etched with floral vines.

A low table in front of the couch was draped with a black silk scarf,
exquisitely embroidered with flowers and leaves in gold and red thread. A
TV remote and small crystal dishes holding nuts and candies sat on the silk.
The opposite wall held an entertainment center with a large TV screen, cable
box, DVD player, and music components. A neat stack of CD's was atop one
of the speakers, DVD's stacked on the other speaker.

In answer to the annoyance blooming in Mr. Farsadi's eyes, Hermie made
a point of sitting in the chair that directly faced him, without waiting to be
invited, without offering a handshake to the seated Mr. Farsadi. Both father
and son were not pleased. The son plopped down on the couch, alongside
the father.

"Ma-ra!" the father yelled, the word for "woman" snarled like a curse.

Almost instantly, Hermie heard the soft rattle of cups and Mrs. Farsadi
glided in, carrying a silver tray set with a white porcelain tea service and
three bowls, one filled with cookies, one with dates, the third with tan sugar
chunks, which reminded Hermie of Selah and his lethal coffee.

Hermie instantly stood up for her presence, instinctively knowing this
would piss-off her old man and son, since it showed too much respect for her.

The brief flight of her black chador ceased when she arrived at the low
table, its filmy black wings settling down and enfolding her as she set the tray
down, and poured tea with hands covered with filmy black gloves.

When she handed Hermie a cup of tea, her back was to her husband and
son, so her eyes briefly raised to look into Hermie's and he saw how much grief
had drained her. Her eyes were encircled with black rings set into her pale olive
skin. Her cheekbones announced what the chador hid: a great loss of weight.
Hermie was moved when she left her sorrow for the briefest moment it took
to smile at him. Knowing the view of him was blocked, his eyes returned her
smile as he nodded, then sat back down. "Thank you, Mrs. Farsadi, the tea
smells wonderful."

Her face returned to stone before she turned away to serve her husband
and son. Then she glided out and Hermie's peripheral vision once again saw
the still shadow on the kitchen wall, as the black wings settled and enfolded
her once more, and she listened.

Father and son automatically put tan sugar chunks between their stained
teeth and sipped tea, both glaring at Hermie over their cups.

Now pissed off at the attitude, Hermie rose to the challenge and played it
for all it was worth: He took a cookie from one of the bowls, took a bite and
relished it, as if he had all the time in the world. "Mmm-mmm -- delicious.
Your wife bake these?"

"I do not know." Mr. Farsadi's voice was as rigid as his body language.

"We-ell, whatev-er, these are a very fine welcome to a guest. I'll have to come more often. And you're welcome to come to my place, anytime."

The son choked on his tea. Both father and son were suddenly flummoxed, not knowing where this was going.

Hermie washed down the cookie with a sip of tea, then took another cookie, slowly eating it with a glow of pleasure. "Mmmm . . . wonderful . . . there's nuthin' like a good cookie, mmm--mmm . . ."

The son took a fig from the other bowl and chewed it ferociously, gulped tea too quickly, it was too hot and he flinched while his eyes swam.

"Too hot for ya? Some things you gotta take . . . slow." Hermie slowly finished the cookie, sipped tea, reached for another and was pleased to feel and see the barely controlled rage waft over the table toward him. He took a bite of the cookie, set it into the saucer beneath his cup, set them down on the low table, rubbed his hands as if brushing off crumbs, pulled his little notebook and Green Hornet pen from his pockets, flipped the notebook open and made an elaborate show of flipping page after page, back and forth, back and forth, until seemingly arriving at a blank page, fake-licked the point of his pen thoughtfully, and then appeared to carefully, firmly write something on the page, then lowered the pad and pen and looked up, the full force of his blazing eyes turned on in direct proportion to his heretofore hidden temper. Hot blue met black arrogance and it was the arrogance that blinked. If they hadn't been seated, father and son would have liked to take a step back, maybe two.

"First off, let me once again say that I am very sorry for your loss. My job has taught me there is no pain as deep as the loss of a child. Especially in this cruel way, by a heartless stranger."

Father and son were expressionless, but Hermie had not said these things for *their* benefit; his peripheral vision told him the shadow on the kitchen wall had heard. "I apologize for coming here during your mourning."

"The mourning is over." The son thought he sounded manly, but it came off as childish petulance.

"Mourning for the loss of a child never ends." And the lasers went even hotter into the arrogant son's eyes, who instantly sat further back and looked away. *Arrogant son of a bitch. You talk that way where your mother can hear?* "The reason I'm here, as I mentioned on the phone, is that the investigation is ongoing and I need to ask you some questions about your daughter, sister, in the hope I can find a clue as to who did this to her. I'd like to be brief, but it will take as long as it takes."

The father said it so matter of fact-ly: "Her death was Allah's will. There are no questions."

Hermie instantly dropped his eyes down to his little notebook so they would not see his rage. *Ignore it, ignore it, get on with it.* Normally, he would ask survivors to simply tell him about their child, wife, sister, brother, husband, father, mother. Inevitably, good memories would come pouring out, briefly easing their grief, giving them a temporary strength to then answer painful questions. But he instinctively knew these two wastes of space did not know Amira — his daughter, his sister -- in the least, much less care. The person who did know her and loved her profoundly, the person who was now utterly alone in this void, was hiding just inside the kitchen door, out of his reach. He knew she needed protection from this dour duo, knew that she would not be free to express herself in front of them and would not be allowed to be alone with him for questioning, might even be punished for talking to him, so he protected her by ignoring her, hoping she'd understand.

"She was taking difficult college courses at the school, that must mean she was very intelligent."

The father dismissed her: "She was a woman."

"Do you know who were her friends at school? Or her teachers?"

"No."

"She never mentioned any names of who was in her classes?"

"No."

"She never brought friends home?"

"No."

Considering the welcome they'd get here, this is not a big surprise. So this is why nobody from the school offered her a ride home. This poor girl . . . I hope to God she did have some friends at school, someone, anyone to talk to . . . "She was studying mathematics, engineering, physics, judging from the books found with her. What were her career plans?"

"She had no plans."

"People who work so hard at their studies, education, always have plans, ambitions, dreams."

"Her studies would cease upon her marriage."

"Oh? She was engaged?"

Both father and son shifted in their seats.

"Who was the guy she was going to marry?"

Another stirring in their seats.

Hermie pulled out the Fear of God Card: "You seem reluctant to help with this investigation. Your daughter's *murder.* It's been my experience that people who act like you do so because they had something to do with the crime." *Shot in the dark:* "Did you have anything to do with her death? Do you know who was involved with this?"

The son was the first to crack, but only because he felt that he had some kinda right: "She shamed us!"

Without looking, the father back-handed the son, just missing his face, but landing a sharp blow in his throat that set him coughing.

"A marriage was arranged, but she refused," the father snarled.

"Wasn't that her right? In Islam? According to a Muslim friend of mine . . ."

"A daughter must obey!"

"Let me understand you: she refused marriage. Why? She didn't like the guy? Or, because she wanted to continue her schooling?'

"She went to school to meet men!" The father was now spraying spittle in his rage.

"Well, it was a co-ed school, she could hardly avoid meeting men in classes. About as many men as girls, like herself."

"It is a sin!"

Hermie recalled the thorough file that Nell had volunteered to create on Amira Farsadi, in preparation for when he would go to the school and interview anyone who knew her: "My office has copies of her transcripts -- her grades, evaluations from her teachers -- she was at the top of her class, which tells me she spent her time studying, not socializing. More than one of her teachers said that Amira had the grades and intelligence to get a full scholarship to just about any college she would have liked to attend." *Education was her ticket outta here, and she knew that, God bless her.*

The father folded his arms and looked away, as if ending the discussion.

"I will question her classmates, her teachers, everyone who knew her. What will I find?"

Neither man acknowledged the question.

"What were her days like?"

"She went to school, she came home, she studied, she helped with the cooking for her mother." This from the father.

"Ah, then she *didn't* spend time with all those men she met. Good for her."

The father's eyes snapped back at him, then snapped away.

This is a goddamn waste of time. They're giving me a headache. Five more minutes before I have the stroke. Five more minutes to piss 'em off, just to be sociable. Hermie closed his notebook, pocketed it and his pen. Father and son appeared relieved the interview was at an end, started to rise as one. But Hermie stopped them inches above the couch when he reached for his tea and cookie and slowly ate, sipped, as though he was in no hurry at all. He deliberately waited until father and son, annoyed, reached for their own tea, before he abruptly set his cup and saucer down and got up. Tea cups clattered against saucers as father and son scrambled up. They were stopped dead when

Hermie smiled a crocodile smile and said, "You can show me Amira's room now."

Hermie was surprised when the boy did not argue, but led him down the hall. Until he reached Amira's room. It had been stripped bare of any sign that she had ever been there. A soap scent lingered, as if the room had been scrubbed. No pictures on the walls -- except the white squares in the paint where pictures once hung. No girlie things like knick-knacks or decorative pillows or stuffed animals. The bed was small, the coverlet plain, not announcing whether it was a boy or girl who slept there. He pulled just one drawer open from the cheap bureau: empty. Then he noticed the vanity: the mirror that would have been attached to it, the mirror every girl relied on in her own private room, that mirror had been removed, a few attachment screws left dangling: *No doubt too much trouble for these assholes to remove. Not even a reflection of the ghost of that precious child remained in this room.*

Thoroughly annoyed, Hermie yanked open the door that indicated a very small closet, certain it would be empty as well. It wasn't. It held something only LAPD Homicide Detective Herman Grabfelder would or could find: Amira wafted out to him. The faintest scent of her was still in that tiny closet, where her few clothes would have hung, and Amira came out to *him*, young and innocent and full of flowers and promise.

Hermie had to walk past the son quickly, otherwise he would have thrown a punch into that smug face.

To his surprise, the chador-clad figure swiftly glided past him as he turned toward the foyer, and she opened the door for him, then stood against the foyer wall, eyes down.

Moments later, standing in the hallway outside the closed door, he wondered at her skill at stealth. Because as he passed her in the foyer, he had nodded and said, "Thank you, Mrs. Farsadi. And again, you have my deepest sympathy. For *everything*," and continued on his way, but he *felt* more than saw her turn her back to the watching husband and son and slip something into his hand seconds before he was out the door and heard it close behind him.

Now he looked in his hand to discover a slightly crumpled business card, still warm and moist from her hand, as if she'd been holding it for hours in anticipation of him. The card read: "AIDA'S GROCERY, HALAL AND OTHERWISE", with an address on Western Avenue that was within walking distance of this apartment building.

Hermie was amused by the "Halal", which meant strict Muslim rules, being paired with "Otherwise", which could mean everything and anything else. *Even kosher?* Considering what Mrs. Farsadi risked to give him this card, he owed it to her to find out just what "Otherwise" meant.

* * * *

When he got to the address he wondered if there had been some mistake. It was indeed a grocery store that had Arabic and English signage on the roof, on the windows. *Why would Mrs. Farsadi send me to a simple grocery store? And why did she need to be so secretive about it?* Trusting her, he stepped inside and was met by dozens of wonderful smells that brought his childhood swiftly back, when he'd stepped inside the tiny, family-owned grocery store out in the farm country of Bay City, Michigan. *Ah, the smells* . . .

Fresh green vegetables that still smelled like the dirt they'd come from; sweet fruits ripened just right; brightly lit glass cases arrayed with the gleam and clean blood smell of the reddest fresh meat, pinkest chicken, and immaculate fish; the smelly cheeses his grandpa used to love and tuck under the kitchen sink for safekeeping; and the pleasantly nutty smell of an old, squeaky wooden floor polished by years of farm families' footsteps.

It took a moment for him to realize what was different about this store: Muslim women manned every counter. Head scarves in a variety of colors and floral patterns covered the heads of the female butcher, the woman who was stacking rosy apples in produce, the woman who was straightening up the dairy case –- which had more varieties of yoghurt than Hermie had ever seen –- and another modestly scarved woman was vigorously mopping the immaculate floor with a dust mop that had a bright yellow and fluffy mop-head.

Half a dozen women shoppers pushed small carts down narrow aisles, some bareheaded with stylish haircuts, others with loose headscarves barely anchored on their heads, and two in nearly identical deep gray chadors, only their faces visible, pushing the same cart side by side. Now and then, here and there, female voices spoke in the bouncy tones of Arabic, flavored with some English.

Hermie became aware of being watched, and turned to see the watcher: the stern face of a woman of about forty, whose thick, lustrous black hair was loosely pulled back into a large knot that settled against the back of an elegant, long neck. She wore a deep blue caftan that had silver thread embroidery at the neck and around the armhole seams that held long sleeves. It was similar to that worn by Sunidhi Askar, but designed to flow over a much sturdier, muscular body.

Hermie walked over to her, looking directly into wary, warning eyes, pulling out his badge. She looked at his badge closely but oddly, as if she'd seen it before. "I am the owner of this store."

Instinctively, Hermie looked around to make sure neither shoppers nor clerks were close enough to hear or see. He pulled out the card given to him and showed it to her. "Mrs. Farsadi gave this to me. In secret. I'm investigating her Amira's murder."

He heard her sharp intake of breath, saw her large, copper-colored eyes fill with tears. "You are *he*!"

She reached under the shelf beneath the cash register plopped among displays of several kinds of Arabic candies and Hermie heard the faintest sound of a buzzer sail throughout the store. Instantly, the female butcher left her post and glided over to them. She exchanged knowing looks as the store owner spoke a torrent of Arabic, with ""Amira" and "Sunidhi" and "Saa-Hib" entangled. And Hermie's memory flashed and he recalled Shakey's using "Saa-Hib" as the term for "friend".

The butcher lady looked him up and down and her round face gleamed with a merry, flirtatious smile. "Ah . . . it *is* he. Not bad, not bad at all."

Hermie nearly laughed aloud.

"Really, Farah!" the store owner scolded, embarrassed. "Sorry, she is not controllable."

"And why should I be? Around the likes of him?"

"Ach! Come with me, Detective, while you still can." She glided swiftly down a side aisle to a swinging door marked "PERSONNEL ONLY". Before she went through, she gave out a sudden, brief whistle, and Hermie heard the same whistle repeated by every non-shopper in the store behind them. The door led to a warehouse-type area in back of the store, where crates and boxes, some empty, some full, indicated the store's delivery space. A large cooler with a glass door filled most of the room, inside were crates full of still-wrapped vegetables, fruits, dairy items, other perishable products. Its motor was a not-so-subtle roar. She locked the door they came through, then she worked her way through the clutter with graceful skill and appeared to walk straight to a large hot water heater in the far corner of the room. She reached behind it and found a hand hold, pulled, and to Hermie's amazement the contraption swung aside on a track and exposed a stairway behind, heading straight up. She indicated he should go up.

As he began to climb, she pulled the heater shut behind them and lights flicked on along the walls of the narrow passage up. He hadn't noticed the tiny button beneath one of the lights until she pressed it behind him and he heard a pleasant bell sound reassuringly. Then Hermie got a whiff coming from above -– women's perfume, cooking, and babies.

He already knew what to expect when he arrived at a door at the top of the stairs, even before he heard several sturdy locks being clanked open. The heavy, steel door was pulled open with all the strength of a slender woman wearing jeans and an oversized light grey sweatshirt that had a bright yellow bouquet of daises printed on it. At the sight of Hermie looming up, she hesitated, mahogany-brown eyes wary. "He's okay," the owner called from behind him. Another flurry of Arabic, including "Amira" and "Sunidhi" and "Saa-Hib." The gray eyes lit up. "It's <u>him</u>? Wow! I mean, hello!"

"Hiya. Interesting place ya got here."

Hermie stepped up into a woman's shelter that apparently occupied the entire roof length of the grocery store below. Portable partitions had created a number of miniature bedrooms, some with a single cot, others with smaller child-sized cots or cribs alongside, plus simple t-bars for hanging clothes, and small dressers with drawers. It was obvious that what windows there were had one-way glass, light came in but nothing showed out. He heard a toilet flush from all the way across the building and assumed a communal bathroom was over there. He could see an immaculate kitchen in a nearer corner, with large-sized fridge, freezer, and stove, and a divided sink. Behind glass doors, foodstuffs neatly crowded cabinet shelves. Three toddlers, two girls and a boy, were happily playing with colorful plastic measuring cups, some tiny trucks, and a doll on the gleaming linoleum floor. A television against another wall was playing an episode of *"The Bold and the Beautiful"*.

The women who had been watching stood up from chairs and small couches to gape at him, some hastily replacing headscarfs on their heads. Behind him, a few words of reassurance in Arabic from the store owner, and once again Hermie heard "Saa-hib" and "Amira" and "Sunidhi". The women relaxed, some hankies fluttered up to eyes filled with tears, but they sat back down, watching him almost lovingly as the store owner grabbed a chair in passing and led him to another partition that made a small office out of a corner's walls. Inside, a battered wooden desk was overloaded with file folders, papers, the kind of large phone that had a shelf full of speed dial buttons to accommodate more than a dozen numbers. A few disposable cellphones occupied their own clutter. A computer monitor and keyboard sat on an old metal typewriter stand, the hard drive on the floor underneath.

The partition's walls and the other walls were festooned with photos of Muslim women and their children. Some looked frightened, worn down with sorrow; others glowed with triumphant smiles. On the partition, near where they had entered, Hermie's eye was caught by an enlarged xerox of an old newspaper article, Hermie recognized the typeface of the LA Times. He could easily read the headline, "SAUDI ARABIA: DON'T PUBLISH PICTURES OF WOMEN", and the article telling about King Abdulla advising that Saudi newspapers should no longer publish photos of women to accompany news stories because it could "lead young men astray." Someone had tacked a large photo alongside the article that showed an Arabic woman whose twinkly face was almost entirely obscured by a severe black headscarf pulled tight, and large horn-rimmed glasses magnifying wrinkled eyes and thick eyebrows. Someone had scrawled in English beneath her photo: "Ooh-Baby-Ooh!" This time, Hermie laughed out loud.

He turned to find her standing behind her desk. She had set the chair she'd grabbed in front of the desk, gestured that he should sit. He did, but she remained standing, as if her inner energy couldn't quite be contained. "I am Aida Abdulla. No relation."

He chuckled, "Obviously. I take it you run the place."

"Yes. It's been . . ." She paused for a brief moment of memory and thought, " . . . about seven years."

"They've all lived here for seven years?" Hermie was astonished.

"Oh, no. None are here for more than a few months."

"I don't get it."

"We are relocating them."

"'Relocating'?"

"Oh, yes, no way that any of them can or want to go back to their personal hells." She sat down as if setting down her anger, temporarily.

Hermie thought about the personal hell of his recent acquaintance: "Why did Mrs. Farsadi risk giving me your card?"

"Because she's another of the brave ones. She was trying to arrange for flight."

"Seeing how her husband and son treat her —"

"Not for herself. She wanted us to take her Amira away."

"Jeezus. I saw how much she loved her daughter. But without her . . . now she's so alone."

"She wanted to stay behind so she could stop her husband and son from finding the girl. If she remained, they would not suspect she had a hand in it. Of course, she knew their rage would be rained down on her. But she would bear it. She has done so before."

He was temporarily speechless. Then he became aware of a little girl of about five years old standing at his elbow, gaping up at him with merry green eyes. He turned down to look at her, winked large, and dropped his hand near her, palm up. "Give me five," he said to her.

The girl giggled, slapped his hand, covered more giggles with her hands. "Good job," he said.

She ran away.

Without missing a beat, he turned to Aida, "They'd actually hunt her down?"

"Let me tell you about 'Every Mother's Dream' Mr. Farsadi. His wife, her name is Lela by the way, was sold to him when she was eleven years old.

Her family had a large import/export business in Santa Monica. Farsadi was a distant cousin. He also came from money, his family being one of Lela's father's investors in the business, back in the old country –- Iraq. And he was "traditional", therefore trustworthy. They sponsored his entry into the states and before the wedding he was made a full partner in Lela's family business. Of course, the object of this union was sons. Farsadi raped eleven-year-old Lela on their wedding night, she hemorrhaged and damn near died in the hospital. Over the years, Lela had six miscarriages in six years and was blamed for all these failures. The beatings she received from 'The Beast Farsadi' were not considered a mitigating factor by doctors because they were not known outside the walls of their home. Farsadi asked for a divorce on account of Lela's 'failures' and was about to be granted that divorce when Lela became pregnant again and carried to term. When a girl was delivered, it was the last straw for The Beast, but the Imam at his mosque pointed out that one successful pregnancy could lead to another, a son, God willing, patience was counseled to this good Muslim husband. So another pregnancy within the year, and this time she delivered a healthy clone of the husband. She also tore her uterus so badly she nearly died on the table. There would be no more children. But since there was a son, this was irrelevant."

This time, the little girl brought a friend, a little boy about her age. Knowing the drill, Hermie dropped his hand palm up, the little girl slapped it, the little boy slapped it, giggles all around, and off they ran.

The children know, Aida thought. *They know that this huge man with the scary eyes is safe. And very kind. Lela was right. Oh, how sad that Amira only got to meet him in death.*

Without missing a beat, Hermie continued, "When did she come to you about her daughter?"

"The first marriage contract the Beast Farsadi tried to negotiate was when Amira was ten."

"You're kidding!"

"We arranged for an officer from Social Services, a Muslim, to explain the facts of American law to The Beast. The officer emphasized the kind of jail time sure to come for, in effect, selling his ten-year-old daughter in marriage to a forty-one year-old man who was considering a business merger with Farsadi's inlaws."

"I just don't get it." Hermie shook his head in disbelief.

"But it is easy to get, Detective Grabfelder. It is men using religion to do whatever the hell they want to women. Whether it is Muslims or polygamous Mormons or fundamentalist Christians or Hasidic Jews, it is all the same."

"Yeah. It sure is."

The little girl and the little boy brought friends. Now five children quietly gathered around Hermie, and five little hands gave him five, and five sets of giggles ran away. In the flurry of it all, Hermie smelled the vapors of a very flavorful tea wafting through the room.

"The situation came to a head when Amira reached American legal age. But by that time her startling intelligence was revealed. She came close to genius level in mathematics, physics, universities all over the country were waving scholarships. The Beast refused. Lela managed to persuade him to allow her to take college-level classes where . . . where you found her. And we began making arrangements."

"Where were you going to send her? You don't have to tell me, I get it."

"I know you do, Detective. Oxford to start, on a full scholarship. Harrow was also begging. A Muslim family outside the city was going to open their home to her. They have three daughters in colleges, along with two sons."

"What a sad, sad waste." Hermie had often had this oppressive feeling when he peered down at a murder victim who was too young for the violence that had stopped them forever, stopped them at the very brink of their future, removed them from a world that sorely needed their brilliance, leaving so many longings unfulfilled, so many promises not kept, beloved children unborn, and an old age that just might have been rich with memories of accomplishments.

He remembered the simple beauty of Amira Farsadi, not a sign on her serene face that showed the heartbreak and fear that filled her life. He remembered how tenderly her grief-wracked mother had smoothed her face, as if her hands were memorizing it. "In your opinion, could her father or brother or a like-minded Uncle have 'arranged' her death? The brother mentioned her 'dishonor to the family'."

The gaggle of giggles were stopped by That Look given by a graceful woman in a gray chador who glided up, carrying a tray with a tea service on it. The children scattered away, quietly. The sleeves of the woman's chador were tied back away from her wrists with rubber bands, no doubt to prevent them draping over the tea service or sweeping the tiny cookies off the saucer and onto the floor.

Aida shoved aside papers to make room on her desk, and the woman set the tray down.

"Thank you, Donna."

The woman nodded a smile at her and then Hermie, and glided away.

Aida poured the fragrant tea into cups, handed one to Hermie.

"You *know* I gotta ask: 'Donna'?"

"That is the name that will be on her passport. Donna Sharif, widow of Malek Sharif. You'll find his name in the obituaries, but not hers. She's a woman, not important to mention. Sharif had sons, brothers to mention."

"They wouldn't take care of her?"

Aida smiled, "Detective, she has no connection to the family of Sharif whatsoever. We look for Middle Eastern dead people in the papers, use their names for our women because if anyone asks, they have a name other than their own family's, so they can't be traced. And they can prove it with a newspaper clipping, a death certificate. Whatever it takes, if they are stopped. But they are women, so hardly anyone pays attention enough to stop them, once they are on their way."

"Jeezus!" He took a long gulp of the fragrant, stomach-comforting tea. "I have a friend in the FBI who'll never know about you. His loss. You'd be his teenage idol."

"'Teenage'? I'm flattered." She smiled a dimpled delight before she sipped. "Now, to answer your question: When I heard about Amira, that was my first thought –- that The Beast had arranged for her murder. He's too cowardly to do it himself, of course, but he'd know someone fanatic enough to 'get it done'. But I do not believe this is so, now."

"Why not? So far, he's my favorite –- and only –- candidate."

"Because there came Sunidhi. No connection to the Farsadi's whatsoever. The Beast and his offspring Farsadi, no. They were not involved. I would have been told."

"By who? Whom?"

"The women. The women know *everything*, even the ones locked away know. And they manage to communicate. Against all odds and all fears, they communicate. Amira was slaughtered by a stranger. So was Sunny, Sunidhi. Of this we are certain."

"The killer stole their headscarfs. Is that a message?"

"Oh, yeah. The purpose of the chador, the abiya, all those damnable veils, is to make a woman disappear. Especially the veils that cover the hair, a woman's glory. That's why, to some women, it is the sign of their piety. The headscarf is an adaptation, the minimal, to appease. The killer took them? I'd say the message is 'You're not fooling anyone with this inadequate covering.' In essence, he's stripping them, exposing them for what they are."

"'What they are'?"

"In his mind, whores."

"Holy . . . ! Uh, this is super-confidential: He used a particular dagger, the same kind used in the 11th Century."

"Assassin!" She immediately said.

"You know about that history?"

"I have a Masters in Middle Eastern history. One of my uncles was a professor of that kinda thing, back in the old country –- Saudi, in my case. Assassin! Holy shi –- uh, pardon me. He used a dagger? Had the training? He's a Shiite? How do you know?"

"One stab, then slice. My coroner recognized it. He's French. I have no idea how he knows about such things."

"The French were very large in the Middle East, once upon a time. My God –- we have heard only that it was a stabbing."

"And that must be the *only* discussion of the wounds, Ma'am, I'm trusting you and only you with this information."

"I can understand why. You have my word of honor I will not divulge this to anyone. As I trust you not to reveal what you have learned from us on this day."

"Word of honor, in turn. Hell, Eleventh Century crap is now on our shores. Probably join up with the right wing loons of Christianity, you know, 'Guns and God'. When will it all end?"

"Never. *All* religions are simply political power. If you understand that, you understand *everything*."

Hermie saluted his assent with his cup, drank what was left, in time to be aware the Giggle Bunch had returned. This time, Hermie did not offer his hand, but spoke to Aida in an apologetic tone, "Good heavens, Miss Aida, cookies? You know I'm on a diet. But they must not go to waste. What to do, what to do?" With elaborate gestures, Hermie picked up the small saucer of cookies, looked around mystified, then let his gaze drop on the wide-eyed kids. "Help me out here, huh?" He held the saucer down to their level. To his surprise, each child delicately took just one cookie, moved away so another could reach the plate. "You obviously aren't American kids," Hermie teased. There was one cookie left on the plate. The little girl who had first discovered Hermie picked up the cookie and held it out to Hermie. The rush of tears in his eyes made him take the cookie quickly, pop it into his mouth. "I thank you all," he said, bowing dramatically. A rush of giggles and the whole bunch ran away, but stayed nearby, munching cookies, watching Hermie.

Hermie wiped his eyes quickly before searching his pockets for a business card and came up empty. "Sorry, I had some business cards with my phone numbers, but gawd knows . . ."

"There is no need. You are well known in this community."

Hermie indicated the watching kids. "Yeah, but they don't get out much, do they?"

Aida laughed. Then she stood up, respectfully. "Lela has told us of what you gave her at the coroner's. To see to it that she and her daughter were alone, for a goodbye. This was such a kindness, such a blessing. We are all grateful. You will be contacted if we hear anything helpful, anything at all. About Amira or Sunidhi."

"It goes both ways. If you –– any of you –– need anything from me. Or if someone in authority doesn't take you seriously, give me a call. Or call a friend of mine in the Pacific Station –– Shaikh Mohammed. "Shakey". Mention my name. He'll step up to help you anytime."

"Thank you. This community keeps track of respectful law enforcement officers. After 9-ll, there was no one. There are more than a few, nowadays."

"'Cultural ignorance' they called it. I personally think of it as the 'Dork Factor'." He reached out to shake her hand, remembered, withdrew it. "Sorry."

An unrestrained smile lit up her face, and she reached out her hand to take his, firmly. "I personally appreciate shaking hands with a man –– we are then equal."

"Oh, Lady, you have it all over me, and just about every guy I know." He turned to go and again saw the poster on the wall. "I have-ta ask –– who is she? You must have picked her for a reason."

"A member of parliament, one of only two in her country. After retiring as a cardiologist, she got a law degree, took up politics. While she was running for election to parliament, the Sharia court granted her husband a divorce on the grounds she was an 'unfit, immoral woman', consorting with the men in parliament. He took her four children from her, as the Sharia ruled was his right. She won the election in a landslide."

"Good for her."

"Four months later, someone slit her throat as she was lifting groceries out of her car trunk. Her bodyguard was first shot in the head. She happened to fall on top of him as she bled to death. The husband took this as an 'embrace', proof of her adultery. Only she and some loyal friends knew that her bodyguard was gay. However, the 'embrace' justified his taking every penny of the inheritance she'd had from her family. He bought a yacht and remarried. She was thirteen and an heiress to a shipping fortune. She did not like the idea of raising another woman's kids, so the whole bunch was shipped off to boarding schools, rarely to be seen again. The heiress proved to be fertile, but so far two girls only, so she's on borrowed time at seventeen. What irony, huh?"

Hermie just stood there, stunned.

Indicating the photo, Aida smiled, "She was known for her sense of humor. That's why we used her picture for our little political statement. She'd have loved it. Probably would have made bumper stickers with it. Come, I'll walk you out."

As they walked through the shelter, Hermie answered the smiles from the women, even though he was aware that these smiles did little to lighten the deep shadows of fear and loss in their beautiful eyes. *This is a roomful of women that need hugging, bad,* he thought. He was trailed by the children, the first little girl he had encountered now held his hand.

Aida heard a deep, thoughtful sigh of sympathy rise up from within this strange man. "Thank you, Detective."

"For what?"

"For more than you will ever know."

She turned to open the steel door, Hermie jumped to help, surprised at its weight. As if by signal, all the children obediently returned to their mothers. Hermie felt a pang when he noticed the little girl give him a wave from her mother's lap. On impulse, Hermie kissed his palm and waved it at her. She imitated him and giggled. Her mother smiled at him as though giving him a gift.

Aida checked the TV monitor that Hermie hadn't noticed was tucked in the wall alongside the stairway door. Its camera swept back and forth the entire length of the warehouse below, showing the place still empty. They descended the stairs, someone pulled shut and locked the many locks on the door behind them.

Later, Hermie helped Aida push the boiler back into its place, hiding the stairway door. She led him through the warehouse, unlocked the inside door, and led him through the store, back to the cash register. Hermie noticed the butcher lady –– Farah –– had tension in her heretofore merry face. "What is it?" he asked, pointedly.

Farah pointed to the windows that viewed the sidewalk outside. Two Middle Eastern men were pacing impatiently on the sidewalk, smoking intensely. Then Farah pointed toward the produce, at a small woman nearly overwhelmed by a deep black chador. When she turned her hardly exposed face to pick up and sniff an apple from the colorful display, tuck it and a couple more in her cart, Hermie saw she was elderly, her ivory skin had deep folds alongside enormous eyes, a delicate nose and lovely lips all recalled what once was a great beauty.

"She's seventy-five years old," Aida said behind him, "And still they wait for her. She's never gone shopping or anywhere alone, in her entire life. You see, it is *her* family that has the money. Not her, of course, but she'd be valuable in a kidnaping."

"My God," Hermie breathed.

"Mine, too," she answered. "There is a message tucked inside one of those lovely apples. We are going to get her to the South of France. We have already secretly moved most of her money there. A cousin's son and his wife and children await her. She will have her own room and a life of leisure, and be close enough to smell the sea. She will be loved, and there will be no more fear, no more longing."

"How? I mean —- you don't have to —-"

"In two weeks Safia will make her usual visit to the services in the women's section of her local mosque. And she will vanish."

"She went 'grocery shopping'?" he twinkled.

Aida laughed. "Well, we will actually be having a sale on nectarines then, her favorite."

Hermie felt his eyes fill again, and could think of nothing more to say. He gave Aida a last look, a look instead of the hearty hug she deserved, and saw that she understood.

He walked out the door, behind the men outside, who didn't notice him. When he reached Roberta down the street, he looked back at them as he opened the car door. Both men were checking their watches, impatiently.

CHAPTER ELEVEN

"Three things in human life are important:
the first is to be kind; the second is to be kind;
and the third is to be kind."

Henry James, American Author

Outrage was nothing new to Herman Grabfelder, considering his profession. But this outrage was over the top. *To those ignorant bastards, if you're a woman, you don't matter. Even Mohammed had a mother, for chrissakes, show some respect!*

He really, *really* needed to calm down, but the outrage was pounding in his ears like a hot surf and his foot was stomped down on the accelerator as he used a rare break in traffic on Normandie to blast twenty miles over the speed limit. Roberta began her usual shimmy to warn him of the consequences of his folly, namely a tossed rod or two, so he lifted his foot, pounded the steering wheel instead, as Roberta slowed down. His cellphone rang and his first impulse was to throw it out of the car, but it was The Job, so: "WHAT?!"

"Oh. Ah'm so sorry, Mista Grabfeldah, I know Ah'm using your private line without y'all's permission, but . . ."

Sharon. At the breaking point I knew she'd reach after all these days without a phone call from that sonuvabitch Gordie. Pulling on calm, he checked his watch. *Good.* "It's okay, Sharon, no problem. Can you do lunch?"

"Raht now?"

"Raht now."

"Yes! Anythin' you say." The relief in her voice was touching.

And he gave her directions to a hidden treasure in Torrance, tucked between some low office buildings, unfortunately located beneath the flight path of the Torrance airport, but a treasure nonetheless. It was the place Gordie had taken him one twilight after finding him passed out cold at his desk from insulin shock, the result of trying to quit drinking cold turkey without medical supervision and failing to eat regularly to help his body adjust to the sudden loss of all that alcohol sugar.

He was sitting at the table under a bower of deep purple Bougainvillea, listening to the man-made but artfully designed stream splashing over rocks and through flowers, emptying into the calm pond beyond, where ducks were discussing events of the day while the scent of garlic, fresh baked bread and subtle spices wafted from the Italian restaurant alongside.

She didn't yet see him as she approached, she was so occupied looking around at the masses of bright flowers following the miniature stream, hearing the music of the water as it danced up and down smooth, artistic rocks. Everywhere, birds chattered and twittered and whistled in the branches of trees that seemed to want to bend closer to the stream, shivering their branches with ease, spinning leaves according to the direction of the breeze: dark green, light green flashing in turn. It was only when she heard ducks quacking that she looked toward the sound and saw Grabfelder quietly looming in the dappled shade of masses of royal purple Bougainvillea.

She had first seen him in the soft lighting of Gordie's apartment, and at that time was only made aware of the overwhelming presence of his large frame and the blue intensity of his eyes. Now, in daylight, she was struck by how good looking that man was, with his unruly hair above a strong face with glowing skin, the smile that tilted the dangerous eyes into an unexpected kindness that instantly flooded her with relief. *I did the right thing to call him and he's lettin' me know by his welcome.*

Hermie stood up to shake her hand. "Hi. Good to see you."

"I nevah knew there was such a place out heah," she breathed. "It's just beautiful."

As if on cue, a small plane accelerated overhead. "If you don't mind the noisy flight path," answered Hermie. "I'm surprised that nasty letters haven't persuaded the FAA to re-consider and re-route."

When they shook hands Hermie felt the loss of weight on her frame was even in her hand, he felt cold bones. "A friend told me about this place some time ago." *I'm not going to be the one to mention his name first. Goddammit.* "You hungry?"

"Well . . . not really."

"I gotta eat, so you do, too. Wait here." He hurried away past the pond, startling ducks when his large shadow fell on the water as he took the path to the Italian restaurant.

Sharon sat at the table wondering why there weren't other people enjoying this arbor, checked her watch and noted that the lunch hour was way over, and she could see people bent over computers and phones in the windows of the offices and medical buildings surrounding this hidden paradise.

She had absolutely no desire to eat. She'd started to basically force-feed herself after the day she'd nearly fainted while driving down Crenshaw Boulevard and realized the headache she sometimes wished was a stroke was actually low blood sugar, near starvation level. But Gordie had not called in over two weeks, had not answered the few messages she'd had the guts and/or humiliation to send, and the pain inside her love had taken over her entire body, the worst in her stomach. She now hoped she wouldn't vomit in front of Grabfelder, in this lovely, lively garden. At the same time she wondered if the pond was deep enough for drowning. For sure it would be a nice setting for that occasion. *Note for the future.*

She heard another small plane pass overhead, again disturbing the peace of quacking ducks, whispering trees and the brisk breeze that sailed through Torrance from the ocean at this time of every day. Suddenly she realized that some of the tenseness in her skin and muscles was easing. She took a deep, grateful breath, hoping it would influence her stomach.

Soon Grabfelder returned, carrying two bulging takeout bags from the restaurant. Her stomach clenched, but she smiled and got up to take one of the bags. When they set the bags on the table, Hermie went to work — he snatched out two large Styrofoam cups of iced tea, opened the lids and handed her one. "Drink this down," he instructed, "it's unique."

Sharon tentatively sipped and tasted a crisp tea flavored with the surprise of a hint of fruit. It cooled and delighted her tense stomach. "Oh, this is verah good," she smiled.

"Told ya."

Then he snapped open the takeout boxes and tantalizing fragrances exploded into the breeze — garlic and olive oil and tomatoes and the sweet scent of braised seafood. She saw gleaming Angel Hair pasta festooned with browned scallops and shrimps, speckled with tomato bits and parsley flakes. He put napkins and sturdy plastic utensils at her hand, sat down to dig into his own plate, this rude activity masking the fact that he was watching her every move.

Determined to at least appear like she was eating, Sharon got a forkfull of shiny pasta and a bit of scallop into her mouth and was instantly a goner. The sunny flavors warmed her constricted throat and relaxed her tense stomach, which gurgled with pleasure and want, and she forked up more.

Thank God, Hermie thought. *She's been starving,* he could see, her inner turmoil a barrier against hunger and sense. He figured ten pounds were gone from her and the loss had turned a slender woman into downright skinny. And he could see purple circles beneath her Bambi eyes, the cocoa-colored cheekbones had gone pale and sharp. "Beautiful day, isn't it?" he said affably, glad she'd called, glad she came, because he could feel the rage leaving his own bones, even though he knew why she'd called and why she came and he hadn't any idea what the hell he could tell her without breaking faith with that shithead Gordie.

Later, their takeout boxes scraped clean, they both relaxed while sipping the last of the fragrant iced tea. He waited for her, mainly to spare himself the task he had to perform with understanding, delicacy and a pack of lies.

Luckily, she started small: "I know ya can't tell me much, 'cuz I'm sure Gordie swore ya to secrecy, but I haven't heard from him in so many . . . I guess I want to just *know* . . . Have I been dumped?"

Startled, he yelled, "No! Hell, no!"

A sad little smile, "Y'all sure?"

"Positive! 'Swear! Look, you're right, I promised that dork I wouldn't say anything to you. He's wrong, *SO* wrong, and he's not being fair, but what can we do? He's an ass, but it's his call. I can only ask you to give him the patience he does not deserve, and when this 'crisis' is over, we'll both give him a good smack upside the head."

"Is he . . . is he sick?"

Goddammit! Woman's intuition! Now what the hell do I say?! Well, she guessed, I didn't tell her, so I'm on solid ground here, alibi-wise, right? "Uh, what makes you ask that?"

"I just love that man. I know it must be somethin' serious for him to go into hidin' like this. If he ain't dumpin' me, he's protectin' me."

"Well . . . he *might* be. He's getting some tests done, but at this point, there's nothing, *nothing* to worry about. 'Swear."

She took a deep breath that shivered at the end. "I thought so. I was so *afraid . . .*"

"Don't borrow trouble. There's nothing to be afraid of yet." *How easy it is to lie to spare someone. But then comes the reckoning. If it all goes wrong, I'll be on both of their Shit Lists for the rest of my worthless life.* "If you can just wait him out. If you want to, that is."

"I *don't* want to. I want to be *with* him, no matter what comes. But he doesn't want me theah. What does that say about how he feels about me?"

"That he's a guy. And it's a biological fact that guys do the exact wrong thing when it's crucial that we do the right thing. I speak from experience. He's making the biggest mistake of his life. And if he loses you because of it, I will be saying 'I told you so' every day for all his rotten years."

She smiled a little, sipped tea, ice cubes bumping styrofoam.

He leaned closer to her, over the table. "Sharon, I won't tell ya what to do. Except to say no guy is worth suffering for. He's not being good to you, so you be good to yourself. If it's going to hurt you this bad to wait him out, then kick him to the curb. You gotta right."

"Bull shit," she said, delicately.

He laughed, bowed his head as if embarrassed. "Yeah, I make a lousy Dr. Phil." Then the blue-fire eyes came up to look at her in all seriousness.

Lordy, those scary eyes! He sees ever'thin', probably knows I been have-in' to take pills to sleep this week. But she couldn't look away from those eyes, she had to let them take over, and she was willing because she knew from the first moment they met that she could trust this man. Trust him absolutely.

"Okay, here's all the truth I can tell: I hope you can hang on, wait him out, because you're good for him. I promise you, I'll be in his face and watching his back. And I also promise I'll bring you in, should the situation warrant it, whether he likes it or not."

She suddenly felt the tension inside her let go, almost all of it except the part that was terror. *He'll take care of us,* she thought, *he really will take care of ever'thin', even if somethin' bad happens.*

He was relieved to see her slender bones relaxing, the rigid shoulder line rounding to nearly normal, her spine lift up. *Thank God I pulled this off!*

"Okay, Mistah Grabfeldah."

"Hermie, please."

"Thank ya kindly, Hermie. I appreciate your time. And the wonderful lunch." She stood up, picked up her purse, held out her hand.

He shot to his feet, held fragile bones that were no longer icy with fear, but warm and relaxed in their gentle grip.

"I'll wait. Long as I can." She turned to go, noticed their lunch trash, reached for it. "Oh, let me help clean up."

"I'll take care of it." He started gathering up napkins and boxes and bags.

"Okay. Thanks again. Hermie."

And she walked away alongside the flowering, bubbling stream, scattering song birds and leaving the faintest scent of lilies in her wake, even amidst the variety of floral competition on the breeze.

When he got back to the oven that was Roberta -- the blasting consequence of some idiots deciding to chop down all the colorful Oleander shade trees that once ringed this parking lot and replacing them with trees that wouldn't grow to offer blossoms or shade in anyone's lifetime -- he left the car door open to air out the heat and grabbed his cellphone, punched in Gordie's number at the Sheriff's station. Gordie didn't even get past "Hello" before Hermie yelled, "We have to talk!"

"You're damn psychic, Herms, I was just about to call you. I got an appointment, at nearby City of Hope. A prostate cancer specialist. Does all sorts of innovative stuff. He's even famous, they said."

"When?"

"Day after tomorrow."

"Want company?"

"Not for this. It's like a go-see, I sent him all my records, it's like starting over with someone new. We'll see what he says."

"I hope that 'we' is literal!"

Gordie chuckled deep and mellow like in the old days, pre-terror, "Yeah, Herms, I'll call you, no matter what. Honest t'God."

"Good."

"Thanks. Oh, why did you call me?

"Damned if I know!" And Hermie hung up.

* * * *

The next morning began with Hank O'Dell calling to report that "Kevin Costner" was still unresponsive, according to the child psychologist that Hermie's friend, Babs Matthews in Social Services had gotten to interview him. The psychologist, George Colewell, said the catatonia gripping "Kevin Costner" was a protective psychosis, and intensive therapy plus Time would be required to break through to what threatened "Kevin's" sanity. He offered his services, gratis, but it would require moving the patient out of Juvenile Hall and into a controlled environment, such as a private clinic that he partially owned. Until such time, he approved of Hank O'Dell's constant presence with "Kevin", a reassurance he was certain that the boy felt.

Hermie called Babs Matthews on her cellphone, since she was still out on the picket line, and once more thanked her for getting some help for "Kevin Costner", even though she was beaucoup pre-occupied. He knew her down to the ground from years of experience, so he knew it tore at her heart to have to abandon "her kids" because of the strike, necessary though it was. "Hang in there, Baby, and you know my number if I can come rescue you and yours."

"Hermie, as always you're a gentleman and a scholar. Or something like that."

"Everyone tells me that. Mostly women. Ain't it odd?"

Babs was laughing when she hung up. It occurred to him that it might be her only laugh of the day.

Then he got an idea: He checked his watch and was relieved the lunch hour was well over, so as not to interfere; then he called the Madame de Lis Restaurant and asked to speak to the proprietor, Charlemagne Junot.

Junot took his call immediately and graciously. "Monsieur Detective Grabfelder, what a pleas-aire. When may we expect you?"

"Don't know. Actually I'm calling to ask an enormous favor. And you can turn me down if it interferes with today's business. I can understand that."

"I am filled with curiosity, mon Ami. What is zis favor?"

And Hermie laid it all out, relieved to hear Junot listening raptly, and obviously writing things down because he asked for an address and approximate number of "guests".

When Hermie insisted on paying for the whole thing, Junot would have none of it. "Non, non, it will be our pleas-aire, Monsieur Detective. We know of their work." Since time was of the essence at the moment, Hermie didn't argue.

Reporters from all the local newspapers, TV channels, radio stations were soon descending on the Social Services picket lines, some too flabbergasted to interview the picketers, who were even more flabbergasted and delighted. And in mere minutes, it was all over the Internet, to pro and con response: Pro because the people at Social Services were the unsung heroes in this city and deserved not only what they were picketing for, but today's surprise gifts; con because of recent sufferings and deaths of children trapped in an outdated system of limited funds and over-burdened personnel missing or ignoring vital clues due to lack of the training that would identify and galvanize a sense of urgency.

All this fuss was caused when large vans marked "Madame de Lis" turned up near the picket lines, doors banged open, and a flock of French waiters emerged with tables, portable shade umbrellas, folding chairs, place settings, napkins and numerous covered and steaming platters of food whose fragrance made the weary picketers nearly swoon. In a nonce Proprietor Charlemagne Junot and his Chef, Henri Chabot, directed with military precision the arranging of tables and shade umbrellas, and then the filling of plates and glasses, and the placing of them in the disbelieving hands of the picketers, accompanied by a flourish of napkins and utensils and guiding them to the nearest chair and shade. Some waiters offered to hoist picket signs while the picketers sat and ate. Other waiters carried frosted pitchers of iced tea and glasses, and poured graciously for those too blissed out with the food to notice. Once the picketers were served, the waiters turned their attention to the cops that had been guarding the picket line with aching feet and sweaty brows. Unsure whether they should or could let their guard down, the cops hesitated, resulting in waiters gently pleading in French, waving cold tea and hot food. Then someone in charge yelled, "What the hell — go for it!" No one bothered to check to see if it was a uniform that had given permission, things being at the point of no return by now.

Picketers were fed and tea'd, cops were fed and tea'd, and all returned to their mission at hand with soothed feet, cooler brows, renewed energy and calmer resolve. And everyone blessed whoever had made sure plenty of port-a-potties were on site.

Days later, Hermie asked for the bill, but none ever came. When he sent a check anyway, a note came that his check had been endorsed over to Social Services as a contribution "for the children." In French.

✳ ✳ ✳ ✳

When Hermie read the coverage of the "French Cuisine Supports Picketers" it was the one bright spot in the news. There was another story on the murders, and he was relieved to read they were still called "stabbings" and not "assassinations", Eleventh Century or otherwise.

And he had seen two more items of interest: Sunidhi "Sunny" Askar, Victim Number Four, had been buried, attended by hundreds: friends from school, from her work and her father's business, her mom's bank, along with dozens of other family friends and relatives and neighbors. The second item announced that today marked the funeral for Miriam Pincus, wife of former Judge George Patton Pincus. Judge Pincus had provided Hermie his file archives about the San Francisco serial killer, crucial to solving Hermie's own serial killer case. He would miss the funeral, but the article noted that a reception was being held this afternoon at the Pincus' home.

He remembered that big, white wedding cake of a house whose major charm was its lot -– on a large, flower-ringed cliff above the sea, whose salty, fresh breath cooled and scented the air, whose waves whispered day and night.

The lawn held several mourners in somber but elegant dress, holding plates of delicate finger foods, either standing shoe-arch-deep in the lush grass, or sitting on a variety of comfortably upholstered lawn chairs.

Some of the guests looked at Hermie curiously, since his blonde hair and vivid blue eyes did not match most anyone else's ethnicity; others recognized him, no doubt from the news, and elbows nudged. He found George Patton Pincus in the immaculate kitchen Hermie had once found dazzling, quietly towering over a circle of guests that were talking to him but not quite reaching him. There were deep shadows on the still handsome, patrician face, and his shoulders curved inward around the burden of his grief.

Hermie stayed at the edge of the small group, waiting his turn. Judge Pincus spotted him and lit up with recognition. He excused himself and went to Hermie with an outstretched hand. Those in his wake wondered who was the stranger, then got a good look at him and some more discrete nudges were made.

"Detective Grabfelder! So good to see you." His handshake was warm, accompanied by a sincere pat on Hermie's shoulder.

"Sorry I'm late, Judge Pincus. I just read the notice in the paper. I'm so sorry for your loss."

"You read the notice and you came right over? How very kind of you."

"How ya holding up?"

"Not too bad. Actually . . . let's go somewhere we can talk. Would you like something to eat? A beverage?"

"No, thanks, I'm fine."

He led Hermie outside, to the opposite side of the property from where the guests were mingling. This part of the yard had a small, antique gazebo near the edge of the cliff, gleaming with white paint, the ocean spraying on the rocks below, so close Hermie could smell the kelp beds and sunshine and new, warmer weather approaching from the southeast. *Damn, summer's coming. Hot heat. I hate that.*

They went inside the gazebo to find encircling benches lining two walls, padded in puffy peacock blue cushions. One of the benches had a computer stand in front of it, stacks of paper on shelves below, the upper surface probably sized to hold a laptop, Hermie figured. *Although how you'd get any work done in this wonderful view is a question.*

Judge Pincus gestured he should sit, and Hermie sat opposite him. "This is my retirement office. I bring the laptop out here, doodle and Google."

Hermie remembered the inside office he once saw, with its antique desk taken from his court office along with his well-used brown leather chair, and the vast built-in file cabinets whose drawer fronts were disguised as plantation shutters. Hermie breathed in the clean air, the sea's loud rhythm slowing down his metabolism to keep time. "I'll say it again, I do envy you your yard."

"Yes. The house was never my taste, really, but the yard . . ." Pincus took a deep, contented breath.

"Again, I'm sorry for your loss. Even more sorry I didn't get to meet her when I came here that day."

"You would have liked her. Everyone liked Miriam. She had a talent for being liked."

Hermie suddenly sensed something, and then *knew*.

"I liked her a great deal," Pincus said, "but . . ." Then he got a little embarrassed. "Sorry."

Hermie helped him out. "How long were you married?"

"Nearly 43 years. We married right after college. Our parents . . ."

"Encouraged it'?" Hedrmie asked, helpfully.

"Nice way to put it. Our fathers were business partners. Jewelry stores. We practically grew up together. So, everyone assumed . . . Well, we were friends, so why not get married?"

"Sometimes that turns out to be a good reason. Marrying your best friend and all.

"Oh, yes, friendship is –– is *essential* in marriage. But . . . We had only one child, a son. Lost him in Iraq."

"Oh, I'm so sorry."

"I mis-spoke. He wasn't *killed* in Iraq. But he came back ruined. He's been on drugs and lost ever since. I didn't even know how to reach him to tell him about his mother."

"Has he ever been arrested?"

"Several times. We stopped bailing him out some time ago, as doctors advised. Stop 'enabling' him, they said. So we did. And that made Evan tell us both to drop dead, before he left and never came back."

"If you want, I could make some calls, find out where he is. I used to be in Narcotics."

"That's kind of you, Detective. But . . . maybe later. Right now I don't think I want to know. A terrible thing for a parent to say, isn't it?"

"No. I've met a lot of parents who felt the same way. Not knowing left room for hope."

"Yes, that's it exactly." The Judge sighed deeply, looking out toward the two blues of the horizon, a pale aqua sky resting upon the deep blue of the ocean. "Detective Grabfelder, I have a confession to make. I'm choking under this burden, but I don't know who to tell it to."

"Your Rabbi?"

"He's a cousin. Clueless. And the worst gossip in the family."

"A close friend?"

"Do you have a close friend you would trust with something terrible?"

"Yeah. But he's a six-foot-six black cop who grew up in Watts –– nothing fazes him. Almost." Hermie thought of how Gordie's eyes looked that night when he said the word "cancer."

"This time . . . My wife's death . . . has been an epiphany for me. I suddenly saw my life with a harsh, inescapable clarity that has shaken me to the bone. I haven't felt a shock like this since . . . Well, I told you about the polio when I was a kid."

"Yes, I remember. Overcoming something like that, you should give yourself some credit for guts."

"Yes . . . yes . . ." His gaze drifted back to that horizon of blues. A flash of white wings sparkled past as a noisy group of seagulls headed north, arguing along the way.

Hermie could feel it, radiating off Judge Pincus in waves of guilt and pain that were almost palpable. *The man's tilting on the edge. For godsakes, did none of his friends or family notice this, offer to help?* The breeze brought whiffs of the Judge's pleasantly clean, soapy cologne, but he also picked up a scent of wine, a heavy, fruity smell that indicated a lot of wine was inside Judge George Patton Pincus. And he knew instinctively that this was unusual, that the Judge was ordinarily not a drinking man, since discipline radiated from that correct posture, those keen eyes. But having gone through the loss of a wife himself, Hermie knew enough to make allowances, but he also knew what could happen if *something* or *someone* didn't intervene _now_, *at the beginning*, before the spiral of guilt began its sharp turn downward, down toward Stingers and days and nights he couldn't remember, and a liver that got nearly unredeemable. "Well, your Honor," he said, gently, "You brought me out here, away from your guests. The view's great, but I think that was beside your point. Whatever it is."

Judge Pincus nearly smiled, looking sheepish. "This is going to sound very odd. But when I saw you in the kitchen, among people I've known most of my life, I suddenly felt that they were the strangers and you were the one I knew best. It was such a . . . *relief* to see you."

"Good. So . . . if I can do anything, like maybe just listen?"

The Judge suddenly brought his haunted eyes up to look directly at him. "I never loved my wife. And I think she knew."

Careful, careful, Hermie thought, seeing the enormous load of guilt that lay exposed and raw. "How do you know?"

"Looking back. Friendship instead of passion. Both of us being so . . . We never had a knock-down, drag-out fight. Because it didn't . . . matter."

"Were you unhappy? Either of you?"

"Not that I could tell. We were . . . polite. Easy going. Friendly."

"That's a helluva lot more than most people have."

"Of course. I know. But I looked at her casket today and was suddenly filled with the conviction that I cheated her. Cheated myself. All those years . . . without . . . *joy* . . . or *even upheaval."* Now it was a pain-filled sigh of profound loss. "What a waste. What a waste of life. Of *her* life."

Suddenly Hermie remembered something: "It must have been in the dentist office."

"What?" The Judge turned to look at him, startled.

"Only place with all those women's magazines in the waiting room. I was early for a change, they were still shut for lunch. So I picked up this female-type magazine, since there wasn't even a Readers' Digest to be had. Damned-est thing, one section full of diets, the next section recipes for desserts. Didn't make a helluva lot of sense to me." To his relief, the Judge's face had softened to a bemused look of interest. "Anyway, there was this one article about women and their houses, some psychologist wrote it, I think. The gist of it was, if I can remember right, it was that you can tell how a woman feels about her body and her life by looking at how she decorated and kept her house. Pride and contentment in her home was pride and contentment in herself, in her life. I got a couple looks around your home when I first came here, Judge. I'd say she thought a lot of herself and her life. Wouldn't you?"

Judge Pincus stared at him as if he was seeing him for the first time, or as if a brand new thought struck him and grew. Suddenly his eyes filled with tears and spilled, a soft moan escaped his throat, he snatched an immaculate hanky from his suit pocket and hid his eyes, sobbing.

Aw, hell, I said the wrong thing! "Aw, hell, Judge, I'm sorry!"

The Judge shook his head, waved his hanky at him as he struggled against his tears. "No, no Detective. You said the exact *right* thing. I had been too ashamed to weep for her. Now I can." He shook with soft sobs for a moment, then caught his breath, breathed deeply and calmly, wiped his eyes, nose. "She did take pride, was content, I can recall that now. Can't count the number of dinner parties and picnics we had, she loved having people over, being entertained in her home. Made *cheerful* in her home. Like her."

Now his smile had no strain, as if something tight and binding had let go inside of him. "Can't thank you enough, Detective Grabfelder."

"'Hermie', please. If I really did help, I'm glad."

"I don't doubt there will be some rough times ahead, but I'll remember what you said and look around our house, perhaps feel . . . a little better. She did take pride. She really did. I will now see that, see her *happy* . . . everywhere." He stood up, now his shoulders were set back where they belonged, and he did a last wipe of his face, tucked the hanky back inside, neatly. "I should get back to it."

They started across the lush lawn. The Judge recited, "There's some truly ghastly punch, or passable iced tea but thick with sugar, you know my people. Or there's coffee, liquor, hot food, cold food, you name it."

Hermie couldn't help echoing the Judge's own words of the first time he was here, when Pincus had recited a delightful luncheon menu of food left by his thoughtful wife, ending with what Hermie now repeated: "And, of course, there's cake."

Pincus turned to him, obviously also remembering, and flung a long, slender arm around Hermie's shoulders as he laughed out loud. "Of course!"

And some guests wondered, to the brink of a mental scold, but most who loved him were relieved that the Judge could now laugh alongside that large, dangerous-looking Detective, on such a day as this. It meant that their grieving friend was coming to terms.

CHAPTER TWELVE

"What we have once enjoyed and deeply loved we can never lose."

Unknown

The next day was spent with paperwork, writing up his notes of the visit to the Farsadi's. He did not mention his experiences at the grocery store shelter, so it would remain unknown by anyone, including the D.A., and thus not end up with Aida having to testify in any court about the escape plans for those remarkable women.

Nell, wearing pink today which made her eye color their original moss green, had called and questioned every weapons and antique store in the area about the type of dagger used in the killings, telling none of them that the reason she was asking was she was trying to track down a murder weapon. Instead, she was a "collector" looking for a special gift for a Middle Eastern friend. Nobody had sold such a dagger recently, four antique shops had one for sale, as did two weapons stores and one store that specialized in cast-off military supplies.

It was mid-day when Hermie had time to call the parents of Sunidhi Askar, first to offer his condolences and then to ask when he could stop by to ask some questions. To his surprise, Mr. Askar invited him to come over "any time", even this afternoon, if it was "agreeable."

The two-story house had a French feeling, with windows rounded on top, silvery wood shingles decoratively used to add a country French touch. However, this being Redondo Beach, the yard was minuscule, but it was tastefully encircled with cement posts supporting wooden railings that were buried under the weight of rambling roses in pink and scarlet. Two tall Royal Palms flanked the house like sentries, set into the scant ten feet that separated this house from the neighbors on either side. The neighbor on the right had erected a tall, wooden fence to mark his property line; the neighbor on the left opted for a hedge of coral Bougainvilleas.

The neighborhood all around was a mix of older craftsman wooden houses that were well cared for and didn't crowd out their lots, side by side with stucco monstrosities too big for their lots, and fake Spanish or Italian touches did little to disguise the fact they looked like they didn't belong here. As always, Hermie noted that these new stuccoes could cost a million-plus dollars for the privilege of hearing your neighbor's toilet flush and their alarm clocks go off in the mornings. It was all so–o L.A., even though it was over twenty miles southwest.

Hermie paused on the front walk for a moment, noticing a hedge of Hydrangea bushes in full bloom of deep blue while gathering some defenses against the grief he was about to intrude upon. To his surprise, the front door opened and both Mr. and Mrs. Askar were there, with welcoming if somewhat strained smiles. Both of their attractive faces were ravaged by grief, hollowed by weight loss, shadowed by sleepless nights and weeping. But they both were beautifully dressed in casual clothes: he wore an ivory linen shirt tucked into dove grey twill slacks; her ivory linen shirt was like a short caftan, with white embroidery circling the collarless neck, the sleeve edges and hem. Underneath, her slacks were pale peach linen. They stood very much together, their shoulders touching.

As Hermie walked past them on entering their house, he caught their scents: soap and flowers and an intriguing touch of musk. The house smelled like oranges, furniture wax and sugar, the latter coming from an array of cookies and small pastries that were arranged on a large ceramic tray set on a low table in the livingroom, alongside an elegant silver coffee service, with cups and small saucers in delicate white porcelain sprinkled with a pattern of violets.

"Please, detective, sit anywhere you will be comfortable. Coffee?" she asked, graciously.

"Oh, Mrs. Askar, you shouldn't have gone to this trouble," Hermie said, sincerely.

"Oh, we didn't. Friends, relatives, neighbors, everyone brings wonderful things to eat."

He instinctively knew they would sit side by side on the couch in back of that low table, so Hermie took the nearest comfortable-looking chair that looked his size, and comfortable it was –– the brocaded upholstery was stuffed with goose down, his heavy bones sank into air and relaxed.

While she poured coffee into cups her husband helpfully held for her because her hands trembled, Hermie looked around so she would not feel he was watching.

The room was a combination of elegance and comfort. The walls were pale celery green, an exact match to the carpeting. The furniture was soft brown pecan wood, with delicate French curves. There were a couple of dainty French chairs, charming if hell to sit in, but most other chairs were the deep, soft kind Hermie relaxed in. The couch was also down-filled, and the brocade of couch and chairs was a delicate pastel floral pattern of aqua, yellow and pink against a light beige background, this print picked up by the drapes alongside the tall windows. On the walls were original paintings of lush landscapes, seascapes and floral still-lifes that picked up the colors of the upholstery.

A side board of pecan wood contained floral inserts carved in a lighter wood. On top of the gleaming surface stood several silver-framed photographs of Sunidhi, from her baby pictures to school photos, to a recent photo of her arm in arm with a group of girlfriends, all of them laughing. The girlfriends wore t-shirts and jeans, while Sunidhi wore a short caftan and slacks and a flowery head scarf. Hermie had a sad thought: *Her headscarf, is it similar to the one taken from her while she lay bleeding on the cement of that parking garage?*

Once the coffee was poured, a steaming cup handed to him after he declined cream and sugar, Hermie once again said the inadequate words: "Mr. and Mrs. Askar, I'm so sorry to intrude at such an awful time. You have my deepest sympathy for your terrible loss. And if at any time, you want me to leave . . ."

"Thank you, Detective Grabfelder," the father answered. "We know you have a job to do, to find out who . . . who did this. We will do *anything* . . . to help." He surreptitiously took his wife's hand and she clung to his.

"I could tell from the time we first met that you were very close to your daughter and she with you. She would speak freely to you, I feel. Did she ever mention that she noticed someone following her, or bothering her in any way?"

"No, never," said the wife. She now appeared to be concentrating intently on Hermie, as if this effort would steady her.

"I know she had a wide circle of friends, co-workers. I can assume some of them were boys or men. Was she dating anyone in particular?"

To his surprise, both of them suddenly looked at each other and smiled as if over a private joke, before grief constrained them again. The husband put his arm around his wife before answering, "Forgive us, Detective, you've stumbled on our family joke. We used to encourage Sunny to date, in groups, of course, double date' or even 'triple date'. And she would 'scold' us, tell us we weren't doing our jobs, it was up to *us* to find her a suitable husband. 'Before I wither on the vine,' she'd tease us. She was more Muslim than her Imam, I used to tease her back. And we'd . . . laugh." His smile was cut off by his eyes filling with tears. He swiped them away with his free hand, regained control. His wife leaned into him for a moment, as if giving him what strength she had left, then she re-focused on Hermie. "She did have friends among the boys in her classes, in high school, in college. Now, young men at work. She brought most of them home for cook-outs in the back yard, along with her girl-friends, that sort of thing. We knew them all, none would do . . . this. No." She shook her had, sadly.

"I'm sure some of these young men were interested in her, for dating."

Recovered, Mr. Askar answered, "Yes. They would ask her out, she'd tell them to ask us for permission. Only a few did. When she was in college. But . . ."

"What?"

They checked with each other with A Look. The husband answered, "Frankly, they were too traditional for our comfort. Look, Sunny was religious, but we didn't want a religious man controlling her life. Like locking her in a marriage where she'd have no freedom to be herself, fulfill her potential as an intelligent, gifted *person,* as well as a wife and mother."

"Would it give offense if I ask how you came to be so . . . enlightened?"

"No offense at all. I come from one of those traditional marriages. My mother was thirteen when they married her off. She had ten kids in fourteen years and wasn't allowed to leave the house without my father, one of his brothers, or one of my brothers going with her. She was barely taught to read or write. I once tried to teach her and my father beat me for it. I was nine years old. I was the youngest. I was the last son to leave for college. My father had already "arranged" marriages for my four sisters, five brothers. Because I was away at school, my mother was left alone with my father for the first time. She drank a bottle of drain cleaner. She died in the hospital after much suffering. I alone got her to that hospital. I alone stayed with her. Even in her agony . . . she was almost happy. Because she was out of that house. That life." He took a deep breath of remembered sorrow. "So, you see, we were hoping to find for our Sunny someone who merely . . . loved her."

Both of them dabbed at spilling eyes, smiling painfully at Hermie as they fought for control. In desperation, the wife offered a delicate plate of small, golden cookies to Hermie. To ease her, he took one, smiled, "Thank you. My weakness, cookies." He bit into a cookie he thought would be too sweet, but instead was pleasantly surprised to taste butter and almonds and just a hint of vanilla. "These are delicious," he said, and was once more struck by how mundane things could momentarily lighten grief as he saw her face reflect how pleased she was that a guest was well served.

"I'd like to interview her co-workers. Starting with her boss, Mr. Amitabh Khan?"

"Yes," he answered. "You met him, he's the leading attorney at the firm. We've been friends since college, USC. We remained friends, our families get together for tennis, barbecues, vacation traveling. When Sunidhi began pre-law, he offered her a job as a paralegal, part-time while she was in school, full-time when she was not. He had plans to hire her as an attorney after she passed the Bar. She was going to specialize in corporate law –– can you imagine?" He ended proudly.

"She kept surprising everyone with her gifts." Hermie said.

"Yes! Yes!" They both said, as if delighted this stranger somehow knew their Treasure.

For a moment, Hermie remembered another young girl with great gifts, who had to hide them from everyone, except one, her valiant mother. "I'll need a list of her friends, co-workers, the people you know who were especially close to her."

He was startled when the wife immediately got up and left the room. He shot a look of apology to the husband, but he gestured calm and said, "It's all right. Wait for her."

She quickly returned to hand him a deep green, leather-bound address book. "This is the address book of Sunidhi. All of her friends, family is in here. Phone numbers, e-mails. She was very organized."

When Hermie took it, he saw the look in her eyes and what it meant. "Don't worry," he said, "I'll have it photo-copied and return the book to you immediately."

Her eyes relaxed. "Thank you, Detective. It's something we don't want to lose. Like so many of Sunny's things."

"Mr. Askar, what do you do for a living?"

"I own a company, Fanciful Designs. We make greeting cards, gift wrap. I employ over two hundred people, writers, designers, cutters, office staff. We are located at the eastern edge of Gardena. My wife is an officer at Thornhill Merchants Bank."

This was a bank Hermie knew, with a guard he also knew: George Toomey, who would know *everything* about Mrs. Askar, just as he had known about Helen Litton. But not Helen Bradford, or Helen Lawrence. Hermie turned his mind away from her memory. "Greeting cards. Then I guess you wouldn't know of anyone, business-wise, that would want to hurt you."

"My God, no. I've been in business for over twenty years. My customers, my suppliers, employees, they are like family."

"No disgruntled employee that gave you some problems?"

"No, no. Most have been with me since I started. I have had people quit, of course, but usually for better jobs or because they moved. I still get Christmas cards from most of them. You are welcome to my personnel files."

"Mrs. Askar?"

"I have been with this bank for six years. I am now in New Accounts. I began as a teller, at another branch. I have had no problems from a customer. Or my co-workers. Most of them knew Sunny, she used to come by and we'd go to lunch very often. My co-workers . . . the president closed the bank for the day, so they could come to Sunny's . . . burial." That last word was a struggle to get out.

Hermie could tell she was near the edge. He helped her out by standing up. They both rose with him. "Would it be all right if I saw her room?"

"Of course. Come with me." She led the way, the husband following behind Hermie. They went down a shady hallway that had walls festooned with beautifully framed photos of happy family occasions with dozens of relatives, more photos of Sunidhi, a couple of studio shots of the daughter backed up by her proud, happy parents.

Hermie noticed the parents hung back when they arrived at an open doorway, letting Hermie go into the room alone. It occurred to him they may not have come into this room since her burial, avoiding the emptiness, the stillness, the finality of her room.

It was a corner room, with two sides of windows bright with the sunshine that filtered in through filmy curtains delicately embroidered with a floral pattern. There was a faint scent in the air: young, saucy. Except for a jumble of law books, folders and papers alongside the computer on top of a wooden desk, with a smaller stack of books on the padded desk chair, the room was neat as a pin. Hermie noticed a bright red cellphone and what he took to be a Palm Pilot was on the desk. A pair of blue fuzzy slippers waited alongside a large bed covered with a pale blue satin bedspread, piled with smaller satin pillows of various colors, and a large stuffed Bugs Bunny, nearly three feet tall. It was undoubtedly Sunidhi who had painted a mustache on Bugs with a black Magic Marker, and tied his long ears up in a fashionable knot.

The pale blue walls had several framed photos of Sunidhi and her friends, boating, on a school campus, and a large group alongside the Eiffel Tower in Paris. There was also a large framed piece of parchment, dazzling with Arabic writing of verses surrounded by painted vines and vivid flowers touched with gold.

"It's a verse from the Koran," the husband called out, helpfully, "That's all I know. I never read the Koran. My father used to quote it all the time, which killed any interest I may have had about it. Sunny didn't hold it against me."

Hermie hesitated at opening a closet door. "It's all right, you may open anything you need to." the wife called out from the doorway.

Sunny's fragrance was stronger in here, teasing. There were fewer clothes than Hermie expected of a young woman with such beauty and busy-ness.

There were several caftans of the style she wore at her death, most in muted jewel colors of dark green, royal blue, and deep garnet red. There was one in sunny yellow. All had the delicate embroidery encircling the neck, sleeve edges and hem, but on each the embroidery was different; sometimes a scroll pattern, others were flowers and vines, still others had colorful stones glittering inside the embroidery. The sunny yellow caftan was the only one that had lace in place of the embroidery. Head scarves in various pastel colors and brilliant floral prints formed rainbows neatly draped on three hangers. A few pairs of jeans and slacks were probably topped by the assortment of long, loose shirts hung alongside. Several pairs of soft boots and leather shoes in a variety of colors were neatly arranged on the closet floor, all with low, comfortable heels. He gently closed the door on Sunny's bright and happy scent.

Hermie was about to leave the room when he saw again the computer, cellphone and Palm Pilot on the desk. "I'll also need to check her computer, phone and that other thing."

"Take them with you?" the father asked.

"I wouldn't know what to do with them if I did."

The father chuckled. "I cannot keep up with this endless technology either, in spite of Sunidhi's best efforts to instruct me." Another precious memory briefly warmed his eyes.

"I have a friend name of Hank O'Dell. He's a techno-whiz who helps me out, makes me look like less of an idiot. May he call you to set up a time he can come here and get her computer, phone and whatever? He'll be looking to see if anyone in cyberspace was bothering her — if she got any e-mails from someone she didn't know but sounded like they knew her, that sort of thing. He'll be checking all her contacts against the copies of her address book. And he'll be returning everything as soon as possible. You needn't worry."

"She never mentioned to us of any such thing, coming onto her Internet," the wife said, both helpful and worried.

"She wouldn't worry you about something like that. But she may have confided in one of her friends."

"Start with Sara Bandar, they've been friends since the third grade. She lives on the next block. They are as close as sisters. She would know everything about Sunny's internet."

Hermie checked his watch. It wasn't quite the dinner hour yet, "Would today be too soon?" he asked.

"Let me call her," she said, "She has been in a very bad way since . . . But, like us, she will want to be of help." She hurried down the hall with a silken grace. Her husband lingered.

A thought, he asked the husband, "Oh — do you know her password?"

"Yes. It's 'Gilbert'."

"'Gilbert'?"

"Sunidhi was a passionate fan of silent films. The actor John Gilbert was her special favorite. In our livingroom, there is a cabinet that is stuffed with her collection of DVD's, VHS's, tapes she made of silent films. Every film John Gilbert made, silent or talkie. Countless biographies and photographs of him and other silent film stars. We had to move the whole lot out there when she ran out of storage space in here."

God, I wish I'd known this brilliant, surprising girl! What a loss, what an endless loss. "I can relate to the silent film addiction. In my case, it's coupled with Korean TV serials. Obviously, I live alone."

The husband chuckled with understanding, then moved off down the hall. At the door of Sunidhi's room, Hermie took a last look back at all the love still living in there, and remembered the room where Amira Farsadi had been completely removed. In the hallway, he took a last look at the exquisite face and the merry eyes of a young woman that was so precious in this house, in these hearts.

* * * *

Sara Bandar had until recently been sweetly plump, with a round face dominated by enormous round eyes with eyelashes thick as hedgerows, and a body once lush and curvaceous. But Hermie got the immediate impression that her appearance shocked those who knew and loved her because her roundness was now gaunt and stark from grief, round cheeks were now sharp with bone, round eyes circled with deep purple shadows, her figure worn down to the essentials of bust and hips, with arms like sticks and a shockingly thin neck. Sara's thick, black hair was held tight in a ponytail that cascaded halfway down her back. She wore jeans and a black t-shirt that was embroidered with a small pink rose. The clothing hung on her now thin frame. And she looked at Hermie as though he was a lifeline, a hope, a chance.

With Hermie's careful questioning while her parents looked on, she painted a picture of Sunidhi Askar that mirrored her parents' vision of her. "Sunny was spooky-smart, generous, funny, and so kind, everyone loved her, even those who were not religious," Sara began. "She had both kinds of friends." Even Sara knew that Sunidhi was leaving it up to her parents to find a husband for her.

"How did you feel about that?" Hermie asked.

"I thought it was entirely Medieval! Sorry. I'm so-o not traditional or particularly religious, my parents not at all, thank God. So to speak. You see, they have friends that escaped from the Taliban, so they *know*. But I went with Sunny to the mosque a lot. After all, that's where most of the men are." She nearly giggled, then looked guilty when from the kitchen her father cleared his throat, pointedly. She blushed. "Sorry. But it seems to me religion is the cause of most of the troubles in the world."

"You may have a point."

"Sunny thought religion was the *hope* of the world. But she never tried to convert anyone. It was hard to believe she was so traditional, because she was so 'live and let live'. That's what made her so . . . special." The hedgerows around her eyes clotted with barely held back tears.

Hermie gently got down to business: "Did she ever mention to you that someone, a man, was intimidating her, scaring her?"

"No, never. The men she knew were our friends. Most of them from school. She made men friends at the office, we went to dinners or movies, concerts with men now and then, always in a group. A couple took Sunny on double dates and such. But nothing clicked. They were either too religious and wanted a traditional marriage with dozens of kids –- sons, *instantly* -- or they were not religious at all and didn't respect her beliefs. A couple just liked to hang out with her because she was fun and gorgeous, made them look good, y'know? But they weren't interested in marriage at this young age."

"Did she correspond with any men friends on the Internet?"

"Of course. Cellphone, text and stuff."

"And she never mentioned someone making her feel un- comfortable or uneasy?"

"No. And she'd tell *me*, that's for sure. We told each other . . . just . . . *everything*." And the tears spilled past the hedgerows and down her face. She yanked a well-used wad of tissues out of her jeans pocket and dabbed and sniffed.

They were sitting on a patio in the backyard of the gracious house that was a couple blocks from the Askar home, cooled by the shade of a large Crepe Myrtle tree shivering fuchsia blooms nearby in the breeze. A chatter of birds was all around from flowery bushes and neighboring trees in the close-by neighbor's yards. Sara's parents had offered him tea and the privacy of their patio. They hovered in the kitchen nearby, keeping watch through the open window over the sink and listening to every word.

Hermie stood up, once more fighting the impulse to hug yet another one, this thin, lost girl. "I am so sorry you had to lose your 'sister' in this terrible way. If you think of anything that would help me in my investigation, just call me, day or night. That goes for Sunidhi's other friends, too. Get the word out for me." Teenage gossip was worth harvesting, but better the gossip was unfettered by questioning at this stage. He handed her a few of his cards, having remembered to replenish his pockets this morning. "Now, you sit there, rest. I'll see my way out." Hermie went into the kitchen to be greeted by another set of purple-ringed, desolate eyes. Mrs. Bandar had the same roundness her daughter once had, her husband looked twice her height and was rail thin. Their clothes and house had the same quiet elegance as the Askar's, with the addition of a collection of precious small statues and objects from antiquity, since Mr. Bandar was a Professor of Archeology. Hermie was tempted to ask him about Eleventh Century Assassins and their daggers, but did not know him well enough to trust with this must-stay-secret information.

"Mrs. Bandar, Mr. Bandar, thank you for letting me speak to your daughter."

"Was she able to help?" he asked.

"She confirmed most of the information I got from the Askars. And I'm hoping she'll get the word out to Sunny's and her friends that they should call me if they noticed anything suspicious."

The father had to ask, feared to ask, and clearly wished his wife was not present for this, but: "Is . . . is our Sara in danger? Because she was so close to Sunidhi?" Both he and his wife suddenly showed their secret terror.

"Oh, no, I don't think so at all. No, these were all unconnected killings. None of the victims knew each other, not in the slightest way." *Except they were all Muslims, except the first one.* Hermie wasn't about to bring *that* up.

"Who would do such a thing? I hope he rots in the deepest hell!" Mrs. Bandar was immediately embarrassed by her outburst. "So sorry." Her husband patted her shoulder, sympathetically.

"Mrs. Bandar, I agree with you. And when I find this sonuva- -- uh, this *guy*, the deepest hell is where I'll put him."

At the front door, Mr. Bandar's handshake was firm and friendly. "If there is anything we can do to help, you have only to ask."

"Keep *listening* –- to Sara, to her friends, to neighborhood gossip. Has a stranger turned up? Kinda short guy, someone very religious, conservative, that sort of thing. And call me anytime, nothing is trivial, understand? Thank you, Sir. Thank you both."

Later, Hermie sat in Roberta and leafed through Sunhidi's address book, looking at names, addresses, phone numbers, e-mail addresses, written in purple ink, in a graceful handwriting in English, noting there were just as many male names as females. He put it aside, took a look around the neighborhood of nice, family homes. *Two young Muslim women, bright, beautiful, from such ordinary backgrounds, what the hell did he see in them? What was his trigger? How the hell did they relate to a dangerous cyber genius who didn't exist and an undercover FBI agent-slash-call girl who loved him? I'm gonna blow some circuits over this damn --!*

His stomach sounded dinnertime and he knew better than to ignore it. He knew everyone would be gone by the time he got back to the stationette, so he stopped at the New China Buffet and got a takeout of crab and cheese casserole, broccoli, shrimp and vegetables, hot and sour soup, and a large container of steaming Jasmine tea. He took it all back to the office, let himself in, locked the door behind him, ate, drank, and photo-copied Sunidhi's address book.

On his way home, he stopped by the Askar house again, in order to place the precious book back in Mrs. Askar's grateful hands. Because he knew she'd be waiting.

When he got home, he called Hank O'Dell and inquired about "Kevin Costner", didn't know if he was glad or not that there was no news there. Then, in exchange for large money out of his own pocket, not wanting to wait for the LAPD to find an officer who had lots of time and was the expert computer geek he needed, he asked O'Dell to take some time in order to phone first then go to the Askar house and pick up their daughter's computer, cellphone and Palm Pilot.

He gave him some background on the tragedy, and knew that it was in the nature of Hank O'Dell to be sympathetic and kind when he came to call at the house with the empty room that was still so filled with love.

CHAPTER THIRTEEN

*"What makes humans so dangerous are their emotions;
it allows them to kill for what anyone else believes is no
reason, but what they believe is the only reason."*

Lt. Joe Kenda, *"Homicide Hunter", I.D. Network*

The Torrance Station got the 911 call because the body was found in the parking lot near a now just about invisible department store in the newly massive mess of the Del Amo Mall, which was less than a mile from the Torrance Station. The mall was undergoing an "exciting re-design", which meant EMT firetrucks, paramedics and LAPD forensics techs spent infuriating minutes trying to find an entrance to the right parking lot, all former landmarks —- and gracious shade trees -- now gone. This frustration they had in common with shoppers trying to fathom this "exciting redesign", the entrances to their once-favorite shops now known only to God and that "exciting architect".

Several sides of the mall were still under re-construction, the improved economy having placed stars in the eyes of developers who saw the complicated expansion of the already gi-normous mall as a good thang, did no-one mention traffic? Where the economic toilet had claimed some larger stores, several other smaller shops had also done their swan songs, so this particular end of the mall had the crumbled look of either being completely demolished or completely re-designed (at this point and no doubt future points, no one was sure which), but it was where a forklift driver grandly named Alfonso DeLeon was getting an early start when he puked his breakfast of elephant ear pastry and coffee when he came across the carnage on this, his job site. Torrance police took one look at the wound and called Hermie, and everybody censured themselves, calling it a "stabbing" because word and threats had gone down the ranks in all the South Bay stations from exceedingly high above.

Hermie got the call while he was on his way back to his stationette after having gone to Amira Farsadi's school and interviewed the Principal and a couple of her teachers. All freely offered sometimes tearful testimony of how dear that girl was, how eerily intelligent, and of how her fellow classmates had "taken her in" with affection and protectiveness once they'd gotten wind of her situation at home. Not that Amira talked about it much, but everyone got clued in when The Beast and Son occasionally turned up to make sure she headed home and nowhere else after classes. None had met Amira's mother, but apparently Amira had told *All* about her because nearly everyone asked Hermie, with sincerity, "How's her Mom doing? Is she all right?" Absolutely no-one inquired about the feelings of the Beast and Son.

Now Hermie crouched down alongside another wreckage that was once a lovely young woman. She was laying next to a car which turned out to be hers, a cream-colored Volkswagen convertible that still had dealer plates on it, and now blood splattered the creamy flanks of the closed driver's side door. *Her car keys were fallen directly alongside the door, she didn't even get the chance to press the door-unlocking button or the alarm button on her keys, Hermie realized.* He looked some more, studied the scene. *He'd come up from behind this time, his dagger nearly decapitating her and severing the top of her spine. She had fallen forward onto the car, slid down and landed on her side, then half rolled onto her back. Did she get a look at the monster before she died? Christ, I hope not. I hope Pierre will tell me she died instantly, with the briefest fear or pain.*

The smell of blood nearly obliterated a somewhat unpleasant perfume lingering within her clothes -- oranges and vanilla and a dash of something that smelled like black pepper. She was tall and shapely, wearing a charcoal grey suit-jacket and modest-length skirt, in a fine fabric that looked to Hermie like wool gabardine, which he recognized because his father's one good suit was in that same fabric. In those days, in Bay City, Michigan, everybody's "Sunday Suit" was made of wool gabardine. Beneath the wash of blood and sliced fabrics, her blouse was ivory silk, with a froth of lace cascading from the collar, more lace peeked out from her jacket sleeves, covering a gold bracelet on one wrist, a gold watch on the other. A pale green jade ring was on her right hand. A slim gold chain around her neck had been sliced in two, its pale green jade pendant -- a small bouquet of flowers -- had fallen into the pool of blood beneath her savaged neck. Her face had round, cheerful cheeks, slightly slanted eyes above a straight nose. The eyes were half open, and Hermie got a glimpse of their dark brown. She wore the nearly brown lipstick that was now in fashion and which Hermie hated. Once again, Hermie could tell by the way her hair was slightly matted that she had worn a headscarf, but it was missing.

Andy Cho Hui and his tech team were unfurling body sheet and bag at a respectful distance. Andy quietly came closer, within Hermie's peripheral vision, just in case. He carried the evidence bag that held the Vic's purse.

"What time?" Hermie asked, aware of Andy hovering.

"Between ten and midnight, thereabouts. More later. Nine-one-one came in at eight-ish A.M. Blood had a lot of time to dry." He held up the evidence bag, indicating a driver's license showing. "She was Shirin Batawi, twenty-six, lived over on Benson in Torrance. Brand new license, I checked — she'd just gotten it months ago, because she'd just moved here and into that apartment. She also had a work I.D. — she worked in one of those department stores in the mall." Andy held up that I.D., helpfully.

Hermie recognized the department store I.D. because he knew someone who worked there. Hetty McDougald had given him the key to the fragrance left behind on the sixth victim of the South Bay Serial Killer: The scent of almonds, made beautiful. Hetty knew all about fragrances and what type wore what. "Well, I have a place to start. I know someone who works there."

Andy, who had expected to see just about everything on the horror scale when he signed up for this job, was pretty much dangling on his tether, if not quite at its end. So he just had to ask: "Hermie, what the fuck is going on here?"

"I ask myself that every hour of every day." He loomed up past protesting knees, flexed them and his back. The look on Andy's face moved him to give a sympathetic pat on his shoulder as he passed by. "Hug your Grandma today, it might help."

"Always does."

Last night's fog was nearly blown away by rush hour traffic slogging past on nearby Hawthorne Boulevard. A clog of cars were attempting to get past the yellow police tape in the mall parking lot, as mall workers, shoppers, construction workers, and coffee seekers arrived and found their routine route disrupted, thus their day starting with more aggravation than usual. All they could see was a jumble of police cars, ambulance, unmarked police vehicles and cloth screens hiding something on the parking lot pavement.

Adding to the aggravation quotient, news media arrived. SUV's with TV station logos began barging in, honking, as if expecting the civilian cars to get out of their way. *NOT!* Obscene hand gestures and pithy comments flew about, just as a TV news helicopter did a dip overhead, blowing dust into everyone's eyes and hair. Word had gotten out among the media that the Torrance Station had called out LAPD Homicide Detective Herman Grabfelder, which should be big news except that, "You know how he is!", so there would be no cooperation from Grabfelder whatsoever. And the rank and file knew from past experience with his wrath that they dare not give the media any quarter or tidbits they happened to learn from watching him and his nose interact with the body. Thus, ever resourceful, various reporters were already spouting off news reports into minicams, consisting of rumors, conjectures, creative license, and outright lies they hoped would prove to be true by broadcast time. Or eventually. Just enough colorful crap to give legal cover if, down the road, her family decided to sue for invasion of privacy and/or mental anguish. Grabfelder was grateful to hear "stabbing" here and there in their commentary. *Nobody knows what kinda stabbing yet, thanks be to ALL the gods.*

The breeze sneaked under the screens and ruffled her hair. *Did the slime yank her headscarf off before or after he killed her? Did he wash all those headscarves clean or did he like to save the blood on them? How did he know that all these women would be momentarily alone, long enough for him to strike? Most days this area of the mall was shut down completely by construction, other areas were shut down off and on, depending on the complications of safety issues. Did he know that? Did he stalk this girl, too? What the Sam Hill has he got against Muslim girls?! If he's a racist pig, wouldn't his beef be against Muslim men? Or is he too slight, too short to come up against a Muslim man? Small feet, remember the footprints around Lila Miller? But why and how did he kill a big, strong Muslim man on that first round? Hashemi came out of the car to face him. Why? Lila wasn't Muslim, obviously. Why kill her, then kill a Muslim man, and then kill only Muslim girls after that? Doesn't make sense. What is the goddamned key?! Different victim, same questions, no answers.*

He looked around and noted her car was nosed into a parking space that was in a corner formed by low cement planters holding tall, Juniper pines which had been allowed to die because they were soon to be yanked out like the rest of the once-shady landscaping. Their twisting branches always spooked Hermie because they looked like agony. At the foot of the pines, dried-up red and pink petunias curled up within a scatter of paper litter, crushed soda cans and cigarette butts.

Those pines would cast shadows at night, hiding the sonuvabitch. Is that why he picked this spot? But why this girl? Her headscarf . . . she was picked because she was Muslim. Who she was otherwise didn't mean a rat's ass to this sonuvabitch. But Lila was obviously not a Muslim. Was Hashemi? I assume. How would the killer know that, since Hashemi didn't exist. I really, REALLY need a Stinger! His large fingers scraped in and out of his hair, mixing up the blonde and the scant silver strands.

So when Hetty McDougald first glimpsed him a couple hours later, to her he looked like he'd brought a whirlwind with him that had stirred up his wonderful hair and now was coming to stir up her life once again. *Thank ya Jeezus!*

Coming to work earlier, Hetty McDougald had gotten off on the wrong floor again. When she took the elevator up from the employee section of the parking garage each morning, at least twice a month she got off at the floor that held Men's Clothing and Accessories, which had been her happy post for twenty-and-then-some years. Happy, because Hetty thoroughly enjoyed looking after men, as only a middle-aged — make that "seasoned" — unmarried lady can.

Hetty thought men were *fascinating* because they were so different. She studied them with the open mind that only an optimist has. It didn't really matter to her if men were bright or successful, what mattered to her was what she instinctively knew: All men needed help because all men had an insecurity they were masters at covering up. Therefore, when they didn't have a clue about picking the right clothes that actually flattered their shapes, whatever they were, or choosing the right colors that not only enhanced their skin tone but made a personal statement as well, Hetty stepped right in with a knack that charmed, persuaded, educated, and brought straight men an ease and some laughter, and caused gay men to give her heartfelt hugs and kisses and sometimes send her flowers. More than a few called her "Mom". As a result, Hetty McDougald — woe to anyone who ever called her "Henrietta", the name her parents cursed her with and which she had abandoned by the second grade — happily sold the hell out of Men's Clothing and Accessories for all those years, the top seller in not only that department but the whole damn store; surpassed only by some guy in Major Appliances, but how can they compare those big ticket items with the gross totals cranked out by Hetty on things like belts and socks, as well as suits, shirts, ties, coats, fragrances, and even scarves. Selling scarves to men — in California weather? — nobody but Hetty McDougald managed to do that. By the gross.

So, naturally, after racking up all those sales for all those years, her reward was to be kicked out, just when retirement loomed. They lied their asses off, Management did, to convince Hetty that she was being "kicked upstairs, with a raise", where her "awesome sales talent" was "desperately needed" . . . in Small Appliances and Bedding. Which meant Hetty McDougald, at aged never-mind was schlepping her tired feet and varicose veins back and forth between two dismal departments, in Boring Small Appliances and Double-boring Bedding, where men never came.

Worse still, she knew this being "kicked upstairs" — with a raise, yet — was a crock of cow poop, specifically designed to prevent her from having grounds to sue their dicks off for discrimination: She was kicked out of Men's Clothing and Accessories because she was too old. She didn't fit in with the new hires there, none of whom neared thirty years old; all of them tall, shapely new hires for the newly shaped-up department, heavy on the chrome and booming with hip-hop music. And most of those new hires were spending their salaries on surgical enhancement of their boobs and lips. And in one case, Hetty knew for a damn true fact, surgical enhancement of the buttocks, the Kardashians continuing their destruction of civilization as we know it.

A couple of the winsomes were going to school, and using their salary in the endless chipping away at student loans, and glad that the job was mindless, of limited hours, and had the bonus of meeting all kinds of men. Most of the men were married, of course, but in this day and age that wasn't an iss-yue. And as for most of the rest being gay, well who was a better date than a sophisticated, moneyed gay man? Most of them had straight friends and a matchmaker's heart.

Hetty had never been afraid of anything before. Orphaned as teenagers when both parents, smokers, died of lung cancer within months of each other, Hetty and her sister Nancy went to work, went to school and lived on their own instead of being sent to relatives. Nancy managed to land herself a doctor –- a proctologist, big deal. And "Eeew!".

But Hetty was simply too busy to notice marriage was passing her by, what with her store hours and her many hobbies, which included rollerblading or bicycling or busing from Torrance to Malibu or Santa Monica on weekends, depending on where the best foreign films or street festivals were to be enjoyed; and her weekly poker game at the Redondo Beach VFW –- being the daughter of a veteran, she had an In and regularly cleaned those Vet's clocks; and the Japanese garden club that landscaped empty lots that were too small to put a condo building or a Starbucks on. They planted trees, flowers, vegetables to both entertain, feed and educate the neglected kids in the surrounding rundown neighborhoods. The fact that Hetty wasn't Japanese never crossed anyone's mind, such was Hetty's "people person" personality. That and the fact that when she tried to learn and pronounce Japanese, her Asian co-volunteers fell down laughing.

If asked, which she regularly was by her smug sister, Hetty would say she had nothing against marriage. And, no, she wasn't gay. No, she wasn't still a virgin ("I'm not a nun, Nancy, goddammit!"). She was simply too busy to think about it. Much.

But when they shoved her "upstairs", Hetty had time to think about lots of things because she didn't have enough money saved to tell them to take Small Appliances and Bedding and shove them both up their nethers. Her rent at the nice one bedroom apartment in east Torrance had been raised again, she was beginning to wonder about the smog and fumes she was sucking up by rollerblading or bicycling everywhere, so she was trying to figure out how to afford a car, its gas and insurance, just when her employer lowered the damn boom. After taxes, the raise was a little over piddling, like always, so "shoving them" was out of the question, finances-wise. And an early retirement would shrink her future Social Security checks. So she would have to bite the bullet while looking for another job on the sly.

The problem was, the economic toilet flushed retail down right and left, stores were merging, closing, or laying off, or switching full-time to part-time in order to avoid paying health insurance, so nobody was hiring. And the few trendy boutique stores in places like Beverly Hills, or Malibu, or anywhere in Orange County where the rich never lost anything no matter what tanked the economy, did not hire women who had lived through those rollicking Jimmy Carter years. Beverly Hills and the like hired girls who "had some college" at all the best schools, had new cars, designer clothes and expensive watches, and did not need a job at all, but wanted "something to do" while making better plans.

The shock of Time passing was doubled when she last voted for a president and realized it was the first one not only who was black, super-smart and elegant, but wa-ay younger than she was.

So, Hetty McDougald, who had never been afraid of anything, *ever*, now felt that flutter of fear that comes when one looks to the future and doesn't see much beyond a Social Security check that would at least buy her Supplemental Medical Insurance, thank gawd and the AARP. Unless the Republicans made good on their obsession to take that away from her, too. Vouchers smouchers!

It was with this burden of a mind full of worries that Hetty dusted the appliances in Small Appliances, with a feather duster that had seen better days from better birds, and she watched the dust puff up, drift and settle back down on almost the same surfaces, and she didn't give a rat's patoot. She'd be fluffing up the bedding in Bedding next. It was her morning ritual before the mall and store opened, and since she came into the store directly from the employee parking area where she roped her bicycle to a cement pillar with a chain thick and strong enough to discourage a Man of Steel or a teenaged Meth addict in a hurry, she hadn't noticed anything unusual, so was genuinely shocked when Fran Nielsen came onto the floor, all wide-eyed and breathless because she had nearly *run* her 200 pounds to tell Hetty they'd found a body in the outside parking lot and she'd heard it was a mall employee. Little did Fran or even Hetty know that when the mall opened at ten, Hetty would hear most of the grisly details, straight from the Homicide Detective in charge.

Now, Hetty was bent over, trying to ignore her aching back and the slide down her nose of her cherry red half-frames as she checked a pallet filled with boxes of electric can openers (*All in black. Who does that?!*), when she heard heavy steps at the same time she saw shoes approach. A *man's* shoes — a BIG man's shoes -- large oxblood loafers in need of a shine. *He doesn't work here.*

She shoved up her glasses as she shot upright, and saw Detective Herman Grabefelder grinning at her with his blazing eyes tilted in that sly fox smile, unaware of the tousled results made by the wind in his hair. And his first words reminded her of why she simply adored this blue-eyed boulder: "What the hell ya doin' up here?"

Because he *knew* — he *knew* she didn't belong "up here" in the isolation and boredom of Small Appliances and Bedding. He also knew she had not gone willingly because he had gone to Men's Clothing and Accessories to find her and he'd seen why she was no longer there. And he knew how she was faring after that insult. And once again Hetty felt the thrill and the comfort of wanting to tell this man *ev-v-er-r-y-thing* because this hulking life force could figure it all out for her.

But she didn't want to waste the man's time with her troubles because she wanted to hear everything that was on *his* mind, because he was the most fascinating man she'd ever met, and she'd certainly met more than a few.

Instead of flinging her arms around him in sheer relief, she restrained herself down to a happy gush and handshake: "Detective Grabfelder! How are *you*?" Which was inane, since from the looks of him he was double-damn fine.

She noticed the weight loss first, then she saw the outline of his body within the trimmer suit had gone from soft to rock-hard with muscles. His skin still had that rosy-gold glow, but now it was good health in addition to the sun seeking him out. But the real change was in his eyes. Their previous meetings had involved testing fragrances to track down the brand of scent left behind by a serial killer — *"A serial killer, honest t'god, Nancy! —* that scent of almonds made beautiful. This necessitated Hetty taking him over to Fragrances and Cosmetics, which was right across the aisle from her then post, and the assault of smells from the thousands of perfumes, makeups and powders had overwhelmed what she would later read was his infamous and eerie sense of smell, and burned up his worn eyes, sending them streaming tears into the tired shadows below. But now those shadows were gone, the eyes bright and clear, blue doubly dangerous except when he was smiling, like now.

"What are you doing *here*?" She asked and hoped.

"I've got another case."

"Oh, my God, you mean — someone just ran in to say there was a body found in the parking lot."

"Yeah, that's mine. A bloody mess. Pardon my French. And do not get me started on that 're-designed' parking lot out there! So, naturally, I need your help. How ya been?"

It was that sincere smile, a real dazzler he sent directly into her eyes, that was why she felt the roof lift off the building and full sunshine fell all over

Small Appliances and Bedding. And she took a deep, happy breath of what she was certain was the same fresh air that had mussed up his hair and answered, "I'm just fine," she lied. "It's so great to see you," the happy truth. "How can I help you this time?" *Oh, for godsakes give me something interesting to do!*

She was only dimly aware of leading him across the aisle to Home Furnishings and picking a large, soft couch that she knew would suit his great and sheltering bones, and they sat together and Hetty felt the thrill of being the object of not-so-surreptitious attention by several male and even more female employees as they found excuses to walk not-too-close-by to check out Hetty and the dangerous-looking man she was sharing a couch and intense conversation with. A few customers also passed by, but most merely smiled politely because the two of them looked so companion-able. One lady even checked the price tag on the couch, nodded, smiled at them, then moved on.

"Shirin?! Oh, no!" Hetty exclaimed, horrified, a rush of tears made her grab for the tissues she always kept inside her sleeve. A dab and a wipe, "What happened?"

"As far as I can tell right now, she was attacked when she reached her car, after ten PM last night."

"Is she –?"

"I'm sorry. Yeah, she's dead. She's the fifth victim in this case I'm on."

"Five? Here we go again," she said, and then thought that might sound critical. "Oh, sorry."

"Hell, don't be sorry. I've been saying that from the first scene. But this guy . . . this guy . . ." He shook his head with what Hetty knew was rage held in, just beneath his helplessness, and alongside his grief over the slaughter of strangers, especially the young ones.

"I'm so sorry," she said and patted his hand. Hetty had often patted men's hands reassuringly in Men's Clothing and Accessories, whenever their wistfulness touched her. And behind the intimidating aspect of this powerful man was a secret, wistful soul. She just knew it. Treasured it.

"We found her employee I.D. and I realized she worked in this store, so I knew you'd know her and could give me good background info."

He knew she knew! "I did know her, almost very well."

"'Almost'?"

"She started work here, oh, let me think . . . about six months ago, I guess. She was hired in the Executive Department, in Finance. That meant she was checking the books, the word 'audit' was heard here and there. But, of course, she didn't talk out of school at all."

"You didn't like her perfume, did you?"

"How'd you know?! Oranges and pepper? Just *ghastly*. Didn't suit her at all, as she was delicate, shy, a real lady. I often thought of how to ease into *that* advice." She sighed with memory. "But when she came, there was some trouble."

"What trouble?"

"Oh, it made me so mad. Just because she was a Muslim –- the headscarf, see? The snide remarks were like these people were back in high school. Like that poor girl had anything remotely to do with Paris or Syria or goddamn Isis, for godsakes. She was born here, so were her folks. 'Grow up', I said more than once to more than one ass–- uh, idiot."

"Did it help?"

"Not really. But what I meant about 'almost' knowing her, well, when the comments started, I made it a point to befriend her. Just a little, it turned out, because she was very shy and reserved, plus she was in Management and I sure wasn't. I understood her being stand-offish. But I spoke to her whenever I could, invited her to lunch even when I knew she had to say 'no'. I walked her to her car a couple times, because the employee parking area was where the yahoos gave her the hardest time. It wasn't on the work premises, you see, so they could do whatever their tiny little minds wanted. But after we found eggs splattered all over her car one night, she stopped parking there. Started parking in what's left of the public lot along Hawthorne Boulevard. Employees aren't supposed to take up public spaces, but I told her if Management gave her any flack, I'd be her witness as to why she was refusing to park in the employee spaces, and I'd name names. I told her she was a harassment and intimidation lawsuit waiting to happen, so they wouldn't dare stop her from parking where it was safer. Last week she told me she got a new car, in fact. Probably so they wouldn't recognize it as hers, even though she was parked elsewhere."

"She was found parked not far from that humongous book store. Was that her usual spot?"

"I doubt it. She used to park in a different place every day. Just in case."

Then how the hell did he find her?! His thoughts yelled.

"What?" She asked, instinctively feeling the rage in his thoughts.

"I can't figure out how or why these girls were targeted by the same guy who first murdered two people who lived in entirely different worlds."

"Hmmmm. Maybe, to him, they were all in the *same* world. Whatever, wherever that is. Find out why that world pisses him off, and you got him."

His grin was warm, "I gotta get you a badge."

She laughed, delighted, young.

"We got her home address. Was she married or living with family?"

"No. She was living alone, unusual for an unmarried Muslim woman, I hear. She mentioned her family lived in . . . oh, where was it? Can't remember, except it was in another state. East. She went to UCLA and just decided to stay

--- loved the weather here. Yes, she came from someplace with lousy winters. Was it Minnesota? Ohio? I'll think of it. Maybe."

"You got lights dimming in the attic, too?"

"I bought stock in gingko biloba."

They both chuckled. Then his huge frame rose up. "Well, I guess I'll let you get back to work, and I'll get on with mine. If you hear anything useful about Shirin Batawi give me a call. Start with a list of the yahoos that gave her a hard time. You still have my phone number?"

"Yes." In her wallet, in the very first plastic photo sleeve, ahead of the photos of Mrs. Proctologist and her two spotty kids.

"See ya when I see ya." As he turned to go, it was as if the thought tapped him so hard on the shoulder it stopped him in his tracks. He turned back. "Don't mind me asking, Ms. McDougald, but are you married?"

"Never had the pleasure. So to speak. Not that I didn't get the breezes."

Her standard line made him laugh out loud. "Reason I'm asking is that I have a friend who'd think you're a treasure. As well as a sketch. George Patton Pincus. How's that for a name? I'll put him in touch." And he gave her a little salute, and turned and walked away. The floor dipped a little at his passing.

A 'treasure' and a 'sketch'? 'George Patton Pincus'? Sheesh! Name like that, he just has to have a sense of humor. And imagination got her through the day with hardly any boredom at all.

*　*　*　*

The flutter in his gut and the growing heat within his skin warned him that his blood sugar was plummeting. It had been too long since his post-sweat granola break at Bud's body Works. Of course, the mall's "re-design" had moved the food court wa-ay inside the bowels of the mall, so he was on the brink of breaking into the sweat and shakes of full-blown hypoglycemia just as he finally arrived at the mall's "newly-designed" vaster-than-VAST food court, having walked miles through loudly irritating music and loudly strolling shoppers. Although he had a choice of Italian, fried everything, Greek treats, chicken in several ethnic ways, spicy and not-so Korean bowls, he picked Chinese because he was able to be second in line.

Minutes later, he was overwhelming a small, round table and its accompanying child-sized (to him) chair, halfway through soy noodles sprinkled with lots of cashews and faint brown sauce, crispy chicken morsels on a stick, some gently cooked broccoli and carrots, lots of iced green tea, and feeling his skin begin to cool as his blood sugar slowly began to rise. He sat back and relaxed, glad to be rid of that helpless, weak feeling that plagued him whenever he forgot to eat on time. Bud the Cheerful Fuhrer at Bud's Body

Works had once told him to carry a pack of almonds as "emergency food", and now he was thinking it wasn't such an annoying idea.

He was just about to open the fortune cookie when a vaguely familiar male voice, flattened with the Midwestern twang of his youth broke in, "Detective Grabfelder! Surprised to see ya here. How are ya?"

It was still there, deep in their eyes, the profound grief of their loss, but both of their faces were somewhat eased now. Gone was the harshness of bone revealed because of weeks of not eating, not sleeping, and not being able to stop the tears. Frank and Millie Harrison were the parents of one of the victims of the South Bay Serial Killer. Brad Harrison was their only child, was gay, the handsome and talented, teasing light of their lives, whose loss left an incalculable void; but whose loss also caused his father to remember something that not only led Hermie to the motive for the killings, but to the protection of the future victims the killer had in mind.

Hermie shot to his feet, delighted, shaking hands. "Mrs. Harrison, Mr. Harrison, so good to see you!"

"So . . . how are ya, then?" The echoes of an upbringing in Winona, Minnesota, were vivid in his Midwestern twang. But his voice no longer drifted away, his gray eyes no longer drifted away, toward the void. He was looking Hermie up and down with admiration and humor, "See ya dropped a few. Looks right good on ya."

"It sure does," her voice was a little less Midwest, having been raised in Indiana, which her husband once joked was "On the cusp."

"Thanks. Did it the hard way -- sweatin' and swearin'."

They both chuckled, and Hermie noticed they stood very close to each other, shoulders nearly touching, holding hands. Hermie suddenly and fervently hoped they hadn't yet heard of the murder in the parking lot, dreading the memory of horror it would call up for them.

"Ya been shopping, Detective?" she asked.

"Call me 'Hermie', please. Yeah. Also visiting a friend in a department store. How've you been?" He made a move to pull up another chair. "Have a seat."

'Naw, you go on with your lunch, then. We were takin' the long way to Sears. Our icebox went kaput, lookin' for a replacement," he said. "First stop is always Sears, ya know."

"Ya got that right," Hermie grinned with memories of a small town of farms in Michigan, depending on Sears for *everything*. Their yearly catalog growing dog-eared from use, packed as it was with everything from appliances to furniture to kids' toys to car parts to farm equipment to men's and women's clothing to baby supplies. And back then, a refrigerator was called an "icebox". And it literally was one, back in his Grandma's and Grandpa's day. He knew that because as a kid he had sneaked a peek inside, "just lookin' for wieners" and saw that big block of ice. "What ya hadda buy in summer, you could go out and cut some out of the creek in-a winter, ain't that right, yeah-huh?" Grandma's teasing voice.

"Actually, it's lucky we're comin' across ya. We were thinkin' of calling' . . ." She looked at her husband and they exhchanged That Look that long-time marrieds use to instantly communicate, those that were still in love that is.

"Couldn't hurt, Hon, cuz he would know." He answered her eyes.

She turned to Hermie with a mixture of shyness and hope. "We were signin' up to be foster parents, ya know, but because of our age, well, we're thinkin' we been shoved down the list."

"Oh, I doubt that," Hermie answered. "There's always a chronic shortage of caring fosters. Older people usually have more experience with kids. Besides, you're not that old."

He saw Frank Harrison squeeze his wife's hand with another silent communication before he spoke, "Ya think how we . . . how we lost . . . lost our boy would count against us? Them thinkin' we're . . . damaged goods 'n all?"

Hermie was careful as he tread on this pain-filled ground. "The kids who end up in the foster system, they're damaged, too, some of 'em beyond repair unless someone who understands steps up and hangs in there for them. It takes more patience than Job, nerves of steel. And the worst is you gotta let 'em go when the time comes."

Again, they exchanged looks that spoke volumes. "That's what we thought," she said. "We know we're 'substituting'. What we don't know is if this is a good thing or a bad thing. For a child."

Because of years of experience getting to know those left behind a violent crime, knowing them down to their shredded souls, most often to eliminate them as suspects, just as often to pull clues out of them that they were unaware they had, Hermie could say this to Mr. And Mrs. Harrison with absolute conviction and a smile of reassurance: "In your case, it's a *good* thing. No doubt about it."

They both actually blushed. She beamed at him gratefully, he ducked his head but couldn't hide a relieved smile. "'ppreciate that," he said.

"I know people in the system, I'll make some calls, give you a reference, if you want," Hermie said.

"Wouldn't want to impose," Frank Harrison said, politely. "'Sure your plate is full, like always."

"It's no trouble at all. Happy to do it."

"Thank you so much, Detective . . . Hermie," she smiled, "We'll let ya get back to your lunch, right Frank? Hope it hasn't gone cold."

"Sure, sure. Come by the house, sometime. Good t'see ya," her husband said, with the sincere handshake of his farmer ancestors.

With another grateful smile from her that took years away from her face, giving a glimpse of what she was like as a teenager, with dimple-lifted cheeks pushing giggles up into her eyes. Then they walked away, hands holding, shoulders brushing, taking the long way to Sears.

The noodles, chicken and broccoli had indeed gone nearly cold, but Hermie finished it all anyway, aware that what had begun as a colossally awful day had given way just a little to hope. Because he knew a motherless, fatherless boy who was damaged, perhaps beyond repair. But the Harrisons were a loving shelter that just might begin to heal that damaged boy. As he ate, phone numbers and a plan began to flicker in his mind. It would start with pulling Babs off the picket line, but she'd manage, he knew. She was one of the warriors where kids were concerned.

He had no idea that this day would have him doing a lot of warrior-ing himself.

CHAPTER FOURTEEN

*"I am circling around God, around the ancient tower, and
I've been circling for thousands of years, and I don't yet
know: Am I a falcon, a storm, or a vast song . . ."*

Prayers of A Young Poet by Rainer Maria Rilke

Claire breezed in to the stationette, fresh from a community Crime Watch
meeting at the Wilmington Chamber of Commerce, at which several Muslims
were present, including the father of Sunidhi Askar, who gave a sincere vote of
confidence for the investigation into the death of his daughter and the others,
with special mention of Detective Herman Grabfelder. And he touched even
prejudiced members of the crowd when he ended with, "These were not just
Muslims who were killed; they were daughters. *Daughters.* Like yours."

Claire stopped by Nell's desk to share this news and pick up her phone
messages, when she felt the floor shake. "He's pacing?"

"Oh, yeah," breathed Nell. "Del Amo was a bitch. Another one. He's on
Overload."

"Well, wait for it. It'll come. Duck and dive."

The floor let them both know Hermie was coming out. He was pulling
on his jacket when he emerged, spotted Claire. "Good, you're here. I was going
to look it up, but maybe you know."

"Hello, to you, too, Hermie-dear." Cheerfully to the point.

"What? Oh, sorry. Hello, how's it goin'? How's the family? You look great,
as always. And do you know where I can find the nearest mosque? Or do I
have to look it up in the Googley thing? Oh, wait –- I can call Shakey, he'd
know. But, this time of the morning, he might be out on a call . . . Still --"

Claire had a passing thought that, relations between American and
Muslim officialdom being what they were, was *anyone* ready for Herman
Grabfelder? Scary, impatient and tactless as he was? But on the other hand,

nobody else could do this. So she gave him the location she happened to know because she drove by it every day to and from work.

It was the kind of place of worship that indicated "paid for by donations" by middle class members. It had previously been a book store, its once large front windows now replaced by smaller ones with elaborate metal frames that depicted climbing vines. The frames were dazzling white, to match the white stucco walls. Expansion of those walls was noticeable on both sides and probably in the back. Fresh white paint did not quite obscure the spots where additions were connected, then patched with stucco. Large bushes of scarlet roses grew along the bases of the walls. They had just begun to climb, and would one day obscure the patched stucco.

Two young olive trees flanked the walkway that led up to some steps and the double doors. Hermie could imagine them years from now, when these trees would be tall and joining leafy branches above to form a shady canopy over the walkway.

Hermie checked his watch and then wondered, since he didn't know if this was on or in-between one of the five prayer times he'd heard about. There was no one around, so either they were inside for prayers, or due to arrive.

Suddenly, he became aware of the familiar musical sound of children playing nearby. He walked to a space between the mosque and a nondescript, boarded up building next door, "For Sale or Lease", so he could look through an alley-like space to see a chainlink fence circling a playground in back of the mosque. Brightly colored plastic swings, slides, sand boxes were crowded with small boys and girls in just as brightly colored shirts and slacks. They were all about five or six years old, most of them laughing, all of them bursting with the energy of the very young. Since some of the girls were wearing headscarves, he assumed they were in a school attached to the mosque. He was scanning the playground for a teacher, when:

"May I help you?" Behind him, her voice was distinctly no-nonsense and a direct challenge.

Hermie flashed: *A man, peeking at a playground full of little kids! Aw jeez!* Before he turned around, he whipped out his badge and held it up where it could not be missed. "Sorry to intrude. I'm here hoping to speak to the --" *Pastor? Priest? Reverend? What the hell was it? Oh!* "The Imam?"

For once he was relieved to see a flash of recognition when she looked at his badge, then her dramatic, dark eyes looked him up and down as if searching his character. She was wearing a headscarf colorful with a floral print and a moss green chador. Her shiny face had no sign of lines or softness to indicate her age, except those eyes that radiated an intimidating wisdom.

And she was just a smidge over five feet tall. He towered over her, but knew he had met his match.

"You're Grabfelder."

"Yes, Ma'am. Miss? Miz?"

"Well, it's about bloody time! C'mon!" she snapped, and turned to walk away. He dutifully followed her at her brisk clip, up the walk and steps into the mosque, through the wake of her scent, which reminded him of peaches. Just inside the door was a wide foyer, where she turned to him, but he was already removing his shoes, remembering his bare-bones education from Shakey.

"Well," she said, as if impressed. He grinned at her, but she ignored it, and slipped off her own shoes, which were child-sized, black leather flats with a golden oval buckle on the tiny toes. She pulled a pair of immaculately white, rolled-up satin slippers out of the depth of her chador, slipped them on.

Master Craftsmen had lovingly restored this place, Hermie saw. Gleaming blonde wood floors had been laid with pegs instead of nails; what were once ordinary square door frames had been changed to graceful peaked frames, some flanked with hand-painted vines and flowers that traveled upward delicately, only to burst forth in arabesques on the ceiling above. Someone had changed an ordinary ceiling to one that curved up and then down to meet the walls. He got a glimpse of the prayer room as they went past and was startled to see the ceiling had been partially removed, replaced with glass panels that opened to the sun and sky at the moment, but could be closed against the elements. A breeze drifted into the room that was not as vast as he'd seen in pictures of other, richer mosques; but prayer rugs in blazing colors contrasted dramatically with the gleaming, pale wood floor. The moving air carried smells of soap, floor wax, and a touch of the traffic smells outside.

Just as the question formed in his mind, she piped up: "Because we don't have the space, we pray in shifts — the men come out, we women come in."

"Efficient."

They entered a hallway that had been made less narrow looking by replacing one wall with floor-to-ceiling windows, where sunlight dazzled in. At the end of the hall a gleaming wooden door was half-open. Before they got to it, she lifted a tiny hand that wore a gold ring shaped like a flower, to halt him. "Wait here, please."

"Sure."

She glided through the open door, closing it behind her.

Hermie barely had time to turn and examine the photos of various and spectacular mosques on the walls, because the door banged open and a very old and fascinating man dashed toward him. His robes were white, his long beard was white and shimmering like silk against his dark skin, and his merry eyes were a startling aqua below thick, white eyelashes. He raised a finger to point skyward and he said with an accent warmed by the Middle East, "I was going to give Allah one more day — *one more!* — before I came to get you myself!"

Hermie just had time to remember to place his hand over his heart and nod, before the Imam grabbed it and pumped it, eagerly. "Detective Grabfelder, I hate why you are here, but I am nevertheless glad to meet you, having heard much about you. I am Mirwais Hanna. Come, come!" He shoved Hermie into his office as the tiny woman slipped out. "Yes, I am a packrat. My parents named me 'Mirwais', which means 'light of the house' — had they but known! My apologies. Nobody believes me when I swear I know where everything is."

"I can relate," smiled Hermie at this kindred spirit.

Hermie carefully entered the small, cluttered office, filled with shelves sagging under the weight of hundreds of books, both old and new. A brilliant blue tapestry draped one wall, with golden thread embroidering Arabic words. He recalled the embroidered tapestry in Sunidhi's room, wondered whether the words were the same.

A sweet fragrance reached him, through the other smells of books, dust, apples, and Hermie noted a bouquet of white and yellow lilies and orange roses filling a blue porcelain vase placed on a small table in front of a window. The table was a warm-brown wood imbedded with tiny silver pieces forming flowers and vines. A large, old desk dominated the room, its dark wood incongruous in a building filled with lighter colored wood, scratches and chips marred a surface that looked futilely waxed and polished. Stacks of folders, papers, stuffed IN and OUT trays, a black phone with several buttons, and a delicate-looking brass lamp with a pale pink shade crowded the desk top.

Jammed against one wall was a row of dented metal file cabinets piled with colorful file folders stuffed with papers; on top were small woven trays holding a variety of cellphones in different colors. A computer, printer and monitor was on a small wooden cart shoved against one side of the desk, as if adding a wing of space.

The Imam scooped a stack of newspapers off a worn leather easy chair and dumped them on the stack half-filling its twin alongside, indicating this is where Hermie should sit. Raised right, as they said in Bay City, Michigan, Hermie respectfully remained standing while the Imam slipped past him, leaving a scent of baby powder and peppermint as he went behind his desk to abruptly sink into a protesting chair that was once upholstered in puffy green leather cushions, but now the cushions had been punched and hollowed by the man who had been plopping down on them for a lot of years. Hermie then sat in the easy chair, which was large enough to fit him, but its worn, wine-colored leather squeaked unpleasantly.

The Imam leaned forward toward Hermie, elbows on his desk, hands folded on top of papers stacked on the desk top, his intense aqua eyes appearing to drink Hermie in. Then a flash of annoyance. "This is too far away!" He jumped up, coming around the desk.

Hermie got up, too, confused, but the Imam patted him back down as he passed on his way to the other easy chair. He scooped all the papers out of it, plopped them on top of the now-sliding papers on his desk, then pulled the chair around to face Hermie, sat in it, scooted the squeaking leather chair and himself forward, and Hermie found himself nearly knee to knee with this energetic old man. Peppermint wafted from his breath.

And now Hermie could see that he was, indeed, *very* old, his dark skin leathery and lined, except for the smooth and glowing pink cheeks just above the snowy ridge line of his beard. His tangled white eyebrows made nearly perfect half-circles above his now evaluating and brilliant eyes. "So . . ." he said, "what monster is doing these horrors? And what are you doing about it?"

"That's why I'm here."

"These are a hate crime, are they not? Against our faith?"

"Oh, it's a lot of hate, Sir, up close and personal. But . . . I'm going to tell you some confidential details we haven't released, for good reasons."

"I understand. You have my word this goes no further."

A soft knock on the door interrupted. "We must take some tea and cookies, out of respect for Yasmina's feelings. She's my great-granddaughter, and the best assistant on this planet. Believe me, I know from experience, from *centuries* past." He twinkled a smile before he shouted toward the door, "Come, Dearest!"

The door clicked open and the tiny woman returned. Hermie got to his feet, but she echoed the Imam: "Sit, sit." She was pushing a small wheeled cart that held a porcelain tea service, cups and saucers, none of which matched, and three plates stacked with fragrant goodies: dates, cookies lumpy with nuts, and tiny layer cakes with ribbons of fruit puree — apricot, raspberry, pineapple — tucked between their golden cake layers. A stack of neatly folded ivory linen napkins rested to one side. Hermie's nose was quickly overwhelmed by the scents of fruit puree, vanilla cake, and strong tea.

"What bounty!" the Imam teased. "We can serve ourselves, Yasmina, thank you."

"Holler if you run out," she said, matter-of-factly, before she swept to the door. "I assume no calls, no interruptions."

"Once again, you read my mind, my Angel."

The door clicked shut. The Imam expertly slipped back the sleeves of his robe, snatched up the tea pot, poured for Hermie and himself. The tea was black and smelled of rich leaves. "Sugar? Cream?" he asked.

"No, Sir. I like it straight."

"I, too. Full-blown caffeine to goose the carburetor." The Imam took up his cup and one of the folded napkins. They both blew on their cups and sipped. As if it were a habit, the Imam immediately tapped the folded edge of his napkin onto the bottom of where his mustache had dipped into the tea, dabbing away any moisture, but making no change in the stain.

Hermie felt the whomp of caffeine almost immediately. *Almost as lethal as Selah's coffee.*

"So, go on." The Imam's eyes once more trapped Hermie.

"It all started with the murder of a woman and her man. I'd call them 'lapsed' Muslims, if anything."

The Imam was almost startled, "Someone took offense at their union?"

"Well...could-a been, in a kinda way. Because she was FBI, he was Most Wanted by the FBI and everyone else 'Official' and 'Guv'ment'. But these first Vics — victims — were the point, not their relationship. For sure, because the next victims were three Muslim women. Young girls, actually."

"Why? Why?! There is the hate." The Imam moaned as if in pain.

"These are hate crimes, yes, and I once assumed the usual: A god-fearing white guy with a grudge."

"Good assumption these days."

"Yeah. Sorry. Or, a Muslim fanatic with his own version of Islam. No offense."

"Hmmph!" The Imam's shrug spoke volumes. "What next, do I not want to know."

"I was only half wrong. Oh, it's a Muslim guy, for sure. Sorry. Short, light, small feet. But his weapon was a dagger. An Eleventh Century Shiite Assassin's weapon. And the cuts — he has been trained in the skill of how to use that dagger."

Shock widened the old man's jewel-like eyes. "An Assassin!"

"Yeah. As soon as we realized what we were dealing with, we made sure nobody knew from nothing but a stabbing. For . . . reasons. I think you understand."

The Imam closed his eyes for a moment and slightly swayed as he softly murmured in Arabic what Hermie assumed was a prayer. Then, the Imam sank back into his chair in shock. "A Muslim man assassinating Muslim girls? This is not . . . *not* . . . ! Allah, Islam forbids — *forbids* —! Is there more?"

"All the Muslim girls were wearing headscarves. The killer took them."

The Imam's thin, freckled hand shook as he brought his cup to his lips, sipped deeply, held the napkin to his lips for a long moment, then pulled it away to say something that gave Hermie confirmation in his own mind that he was, at least, on the right track. "Because he is traditional. Pious. And he was showing that they were not. And should be exposed. And . . . punished."

"Yeah. Sir. It's the one thing that makes sense. Even when the rest of it don't. Frankly, it's all I got."

Tears suddenly fell from the Imam's eyes, in rivulets that ran down and disappeared into the snow of his beard, and his shoulders shook with silent sobs.

Feeling awful, Hermie set his cup down, took the Imam's and offered his own fresh napkin. "I am so sorry, Pastor — uh, Sir."

The Imam took the fresh napkin with a thankful nod, covered his eyes with it for a moment, then wiped and sniffed. "My apologies. I sit here weeping when you saw, you *saw* it all . . . such horrors."

"Yes. The worst . . . of my job, my life."

With a sudden understanding, the Imam reached over and patted Hermie's hand, a fatherly gesture that made Hermie's eyes moisten. Then the Imam retrieved his tea and drank, dabbed, took a deep breath, then his remarkable eyes were calm when he looked at Hermie and said, "What do you need of me? Us?"

"Were any of the girls or their families or friends members of this mosque?"

"No. But some were known by my members. Schoolmates, business acquaintances, that sort of thing. And the parents were known by their reputation, in particular Mr. and Mrs. Askar. Their home was open to so many in our community. And their daughter, Sunidhi, 'Sunny' . . . she was indeed a light. Such a light . . ."

"Yes, I met them. Very good people. Whereas Mr. Farsadi—"

"Whush!" The Imam blew out a breath of annoyance. "Pious pig! He came to ask me to perform the marriage of his *child* after his own Imam refused."

"I thought . . . with a mind-set like that, it's kinda simple to go over the edge. He was strongly against his own daughter's ambitions and lifestyle. But a good source told me he hasn't the guts."

The Imam nodded emphatically, "Quite correct, your source. It's not him, or his son. Farsadi is a coward. He would beat his daughter, his wife, I grant you, but they are not strangers, they are not the 'unknowns' — understand?"

"They are predictable in their reactions."

"Precisely. Farsadi has no power over a stranger, even if the stranger is a girl. Especially not in this country — some of our girls know karate, go to self-defense classes. Can you imagine how such would react to that man?"

"I'd like to see that, frankly. Sorry."

The Imam nodded, understanding. Then his eyes once more filled with grief and desperation. "What can I do? What can we *do*?"

"You can save me some time, and a lot of footwork. In confidence, can
you consult with the other Imams in the South Bay area, ask them if they
know of a Muslim man who is known to have a hatred of non-traditional
women, successful, ambitious women who work, who go to college, who are
active outside the home. He's short, as I said, well under six feet, and slender,
with smallish feet for a guy. He owns that historic dagger and was taught
how to use it. Maybe he bragged about that, being part of ancient history,
yada-yadoo. Sorry. He's undoubtedly a Shiite, because of that history. I don't
think he's a collector — we checked dozens of weapons and antique stores that
stock daggers and nobody's sold anything like that to someone who collects.
So maybe he brought it here from the old country, or inherited it, it's been
in the family, or carried such a thing in an army back in the day — *anything*.
But don't let anyone talk about *how* these girls were killed. We're keeping
it to a stabbing by an unknown white guy so there's no backlash against
Muslims. We — and I'm sure *you* — don't want this monster to be the poster
boy for more anti-Muslim propaganda, especially by all those 'real American'
politicians. There's enough of that going around these days."

"There is indeed. Tell me, do you think this 'anti-Muslim propaganda',
as you say, will die down after the elections?"

"Hope to God. Sorry. It probably will because it won't be useful anymore."

"'Useful'?"

"It's being used these days to attract votes. It's votes by ignorant yahoos,
but still votes. After the elections nobody needs votes. See?"

"Yes. Thank you for being so candid. I know the police, your colleagues
who defend us, are being accused of being 'anti-American', at the same time
as they are being fair. A position impossible most of the time. You have my
sympathies. Most of the time."

Hermie couldn't tell what those colorful eyes were conveying at the
moment. "We appreciate it. *All* of the time."

The eyes now mellowed with kindness. "I will contact my colleagues in
confidence, as you say."

"A Muslim woman told me that this monster thinks he's doing the work
of Allah, so it would make sense that he's super devout and goes to the mosque
more than the average."

"Smart woman. My compliments. She's right. In a monstrous way, he's
making a great show of his 'piety'."

"I've also been told by her that people in your community, especially
women, see things, know things, and share information."

A smile lifted up the top of his beard. "This is also true. We all come from
villages, where the favorite entertainment was gossip. It stays in our blood no

matter how far we travel or how 'modern' we become. It was invented by the women who were confined, the women who were never thought of at all."

"My fear is he'll get wind we're on to him and if he runs, he'll take that dagger with him. To God knows where."

"I understand. But we are not looking for a dagger, we are looking for a piety that constrains, judges women."

"Exactly."

"But I must ask to share this confidence with others who are not of our community, but trustworthy nonetheless."

Hermie questioned him with a look.

"We have had these others come to us in sympathy and guilt –- Rabbis, Christian Ministers, Priests –- may I tell them they have no blame? May I tell them the monster is not of their faith, but one of our own?"

Heremie felt a deep sympathy for this man who was so pained by this horrible knowledge that the hate crime that had cut down the flowers in their midst had most probably been committed by a member of his own faith, doing it for God.

"Sure," was all he could say.

Later, Hermie left the mosque with two linen napkins filled with cakes and dates and cookies, pushed on him with a smile of insistence from Yasmina. When he arrived at Roberta, he used his cellphone to put a call in to Shakey and told him of his meeting with this particular Imam and having to tell that ancient, charismatic man that a self-righteous little shit who owned an historic dagger was a Muslim serial killer, and asking him to keep this horrible information confidential while keeping his ears to the ground about his own people.

When he had somewhat recovered from this information, Shakey floored him with news that illuminated again how little he knew about these people of a maligned faith: "Did you meet Yasmina?"

"I'll say! Five feet of intimidation. The Imam said some of their girls know karate –- she's a black belt for sure."

"Got news for ya –- she's the light of that Imam's life and she's taking classes to be a cleric. If he has anything to do with it, she's gonna be the first female Imam in the U.S. of A!"

Hermie couldn't resist; it had been his experience that only the Jews have perfect words for such things, so he said it: "Oy! What a tzimmis that's gonna make!"

Shakey bellowed with laughter, even after Hermie hung up.

CHAPTER FIFTEEN

"I am only one, but still I am one; I cannot do everything, but still I can do something; and because I cannot do everything, I will not refuse to do something that I can do."

Edward Everett Hale

He took a traffic-avoiding shortcut to get back to his stationette and it took him past Amira Farsadi's school. In days to come, he would wonder why he re-visited the school, some strange compulsion that he couldn't explain. He had already interviewed faculty and some students, instinctively knew that if any one of them knew something that would help find Amira's killer, they would have told him so; everyone was desperate to help that dear girl.

So, perhaps the seed had been planted long days ago, upon reading the newspaper coverage of the vast outpouring of love that was demonstrated at the funeral of Sunidhi Askar. Hundreds of people of all races and religious persuasions mourning that special, "Sunny" girl. And that's when the seed sprouted: Where was coverage for Amira Farsadi's burial?

He pulled into the parking lot of the school and guessed it was between classes because the campus was filled with students obviously hurrying on their way to the next class because hardly any of the kids stopped to chit-chat. Then he suddenly noticed that nearly every student he passed was wearing a bright red, makeshift armband. Some were made of men's neckties wrapped around the arm and knotted; others were woven of satin ribbons; others were scarves or neckerchiefs; some were simply strips of cloth cut from who knows what. All in bright red.

"Red was Amira's favorite color," said Principal Harry Danforth, his eyes once again moistening to the point of flooding. "A group of her classmates came to me and asked if they could show their loss for 'our Amira'. They had come up with the armband idea, only not in black, but in red for Amira. Since I was sharing their feelings, I gave permission –– to hell with it if I get flack from the District."

"She was one of the special ones, I found out," answered Hermie.

"Special and brilliant and touching. You saw the brilliance first. Did you know she got a letter from NASA, offering her a full scholarship in exchange for just five years of her service?"

"Jeez, how did NASA know?"

"Well . . . I told them. I knew *she* wouldn't. Too shy. But such a mind must be allowed to flourish, reach its full potential. But I soon learned how much she was hiding behind that brilliance."

"Her father? Someone called him 'The Beast Farsadi', and I thought that was right on."

"Oh, yes. He showed up some months ago, tried to drag Amira bodily out of her classroom, shouting Arabic that, mercifully, kept us from knowing what he was yelling at her."

"How'd you deal with him?"

"Fortunately, on that day and time our Security Guard was Giant John."

"Giant –?"

"John Rawlings, six foot seven black man, retired Navy Seal. He never had kids, which was a pity –– he's a Pied Piper to all kids. Well, it was a beautiful sight: he hauled Farsadi up by his shirt collar and carried him out and off campus. Told him the next time he trespassed on this campus he'd be arrested. And he threw out a bald-faced lie he knew would impress a jackass –– pardon me –– a *man* like Farsadi: he told him Amira was under police protection and if she was harmed in any way, physically, he'd 'have the crap pounded outta you', was how he put it. Coming from a counry where the police did that kind of thing, Farsadi bought it."

"Beautiful. I am filled with admiration for your tactics. And I may send a fan letter to Giant John." Hermie grinned.

"More importantly, it worked. He stopped hovering, spying on her, stopped waiting for her to make sure she went straight home. Amira had a little breathing space. Till . . ." Once more, his eyes blinked back tears. "We didn't protect her at all. He got to her anyway. Or was it that brother of hers?"

"No, no, Mr. Danforth. It wasn't either Farsadi."

"It wasn't? But who ––?" Danforth was at a loss.

"Different monster. And our Amira was his third hit."

"'Our Amira'? You too? You knew her?"

"No. And I'll always regret that. But I've met her mother. Very brave woman."

"Ah . . . yes. Amira spoke of her mother. We were all relieved that at least she had someone at home who was on her side. But . . ."

"What?" Hermie encouraged.

"Maybe you're not the one to ask, on the other hand . . . The students kept asking, so I called the Farsadi house to ask when Amira's funeral would be. This entire school, her classmates, teachers, John and the security crew, the cleaning crew, even the landscaping guys — *all* wanted the chance to say goodbye to her."

"Her mother would very much appreciate that."

"But Mr. Farsadi shouted into the phone, 'That's none of your business!' And a torrent of Arabic that made me hang up. How do you deal with such a man?"

"He's not a man."

"Oh, I fully agree!"

"Let me see what I can do. I'll be right back."

With that, Hermie walked back to Roberta and grabbed his cell phone. The walk and grab betrayed his growing rage. He remembered this number without effort.

"Pierre, it's me."

"Ah, 'erman, you are, as always, how you say, 'spooky'?"

Pierre's pronunciation of 'spooky' calmed things down a bit. "Okay, what did I do this time that spooked ya?"

"I was going to telephone you yesterday, but got so busy, you understand."

"Yeah, I sent you another tragedy."

"Ah, oui, and in answer to your thought, oui, the Mademoiselle Batawi is yet anozer victim of ze dagger. I have yet to do ze full autopsy, but I recognize zat stab and cut. Mon Dieu, zis kill-aire is wizout heart, wizout soul."

"If I ever get my hands on him . . ."

"You must stand in ze line, mon Ami, behind me."

"We'll be in a very long line, Pal. Oh — you said you were going to call me? About those wounds?"

"Ah, no. I was going to ask, since it is your case — ze Amira Farsadi?"

"That's what I was calling about! We're *both* spooky! What about her?"

"I still have zis poor child. Zey will not come to get her. Nor send ze funeral home."

"WHAT?!"

"I have called ze Farsadi home — merde! Zat man!" He paused, listening to the rage in Hermie's breathing. "I agree, 'erman. What shall I do? I await."

Hermie's voice was tightly controlled. "Get her ready. Someone will come for her. I will make sure." And he hung up.

His thoughts were not only on Amira, alone and unclaimed; but on her mother, who must know her daughter is not buried, must know that she's somewhere unclaimed, somewhere lost, and there is no one in her house or world who knows where she is, so she could not claim her even now.

He got his wallet out, found the business card that Mrs. Farsadi had the courage to sneak to him. Dialed the number. He knew the voice of who picked up -- Farah, the flirtatious butcher, whose cheery voice nearly eased him. "Hello there, this is Aida's the grocery. And, yes, we got the first cherries in. Get them while they are hot. Uh, cool. Uh, ripe. Whatever, they are perfect and supplies are limited because global warming has screwed with the harvest, so come on down. Can I help you?"

"Miss Farah, this is Detective Grabfelder and I need to speak to Aida. It's important."

"Ah, Detective, how I enjoy your voice. And the other parts. Please hang on, Aida will be here right away."

Aida's cheerful voice was instantly dampened when Hermie said the awful words: "Aida, no one has come for Amira Farsadi. She's still in the morgue. Farsadi won't send a funeral home."

"WHAT?!"

"Look, this may not be permitted, Islam-wise, but I want to fetch Amira, but I can't do anything 'official'. Understand?"

"I understand. I will make it happen."

"Contact a funeral home, *I'll pay for everything* -- pick her up, get something wonderful for her to wear . . ."

"'Something wonderful for her to wear' . . ." Aida's voice trembled.

"I want her to have the finest casket you can find. I'll pay for that, too. And the burial plot. Somewhere that her Mom can maybe walk to or take a short bus ride to. Get two plots, side by side, so her mother will know she will be beside her again, one day."

"Oh . . . oh . . ." Aida was sniffing and blowing by now, she struggled to control her voice, "Detective, please take no offense. But in Islam, there are no caskets. Only a plain wooden coffin, to conform to State law."

"Oh. Sorry. What kinda wood?"

"Oh, any kind will do."

"I hear cedar wood is kinda special. Is that permitted?"

"Why, yes, but it will be --"

"Don't mention the expense, I'll take care of it. Just get the best for her."

"And, the usual isn't 'something wonderful to wear'; it's a simple white shroud."

"Oh, sorry again. But this time I insist -- Rachel's favorite color was red. She won't go to hell or anything if she's wrapped in red, will she?"

She was close to bawling out loud, "No, no, Allah is merciful and understanding."

"Then get the finest red cloth you can find — maybe pure silk. Or even cashmere. She's special."

"She is not the only one."

"What about a headstone? Is that kosher?"

"'Kosher'?"

"Aw, sorry — I'm so pissed off at this whole damn thing, I've gone loony. Is a headstone permitted?"

"You would do that?"

"It's done."

She paused, then: "Uh . . . there's one thing."

"Name it, Aida, I'll do it."

"You must not come to the burial, Detective. For one thing, the Beast Farsadi will hear of it and he will make your life a living hell — I wouldn't put it past him to go to your Chief and accuse you of having an affair with his daughter and that's why you came to her funeral."

"Jeezus H. —! Sorry."

"And there's one other thing. And I thank you mightily for giving us this opportunity, we had been unable to find one."

"What do you mean?"

"Another reason you should not come is because Lela Farsadi will disappear at her daughter's burial."

"Huh?"

"She will vanish. And we will be getting her out of the country, to safety, to a better life, like we planned for Amira. She would not go, not knowing where Amira was. Now, she will know, and now we can take her away from so much sorrow."

"A lot of her sorrow will stay with her. With all of us."

"Yes, it will. Sorrow for the others, too. We read about the other victims. They are not strangers, to us."

"Look, for the funeral and the taking, I can send plain clothes cops to help out — they'll be women, too."

"No need. We've done this before — we know the drill. Besides, the Beast and his Spawn will not come to the burial. Word will get out that they did not make the arrangements but strangers had to. The community did. And when Lela does not come home he will not be able to complain, because everyone knows why. It will shame him. You will not be mentioned, but all will know. All except him and his."

"Look, if there's anything — *anything* else I can do."

"We know you. Blessings upon you."

"And you. And yours. *All* of 'em."

She hung up, and Hermie filled his lungs and let it go. It came into his mind and made it rest: *Don't worry, Amira-Honey, we're going to take care of you. And your Mom.*

Three days later (*She did all this in three days?* Hermie marveled), he read the story in the local paper about another young Muslim girl buried, Amira Farsadi, another victim of the serial killer's stabbing rampage. A photo showed that nearly the entire student body and faculty and various work crews attached to her school attended the burial, Giant John looming in the background, red hanky to his eyes, all of them wearing bright red armbands, most carrying small nosegays of bright red roses, which they gently laid along her grave. It was noted that none of the mourners from Amira Farsadi's school were Muslim; it was also noted and pictured that a large contingent of Muslim women attended, all wearing full length black chadors and the veils that showed only their eyes.

Hermie nearly laughed out loud: *All those chadors and veils covering them up, you couldn't tell one woman from another; so you couldn't tell who suddenly went missing . . . godspeed, Lela.*

The next day, the stationette's mail brought him a 4"x6" envelope marked "PERSONAL", which Nell had put on top of his other mail, unopened. Inside, a small note fell out which read: "Lela Farsadi wanted you to have this. It's a copy we had made for you, for all of us." It was signed, *"Aida".* Accompanying the note was a 4"x6" color photo of Lela and Amira Farsadi, the happier version of the photos he'd found in Amira's wallet: both of them smiling fully; both of their headscarves loosened so they framed rather than constricted their faces; touching lightly their dark, shining hair; and no sign of their burdens in their merry eyes. Now knowing their story, he wondered: *How did she manage to get pictures taken of herself and her precious daughter? Where did they go? If it was at a photographer's studio, was the Beast Farsadi waiting outside, impatient for this nonsense to be over? She knew . . . Lela knew, even back then. She knew she must have photos of her Amira; she must have them, just in case . . .*

In order not to bawl just yet, Hermie quickly took two color photo copies of the photo, put the copies in a drawer in his desk, took the original when he left the stationette in a wordless hurry that had Nell wondering.

He'd already ordered the headstone, having gone to the stone mason just after his phone call to Aida that enraging day. Now he remembered something that happened at the morgue those other terrible days ago. Before he started up Roberta, he called Shakey on his cellphone and caught him having a sandwich at his desk. Hermie didn't want to give anything away, so he simply asked him for a translation of what he'd heard Rachel's mother keen over and over as she bent over her dead daughter's face, memorizing it with her hands. He hoped he said it correctly phonetically, he very nearly did, so Shakey instantly knew what the phrase was and conveyed it. And since Shakey had heard the catch in Hermie's voice and knew he was dealing with the slaughter of young, innocent Muslim girls, he didn't question Hermie about why he needed the translation; that could keep for an easier time; if easier times ever came.

Now Hermie hoped it wasn't too late to make a change in the headstone's design, to accommodate the photo and the phrase he remembered. Luckily, Aristotle ("Hey, call me 'Ari', *puhlease!*") Theopolis of Athena Stonemasons assured him he could accommodate, "Not a problem at all." And when he asked which of the women in the photo had the stone been ordered for, and was told it was the younger at present, the older when her time came, his eyes got moist as well. "Not a problem at all, they will be lovely."

And so the photo of the smiling mother and daughter was carefully framed and glazed against what would be years of sun and rain and smog, and then perfectly set into the headstone, in an oval just below the carvings of roses and vines that outlined the wording of: "Amira Farsadi, 1996-2016" that was on one side of the headstone, leaving a space on the other side for the future welcome of her mother. And below that, Ari carved the phrase that Hermie wrote down for him, the phrase heard in Lela Farsadi's pain-filled voice in Arabic, now to be carved in English: "Take me with you, my Beloved."

* * * *

But late in the day thence came the comeuppance.

After days —- weeks? —- of avoiding the phone calls and e-mails, an Aide in a uniform bristling with medals and complete with sidearm had turned up to personally escort Detective Herman Grabfelder to the new LAPD headquarters for a meeting with the Chief.

It went colorfully, just like so many such meetings in his past.

The first problem was that this was yet another Police Chief who had a temper to match Hermie's, both honed and festered in the trenches of the frustration of law enforcement by guys who cared deeply about these things. Los Angeles profanity battled Midwestern profanity to a spittle-spraying, breathless draw. Intelligence efficiency was questioned, bureaucratic interference was blamed, manhood was impugned and then both got down to it.

"The bodies are piling up and I don't see any progress, Grabfelder! What the hell is going on here? I offered you whatever help would help, but you haven't asked and you haven't done diddly. Five girls!!"

"Actually, four. One of the Vics was a man. One of the *first* Vics."

"Split hairs and it's still the same — you're no closer to solving this crap! Are these hate crimes? Against Muslims?"

"Maybe. Maybe not."

"Shit!"

"I can relate."

"White supremacists? 9-11 nutcases?"

"In Torrance?"

"These days . . ."

"True. But I don't think so."

"Why the hell not?"

"The dagger."

"Ah, yes, the dagger. Instead of a gun? Bomb?"

"Uh huh. It's a strictly Muslim symbol."

"Of what?"

"Eleventh Century Assassins."

"WHAT?!"

"Eleventh Century *Shiite* assassins. To be precise."

The Chief merely gaped at him, speechless.

Hermie helped him out. A little. "That's why I know this isn't no white guy on a 'Muslims must die' crusade. But *nobody* who *shouldn't* know *doesn't* know that these aren't simply 'stabbings'. You can see why."

The Chief found his voice. "For chrissakes, Hermie, there's been *five*! We gotta stop this fucker! I'm getting phone calls from 'Muslim delegations', Imams. Visits are next. And don't get me started on Tommy Velasco!" His voice pitched into an annoying whine familiar to all: "The people have a right to know. Is this, y'know like *'political'*?" The whine dropped, got changed to a sneer: "'Political'! Makes me puke."

"He has that effect."

"I'm thinking of issuing a public warning. Muslim women should go out in pairs, or with escorts . . ."

"Good idea, practically. Bad idea PR-wise. Besides, you're too late shmart — word is already out, most Muslim women are now going everywhere with a male along. And most are packing —unregistered, I'd guess — but these are times for allowances."

"Allowances, for only *now*! I hope they know that!"

Both men sat back, breathed, picked at cuticles, sipped cooling coffee.

"You need more troops?" he offered.

"To do what?"

"Go door to door, nosing around?"

"That would be insulting. Because you're Muslim the police are knocking at your door? Dejavu from where they fled. Besides, which streets? This guy's got no territorial pattern, other than strictly South Bay. So far."

"More police presence, cruisers, might —"

"Might. Do that. Nothing dampens enthusiasm like police cruisers cruising by, snooping. Especially for a stalker."

"He stalks 'em?"

"Oh, yeah. Obviously. How he knows where these girls would be where he could get at 'em is the first thing I'll ask when I get him."

"Optimist."

"I know. This guy . . . this guy . . ." Hermie decided against going on to prevent blowing a gasket in this meeting and exposing his complete frustration. Better only *minor* frustration show at this stage. *Complete* might get him pulled off the case and locked up in Psychiatric.

"Give me something I can tell the governor."

"The governor?"

"It's coming onto an election year."

"*Again?* Christ. Aren't there term limits? What about the mayor?"

"No pressure there. He calls for updates, he's been talking to the Muslim community without cameras being around, reassuring. He's cool. Yet."

"Yet."

"For now. Pressure will build. He's only got so much charm to go around."

The Chief's eyes suddenly told *All*. "Fuck, Hermie, young Muslim girls sliced in half? This is just —"

"This is one sick sonuvabitch, is what this is. And he's doing it all for God."

"Then get that asshole off the goddamn streets! I don't want politicians using this issue for anti-Muslim TV commercials hinting not so subtly, 'It's time for an immigration 'change'. And those pseudo-Islamic groups filing lawsuits claiming that 'If the victims weren't Muslim there would have been an arrest by now'!"

"Is this why I was summoned? Wasting my time, so you can point out the obvious?"

"Fuck you! And the jalopy you rode in on! On that subject, you *know* you can get a newer retired squad car, you just have to ask! You're damn embarrassing in that heap!"

"To who? Whom? I get where I'm going."

"And the next time I call you, you better goddamn be available! Who the hell do you think you are?!"

Hermie was a reasonable man –- well, maybe not reasonable, but understanding; well, maybe not understanding, but wise to the direction the wind was blowing: the once movie-star-handsome Chief now ageing rapidly beneath the burdens of heartbreaking instances of stressed-out, panicky white cops shooting black kids, seemingly without sufficient cause, on top of home-grown terrorists bristling with firepower and dreams of glory shooting anyone, anywhere, with a special hard-on for cops with less firepower –- so Hermie stood up, loomed over the Chief, his desk, and a couple of chairs, and gave him an easy Out this time: "You want my badge? You can have it."

"Who the hell would I give it to?"

"Who the hell would take it?"

A pause for more inner fury breathed over.

Kinda mellow: "Hermie, throw me a bone. So I can sleep nights."

Suddenly, it erupted –- all the frustration and heartache and rage Hermie had been living with since seeing the first victim, Lila Miller, so horribly slashed; and then the others, so lovely, so full of promise, so loved; it all erupted with a helpless cliche', "When I find that sonuvabitch, I'm gonna rip his heart out, tear his balls off, stomp his head in until I land on brains, and then set him on fire and flush his ashes down the sewer!"

The Chief, having seen his share of mutilated bodies of the young with all their promise ended, understood, and nearly flinched beneath the two hot blue flames that were now Hermie's eyes. His hand made a calming gesture without his volition, "Understood."

Hermie turned to go, got to the door.

"Hermie?"

He turned back, his eyes now down to low, but his jaw still clenched.

"Anything you need. *Anything*. Including a good defense attorney, should your future call for it."

Hermie nodded his thanks and left.

The Chief picked up his phone and buzzed his secretary, who no doubt had taken over a dozen messages during the ten minute meeting with Detective Herman Grabfelder. "What?" was all the Chief could get out, his throat still being more than a little tight, his eyes still more than a little moist.

* * * *

It was now days after the discovery of Shirin Battawi, slaughtered at that same mall, days of him interviewing anyone and everyone remotely connected to her, writing more in the blue Murder Books, even more in his own personal spiral notebooks.

Hetty McDougald had given him a list of the names of the yahoos that had given Shirin Battawi a hard time. He started first with Management, realized they hadn't a clue because she hadn't complained, but they seemed sincerely shocked and saddened. Shirin hadn't been with them long, but she was a brilliant, meticulous worker and "easy to get along with."

As for the yahoos, they were shocked-*SHOCKED*! that *anyone* would insult her, yada-yadoo, lying like caught-out little kids all around. But they were so obviously cowards that Hermie did not take them seriously in terms of suspects. And all volunteered for lie detector tests; no doubt because they knew they needed them.

A visit to Shirin's apartment showed that Shirin apparently meant to stay awhile — according to her landlord, all the furnishings and decoration inside were hers alone, the apartment having been empty when she rented it. And it was tastefully done in pastels, with comfortable furniture, lots of plants, coordinated yellows in her dishes and pots and pans, a refrigerator and cupboards supplies showing that Shirin was a gourmet cook.

Shirin had a corner apartment, so there was only one next door neighbor. The neighbor was an elderly gentlemen named Sam Ordway, "ex-Marine" he said as if it was a hyphenated part of his name, a stocky man who looked like he'd been a street fighter in his youth, his nose being shifted a little to the left, and there being small, old scars here and there on his still-strong, Favorite Uncle face.

Sam guiltily confessed that he had at first taken offense at Shirin's headscarf, having a nephew who served in Iraq and had plenty of tales to tell about "them ragheads". But he warmed to Shirin when she'd taken to leaving his own newspaper at his door when she got hers from the lobby, so as to save him the trip.

Thanking her led to a conversation and it turned out she came from the same state he did, Minnesota, so a discussion of the winter weather back home led to some mutual grousing and humor. Plus, neither of them had family around, so they were both lonely. Sam had gotten used to it, but for Shirin it was something new yet, Sam recognized that, and stepped up.

Sam told Hermie that Shirin had tried to jog through the neighborhood, but her headscarf led to some yelling at her. When she stopped going, Sam noticed and asked and she reluctantly told.

Sam's doctor had ordered — well, hollered — that Sam needed to get some exercise to get his diabetes under control or he was facing a future of chopped off limbs, so he asked Shirin if she'd go walking with him, telling her this tale of medical necessity which was only half-true, in order to spare her the knowledge that he knew what the hell was going on and he was damn pissed off about it.

"Yelling at a defenseless woman — over her *babushka*?! Who the hell does that?!" Sam groused to Hermie, who found it endearing to hear that familiar mid-western word for a headscarf. With a kind of pang he briefly wondered whether ladies still brought out the babushkas when it got briskly cold in Bay City, Michigan. *It's been so long since . . .*

So, the old man and the young woman with the headscarf began to walk through the neighborhood virtually every day when Shirin came home from work. A long-time resident, Sam was well-known in the neighborhood and there were rumors: Sam, a long-retired security guard, sometimes packed heat and knew how to use it. The only thing missing from the conjecture was the caliber of the gun. But that rumor served to stop the catcalls when Shirin and Sam walked the sidewalks. Sam's glucose level went down nicely and Shirin was less afraid.

When Sam related all this to Hermie, it was obvious he mourned her as though she was the daughter he never had. It tore Sam up that Shirin's family had not come to get her; they simply called and asked a funeral home to pick her up at the coroner's office to ship her home for burial. When he asked Hermie if it was possible to see Shirin before she was shipped, Hermie said, "Mr. Ordway, you don't want that memory of her. Trust me."

Sam's eyes flooded, a wrinkled hanky was yanked out of a back pocket and swiped at eyes, nose, as he nodded.

"I should get her folks' number, ask where to ship all her things."

"I'll have my office get that to ya."

As if relieved for something else to say, Sam said, "You know, she was one helluva cook. She fixed me a trout one time. Hell, I used to pan fry them out in the woods back home."

"Me, too," answered Hermie.

"Well, then you know there's nothing like it. But how *she* fixed 'em, I don't know, but man-oh-man, dee-licious."

Again, a simple memory lightens the grief, if only for a moment.

* * * *

She no longer got the urge to puke when she was confronted by these photos of the crime scenes and their slaughtered victims. But it was still kind of a surprise for Hermie to come back to the office past quitting time to find Nell walking along the carnaged wall as if studying it. She walked past the map he'd made, with red push pins stuck into it here and there, marking the sites of the murders. He pointed it out, "See those push pins? All these murders were within less than a five-mile radius. The guy wouldn't even need a goddamn car. Not that *that* would make sense — he had to have a car; he's carrying a bloody dagger and blood-soaked headscarves, so he'd get noticed. Or would he? Even if he was, would anyone have the guts to call a cop?"

"Yeah . . . Oh, hi, Hermie . . ."

She was distracted by . . . what? "What?" he asked, firmly.

She hesitated, as she always did before offering her opinion.

She's thought of something! Please gawd! "What?!" he asked again, short of a shout, with the reassurance he always used in order to convince her he actually wanted to hear that opinion.

"Just had a thought at 2 o'clock in the morning yesterday, hanging around here this late now for a look-see, when the phones are finally asleep."

"Wouldn't want you to think such dedication will get you Overtime or a raise or anything." His eyes danced with humor for an instant, then changed to that haunted look he'd gotten since this case started. "What's your thought? I'm desperate. Or incompetent. And thus in the cross-hairs of our Chief."

"Okay . . . I had two thoughts. I'll start with the killer."

"Good place."

"There are two possibilities, both cowards. First, he's not a Christian white supremacist fighting on God's side to protect the white race."

"He's not?"

"No. They use guns. They *lu-uv* their guns, have closets and car trunks full of guns because they are 'real Americans' who have the right to these guns. And they nearly always use guns to make their point. Points."

"Go on."

"And he wouldn't be such a secretive killer, hunting down one or two Muslim victims, anonymously. He'd leave a 'note', so to speak, so that when he's caught he'll already be famous for protecting the white race from the enemy: Muslims. Fame is what he's after, since it's the best prize American culture offers, God help us all. He'd be the most famous 'real American' in custody."

"Okay . . ."

"Second, he's not a home-grown Muslim terrorist, either. He'd use guns and bombs to take out *lots* of numbers, people, then he'd blow himself up as his grand ticket to fame and Paradise, to make his Muslim fanatic idols think he was brave. But he's actually avoiding the consequences of his crimes, so he's also a coward. And he's not a real Muslim — Islam forbids the killing of the innocents, women, children."

"Okay . . . two possibilities shot down in flames. Gee, thanks."

"Wait! The killer is a real, from-the-cradle Muslim. Only such a Muslim would know the significance of the dagger and the taking off, stealing of their headscarves. This is meant as a grave insult, a *public* insult. In his mind, they are not 'innocent' women, therefore Islam permits them to be killed."

"Yeah. The headscarf thing — he's calling them 'whores', I was told."

"He's also killing them up close and personal. Because he wanted to *speak* to them as he killed them."

A chill swept through Hermie as he thought of "Kevin". Did he hear as well as see? "Jeezus! Okay, that fits the killing of those young girls. But Hashemi and Lila? Where do they fit in?"

"Well, here's the thing . . ." she hesitated.

"Oh, hell, 'the thing'," he groaned.

Nell went over and unpinned the photos of Hashemi and Lila's murder scenes and moved them away from the slaughtered girls. "I think the murders of Hashemi and Lila were the main event. The murders of the girls were also-rans, to prove his point."

He merely stared at her, stunned.

"He didn't actually stalk the girls, per se. He *saw* them, the headscarves and where they were — alone, without a male escort — and he watched and waited and then struck. Only Hashemi and Lila were *truly* stalked. Stalked for *years*. Hashemi went through years of computer inputs and outputs to make them disappear. They didn't exist, so they had to be stalked in order to get to them. So to speak. And the killer of all of them was a Muslim from the old country, because only such a Muslim would know the history, the weapon, and would have gotten the training there."

His rage was let loose: "'Also-rans'? 'To prove his point?!' WHAT THE FUCKING HELL WAS THE GODDAMN POINT?!" He took a breath, "Sorry, sorry. But this is all your fault. Do you *know* the goddamn point?"

"Starting with Lila and Hashemi, *All* these victims have one thing in common: They were happy."

Hermie gaped at her, stunned.

Nell went on to puncture the silence and the rage she could still feel filling the room. "Hashemi and Lila were in love, raising her boy together. In spite of a real danger that stalked them, a source we don't know about, they were happy, an odd but a happy family."

Hermie suddenly flashed on what Selah had said: *"They were two empty people who found each other."*

Nell was going on: *"All"* the girls: Sunidhi, so loved by family and friends, so happy in her whole life, with such a happy future; Shirin, independent, on her own in a new city, a new job with a future; racist comments didn't stop her, she was a happy woman with a life she alone created that was only going to blossom further. Even Amira Farsadi, in spite of the hell she lived in, she was secretly happy — she'd started college, was liked and supported by new friends, classmates, teachers, and was appreciated for her brilliance. And soon she was going to be transported to a country and a freedom that would bring the career she dreamed of, a career that would have allowed her to save her Mom."

Hermie's voice was flat, "They were all killed because they were happy."

"Close. They were all killed because they stepped outside of the killer's version of Islam and they *thrived*. Yes, they were *happy*. The killer is *not* happy. The killer thinks they should be punished. So he punished them. He will continue to punish women he sees who have stepped outside of *his* Islam, as if they have the right. He will look for headscarves where he thinks they don't belong. And he will punish them."

Finished and drained, Nell held onto her own hands and waited.

Hermie stared at the re-arranged photos. "The main event was Lila Miller and Jordan Hashemi. And "Kevin Costner". And he spoke to them as he killed them."

"Which means?"

"The boy not only saw, he *heard*. Probably just before his mother screamed."

"Oh, Hermie, that poor boy."

"Yeah." He started to leave, stopped at the door to turn to her. "Good work. No, *great* work."

And he turned and left. And Nell felt like the deep breath she took was the first time she'd breathed since he'd come into the room.

CHAPTER SIXTEEN

"If you want to go fast, go alone.
If you want to go far, go together."

Old African Saying

Hermie got into his car to find his cell phone ringing. *Oh, that's where I left it*, was a passing thought before he answered it to find Babs Matthews in a tizzy. "Oh, Hermie, I am so goddamn sorry!"

"What's happened with 'Kevin'?" He knew it hadda be "Kevin" or she wouldn't be so upset.

"Whale Tail found him on a visit to the psychiatric. Didn't recognize him, wanted to see the paperwork. Everything's hit the goddamn fan. I've been ordered to get him into a foster or my ass is grass. *Again*. But, with the strike going on I may have no cover. Ass-wise."

"Whale Tail" was Bab's supervisor, with the power to hire and fire, mostly fire, and Hermie knew that Babs was taking a large risk for him and more for "Kevin". But that's her way. The kids came first, last and always.

"Where are you and 'Kevin'?"

"Still at psychiatric. I stole his clothes --"

"What?!"

"Slowing down the getting him dressed to leave. I stuffed them in my purse. But --"

"I'm on my way. How can I get him outta there?"

"Simple. Arrest him. He witnessed a murder, n'cest pas?

"'Pas' all over the place -- because I'd need a warrant and at this hour, good luck. But not to worry."

"Love you to death, Hermie."

"You, too, Babs-Baby."

He dashed back into the stationette, startling Nell who was on her way out the door.

"Feeling creative?" asked Hermie with an impish grin.

Some time later, Roberta spun out of the stationette's parking lot with a squeal and a semblance of grace, and Hermie was off on his mission. It was going to be strange night. Hope Eleanor would cooperate.

He owed Babs a trip to Hawaii with the hubby and kids, because it was she who snuck the deeply sleeping "Kevin Costner" out of psychiatric and into Hermie's waiting arms. "Kevin's" sleep was so deep because Babs had slipped him a mild sedative to make him sleep that deeply. Good thing, because it wasn't until after midnight that Whale Tail stopped a rare show of efficiency and went on a coffee break with his toadies, so as soon as his back was turned . . . so to speak. Babs made a break for it, clutching 'Kevin'.

While he was waiting, Hermie made a phone call to the only people he trusted with this, but was surprised to get an answer machine at this late hour. He hadn't time to think about that just now.

"Whale Tail won't know it was you, will he?" asked Hermie of Babs as they strapped the sleeping "Kevin" into Roberta. He was worried some nasty retaliation would affect Babs' job.

"Do you have that arrest warrant?"

"Yeah. Sort of." Hermie pulled it out of his breast pocket.

Babs did a quick read, grinned. "You're so artistic, Hermie, dear."

"Will it work?"

"Oh, yeah, Whale Tail is not that hip when it comes to documents from the Prosecutor's office. He should be, but he isn't. Do not get me started. How did you get this letterhead?"

"I have a secretary who does my bidding. On occasion. She's aware of what the kid's been through, so she diddled her computer and came up with the fake Official. My Captain caught us, and woe-woe-woe, until she was told the purpose of this whole thing. But if it hits the fan, we gave her total —- and I mean *total*, like until we are all in unmarked graves — deniability."

"Good, good."

"That goes for you, too. You did not know nuthin', I broke into this premises and spirited the boy out and away. With my reputation, Whale Tail will buy that hook and sinker. Won't he?"

"He will. Don't sweat it. Where are you taking him?"

"First stop my house, where he can get a night's sleep. Then . . . well I know some people who will step up and do what it takes to shelter him, keep him safe. I'll call with the details when I have 'em. Okay?"

"Always okay. I better get lost." She kissed him on the cheek, he kissed her on the cheek, they both fell into a hug that betrayed how worried they were, and then Babs left for her car and Hermie got into Roberta, relieved to hear "Kevin" was snoring, a manly-man snore.

He drove to his house and tucked "Kevin" into his bed. He could tell the boy was awake by the time he carried him across the threshold of his bedroom, but the vacant stillness was still there on his face, deep in his eyes. The trembling was gone, however, for which Hermie was grateful, because he took that to mean the terror was down a notch.

While he tucked the boy's long, light bones inside Crazy Aunt Fern's flowery quilt, he talked to him: "I hope you can understand this. I didn't want to lose you in the system while you're — well, this way. I have to keep you safe. I need you. I need what you've got locked away inside your head. I know what you saw, I know what you heard, and I know that if you don't let that out, tell someone about it, you'll be this way till you're an old man like me. And I won't catch the sonuvabitch who did this. To you. To your Mom. To Hashemi. And to three other precious girls."

The boy's eyelids slowly sank down, tucking away the deep and empty blues. He made no move to indicate he'd heard the phone, but it startled Hermie and he leaped to grab it off the nightstand and pull the full length of its cord to get it into the hallway outside.

"Yes?" he whispered into the receiver.

Mrs. Harrison's voice was gracious with apology. "Oh, Lordy, we woke you up."

"No, no," Hermie whispered.

"But your phone message — you said call immediately. We were at the midnight movies, y'see, and — Aw, Jeez, it's past two!"

"Thank you so much for calling Mrs. Harrison. You can't know how much."

"What can we do for ya?"

"You know the case — cases I'm working on."

"Sure do. We see the news. Such an awful, awful thing. The parents . . . We *know* . . ."

Yeah, they knew. Which makes them the only ones who would completely understand, and know what to do. And so he told her how it all started with "Kevin Costner", a kid with no real name anyone could find who was there at the first stabbing, who'd witnessed the slaughter of his mother and his father figure, who'd run away to God knows where, and the terror had shut off his mind. He explained why he didn't want the kid's fragile mind to wake up in a foster care setting he, Hermie, couldn't control; in other words, strangers.

Because he needed what was locked in this damaged boy's mind in order to solve these horrible murders of innocent young women.

It was then that Millie and Frank Harrison were revealed to be saints upon the earth. "You bring him over in the morning, Detective," she said.

"In time for breakfast," Frank said, obviously listening in on an extension.

"Wait, wait! You're being – well, you're –" Hermie couldn't find the words, but felt obligated to add, "This kid is damaged to the max. I don't know what will happen, what he'll be like, when –- *if* -- he snaps out of this. He could be dangerous. Considering what he saw and heard, I wouldn't blame him if he was."

There was a silence on the phone. Hermie could hear them both breathing, could hear hands twisting phone receivers. It suddenly dawned on him that Millie and Frank Harrison were looking at each other, like they always did, exchanging thoughts without a word. Frank spoke first: "You bring that boy here. We'll keep him safe."

Millie added, "You got our word on it, Detective Grabfelder. We'll figure things out when the time comes. But he'll be safe with us, and we'll make sure he knows it."

Hermie's eyes stung as he spoke entirely inadequate words of thanks.

When he quietly re-entered his bedroom to replace the phone, Eleanor was just completing her inspection of the sleeping stranger in the familiar bed, whiskers waving as her pink nose took in his essence, exploring, evaluating.

Hermie pulled up Crazy Aunt Fern's vanity bench alongside the bed, realized it had no seat back to lean against, so he pulled it flush against the chest of drawers, sat and leaned back against the drawers and realized this was going to be a very uncomfortable night. But if he used the couch in the livingroom and the boy woke up alone in a strange room . . .

Eleanor made her normal gliding leap up as she attempted her usual sleeping place on his shoulder, but it was no go because he wasn't lying down like he should be. So, she turned and this time she did a flying leap from his shoulder to the bed, and delicately sought the shoulder of the sleeping boy. It was too thin, but it was against the pillow and thus would do in this pinch.

"Fickle," noted Hermie.

The next morning, he was glad the boy could walk, not only because he didn't have to carry him to and from the bathroom, but it would have undoubtedly caught the nosy radar of Maybelle Comstock if he emerged from his house carrying what would look like the body of a young boy. *Yeegods, what a yarn that would spin!*

The Harrison's front door opened before they had even reached the front steps. And out wafted the homey fragrances of bacon and cinnamon buns.

Hermie paused there on the stoop. "Mrs. Harrison, Mr. Harrison, uh, this is 'Kevin Costner'".

Both Harrisons raised eyebrows at the name.

"Seriously. Nobody knows why. Yet." Hermie answered their looks.

With a small shrug of acceptance, both of them looked at the boy with keen, evaluating eyes. Then Frank stepped forward and took his hand, like a father his son's. "Good morning, 'Kevin'. I'll bet you're dyin' for breakfast. Wait'll you taste the wife's cinnamon buns." And he led him into the house.

Hermie could see there was no resistance, no fear in the damaged boy. Merely that eerie, distant stillness.

Mrs. Harrison turned to Hermie, "Well, how about you? Breakfast is ready." And she wouldn't let him refuse, so he sat in a sunny kitchen and ate his fill of bacon and eggs, fresh squeezed orange juice, and allowed himself just one-half of a cinnamon bun with a cup of coffee. Then ate the other half, helpless.

All the while he watched Millie and Frank -- who were the still-grieving parents of an adored murdered son whose photographs festooned their home -- look after this silent boy, unobtrusively getting him to eat, drink. This silent boy who was not like their son at all, but who had what they did: *need.*

Later, Hermie drove away through glaring sunlight, knowing he'd done the right thing.

* * * *

Claire stopped by Nell's desk when she came in to the familiar vibrations on the floor. "He's pacing? Still? Or again?"

"Again. And probably my bad."

"You? Spill."

"I gave him an idea."

"With him, that's never a bad thing." Claire looked toward Hermie's office door with sympathy. "What was your idea?"

"It's Muslim perp, not a white guy."

"A Muslim man killing Muslim girls? Jeez! What's his motive?"

"All the victims were happy, all were not conforming to his version of Islamic rules, so they shouldn't have been happy, and all deserved to be punished for that."

Claire stared at her for a moment while her mind worked over it all. "It's too simple. Too Soap Opera. And thus more tragic. That's what bothers him. That and the fact you may be right on."

"What should I do?"

"Nothing. He'll do the doing."

Two days later, it began small; just a small red bouquet waiting in front of the door when Claire arrived before anyone else and discovered it. The card said, "Blessings", and nothing else. But because she could guess, she put it on Hermie's desk. When he came in and saw it, he claimed to not have a clue. *Lying like a rug*, Claire mused. Nell agreed. But both knew they'd have to wait him out, like always.

Then came more. And more. Flowers. None came from florists; they all looked like they had been picked from gardens and tied into bouquets: roses, tulips, carnations, petunias, or impatiens, all of them red, their stems tied together with red ribbon or red string or even red rubber bands. They would be tucked up against the front door, like the first, and most contained no cards, or just "Grabfelder" crudely printed on a label attached to the bound stems. Hermie assumed Nell and Claire were the ones who arranged them decoratively in makeshift vases and glasses placed on his desk. When that ran out of room, the tops of his filing cabinets soon became festooned. In addition to the bouquets, cards began arriving in the daily mail: *red* cards. Never a return address on their red envelopes, never a signature on the cards; but with a single sentence, sometimes in Arabic, sometimes in English hand printed with great care; always the same words: "Blessings upon you."

Of course, because the flowers and their bindings and the cards were all in red, Hermie knew up front what was going on. More than a few times he had to yank out a hanky and dab his eyes and nose, and whisper, "Ah, Amira . . . how you linger . . ."

Finally, Claire and Nell presented a united front, demanding to know what the hell was going on.

"Are you dating someone we don't know about?" Claire teased.

"You speak Arabic? Who knew?" Nell teased.

Both were kinda friendly but emphatically fishing, so Hermie knew he didn't have a chance. So he swore them to secrecy, even shut his door just in case, and told them about the secret glory of Muslim women. About Sunidhi's faithfulness, about Amira's mother and her genius and courage, about Shirin's dignity and determination, and about the love they inspired in so many. He didn't tell them about Aida, although he'd like to tell the whole world about that valiant lady and her even more valiant charges; but he held their trust.

"And all these flowers and cards?" Claire persisted.

For some reason in his heart of hearts, he didn't want to share his part in Amira's burial just yet. So, he told half of what had been going on: "Well . . . I'm told I'm the subject of a lot of gossip among the females in the Muslim community. This is a good thang, gals, because it gives me a lot of eyes and ears that I couldn't possibly reach on my own, so it will help get me information on these murders. The entire Muslim community, God bless 'em, is looking for that short, pious Shit and his dagger."

Claire could tell, because she knew him right down to the ground, that he was telling only half of it. She began to muse as to who she could call to ask for the whole poop. Shakey crossed her mind just as a sharp knock cracked on the office door, that made all three of them jump.

When Nell got up to go to the door, Hermie pulled out the desk drawer that contained his gun, just in case.

Nell barely opened the door when a small Arab woman who glowed with energy and purpose barged in, blue chador flapping around her. "Ah, Grabfelder, you are here," Yasmina said, seeing Hermie, "Please wait there." And as she swept out, she nodded to Claire and Nell, saying, "I beg your pardon, for both of us. But he commanded."

She was gone just long enough for Claire to say, "Who the hell —?" before Yasmina re-entered, stepping aside to allow the ancient, white-robed, white-bearded Imam Hermie recently met to enter Hermie's office. Hermie shot to his feet, stunned, and could only manage: "Imam, has something happened?"

The Imam's brilliant aqua eyes swept the office, took everything in, from the red flowers to the crime scene photos to the elephants' eyelashes, then he nodded to Claire and Nell.

Nell was so stunned she bent her knee in an almost curtsy. Claire managed, "Sir," respectfully.

Then the Imam focused on Hermie, tears coming into his eyes. And it came out like a prayer, "Amira. We are only now hearing." He came near enough to clap his ancient hands on both Hermie's shoulders, rose on tiptoe to loudly kiss both of Hermie's cheeks with gratitude and affection, saying: "Blessings, blessings without end. Dear, *dear* boy."

"Oh . . . there's n-n-no need . . . r-r-really," Hermie stammered.

The Imam patted his cheek, turned and nodded again to the two gaping women watching. "Such pretty company you keep. My apologies for interrupting your meeting." And he swept out.

Yasmina, clearly amused, took a last twinkling look back at Hermie when at the door, saying, "Just so you know, you've been given a free and certain pass to Paradise should the occasion arise," and she swept out.

Avoiding his emotions, Hermie played it for all it was worth, grandly walking back to his chair, wiping off invisible dust, sitting down in potentate pose. "What can I say? When ya got it, ya got it."

"What's going on?!" Nell managed to get out.

"Don't encourage him!" Claire snapped, mentally making a list of questions to ask Shakey. She went out of Hermie's office, Nell reluctantly knowing enough to follow her, wondering at the whiff of peppermint that lingered in the air.

Speaking of Shakey, he called Hermie later that day. The call was brief because Shakey was helplessly emotional, having heard about Amira's headstone and Lela's disappearance because Aristotle Theopolis had a cousin who had a Muslim wife, who told a friend who had gone to high school with Shakey and who had always kept in touch, Presbyterian though she was, so she told Shakey. There was an additional reaction when everyone talked about the red flowers descending, and then the capper of the revered Imam paying a kissing visit to Hermie's stationette. But now, all Shakey could get out was, "Thanks, Hermie. For Amira. For her Mom. For more . . . for so much."

Hermie tried to be gruff, "I'm not finished yet."

"I know. I'm just sayin'." And Shakey had to hang up before he started bawling.

Hermie said it aloud as he hung up the phone: "I still owe you all the sonuvabitch that took your wonderful daughters away from this needy world."

CHAPTER SEVENTEEN

"Undoubtedly a Somalian in the water supply."

W.C. Fields in *"My Little Chickadee"*

It was the *real* voice of Gordie on the phone this time, familiar and deep, no longer off-key with fear. "Herms, am I interrupting?"

Hermie paused within his new addiction on the computer, having made the mistake of 'just looking up something', and said, "Naw, I'm just browsing the Serengeti. Just got here from Italy. The Pope says 'hey'."

"What!?"

"I'm Googling. This is the absolute nuts -- you can tour anywhere in the world you wanna go. For free."

"Well, *duh!* Where ya been for the last bunch of years?"

"Fighting crime. S'up?"

"You got time for an early lunch?"

"Early, late, whatever." And then it occurred to him: "You got your second opinion."

"Yeah. Like to talk."

"Where, when."

Both of them had a hankering for the cholesterol hoo-hah of the giant omelettes at Five's, which was the second name change and management change and decor change of their favorite lunch stop in two years of the seesaw economy. Luckily, the view from their favorite window hadn't changed: A large, splashing fountain was across a side street, nestled in pink red, purple and white flowering bushes, and populated with the usual beach party: dozens of birds -- red headed Finches, brown and white Sparrows, intensely blue and gray and always screeching Scrub Jays, the whole gang chattering and twittering and splashing in a riot of flashing feathers. A couple whiter-than-white seagulls looked on in fascinated silence. Hermie and Gordie had

229

always enjoyed gazing out at this scene because it was so alive with color and movement and bird song it always lifted the burdens of a lousy day. Now, as they watched, Hermie couldn't help wondering how lousy today was going to be.

They chit-chatted while waiting to be served –- about the latest legal settlement against some patrol cops who screwed up big time, about the legal settlement some patrol cops won against civilians who screwed up big time, and the legal settlement some cops got because LAPD management screwed up, who should know better. And the usual snark about the no longer that new but still lamented police headquarters design, "Nice yard, hope the drought don't burn it up," Gordie remarked, "But why do I think of an ice cube tray whenever I see those windows?"

"Lotta natural light, at least, there's a first. But those sculptures –-?"

"Did you get a gander? That's 'art'? Jeez!"

"Reminds me of wads of licorice gum. Do they still make Blackjack gum? Ah, youth."

They both chuckled, and were saved from eye contact when a sweet-faced Asian waitress slipped up in a waft of a pleasantly powdery scent. "Hi, gentlemen, you look at the menu?" She was somewhat taken aback by this looming pair: the towering black cop in full uniform and dimples, the large white guy in a neat suit and blazing eyes. Those eyes twinkled as he said, "We've decided to go straight to hell: We'll both have the loaded omelettes, stuffed with everything you got, and home fries, and cornbread. Orange juice on the rocks and then coffee. Black. Strong. In a dirty cup. With a spider in it."

It was a relief to hear Gordie's laugh at the familiar jest, which let the waitress know it was a joke, and she delicately laughed, too, relaxing because she now knew these guys would be easy. "Coming up, right. I bring first your O.J."

And so they had another excuse for small talk while they waited for the interruption of O.J. delivery.

Gordie kept up the small talk, "I know it's been a while, but isn't it kinda odd that nobody misses the former Chief? He got things done, I'll say that for him. A lot of dead wood out from behind desks and onto the streets."

Hermie nodded, "Crime went down, retirement went up. He hollered, but he didn't interfere. Me, I mean. That was refreshing."

"Would he have *dared*? You know how you are."

"He was from New Yawk."

"Oh, yeah. He would have dared alright. At least he was replaced with Family. Although they didn't break up the set: middle aged white guy."

Hermie thought better of relating his latest confab with the present Chief, since it was same-old, same-old as far as his relationships with Chiefs went. "Sorry. We'll just have to wait for Claire's turn."

"Think she'll make it?"

"As sure as God made little green apples. Who'd-a thought? Especially since she really wants the job. She's even got 'plans', gawd help her. Even for *you.*"

"Me? What about me?"

"Later. Worth the wait. She's a dusky holy terror and she scares the boxers off'n me at least twice a week. Keeps me within the lines. Have no doubt a-t'all that when she becomes Chief she'll shake up the LAPD like it's never been shaken. Shook. Shacked."

The orange juice arrived in ice-tinkling large glasses. They thanked the waitress kindly, she left, they raised their glasses in salute and slugged some down, both going "Ahh" . . . and "Ooh" with shivering pleasure.

"Still fresh squeezed," said Hermie, appreciably.

"How can you tell? Tastes like Tropicana to me."

"Peasant. Once you taste fresh squeezed, you know it."

"I am filled with admiration that you know all this important crap."

Tension snuck in. Hermie's clenched gut resisted the pleasant down-flow of cold, tangy-sweet orange juice. He had to know or he'd puke. "So?" he asked, pointedly.

"Dr. Homer Nielsen, office near City of Hope. That's who I saw. Would you believe his staff calls him 'Homie'? He's a specialist in prostate stuff. That's why he's who I saw. He went over all the tests. Took some of his own x-rays, blood and stuff. *Lots* of tests. Laid out all the options –- surgery, all kinds, seeds –-"

"'Seeds'?" Hermie hadda ask.

"Radioactive seeds they stuff into the tumor, to kill it over time."

"Oh. Seeds." said Hermie, baffled.

"Then all the side effects of each treatment. I was right about all that. Mostly."

"'Mostly'?"

"Well, he does *all* the latest procedures. Depends on the size of the tumor, position, age of the patient, family history, whether the cancer has spread already, or will soon, or will eventually . . . it's all considered, y'see."

"Good. You got the full picture, then."

"I'll say. Whew!" Gordie gulped some juice, looking almost embarrassed –- an absolute First since Hermie had known him.

"And?" He couldn't be afraid to ask, he had to know. He splashed some more orange juice down onto the tense spot inside his gut.

"Well, he recommends cryosurgery."

"'Cryosurgery'?" The word 'surgery' was the only thing relevant, but: *What the hell's 'cryo' mean?*

"Yeah. He goes in and freezes the tumor with a chemical. It kills the tumor, it shrinks to nothing, and he claims it spares the nerves and veins all around, so side effects are pretty rare."

"'Pretty rare'."

"According to his experience with tumors the size of mine — which he says is not to worry. Yet. Once the tumor dies, it shrinks down to nothing, 'things' pretty much go back to normal. Function-wise. Ya may need a blue pill now and then later on, but chances are the best that you're not going to pee in your pants."

"Which is something to be desired. So to speak."

"Hell, yes."

"Sounds good."

Gordie shrugged. "Yeah. Pretty much."

They both sipped more juice, avoiding each other's eyes.

Ice tinkled pleasantly before Hermie broke the silence between them. "'Cryosurgery'. He goes in and *freezes* it."

"Yeah. Amazing, huh?"

Hermie nodded.

Later, Hermie couldn't even remember why he said it. It just came out, unbidden. Probably a reaction to being so relieved to have a hopeful answer. The terror of the word 'cancer' had suddenly been removed by a hopeful answer. That was it, the *relief* came out, unbidden: "Gee," he said, "kinda gives the term 'blue balls' a whole 'nother meaning, don't it?"

Their eyes met and suddenly chuckles became guffaws of hysterical relief, and people started to stare, so they began to shush each other with their napkins, but that only made things worse; so both of them leaped out of their banquette benches simultaneously and made a dash for the door, nearly colliding with the tiny waitress whose arms were laden with a tray containing their steaming plates.

"We'll be right back, Miss, honest t'god!" Gordie choked at her, and out the door they went.

To the large oak tree that framed the ceiling-to-floor restaurant windows, where they were in full view of most of the diners and waitresses and cooks. Even the dishwashers peeked out to find the source of the hullabaloo, and for once language was no barrier. A couple diners whipped out cell phones and took pictures, as *everybody* watched a towering black man in a cop's uniform bounce off a boulder of a white guy in a nice suit as they both laughed hysterically like they couldn't stop. Hands wiped tears, then hankies were unfurled to take up the slack.

Right in the middle of things, the black cop's laughing face suddenly crumbled as he began to cry, the white man immediately grabbed him in a reassuring, manly-man hug, both clapping each other on their backs. A chorus of "Awww . . ." went up inside the restaurant as an incorrect conclusion was leaped upon. Then they separated and began laughing again, the tree trunk was pounded and hung upon, until they at last ran out of breath. They pointed at each other, shook fingers and heads at each other in a mild scold. After a last clean up of faces and noses, hankies were neatly folded and tucked away, then the hulking duo were panting a little as they walked back into the restaurant to their banquette and table, where their food was waiting, steaming considerably less. They ignored the room full of smiling faces and the smattering of applause.

They tucked into the food with gusto, their good spirits now hungry. And that would have been the quiet end of things if only the hesitant waitress hadn't come up to their table moments later and said, cheerily, "Would gentlemen like desert? Today special is blueberry pie."

This time they merely toppled to a sideways sprawl on their banquettes, strangling with laughter.

Later on, the tip they gave her was very large and needed no explanation. And when they stumbled past and out they left more than a few smiles of strangers in their wake.

* * * *

"You did *WHAT?!*"

Painful past experiences reminded him to tell Claire *ALL* right now -- a little late, but what can you do? -- since his actions affected her reputation and in this case might be -- *was* -- illegal. Kidnaping and all.

"Now, this isn't like the other times --" he protested.

"You got that right! This could get you arrested for *KIDNAPING*, you *ASS!*

"Kidnaping? From who? Whom? His mother's dead, his 'father' is dead, we don't know who he is or if he's got kin --"

"You snuck him out of Psychiatric in the middle of the night! You took him out of official custody!"

"Well. There is that."

"*Who* helped?"

"Not if you stuck hot coals in my shorts."

"That thought makes my mouth water! *Where* is he?"

"Not if you stuck hot coals --"

"You didn't leave him alone at your place!"

"Of course not! I'd never leave him alone anywhere."

"THEN WHERE THE HELL IS HE?!"

"Not if -- you know -- coals. Hot."

She collapsed into her chair with a sigh of exasperation, "Jeezus H., Grabfelder. Can I ask *why* and get a straight answer?"

"Absolutely. He saw his mother get killed."

"How do you know that? He's catatonic, you said."

"Andy Cho Hui. Forensics at scene. Later, the DNA of the blood all over his clothes -- it matched Lila Miller's. Mother, son."

"Maybe *he* killed her. Did you ever think of that?"

"Never."

"Why the hell not?"

"Banana Bubblegum. Remember? I told ya."

She gaped at him, speechless.

"Okay, okay, here's the whole story -- well, most of it. The relevant part anyway. I met this kid through Hank O'Dell at Computer Whammy. Remember when Hank did some computer work for me, back in the day, that little ole serial killer thang?"

She still gaped at him.

"Well, that's when I first met this kid. Calls himself "Kevin Costner" -- gawd knows why -- he'd turned up at a youth center in Gardena where Hank volunteered. Hank had more than a couple uniforms search and he did computer searches up the whazoo, but nobody could find out where he came from or who he really was."

"He wasn't in the system? At his age?"

"Exactly!"

Look at the sonuvabitch, Hermie now all eager, relieved, lighting up like a Christmas morning when he thinks he's got me going down the garden patch. Path.

"Banana Bubblegum. Anytime soon," she glared.

"That kid chews Banana Bubblegum all the time, a big wad of aqua-colored gum. Nuts."

"Nuts. In the gum?"

"No, no. Lila Miller had a Banana Bubblegum kiss on her cheek. I smelled it. Pierre confirmed it. And there were track shoe prints at the murder scene -- Andy said they were from 'Flyaway' shoes the kids are crazy about, currently. Do you know how much those things *cost*? Well, anyway, later, when "Kevin" was picked up, all bloody and catatonic, I went to see him in Juvie. And he wreaked of Banana Bubblegum. Two plus two, evidence-wise. And Lila's neighbor lady -- condo president Pepsi Potter -- by the way, isn't *that* a hoot? –- said a young teenaged boy used to stay with Lila, regular. A white kid with a hip-hop walk." He made a couple of bopping moves to illustrate. "'Kevin' was obsessed with black culture. Talked more rap than –- well, you probably know who the latest rapper is. No offense. I found used Flyaways in "Kevin's" closet in Lila's condo. When he was picked up he was wearing new ones, bloody. I always meant to introduce him to Gordie as a reality check. I should still do that, now that I think of it. 'Course I'll have to wait till Gordie has the surgery and makes up with Sharon and until 'Kevin' comes out of his mental space, well, who the hell knows how long that will be . . ."

"GRABFELDER!"

Hermie jumped out of his musing. "What the hell?! *WHAT?!*"

"One: What surgery? And he broke up with Sharon?! When? Why?!"

"Aw, Jeez!"

"You've been sworn to secrecy?"

"Yes. Thanks for understan--"

"To hell with understanding! You spill it right now! Or, I swear, HOT COALS! RIGHT UP YOUR PENSION!"

And so he told her about the cancer and the cryosurgery to come —- at this moment he did not think she'd appreciate the "blue balls" reference, since she had not yet discovered his and Gordie's new viral fame and all, *Pray to all the gods she stayed too busy to see that!*, so he didn't make the reference. And he also told how Gordie dropped Sharon, asshole that he is, because he was afraid.

"I'll say he's an asshole. What was he thinking?!"

"He's a guy."

"That's no excuse. How's Sharon doing?"

"I had a long talk with her --"

"Oh, CA-RAP!"

"No, no, I was good. Helpful. She knows something's going on –- she assumed it's his health, she's a woman, she's psychic –- so she knows patience and time will tell. Once he has the surgery, I'll be whomping him upside de haid till he calls her and begs –- *BEGS!*-- to be understood. Forgiven is asking wa-ay too much."

"You got that right. *MEN!*"

"True. I am not insulted."

"You haven't distracted me from the issue: *THE BOY?*"

"He'll be absolutely safe and sound, and he'll *know* it, so whatever terror is locked in his mind will lose its power over him and he'll be able to let it out. Hopefully."

"'Hopefully'. Dr. Phil you ain't. Why did you take him away from psychiatric help in a mental facility, since they know how to deal with this kind of thing?"

"Strangers. He's spent his life hiding from strangers. He and his Mom, and then them and Hashemi. More strangers maybe drugging him? I'll think about that as a last resort. Not now. Not yet."

"In the meantime?"

"No one in Social Services or Juvie will squeal. Paperwork has vanished –- no doubt put in the files where no one will look."

"It's all on computer now, you *ASS*!"

"Hell. Well, I have it on a promise that nobody will know nuthin' until 'Kevin' is ready."

"In the other meantime?"

"Oh, that. I'm still looking for an Arab man who's got a particular kind of dagger that was invented in the Eleventh Century, honest t'god, and who can't deal with young women being on their own, out of the house, out of male control . . . and . . . How old was Lila?"

"Lila?

"Vic Number One. Young-forties, maybe. But all the others were hardly in their twenties. It doesn't match. Goddammit to hell and *HELL!*"

His sigh of frustration moved Claire to lowering *ALL* the booms so he wouldn't be blindsided later. "Tommy Velasco from the LA Times called."

"Oh, CRAP-SHIT!"

"You know this case is primo juicy."

"Beside the point. If he does –-"

"He's doing. Coming in Sunday's edition in the California Section. Bios on all the vics and their families and the racism angle -– white supremacist taking down Muslims.

"*Good!*"

"Huh?"

"It's all *wrong*. Which means he won't spook the Perp."

"S'plain."

"Racism has nothing to do with it. Well, only incidentally, since it could be a Shiite perp and he thinks these girls are Sunni, but I doubt that. These girls were out and about and successful, that's what's bugging this asshole. Nell's theory is they were happy even though they were living outside of strict Islam, so they deserved to be punished, and he's just the little shit to do it."

"Oh, Nell's theory?"

"She told you, huh? It's starting to get to me. Farsadi, one of the vics' father was a prime candidate -– tried to marry off his daughter for financial gain when she was just eleven, and she was going to school with boys in the same room. He once tried to drag her outta class. But that Imam and a Muslim lady I spoke to convinced me Farsadi didn't have the guts. And he would have had to go through her mother to get to her. Battered wife though she was, she'd have killed him first to defend her daughter. Amazing woman. One of many I've met on this case."

"Quit tangenting! How the hell are you going to track down this monster? You don't travel in Muslim circles, last I checked. Thanks be to Allah all over the place, you didn't piss off that Imam. How the hell you managed that, I don't --"

"My dear, you forget my innermost charm."

He's twinkling again, a ploy to make me forget the main issue here. She resisted him. "Tell me before your charm makes me puke."

"All those flowers, cards? I gotta Muslim network with ears to the ground: gossiping Muslim ladies who know everything going on in their neighborhoods, that Imam and his clergy friends, plus a Middle Eastern pawnbroker, a secret network of Muslim women who rescue battered wives, not to mention that teeny-tiny gal who crashed into our office towing the Imam -- she wants to be the first female Imam in the USA, and *nobody* would put it past her. So . . . *lots* of ears to the ground."

"What good --?"

"They've turned L.A. County into a village of gossiping spies. Everyone looking for a short Muslim guy, a pious fanatic who's got the time and temper to stalk innocent, ambitious Muslim girls."

And they all know about you, she thought, *they know they can trust you, count on you, in spite of your scary eyes and bad temper and silly name, 'Grabfelder'. They know you will catch this sonuvabitch, you will catch him and stop him or die trying. Like nearly once before.*

"You're staring," he said, pointedly. "We haven't decided who won the argument here."

"You know if this gets out, about the boy, there are other people who'll lose their jobs besides you."

"They've all volunteered. And this won't get out. For once, the system is working to our advantage: everyone's too busy, too understaffed, too underpaid to follow up."

"People -- even *good* people -- talk for money. Giving the Times a call and dangling the 'real' story, for a price: 'We're hiding "Kevin Costner" at our house, come on over and take our pictures and bring a check'."

"Not these people."

"How can you be sure?"

"I caught the asshole that murdered their son."

In a flash, Claire got it all: "Kevin Costner" was being hidden by one of the parents who lost their son to the south bay serial killer that Hermie put a stop to. "Ya could-a told me that beforehand, Bozo, spared me from pissed off phone calls and sundry stomach pains."

"You've got pains — your stomach?" In an instant he was worried and showing it.

"Figure-a speech. You frequently make me puke, you and your winsome ways with officialdom."

On impulse, his face still worried, he shot out of the chair and wrapped her up in a warm, firm hug, then abruptly turned to leave.

"Wait! WHERE THE HELL ARE YOU GOING?!

"Can't you hear my phone ring?"

"No! Can you?"

"It must be ringing. It always is. Ah, my fans. You know."

And he looked back over his shoulder and grinned and winked at her through a glitter of tears, then he was gone.

Claire sniffed, blinked, searched, grabbed up a tissue from her desk dispenser. "Honest t'God, that white guy never fails to get to me. Sneaky sonuvabitch!"

CHAPTER EIGHTEEN

"When you come to the end of your rope, tie a knot and hang on."

Franklin Delano Roosevelt

Hermie fired up Roberta, and then grabbed his cell phone and dialed while her points warmed up.

"'Allo, 'erman. Yet again." Pierre answered.

"Yeah-yeah. First, thanks for all your help for Amira Farsadi. It was appreciated by so many people."

"Eet was my pleasaire. Eet was my honor. I saw ze newspapaire. I am glad she was zat loved in her brief life."

"Yeah. I hope she knew. Uh, listen —-"

"It is most unfortunate zat I have just opened ze chest of a Mr. Franklin. Four of ze bullets went past ze rib cage. Ze gangs in Long Beach are becoming much bettair shots."

"Lots of practice. Same time? Same place?"

"Ah, mon ami, I look forward."

"I got a lot to tell ya. And ask."

"I await." And Pierre hung up.

At the "usual" time and place, inspired by his 'fishy' reminiscences with Sam Ordway, Hermie and Pierre were each serenely enjoying a large, fleshy trout, glistening with butter, fragrant with lemon and garlic, nestled on a plate of brilliant greens and vibrant orange discs: fresh spinach and sliced carrots, also gleaming with the trouts' butter, lemon and garlic. It had all been preceded by the usual dark and sweet onion consomme, and a salad that had the surprise of chunks of apple and slices of almond here and there in the olive oil and wine vinegar drizzle.

Hermie knew the trout was farm-raised, being as wild trout was now scarce. Uncle Benny would be appalled. Fortified by cold amber bottles of Schlitz beer, Hermie's long-gone Uncle Benny taught all the young, raucous cousins to fish for trout, speckled bass, and especially perch back in the day in Michigan. But even before the trout and bass got scarce, and the perch shrank to half their usual size and damn near disappeared, all of the cousins had fled the Michigan winters at the first job-related opportunity. So-well-remembered Uncle Benny didn't make it out.

Pierre was fascinated by the skill and delicacy Hermie showed in perfectly de-boning the trout while eating. Pierre thought: *Zis ees anozer secret about zis man — he grew up a fisherman. Formidable!*

It wasn't until dessert that Hermie felt a twinge of guilt: *God damn, when's the last time I got in touch? Called Auntie Irenie back at the old homestead? She'd be up-to-date on everyone, aunties, uncles, all the cousins. Wonder how her farm is doin'. . .*

Dessert was a bowl of the first cherries of the year reminding Hermie to stock up the next time he swung by Ralph's. *Haven't seen Jasmine and Carmine in over a month, either. The cherries will bring all three of us 'round, that's sure.* And another memory floated in: Climbing Grandpa Grabfelder's cherry tree in his backyard behind the garage, to pluck the giant, dark ruby cherries warmed by the sun or cooled by the brisk breeze, depending on what side of the tree you happened to be plucking.

These cherries were nearly as large and glowing as memory, topping a shallow bowl of made-from-scratch and icy whipped cream. The cherries retained their stems and pits, as God intended, and which enabled them to swirl them in cream by the stem, and eat carefully around the pits, said pits delicately deposited onto a silver spoon and then into a silver bowl.

He does not spit ze pits. Ah . . . zere is a Frenchman wiz-in zis man! Or ze memory of a very good Mammon.

Hermie was down to the last spoonful of whipped cream before he broke the spell: "I gotta ask you another favor."

"I am here. Yet again."

"Lila Miller. Is she still on ice? No disrespect."

You are not capable of disrespect, mon Ami, Pierre thought and smiled, "Oui, she is indeed. No one has come for her, which is unfortunate, because ze FBI has not sent paperwork zat could release her. Neizer has ze LAPD, no?"

"No. Is it do-able to keep her there for a while?"

"Depends upon why zis must be done."

And Hermie told him the entire saga of Lila Miller, FBI Agent, real name Ashwari Begum, and her son "Kevin Costner", real name who-the-hell-knows, witness, catatonic, runaway, kidnaped, hidden away and cared for, but still deeply silent and terrified.

Pierre was riveted by the long story, breaking in on several occasions only to mutter, "Mon Dieu!" in shock.

Hermie finished up: "So you see, the same asswi–– uh, the same monster slaughtered all these women and "Kevin" may have seen him do the first –– his own mother. I need him, but I can't get at him until his mind comes out of this terror. Until then, I don't want to take his mother away from him a second time –– I don't want her buried without his participating, without a proper goodbye for him."

"I understand. I will arrange."

"Arrange what?"

"She must be embalmed, dressed, her dignity restored. I will arrange."

"I will pay all the costs. Done it recently, in fact."

"Zat is known. After she is restored, zey will send her back to me, for ze storage. I will make a place for her to wait for her son to come."

"It won't cause problems? Bureaucracy-wise?"

"Zere would have to be ze people in ze bureaucracy – zey are almost as short-handed as ze rest of us. You read?"

"Yeah. It gave me a new appreciation for the crap you put up with."

"Merci. So, it will be done, wiz necessary excuses should zey be necessary: ze paperwork is 'late'; sometimes ze paperwork is 'misplaced' by absent personnel. Ze 'bureaucracy', as you say, does not have ze people to come down to make an inspection of ze dead or ze waiting."

"Andy Cho Hui, in Forensics, will back you up if needed: 'Let that lady alone till I finish my tests', yada-yadoo.' All you have-ta do is call him and say it's for me."

"Ah, oui, yada-yadoo."

That said with a delicate French accent made Hermie chuckle. Then he remembered the other thing: "Who buried Jordan Hashemi?"

"Ah, zat is a mystery. Your call today was well-timed –– I was about to inform you."

"Be damned –– he's still there, too?"

"Ah, oui. But zat is ze mystery of which I speak. An Unknown came wiz all ze right forms, and a hearse wiz no name."

"An 'unknown' A 'hearse with no name'? Hasn't that been set to music somewhere, sometime?"

"Pardon?"

"Skip it. A hearse?

"Eet was ze funeral home-type conveyance, but zere was no name on ze doors. Ze Unknown was ze driver, a very large man in ze uniform of a chauffeur. It did not look like ze uniform of ze driver of a conveyance for ze funeral home."

"'Conveyance'?"

"Ze automobile. Ze hearse."

"License plate?"

"Ah, who looks? Ze papers were in order to release. How-evaire . . ."

"'How-yadoo'?"

"Zey were fake. Forgeries. Very good ones, but zey were not ze proper."

"How did you know?"

"Ze paper. It was not ze correct paper. And ze type-print, not correct as well. So obvious."

Hermie stared at him in awe. "You knew it was fake because of 'ze paper'? And 'ze type'? Not the forms?"

"Ah, oui. How many years have I seen ze forms? I know of zem. I told monsieur zat Monsieur Hashemi will not be released wizout proper forms. Not zese forgeries. He was not affable. Merde! Zere were threats to sue. But he left after much fuss. I wondaire what happens to him when he tells his boss he could not follow orders."

"I'd rather know who the hell his boss is! Who would come for Hashemi? And why? What good is his body?" Hermie stopped, "Uh-oh."

"Do not be alarmed. I, too, thought of zat after zis incident. So I did ze x-ray of Monsieur Hashemi, head to toe and wiz great care. Zere is noz'ing hidden wiz-in his body. For certain."

"Ya read my mind, as always. But *who*? *Why*?" Hermie nearly got lost in thought until Pierre read him again.

"I will embalm, dress and tuck away him along wiz ze Madame Miller."

"Come to think of it, we should do that, regardless. They were a couple. They were "Kevin's" 'parents'. They should be buried together. By him, when he's ready."

"Ah, oui, now zat you have told me about him, I agree. Zey will be kept togethaire. Till he comes for zem."

It was only later that Andy shouted over the phone: "WHAT?!"

"I'm just double-checking on an attempted fraud, body-snatching, that kinda thing. You *didn't* okay Hashemi's release, forensics-wise?" Hermie asked.

"Without telling *you*? I want to *live*! Have kids someday! I'd *never* release one of your bodies without telling you. Or asking you."

"Then who the Sam Hill tried to steal Jordan Hashemi?!"

Andy came back with: "Next word from our sponsor: the black Jag was hit from behind by a Rolls Royce."

"A *what*?!"

"What. Glass pieces traced. Headlight from a Rolls Royce Phantom."

Hermie's sarcasm salted his rage: "A 'Phantom'! No damn kidding!"

* * * *

He first stopped at a 7-11 and made a very small purchase. When the clerk gave him the eye, Hermie cracked: "Trying to give up smoking." To which the clerk replied, trying to be helpful, "We do have nicotine gum, y'know."

"Don't want to give it up that bad."

The Harrisons didn't mind at all that Hermie wanted to visit in the early evening, after "supper", the Midwesterners still called it. And being Midwesterners, they had a porch swing, only it was on the back porch instead of the front, because the front didn't have a porch, in keeping with Los Angeles' architectural dictates, porches being considered old-fashioned back in the day when this house was nicely built. No idea why it was thought normal to have a garage door taking up a third of the front of the houses back in that day and to this day, but they digress.

The Harrisons had told him that they had at first walked "Kevin" to the back porch swing after suppers, sat him there, and one of them would sit alongside, one toe moving the swing back and forth slowly, while they watched the day close down to twilight, then darkness. Both Harrisons took turns and made small talk while sitting with "Kevin", pointing out the names of birds, or what had just bloomed. "Kevin" made no sign he heard, but he was much more relaxed now than he was when he first came to them.

At first, the darkness falling had made "Kevin" uneasy. But they held his hand, kept talking, calling his attention to the night sounds: the rustle of leaves, a male hoot owl hopefully calling out suggestions to non-existent females; the march of the bright moon or stars through the indigo sky and sometimes through wisps of fog or mysterious cloud formations; and the fragrances of Night-blooming Jasmine and roses and hyacinths and Sweet Peas that nestled in the small garden that was now Mrs. Harrison's pride and joy; it had been their late son's.

Their last report had been that "Kevin" was eating well, no longer needing to be prompted, but the screams of his nightmares were still frequent. Each time, the Harrisons would both come alongside his bed, hold his hands and gently wake him. Once woken, he did not dream again for the rest of the night, or a night or two or three to come.

Now, Hermie found "Kevin Costner" alone on the porch swing, his own toes moving the swing slowly back and forth in a short arc. He stepped into

"Kevin's" line of vision, was pleased to see the swing stop, but "Kevin" did not look up at him.

He's aware. But he's still "not seeing", Hermie thought. Then carried on: "You may not remember me, "Kevin". I'm Grabfelder. The detective? We've met a couple times, thanks to Hank O'Dell. O'Dell says 'Hey', by the way, he'll be glad to hear you're doing better. I'm going to sit down beside you. It's been a long day, my feet are telling me."

He slowly came 'round and sat on the swing, not too near. The swing creaked loudly with his weight. "Hell, all these pounds lost and it doesn't count?"

To his astonishment, "Kevin" turned his head as though to look at him, but he stared, uncomprehending, as though he was trying to will the sight of him into his brain. But it was no use, and a profound look of sorrow darkened his eyes before he looked away.

Hermie's toe moved the swing back and forth slightly. "I know. You're still trapped. Still scared. You don't have to see me. Just *listen.* Nothing like a porch swing to make you feel better. We had one back in Bay City, Michigan. Hell, 'most *everybody* had a porch swing. Kinda stupid when ya think of the mosquitoes. Big as bumblebees they were. But until they got really nasty, the porch swing was like this. Peaceful. Like being rocked by Mom or Grandma when we were little." He moved the swing, sat back and sighed. "I came to see you tonight because you're doing better. The Harrison's can tell, and now so can I. So you might be able to understand this: I know what you saw. I know what you heard. You wanted to stop it, but you didn't know how. And it was too fast, too awful. It was not your fault. It was not your Mom's fault. Or even Hashemi's. I'm going to get him, Kevin. If it's the last thing I do, I'm going to get that guy. 'Swear."

Suddenly "Kevin" shook, shook from deep within then outward, Hermie actually heard his teeth knock, the swing rattled. Hermie quickly wrapped an arm around "Kevin", noticed he was not as thin as he once was, but had not the time to reflect on it; instead he pulled the chilled, shaking boy in an embrace he desperately hoped would warm him. He suddenly heard "Kevin" start to gasp as if struggling to speak. "Let it out, "Kevin". It won't hurt you if you let it out. You're safe here. No matter what. *Safe.*"

To his astonishment, he heard sounds coming from "Kevin's" throat. Sounds that were like an eruption from deep within, not quite a voice, but a pain-filled gasp, one that Hermie heard clearly: "Dad tried," 'Kevin' gasped. "Dad lost." And then he went limp and silent, his eyes shut as though he'd suffered a blow that knocked him out.

Hermie stood, gathered up the long arms and legs and held him close. When he carried him into the Harrisons' kitchen, both of them were waiting there and clearly panicked at the sight of them.

"No-no," Hermie assured them. "He's all right. He's gone away again. But he was *here*, and he'll be back."

While the Harrison's hovered, he carried "Kevin Costner" to his tidy bed and laid him down gently.

"Are ya sure? How do ya know?" asked Mr. Harrison, all his worry evident, as it was on Mrs. Harrison's face, who was gently removing "Kevin's" shoes, revealing immaculate white socks.

He caught both their gazes as he said, "He talked. It was only four words. But he *talked*."

The relief of the Harrisons nearly buckled their knees. Both of them whispered happily, "He talked!"

Before Hermie left the room, he handed it to Mrs. Harrison. "When he wakes up, give him these."

"What is it?" she asked, turning it over in her hand.

"Banana bubblegum," he said, smiling with his own relief.

Later, while he let Roberta drift down sleepy streets, his mind replayed: *"Dad tried. Dad lost." What did he try? When? "Dad lost." No need to guess what that meant. Dad got slaughtered. Why? What or who the hell made him get outta that car? CA-RAP!!*

CHAPTER NINETEEN

"If you're not too long, I'll wait here for you all of my life.""

Oscar Wilde

He was checking the pockets of a jacket prior to taking it to the cleaners when he found it: the list of pubs and eateries Andy Cho Hui had given him at the first crime scene. A list of places that might be the source of the sawdust trapped in Lila Miller's exquisite shoes. He scanned the list while remembering that Pierre had said both Lila and Hashemi's last meal was Italian with "ze incorrect olive oil." And there it was: Poco Pasesano's.

It was in the "betweens" of the afternoon — between lunch and dinner — when Roberta smoked her way into an annoying parking lot. Annoying first because the small entrance could easily be missed unless cars slowed to a crawl or unless this was your favorite place. The small driveway was a sharp turn off the street then snaked past the building and past a small shed the size of a garage. The shed was faded stucco but the door was new and metallic, with a hint of electronics along the top. The driveway then made a small circle around to the parking lot in the back of the restaurant. Said lot was the uber annoyance: entirely too small for a popular restaurant, too-few spaces and lanes, all sized before the invasion of the SUV, RV and other behemoths. But along the street in front Hermie had noticed there was a bunch of what was probably the last un-metered (which meant 'free') curbside parking spaces in L.A., so there was somewhat of a light in the annoyance. Hermie wondered if the atmosphere and food were worth putting up with all this aggravation.

The restaurant itself was obviously a former Chinese restaurant — the red tile roof turned up at all points and edges. Wooden and a-bloom flower boxes and a glimpse of lace curtains changed the aspect nicely. But Hermie noticed that the windows were fake — there was no looking out or looking in.

It was well worth the aggravation.

First off, Sinatra was softly crooning, *"If You Are But a Dream"* from hidden speakers all around. That alone gave Hermie a pleasant pause as he came into the place and took it all in. "Comfortable" was the word. A corner fireplace glowed, the tables were graced with pale yellow linen and the kind of chairs that had enough ruby red padding that made for relaxing, lingering. Small yellow or red candles glowed within etched glass at each table, alongside a large yellow rose inside a tall crystal vase; another vase held a bouquet of breadsticks. The wooden floor creaked pleasantly beneath a generous dusting of gently fragrant sawdust. *Fresh sawdust,* Hermie realized. *Jeez, do they change the sawdust every day? This place is somebody's dream.* Hermie could also smell bread baking, tomato sauce bubbling and cheese melting. *'Incorrect olive oil', what the hell!*

At this hour, only two tables against opposite walls were occupied with a couple at each, both undoubtedly "in between' liaisons because of the way the men and women leaned in close to talk softly into each other's gaze. Hermie's imagination instantly flashed on: Mother's Day, the sight of Hashemi and Lila leaning in close over a nosegay of violets, while "Kevin" looked on and teased them or occupied himself with the breadsticks.

The floorboards creaked pleasantly behind him and Hermie turned to see a somewhat round man approaching, his round belly preceding him, his broad smile lifting round cheeks, his large round eyes very dark, very direct and kind. "Ah! Someone new." he said affably, Italian lilting the English. "A little early for the bread, but not too. The fires we can poke."

Ah, the owner, Hermie surmised, *so he'll know everything about everybody.* Hermie was startled to smell cigarette smoke coming off him, interfering with the delicious smells everywhere else. He pulled out his badge and checked to make sure: "Hi, Detective Grabfelder. I'm here on a case, actually. You the owner?"

The man patted his belly, "What you think?

Hermie chuckled, instantly liking this guy. "Well, it does smell irresistible in here. The music got me, too. Been a long time since Frank."

The man suddenly got serious. "You are the Grabfelder? You have the stabbing murder cases?"

"Yeah, I have that nightmare."

The man's plump hands flew up, "I am guilty!"

"Huh?"

Now his hands pumped Hermie's right hand, insistently, "I was going to call, but I had a plumbing problem you will not believe. Water everywhere but in the sinks, and the mafia plumbers saying the whole system is dying of old age and must be ripped out and replaced. No toilets for the week! Thousands of cost!"

"I'm sorry."

"No-no, *I* am sorry. You are here because of Mr. Hashemi and his lady, yes?"

"Yes. You knew them well?"

"Come-come, we go outside."

He led Hermie through a gleaming kitchen where four young men of varied ethnicity, dressed in immaculate cook's aprons and hats, attended steaming pots and hot ovens for three stoves. The Italian fragrances were now joined by the smells of sweet cookies baking, and something else in rich chocolate. Hermie felt his stomach nudge him with longing.

A small door led outside to a leafy nook blocking the view of the parking lot. Two white plastic chairs circled a small, round plastic table, atop which was a large glass ashtray half-filled with butts. The man rummaged in pockets and brought out a pack of cigarettes and a worn silver lighter. "Pardone-a-me, I am addicted. The wife threatens divorce and alimony, so I am down to only four a day. Unless disaster strikes."

"Like exploding plumbing."

"Ah! You understand!" The man lit up, dragged and inhaled with pleasure. "There. Now I can *think*! I am Roberto Musso. I was born Roberto Mussolini, no relation, but you can understand —" an Italian-style shrug that spoke volumes.

Hermie couldn't help chuckling out loud. "Perfectly. I still get ideas about shaving 'Grabfelder'. So, you have something to tell me?"

Robert Musso's face lost a great deal of its affable roundness as he suddenly got serious, close to tears. "I could not believe what I read and hear. Such violence on such gentle people. Their boy? Was he hurt? The news did not say about him."

"He's been found. He's safe."

All the air went out of Roberto Musso with his sigh of sad relief, and he sank into one of the plastic chairs, indicating Hermie should also sit. Then he took another drag of the cigarette and said, "And then those innocent girls. God damn the man that done that!"

"Amen to that. What can you tell? Nothing is unimportant." Hermie sat and was grateful he was upwind of the acrid cigarette smoke spoiling the fresh, soft breeze making its way into this little nook, smelling flowery and leafy just before it took a turn for Italian spices.

Roberto Musso sighed, "I assumed they were a family when they first came in, oh, months ago, many. And their faces — such love when he looked at her. The same with her. And the boy — a teenager with such manners?

Such respect for Mama and Papa? How often these days with these kids? I speak from experience!"

"You can say that again."

"I thought the guy was South American, maybe, they have that elegance and wealth that shows, but quietly. That man, he wa-ay over-tipped, always. But one of my cooks, he escaped from Syria, God bless him, he say the man was Arab, with the British on top, from schooling. Maybe the woman and boy, too. They had that Arab accent, but not much. American schooling maybe. But live and let live, yes? They were happy, what else is there?"

"Not much."

"But it was their third — maybe fifth? — visit that the gentleman asked for a private conversation. I was not yet surprised, thought he was another Big Bucks who would make an offer to buy my place. You think it is small? I've seen plans for a condo tower on my small lot that would make your head to spin. Thirty-floor ant hill! Underground parking dug halfway to China, they think will do. And once it was a Chinese guy guy who was offering! Fah Napoli!"

Hermie didn't need to interrupt for a translation, the man's arm gesture spoke volumes in any language.

"Big money is always offered, I never tell the wife how much or I never hear the end of it. But I am not interested. This place is *mine*. One day I will drop dead in-a kitchen and then I don't care what happens to it. Basta! But until then, this is *mine* — to love, to serve, and once in a while to curse. Ah, the plumbing! Do not get me started!"

"I understand. So?"

"Sorry, I lose the track. *So*, I am thinking he's a-gonna make me an offer and it will be large, because Arabs have the bucks. But he first apologizes for what he's a-gonna ask and says I must not feel obligated. Then he asks if he can rent out the shed in the back. Huh? Why for that?" A shrug of recalled surprise. "He wants to put his car inside whenever he comes. And I could tell this was a serious matter for him. But not to do with the parking. Since I had already noticed that he never spent a meal without going outside with his cellphone, to check his car. Why for? It was a different car they came in, every time. I later saw it was not only his car — he checked the street up and down and up. He checked the buildings across from here, he checked the parking out front. It took him sometimes ten-fifteen minutes. His lady would very nicely ask to have his plate re-warmed so his food would still be hot when he came back. And she was a bellissima, I can tell you."

"How so?"

"Any wife whose husband leaves the table twice during the meal and she doesn't throw a fit? Her smile when he come-a back and his pat on her hand when he discovers his meal is still hot? This was a love story, those two."

"The shed has a new door, I noticed. So you agreed?"

"The automatics. Solid steel door, reinforced walls inside, he took my shed and turned it into a — how you say? — a *fort*!. And paid me very, very well for that — he must have been psychic about the plumbing, no? Because shed money became plumbing-saving. So, why not? I only used the shed for storing junk anyway. Maybe I clear it out if the wife does the divorce, because I'll be living there. Hah!" He chuckled, shook his head, took another grateful if guilty drag off the cigarette. "As I say, he pay me very well, all the expenses of the re-building. But..."

"Yeah?"

"What was he afraid of? I admit, I spied once."

"And —?"

"This was *before* the talking of the garage. He was checking the street, up and down, up and down, while talking on his cellphone. Don't bother to ask — he was talking Arabic. The only English he said was repeating, 'Be sure, be *sure*.' Many, many times. From the time the garage was finished, they never came into my place from the front door. He always drove into the shed, shut the door, and the three of them went out the door in-a back — he cut that into the back wall, for another steel door – and went into my place through the door we just came out." He gestured, cigarette ash drifted down like snow flakes.

It struck Hermie that this tale was so similar to Pepsi Potter's observation. *Hashemi was being stalked and he knew it and did everything to be on guard, everything to protect his family. Even when going out for a nice dinner.*

"And then there are the cameras."

"Surveillance cameras?" *Please, God!*

"Yes."

"Where?"

"Where not!"

They left the leafy nook and Musso pointed them out in turn: Inside two different trees, high on a telephone pole, tucked beneath the eaves of the Laundromat across the street "One, two, three four, five."

"Jeezus! I'll need to see those tapes."

"No tapes."

"Aw, hell, they're already erased? *Dammit-dammit!*"

"No-sir. There are no tapes. The cameras are — were — on his cellphone. He would check them out — after they arrived, and before they left after their dinner. Only now he did not have to leave their table to do this."

Hermie tried not to grind his teeth. Once again, Hashemi's vigilance was total. And since there wasn't any cellphone on his body or anywhere in that bloody Jaguar or his non-existent office/home, none of that surveillance would ever be seen. "Your restaurant was the last place Hashemi, the woman and the boy were seen alive. As far as we know. Anything unusual happen then? It was Mother's Day."

"Yes. Mother's Day. She carried a sweet, small violets. Fernando, their waiter, put them in a water glass for her. Her face, her smile — she look-a like she had candlelight inside her bones." he sighed, wistfully.

Hermie remembered the nosegay of violets crushed beneath the tires on the street. 'All things...thee...'

"But they left early on that time. Because he saw something on his phone. He came into the kitchen to ask a favor. 'Would I go outside and look for him?'"

"Look for what?"

"A car. A Rolls Royce. He said it had turned into our back lot."

"And?"

"It had, but now it was trying to get out, but it could not maneuver—a-squeeze — out of the lot. He was a stranger to it, the driver. You see our lot. Small cars, she's okay. But the rest –? He shrugged sheepishly. "It takes — how you say? — planning."

"A Rolls Royce?"

"Fancy one. Silver."

"License plate?" Hope sprang eternal in Hermie.

"Did not see. I was watching the maneuvers. The driver was having the fits. Too mad for me to offer advice, understand? I speak from experience."

"You saw the driver?" Hermie now welcomed a thrill. "What did he look like?"

"The windows were too dark. I could see nothing until he rolled down his window to check behind. Tall guy, head way up there in-a car. I saw a big shoulder, big arm. Muscles pushing inside the sleeves. Chauffer's clothes."

"White? Black?"

"The clothes?"

"No. The chauffer."

"It was early dark, but I could see he was not white. Tan."

"Latino?"

"Could-a be. But I remember thinking he's kinda look like Hashemi."

"He was Middle Eastern?"

"Could-a been, could-a been. An Arab Vin Diesel, no?" He chuckled.

Jeezus! Was this the driver who tried to get his mitts on Hashemi's body? Different car, sure, but sized big in a driver's uniform, like Pierre said. "Then what happened?"

"He threw it in-a reverse and fast-backed it out all the way through the lot, down the drive, and out into the street. Missed cars in lot by inches. Great driver."

"What then?

"I went back in. Hashemi was in-a kitchen, waiting, watching the whole thing on that little screen on his phone. He must-a saw the car had left. Now he was clicking on the buttons, I saw the little screen switch from camera to camera on-a street outside."

"He was watching the Rolls leave?"

"It didn't help much."

"How so?"

"His face. He looked...kinda *tight*."

"Scared? Worried?"

"More. For the first time, I could see this was a dangerous guy, y'know? Like he'd have no problem killing somebody."

"A 'specfic' somebody."

"Exactly. He *knew* who it was out there. And he had hate for him."

Hermie got up, walked into the parking lot, turned and surveyed the lot, the cameras, the garage. *If the guy drove into here and then couldn't get out, it hadda be his first time in here. Followed Hashemi, drove back into here thinking it was a parking lot like normal — wrong! So he didn't go inside the place to confront Hashemi because he just found out he could not make a quick get-away. So Hashemi and his family lived for another few hours.*

He came back to Musso. "You confirmed another witness's story about them being stalked. Oh, you said you noticed that every time they came here, they were driving a different car, right?"

"Right. A rental. Why spend thousands in rentals when you could afford to buy a car? Crazy. Oh — he carried a gun, too."

"Where?" *Hashemi had no gun or holster when he was found.*

"In-a jacket pocket. I do not know nothing about guns, but it was pretty big for a pocket."

The killer took his gun. Lila's purse and violets, Hashemi's phone and gun. His first souvenirs, before he graduated to headscarfs. "Can I see inside the shed?"

"Not unless you break down both doors, and you gotta have a cannon. He apologized for not giving me the keys, paid extra again."

"No matter. I'll have a Forensics team come by — they'll get in and photograph, dust the inside, haul away evidence. They'll be quick and quiet, so as not to interfere with business."

"They are welcome. And they will be well-fed. How about yourself?"

"Thought you'd never ask. What kinda olive oil do you use?"

After a heap of overstuffed lobster ravioli crowded underneath a thick and garlicky tomato sauce ("My father's recipe from the old country, Palermo."), sopped up with oven-fresh bread (crust crackling, inside soft as cake), and Roberto Musso not being at all miffed when Hermie asked for iced tea instead of the dangerously fragrant Chianti offered ("I'm on duty, y'see," he lied manfully), Hermie had completely forgotten his intended search into the "incorrect olive oil."

He got the word immediately after Forensics had managed to remove the smaller back door of the shed (it took a controlled explosive device, no surprise to Hermie) — the inside of the shed had weapons galore (Hermie had also expected that), but also an array of computers, most of which were connected to the surveillance cameras that continuously swept the entire property of Poco Paesano and the nearby streets (also not a surprise to Hermie). When Forensics marveled at how deftly concealed the cameras were on the property and streets all around, and how pristine the massive coverage they transmitted was, Hermie could only comment: "What can I say, the guy was obsessive. And picky."

* * * *

The seductive Italian cooking put Hermie in such a good mood, he turned on the Internet, and couldn't resist yelling out his open office door: "Hey, I'm Goo-goo-googling!"

The entire office was fragrant with the Italian take-out Hermie had brought from Poco Paesano for Nell and Claire. There were two more boxes in the small fridge for the two patrol guys to take home when they popped in to say goodnight at the end of their day.

He heard Nell laugh, and Claire's voice sailed out her own door, somewhat muffled as she had to maneuver around a plump and saucy ravioli in order to yell, "I will alert the media. You got Tommy Velasco on speed dial?"

"Up his!"

He managed to check DMV records after a first try resulted in the computer asking him if he had spelled "Rolls Royce" correctly. He hadn't. *Damn typo.* Pressed on, only slightly annoyed. He was astonished by how many Rolls Royces were registered in and around LA County. And he hadn't even gotten to dealerships, who'd have records of sales and where they went, presumably. He checked DMV records for names that might be Middle Eastern and that whittled it down some, but nothing familiar. 'DAMMIT!" sailed out his open door to the curious Nell.

She dared to come to his open doorway, dabbing her lips with a paper napkin in case sauce was lingering there. "What?" she asked, nicely.

"Do you know how many goddamn — sorry — Rolls Royces are registered in LA County and elsewhere in our unfair state?"

"Not a clue."

"That's the goddamn problem! I don't even know if it was owned or rented! A Rolls Royce was stalking Hashemi and family on that Mother's Day. Hashemi saw it on his surveillance cameras at the restaurant they went to often, in the past. He freaked out. And this is a man who does not freak. Out. Why now? He's always been aware they were being stalked. Maybe because-because he had all that surveillance looking, watching and now it all *unmasked* his stalker? It was watching, but that doesn't mean it was *stopping*, does it? But-but-*but*, Hashemi carried a gun. He was ready for it. But his family was there, might be in the line of fire. And then there's the uber-*UBER* question!"

"'Uber-*uber*'? Let me have it." Nell comically braced herself, knowing his frustration needed a tickle to avoid barreling into rage.

"What the hell kinda stalker drives a silver Rolls Royce?! A Phantom, no less!"

"Hmmm.... That *is* a clue. Isn't it?"

Cut grass and clean laundry. Her fragrance drifted in from the doorway, this time among the Italian spices, but for once the distraction didn't soothe him. He was stuck. And frustrated. *And, hell, clueless. So to speak.* "Don'tchya mean 'clueless'?" He voiced his frustration, rage was closing in but not yet here.

"Can you whittle it down?"

"I been whittling. Didn't solve. What's *your* whittle?"

"Well, if we assume Rolls Royce guy is the same who's been stalking them all along, and this was his first mistake — this time Hashemi *saw* him."

"So?" *She said 'we' assume.* His nerves relaxed just a little.

"So, the Hashemi family lived in the South Bay. Wouldn't their stalker also live nearby? Or if it's a rental, rent nearby?"

"Yeah, but wouldn't that pop up in the records if Googled? So to speak?

"Yeah...but it didn't. So...whittle backwards."

"Huh?" He couldn't help smiling.

"Backwards...to the records of a particular Rolls Royce landing on our shores. Shipment records. Somebody here or there had to arrange for it to be shipped here. They're still made in England or thereabouts, right?"

"Hell, I won't live long enough to Google that kinda thing."
"It'll take Hank five minutes. Tops."

* * * *

Hank O'Dell looked like hell.

His face was gaunt, his eyes circled with the blue of lack of sleep, even his usually vibrant red hair looked limp, straggly; the color would be washed out except it was obvious it hadn't been washed for some considerable time, not to mention trimmed.

"You look like the bus rolled onto you and parked. And it's all my fault." said Hermie, guilt-ridden.

"Is 'Kevin' all right?" Hank's one-note worry was always a given when he dealt with Grabfelder, since he'd whisked 'Kevin' into hiding, keeping Hank out of the loop in case down the road came comeuppance for 'kidnaping' outta Juvie.

"He spoke actual words the other day. Four."

Hank nearly collapsed with relief in his battered and saggy office chair, stunned. "He *did?* He really did?"

"That's one reason I'm here."

'Here' was Computer Whammy, where Hank worked and was presently trying to remain upright.

"When's your lunch or break time?"

Hank barely laughed with the irony. "Seriously?"

Hermie got a mental picture of him working all day in this hell-hole — the noise level of which jangled his own nerves after scant minutes — and then up most of the night bent over a computer, doing the searches asked of him by the relentless Detective, "Kevin's" savior.

Hermie had a habit of over-paying Hank out of his own pocket for any time spent on his behalf, LAPD funds being a chronic mirage; but money can't buy adequate sleep and regular food or even a barber that does house-calls.

Hermie abruptly left him, Hank guiltily calling after him, "Hey, Hermie, it's okay. I'm fine. Honest!"

It took just fifteen minutes of badge flashing and a great performance by a gruff Homicide Detective on a mission: Hermie buttonholed the manager of the joint and convinced him that Hank O'Dell happened to witness some aspect of his latest homicide case and he was taking him "downtown" to give a deposition. "Uptown" would have been more accurate, but Hermie was on the fly of lies. He went on that it might take more than one day to get and file these witness statements, so Hank O'Dell was on an 'official' leave, starting immediately and ending when the LAPD released him from the Witness List. And Hank's not going to, like, suffer any 'impairment" as to his salary and/ or job security, ri-i-ight?

Luckily, Roland Chen had emigrated from the hinterlands of China and was used to being cowed by authority figures, so he assured the Detective with the scary eyes that he was pleased to cooperate and Hank O'Dell's salary will flow on and his job will be waiting for his return, because "He is my so-best worker," he embellished with a twinkly smile so intensely sincere it nearly made his merry almond eyes disappear beneath his upturned cheeks.

Hermie took Hank O'Dell to his apartment and shoved him onto his rumpled bed. O'Dell was deeply asleep even before Hermie removed his shoes, revealing socks that had not seen laundry in an age or two.

He checked the kitchen; as expected, dirty dishes were leaning in a stack in the sink, and the fridge was bare except for an over-flowing icemaker and some left-over pizza, which had been left-over for maybe weeks, judging by the height of the green fuzz laced in and out of the dead-red sauce and once-upon-a-time cheese.

Hermie made sure that a volley of howitzers in his own living room would not wake Hank, then he slipped out of the apartment and went to the nearest supermarket.

Recalling the training he'd gotten long ago from grocery-buddies Jasmine and Carmen, he bought a bunch: First, ready-made stuff — a roasted chicken, a tub of Mac and Cheese, a bag of spinach salad, some "vine fresh" tomatoes (a Michigan man knew better, but what the hell they were at least *red*), Italian dressing that claimed "real Virgin olive oil" on the label and the price, three giant jugs of green tea, and a box of blueberry mufins, "Baked fresh right here."

He also got the fridge-stocking stuff: eggs, milk, sliced ham, Swiss cheese, German mustard, a bunch of leaf lettuce instead of a ball of iceberg because his Grandma used to grow it in her backyard garden, pounds of apples named "Envy" because they were something new and thus tempting, a large loaf of grain-heavy bread, a tub of soft butter, a jar of "No Sugar Added" cherry preserves, and a large bottle of adult multi-vitamins.

Next came a four-pack of tissues, a six-pack of toilet paper, four giant rolls of paper towels, a spray cleaner, and a large bottle of dish soap. Good thing, too, since upon his return to Hank's apartment he discovered that one of the reasons no dish had been wash since who-knew was that there was no dish soap in any cabinet.

Soon, groceries were put away, the icemaker was thinned of old cubes, then Hermie used the fresh cubes in a glass of geen tea (the last *clean* glass in this universe), and soon had the kitchen smoking from hotter-than-hot water as he did the dishes and utensils, and washed counter-tops. There was no mop, Hermie had checked everywhere it could have been leaning, but lack of foot-traffic made the floor easily tidied up with damp paper towels and the spray cleaner, leaving it gleaming, thanks to the ever-reliable wonder of linoleum.

It was near sunset when he heard Hank O'Dell stop snoring. He went into the bedroom to find him half sitting up blinking at his surroundings, jerking with shock at the sight of Detective Herman Grabfelder looming in his bedroom doorway.

"Feel better?" asked Hermie.

"How did I get here?" Hank was genuinely puzzled, to the point of almost not recognizing his own bedroom.

"Roland Chen paroled you from your incarceration. Fear not, your salary will continue and your job will be waiting for you, 'after-whenever' the LAPD gets your 'important witness statement'. I figure we can milk this for two days, three days, tops, before Roland starts phoning. Heckuva guy, Roland. He speaks very well of you, by the way. Although, how a Chinese guy gets the name 'Roland' is an intriguing subject for another time."

A full bladder galvanized Hank and he somewhat staggered toward the bathroom.

"Feel free to shower and shave, I brought dinner or breakfast, you choose whatever."

Before closing the bathroom door, Hank turned to look at Hermie with a still-stunned gaze.

Later, scrubbed from hair on down, wearing probably the last clean t-shirt and jeans that existed at this location, Hank opted for dinner, so Hermie heated up the chicken, Mac and Cheese and the blueberry muffins. He put portions of salad in the mismatched soup bowls at hand, decorated them with sliced tomatoes, opened the Italian dressing and gave it a sniff. 'real Virgin olive oil' was actually in there, surprise-surprise. Also, luckily, green tea was Hank's favorite, and he gulped down a fast glass even before touching the food. Then he devoured the food.

"When was the last time you ate?" asked Hermie, sympathetically.

"Can't rememb- ... Oh, I had a cheeseburger and fries...yesterday? Maybe." Hank said around a crispy brown chicken leg.

The last communal bites were savoring the deeply warmed-up blueberry muffins that they both slathered with the cold, soft butter.

Later, because Hermie had noticed and was curious: "You don't have a computer here. Do you use Computer Whammy's after hours, when no-one's around?"

Finishing off a third muffin, Hank got up and walked to a closed door that Hermie had assumed was a cupboard with some kind of metal rooster decal in the door in front, but he had discovered it was locked. Then Hank reached behind the stove to retrieve a key. He put the key inside a hidden hole in the rooster decal, unlocked the door and pulled at something inside — out rolled a computer on a stand, printer, rack of CD's and packs of paper.

"Ta-da," said Hank with a grin. "This neighborhood is iffy, local high school kids do burglary runs on their lunch hour, so I improvised. Left the TV and components out for grabs, tucked the important stuff in here." Hank switched on the computer, printer. "What-dya need?"

"Turn that thing off, sit-sit, and digest. And here — take your vitamins." He handed over the large jar.

"You actually bought me vitamins?" Hank's grin was suddenly shy.

"Had to. I'd be blamed if you keeled over from lack of nutrition. And rightfully so. Look, I'm sorry as hell I've been taking advantage of you, Hank. I have tunnel vision – it's not part of my charm."

"I'll say!" Hank joked, popped a capsule in his mouth gulped more green tea. "But you've been taking care of "Kevin", that's what's important. If he got into the jail system, he'd never get out. All that blood on him and him not able to speak up for himself, alibi... He's a smart-mouthed kid but he's still a kid. He's like the little brother I never had, y'know?" Hank's eyes moistened.

"Let's find someplace comfortable. I need to fill you in on your 'little brother'."

To Hermie's astonishment, Hank sank into a giant, red leather beanbag chair in the small living room, while Hermie took over the small black corduroy couch. *Good thing there's this couch, because I'd never get out of that beanbag alive. They still make those things?*

Then Hermie got right to it, as he was afraid the rush of glucose from good food fortifying a deprived body would soon make Hank nod off again. He needn't have worried — Hank became riveted with Hermie's telling all about "Kevin Costner": his monster father, his runaway Mom, Lila's courageous work for the FBI, the love story of her and Hashemi, the stalking and Hashemi's herculean efforts at defense, what horror 'Kevin' saw on that Mother's Day, and the saints upon the earth who are now waging war against his terrors with unwavering love.

"So, now, as of this date — what is it, by the way? Never mind. I got an almost clue: a silver Rolls Royce was stalking them that awful Mother's Day. And Hashemi saw it and undoubtedly *knew* what it meant."

"Did you say Rolls Royce? Silver?"

"Yeah. A Phantom. And ain't that irony gone postal?" Hermie cracked.

"There's one particular Phantom that I know of."

"You're kidding!"

"No. You remember I gotta baseball team of neglected kids using a field in Gardena for games?"

"Yeah. That's how you first met 'Kevin'. He came around. Joined up. And that's when we knew he was weird because nobody could trace him. Now we know Hashemi taught him and hid him well."

"Uh-huh. And until now..." Hank's face suddenly went serious, somewhat dimming his youthful looks. "We keep an eye out during the games, for cars that come by without real baseball fans, like parents, neighbors coming by, looking on. Because pedophiles also come by, cars circling the field, watching, waiting."

"I'm gonna be sick!" Hermie clapped a hand over his mouth, horrified.

"Tell me about it. Well, we got a system — retired CHP guy name of Barney Holmes photographs the cars, the license plates and runs them all down looking for sex offenders on the state and local lists. Then reports them. If the car comes around again, he's on it like white on rice, makes an arrest."

"Good system."

"Yeah. When we first started at that field, we were catching someone nearly every game. But apparently the word's gotten out, so not so much anymore. One or two a month. Now, let me think... Two months ago? Three? I'll have to look it up with Barns, when the Rolls Royce cruised up and by. A real dazzler. Silver."

"Jeezus!" breathed Hermie.

"A Phantom. CHP from Malibu recognized the model. He does off-time security at celebrity parties, saw that same model there in cherry red for chrissakes. Money don't buy taste. But the important thing is, when Barns ran plates and records, there wasn't none."

"I am shocked all to hell." Sarcasm, Hermie-style.

"Plates fake, car not in any system. So he couldn't track down owner or residence. Barnes got real concerned until we realized the car didn't come back. No sign of it, not even at the usual spy spots in the neighborhood."

"'Spy spots'? No-no, don't tell me," Hermie shuddered.

"And that one time, it pulled into the parking area, stayed with the motor running just long enough for a look-see at the playing field, and Barns' radar perked and he started photographing. Windows too dark to see the driver, though. Then it left, never came back."

Now a chill fluttered within Hermie. "He knew 'Kevin' was there."

"Aw, shit-shit-shit!" Hank moaned.

"He wasn't only stalking Hashemi and Lila, but 'Kevin', too. Goddammit."

"I'll give Barns a heads-up to keep checking."

"Don't bother. He won't find anything."

It was then that Hermie noticed the now glucose-flooded eyelids of Hank were drifting down sleepily, his voice dropping down to low and slow. "There's another way, gonna take time, though."

"Time for later. Right now, I'm leaving and you're going back to bed till further notice."

"No, no, I'm alright, jeez," but Hank was definitely lacking coordination when he struggled to get up and out of that beanbag.

Hermie went over and hauled him up, walked him to his bedroom and kept hold of him so he descended instead of fell onto his bed. "When's the last time you changed your sheets? Never mind, I can guess. I'll get you a cleaning lady for your birthday. Maybe two or three."

Hank managed a sleepy chuckle, "Just don't tell my Mom."

Hermie took off Hank's beat-up slippers, to reveal giant feet smooth and pink as a little kids', then draped the well-used sheet over him. He had a sudden thought: "By the way, did 'Kevin' see that Rolls Royce?" *Damn the thought!*

"Naw. We won that day because 'Kevin' hit a triple in the last inning when the score was tied eight to eight. All the kids' attention was on him, our hero."

"Good." Another, better thought: "I hope that memory comes back."

Both Hermie and Hank smiled that mutual hope, the last one before Hank's eyelids turned out his lights.

CHAPTER TWENTY

"In a world of war, many sparrows must fall."

Unknown

"Oh, God, Detective! We've done something wrong! Something awful wrong!" Mrs. Harrison's normally mild voice was ragged, just short of a guilty scream.

Hermie froze, grasped his home phone so hard he heard plastic crack. *"Kevin!"* Something's happened to *"Kevin"!* "What's happened?"

"We were just walking down the sreet and he *screamed!* Oh, Lordy, that sound!"

"Where is he now?"

"We're all home. "Kevin's" in bed, but he's — he's —"

"Stay there. Keep him there. I'm on my way."

He used his light rack and siren to blast his way through the god-awful traffic of Torrance. He ran up to their front door and didn't bother ringing the bell — his hand was on the doorknob when Mrs. Harrison jerked open the door for him. "What did we do?" she moaned, "What did we *do?*"

"I'm sure you didn't do anything, Mrs. Harrison. It's what's inside "Kevin", coming out. This may be a good thing. A *good* thing."

Mrs. Harrison impulsively hugged that boulder of a man, letting loose an anguished moan of gratitude. Hermie hugged her, patted her, waited.

She pulled away, took a fistful of already used tissue out of the pocket of her slacks and wiped her eyes, nose. "A 'good' thing? Oh, Lordy, let that be."

"Is "Kevin" alone now?"

"Oh, no, Frank's by his side, holding his hand."

"Good. Sit somewhere and tell me what happened."

She led him to the living room, where the first chintz curtains Hermie had seen since his Michigan childhood turned the harsh, intrusive sunlight into a pleasant glow. She went to the comfortable-looking couch and sat to face him. He sat almost near enough to bump her knees with his.

She took a deep, shivering breath, then her Midwestern twang came back full force in her panic. "We'd taken to walkin' with "Kevin" 'most every day. Just a couple blocks through the neighborhood when everyone was at work, so there was little traffic and people 'round about. To be sure, we put "Kevin" between us, I'd have one hand, Frank the other. For so many days, "Kevin's" hands were just...*there*...y'know? But lately, he was *holdin'* our hands — holdin' onto us, y'know?"

"Oh, Millie, that's a very good sign," Hermie said and meant it. *At last, he felt something, he felt their hands and knew they were something he could hang onto.*

"That's what we thought. So we took to takin' him to Cones 'N Cream— it's a small ice cream parlor just three blocks from here. We figured, 'what kid don't like ice cream?" y'know? The schools weren't out yet, so there weren't many people inside. But to be safe, Frank would wait outside with "Kevin" while I went inside and got the cones. We'd put a cone in "Kevin's" hand, Frank held his other, always. And at first "Kevin" was still...*blank*, y'know? Then, when the ice cream kinda dripped down on his hand, he actually licked at the cone! What a day that was! We were — well, Detective, we were thrilled. Every day, a nice walk, and the ice cream, and every day "Kevin" seemed to be...to be...more and more *aware."* She was overcome again, sniffed into the tissues with another moan of guilt.

"Strawberry, right?"

"How's that?"

""Kevin" liked strawberry ice cream." He said it to ease her tension and grief because she needed the simple distraction.

"Yes. Strawberry. How did you —?"

"I always figured that "Kevin" would be a strawberry ice cream kinda guy someday. And now it's come out."

Air and tension went out of her and she nearly smiled into those now calmly glowing eyes. "Bless you, Detective."

"I only answer to 'Hermie'. So, what happened today?"

"We were on our way home, just a couple blocks to go, when all of a sudden "Kevin" stopped dead and *screamed* — a sound I didn't think could come out of a child. And if Frank hadn't been holding his hand — "Kevin" twisted and thrashed and tried to <u>run</u>, God help us, he was trying to run away! Finally, Frank just hauled him up over his shoulder and we got home as fast as we could. "Kevin" screamed till we got home. When we got inside, he went quiet and limp, but when we laid him down on his bed, he shivered and moaned, and we could tell, we could tell —"

"Tell what?"

"He'd gone away again. His mind. And it must-a been our fault!"

"No-no-no. It *wasn't* your fault. This I *know*. What was on the street? Did "Kevin" see something? Hear something?"

"I don't know! The street was quiet, just a few cars, people, the church bells marking the time like always. So quiet I could hear it when "Kevin" took a crunchy bite of his cone. Oh, Mercy, was it the cone?"

"Not possible. The cone was you and Frank, your hands holding his, taking a walk in a nice neighborhood. Something broke that spell. Something only "Kevin" would recognize. And fear."

"What do we do? Do we have to call the child services?"

"Hell, no! Sorry. I'm trying to convince you that "Kevin" is safe here, with you and Frank. Think of it, Millie, weeks ago he was catatonic when I brought him here. Now, because of you and Frank, he's eating a strawberry ice cream cone like a normal kid, and holding your hands."

For an instant, Millie buried her face in her hands and let out a soft cry of relief, then she surfaced, wiped her eyes, and patted Hermie's hand, gratefully. "Bless your heart, Detect — Hermie."

"Let me take a look, okay?"

"Of course."

Hermie followed her into "Kevin's" bedroom to find Frank holding his hand and looking twice the worse for wear as Millie.

"Helluva day, Detective," Frank tried for humor, but his guilt remained.

"Sounds like. But thank God he was with you guys when it happened — whatever 'it' was. Any ideas?"

"Not a one. Did the wife tell ya?"

"Yeah. Something that had nothing to do with you or Millie crashed the picnic. "Kevin" may have seen or heard something, or maybe his wounded brain, his memory picked just that second to fire up, and he lost control. Fear came back and took over, like it had before."

"Jeezus-god," breathed Frank.

Hermie took a closer look and could see the familiar signs: "Kevin" shivering with fear, he had indeed run away again, run away from his mind where the horrors still lived, still threatened. But he knew "Kevin" was safe here. Frank and Millie Harrison would wage war against that horror, holding his hands.

He lingered until the Harrisons were as reassured as he could get them. Then he left and took a walk through the neighborhood, taking the same route to Cones 'N Cream, to discover it was a small ice cream parlor that was a throw-back to the old days: a pink and white color scheme with a black and white tiled floor, a couple of small pink tables and chairs, a long glass counter with pink stools pulled up, and large bins of ice cream underneath, colorful with flavors, some bins lumpy with nuts and chocolate chips, others with striped candy chips. Hermie got a whiff of a clean, creamy and slightly sweet smell.

Hermie was a Butter Pecan kinda guy and at first lick he was surprised to smell and taste ice cream that seemed to be made from scratch, or near-to, like what they were at Danny's in Bay City, wa-ay back when, his Dad always taking Maple Walnut and his Mom Raspberry Ripple, when he was a fresh-faced lad and most of the world still seemed made from scratch, in a *good* way.

He chit-chatted with the skinny guy behind the counter — *How did he stay skinny in this ice cream paradise?* — and learned the guy was the owner, Bud Pitoski, and although he'd be expected to have ears to the ground as a businessman should, he had not heard any commotion in the street earlier.

Hermie thought it best not to bring up the Harrisons and "Kevin", so as not to draw attention to them for the future. *The future. Did "Kevin" have one? Or would his mind always be locked away. Locked away from an ordinary life — like an education, a job, a cute wife and noisy kids; maybe a big, hairy dog and some persnickety cats, who nevertheless curled up on top of or next to the snoring dog to sleep at night; and the whole gang of kids and creatures cuddled up in Mom and Dad's big bed whenever rain and thunder crashed outside.*

Out on the sidewalk again, wolfing down cold and fragrant buttery ice cream and chunky pecans, he noted again the quiet and calm of the neighborhood. *Maybe rush hour jammed and stunk up this street,* he mused, and took a look between houses and yards to see if he could glimpse the whereabouts of the inevitable mall, this being Torrance and all.

He was startled by the delicate sound of carillon bells coming from the church he was approaching. He checked his watch, the bells were marking the hour. The nearly gothic lettering on the sign out front said: "Saint Helge's Catholic Church" and gave a list of Masses and days, times. It was a very old building, interestingly gothic instead of the usual Spanish memory of church design. The visible treasure was the gigantic and gleaming mahogany double doors that topped the few steps that marched up the front. The doors opened to let out a few people, still holding onto prayer books and rosaries, their variety of hued faces all smooth with the calm of having prayed or meditated. A small group of nuns glided out, chatting softly, larger rosaries swinging and clacking down from their belted waists.

Hermie stopped to let them all cross in front of him, surprised to see the nuns were wearing the traditional habits, the white wimple tightly circling their shiny faces underneath the long black veils co-mingling with the long black drapery of sleeves and skirts down to the tops of somewhat masculine-looking black-laced shoes.

Gee, look at that. Don't see many nuns wearing the habit these days. Catholic version of the chador.

And Hermie stopped dead.

Nell tried not to show her disbelief as she gaped at him. "A guy. A killer. Wearing a chador."

"That's how he did it! That's how he got close enough to kill — they all thought he was a woman. A pious woman in a chador. So they let him come near. Maybe he asked them a question, directions, who the hell knows. But too late, they saw his eyes, his face. They didn't even have a chance to take a step back before that dagger struck. "Kevin" freaked when he saw nuns in those black habits. Because he remembered the black chador disguising the monster."

"Wouldn't Hashemi have gotten wise when he was bumped off the freeway by that familiar Rolls? Not exactly dressed for it, how could this guy tie him up in his Jag?"

"Chador Man was a short guy, he had a driver doing the bump-off on the freeway. A really *big* guy, according to Roberto Musso. Someone who could do the heavy lifting, carrying fire power, in order to subdue Hashemi, get the gun he always carried, tie him down. Kept the motor running while Lila was killed, but he couldn't run after "Kevin" because the job wasn't done. There was Hashemi to deal with. But he probably kept the motor running while those other girls were stalked and killed."

"How could anyone just stand by and watch him do such horrible crimes against those lovely beings?"

"Fear. Since he's working for a psychopath. *Large* money. Religion, maybe. The counterfeit kind. Speaking of, once we get 'em both, do pray hard that the driver/thug makes a deal to testify as a witness to all those horrors. Otherwise, he's looking at the death penalty right alongside his boss."

"We live in hope. Oh — how's 'Kevin'?"

"He was shivering so bad, Millie couldn't stand it. She got a slug of wine into him and it worked — he calmed, let go, slept. Close alongside Frank."

"Hope this isn't a setback to his recovery."

"Me, too. But I don't think so. Not with Millie and Frank on the watch."

"What's next?

"I wait until Hank's stomach lining heals, then we'll see if we can find out when that Rolls landed here, to who, from who. Whom. No, I'm not hopeful, just dogged and desperate."

"Or..." Nell put just a toe in. In case.

"'Or'? Lay it on me. Have no mercy."

"The guy at Poco Paesano? Roberto Musso? He said the driver looked Middle Eastern. Take a dog-leg leap."

"A 'dog-leg leap'? Ya fascinate me more every day, Girl." *Oops! Watch-it, watch-it, watch-it, Herms! Damn good thing I'm sitting behind this desk!*

Nell knew she'd gone fire-red in the face, so she pressed on, hoping for relief: "Immigration records."

"From the Middle East?! Ach du lieber, do you know how many — just ask any pissed-off politician! Thousands, running for their lives, little kids running from bombs, being gassed. We used to be the haven for people who have nothing, nowhere to go. And now? Do not get me started!"

"I know. But that's not what I meant. Not from the Middle East. *They* were probably the ones stalking Hashemi. Probably. Maybe. More than maybe, maybe. After the Rasfani thing. But...Hashemi came from England. And not recently. Back in that day, the immigration by people with a Middle Eastern persuasion weren't coming in desperate numbers, like today. Especially not from England. He *did* come from England, right?"

"Who the hell knows!"

"Who came in on the same or near the same day, week, month, even year that Hashemi did? With a Middle Eastern name. But from England."

"Nobody knows when Hashemi came in. FBI and everyone else combed and scraped, but no records were ever found. He just 'appeared'."

"Okay, when did he 'appear'? Did anyone backtrack or go forward from there?"

"Probably. You know how anal the FBI and the rest of the alphabet are. On the other hand..."

He stared at her for long seconds, his blazing eyes hiding his thoughts. She changed feet in her stance, bracing herself.

Then Hermie looked up at the ceiling as if musing.

Nell looked up at the ceiling and noted water stains from many pre-droughts of yore.

Then suddenly Hermie's memory apparently kicked in, he snatched up his phone, dialed, nearly yelled, "Trots-Baby, what are ya do-in'?"

"Classified, Snoopy-Boopy," Trots answered, sounding distracted.

"Fast favor: Search your oh-so-inaccurate intelligence: When did Hashemi come into the USA? I know you don't know that exact date, but when did he, like, 'appear'? I'll wait, oh, so patiently while you look it up."

Trots answered immediately: "April, 1992. First *sighting*, that is. No records of how he got here or exactly when or from whence. So to speak. *Still.* Yes, I am still embarrassed."

"Chronic, ain't it?"

"I assume you will be cautious as to the sharing of that info and its source? Times being what they are? My pension being near, yet oh, so far?"

"Of course. The bodacious Brenda and I are counting on that pension for our getaway and future frolics. Think Bali...or Corfu...the nude beach in Brazil."

Nell went from being startled to stunned at this side of the conversation. *Who the hell is 'the bodacious Brenda'? 'Nude'?!* Before Hermie hung up abruptly, Nell could hear the male voice still yelling on the line.

Hermie ignored it. "Nineteen Ninety-two. So far as the FBI or anyone else knows." He reached for the phone again, but it abruptly rang just as his hand touched the receiver. It was not his private line. He picked it up, said, "Grabfelder here." And listened.

Nell was astonished to see the horror, then the rage wash over his face, making his eyes terrifying, the tone of his voice filled with raw hatred. "God damn them. God damn, damn, damn them. Shoot 'em, shoot'em, SHOOT-EM!!!"

CHAPTER TWENTY-ONE

"More people have been slaughtered in the name of religion than for any
other single reason. That is true perversion."

Harvey Milk

The massacre in San Bernardino exploded into the streets, the TV screens, the innocents; and the minds, hearts, and politics of the bigoted, the wise, the evil and the kind.

Hermie's first call was to the first Muslim he had ever met, long ago: "Hi, Shakey, it's Grabfelder."

"Oh, Hi, Hermie." Shaik Mohammed's voice was strained, gone was the merry Middle Eastern cadence that everyone knew about "Shakey".

"Are you all right?" was the only thing Hermie knew to say.

"You mean have I stopped puking?" Shakey answered, bitterness now apparent.

"What can I do for you?"

"Well, I can think of a couple politicians who could use some spit in their eyes."

"It'd be a pleasure. I'll lace it with chewing tobacco. My Grandpa taught me how."

An almost chuckle from Shakey. "Actually, Herms, we been getting neighborhood watchers coming into the station, offering their support. Rabbis, priests, ladies bringing casseroles and cookies. Surprise-surprise, considering the horrible details that came out about those so-called Muslims. And this was after attacks on a couple Sikhs here-by, yahoos see a turban and assume they're Muslim, dumb dicks. But one guy sure held his own."

"How so?"

"He happened to be packing his ceremonial dagger. He whipped that puppy out and there was a re-consideration all 'round."

"He sounds like a real diplomat. Good for him."

At last, Shakey chuckled like of old. Then: "Hermie, I gotta thank you for calling and for just being . . . Hey, does this screw up your case any?"

"The case is screwed no matter what's going on. You might keep your eye out for a short guy wearing a chador."

"That's nuts!"

"That's also the latest, on account of an eye witness. Keep that on a need-to-know for now, so it doesn't get into the news. We're also trying to trace a Rolls Royce limo, but no records exist. It's a Phantom. Literally. But, hey, you got your own pots boiling, I just wanted to call to see how you're doing. If you need anything, don't be shy."

There was a short pause and Hermie heard Shakey take an uneven breath, then his voice was moistened with emotion: "Hey, Hermie, has a Muslim ever told you, you're a real mensch?"

Hermie laughed, glad to hear that the sense of humor would return in full, in time. "Nope, 'son of a bitch' is still the norm. Later, Shakes."

"Yeah. Blessings, Herms."

"Thanks."

Both hung up gently.

Hermie's next calls were to the broken Muslim families he was desperate to bring justice to: Sunidhi Askar's parents and the parents of her best friend, Sara Bandar; Shirin Batawi's family was out of state, so they weren't in any jeopardy he could do something about. *What was the hate level in Minnesota,* he wondered. But he called anyway, introduced himself, and asked if they were all right. Their surprise was quickly replaced by gratitude. More so after Hermie told them about Sam Ordway, Shirin's good neighbor, who had appointed himself her friend and guardian and kept her memory dear. Hermie gave them Sam's phone, feeling sure they would call him and sharing their loss would help ease Sam's own just a little. He also gave them all his own phone numbers and told them if the local police didn't do right by them, call him and he'd rattle other cages, like those of the FBI. He left them relieved with knowing that if they experienced any kind of threat, someone was on call to help.

He was relieved to hear similar tales from the Askars: of neighbors popping by with casseroles and reassurances, of schoolmates sending cards and letters expressing empathy. To Hermie's personal chagrin and guilt, no one asked if he had any leads as to the murderer of their beloved daughters. They merely expressed their own sympathy for him and other police officers in their dangerous and frustrating jobs.

Hermie did not bother calling the Farsadi household, because he knew that the tender shadow on the kitchen wall had long since departed to a better life. As far as he was concerned, the so-called men left behind were on their own.

He next called his Major Worry, was glad that Aida answered after only a couple rings, her voice cheery.

"It's Grabfelder, Aida. I'm just checking up on you. Are you guys all right?"

"Detective, I've been going through flabbergasting times."

"What does that mean?"

"Well, I was thinking about shutting down for the duration, the store and the you-know-what, because things were getting nasty out here — pickets for godsakes! Misspelled, mostly. Too much of a stretch to correctly spell 'Islam'? Idiots! Then eggs thrown at our windows. They just hadda pick the windows in the sun — eggs got instantly fried from the heat. What a mess! I figured rocks would be next, on the shady side where there's cover. But then we had a visit from the Powell Street Hadassah. Six ladies of the Jewish persuasion marched into our door."

"Aw, Jeez!"

"No-no, they all started *shopping*, shopping like mad — damn near cleaned out my shelves, asked me when I got my produce and bread deliveries so '*in the future*' they'd get a jump on when they were 'fresher than fresh'. And one lady — Adele Schultz — told me she was looking for a part-time job and wondered if I was hiring!"

"You're kidding!" Hermie laughed.

"Since she was a retired financial officer from my very own insurance company, how's that for coincidence, I hired her on the spot. You should only guess at the state of my store books, tax time will kill me again this year — I am constantly shuffling and hiding money for the 'upstairs'."

"Are you comfortable taking on a stranger? I don't mean because she's Jewish, I mean for security reasons. She could be doing inventory in the back room and hear something from up above. Then what?"

"I think we can handle it. She'll only be here two days a week and since I don't have an office in the store, she says she can work at her own home office. She keeps the books for a couple other businesses. Including a veterinary hospital, of all things. So, I think it's do-able."

"Hadassah and Halal. Now I've seen everything."

Aida's laugh was hearty. "Me, too! It's kinda wonderful, isn't it? Right in the middle of these awful times, caused by awful people."

"Speaking of: I've got a lead that makes no sense at all, but I'm gonna share in case you hear anything and you might get the word of warning out."

"Lay it on me, Detective."

"We're looking for a short guy dressed in a chador."

"You're serious," she deadpanned.

"Yeah."

"Holy —-! On the other hand, it makes sense, doesn't it? That's how he got near them —- they thought he was a pious woman."

"Exactly."

"I'll get the word out, eyes and ears. A cross-dresser is a rare one in the Muslim world, I must say."

"But be confidential, I don't want any publicity getting out. If that sonuvabitch hears about it he'll change wardrobe and run and we'll never find him."

"Point taken by one and all."

He also gave Aida all his phone numbers. And couldn't resist: "Shalom 'Aleykum!" and hung up on her laughter.

He next called the mosque and got a chill of apprehension when an answer machine picked up and Yasmina's voice offered greetings, blessings, and "Please leave your number and we'll get back to you soon."

"Yasmina, it's Detective Grabfelder. I'm just calling to see if you guys were all right."

The phone was snatched up and Yasmina sounded slightly breathless: "Sorry for the machine, but some of the calls have been . . ."

"I know. What can I do to help?"

"We're okay, so far. Lots of neighbors have been coming by —- Christians, Jews, even a Rastafarian, who amused the Imam no end. Some of them stayed for prayers. Imagine! We got a rock thrown through a window last night, but it wasn't an important window. So I think we'll be okay till time marches on."

He gave her all his phone numbers and since it was her, he made her promise, word of honor, to call if any more threats were phoned in or more important windows were shattered. And he told her about the suspect.

"A *man* wearing a chador?! That's disgusting!"

"A lot more than that. But that's how he got close to those women —- at first glance, they thought he was a woman. And that's all the time he needed. Now, I don't want this to become general knowledge, enough to end up in the news. We can't tip him off that we know his game."

"No-no-no. We'll be totally discrete. I'll have to rein in the Imam —- a man wearing a chador to murder Muslim women! He will just explode."

"I know. If you want me to come by to do damage control, just call."

"Thank you, Detective. You might be the only one who could, if he goes 'round the bend'."

He'd just hung up the phone when Nell buzzed: "I've got a Sam Ordway who wanted to wait on Hold. Shirin Battawi's neighbor?"

"Oh, yeah, yeah — I got him." Then: "Mr. Ordway, I apologize for ya being on Hold. I was just talking about you, though. I let Shirin's family know how much you did for her. They may call."

"Aw, I didn't do nothing. She . . . she . . . was pretty close with her folks, she knew they were proud of her even though worried. And now . . . more than their worst fears, goddammit. How are they doing?"

"Hanging in. It's not as bad out there, but enough. It helped to know I'd get some FBI on call if they get in trouble threatened or worse. I was FBI in a past life."

"No kiddin'? Good to know. But, hey, I know what's going on out there for you LAPD guys. Helluva thing."

"Yeah, I was just checking on some Muslim friends, making sure —"

"That's why I called. You would not know it to look at me, but my past life was the Marines, and I still got a license to carry."

"I don't understand —"

"I gotta couple pals — ex-Marines, one is ex-Navy, but we hang out with him anyways — well, we all got to talking down at the VFW. You say you got Muslim friends, if any of them need some protecting, just want you to know we old geezers are volunteering. Just tell us when and where."

"That's awful nice of you."

"Well, hell! Those monsters in San Bernadino, and the monster you been hunting — they ain't real Muslims! Innocent, law-abiding folks are being tarred with the same brush and it just ain't fair! Talkin' about rounding them up, forcing them to carry identity cards? God-dammit, one of our guys is Japanese, his grandfather was put in one of those camps in front of World War II — you can imagine how the hell *he* feels!"

"Deja vu all over again."

"Hell, yes! Well, we wanna help, figured you'd know who could use us."

On a hunch, Hermie gave him the phone number of the mosque. Then: "Ask to speak to Yasmina, say Detective Grabfelder told you to call. Yasmina is the great granddaughter of the Imam, and she's a real pip, as we used to say in the Midwest."

Hermie would hear from Yasmina a couple days later, how six ancient ex-Marines and one ex-Navy showed up at the mosque and posted themselves around the property, all day and all night — three in front, two alongside, and two in the playground in back, to the instant fascination of and soon adoption by the kids. Some parents came by and were so reassured they made calls themselves and the kids who had been kept home for safety now returned.

The "guardians" stood at respectful attention when the recorded call to prayer went out and the Imam stood at the door to welcome the Muslims that dared to show up.

The Imam's ebullient gestures now included: "Welcome, welcome, friends. Be assured the Marines have landed, along with a Navy, and all is well. After the services I'll introduce you to our own personal warriors." And he did.

Wariness and fear turned to curiosity, to hesitant greetings, to neighborly conversations, to unique friendships forming and surprising, then finally to the realization that better days were presently way out of reach, but were indeed coming. Because, deep down:

"I still believe, in spite of everything, that people are still good at heart."

The Diary of Anne Frank, 1944

CHAPTER TWENTY-TWO

"You ain't nobody until you do what you want anyway."

The Fonz

Blame it all on the weather. Except California does not have weather; it has *drama*.

After months of meteorologists happily predicting that an El Nino to beat all El Nino's was coming to not only wipe out the drought, but basically turn California into Marshland at High Tide, they first predicted mid-December for the deluge.

Ah.

December did indeed bring rain and snow by the feet up north, but in the Los Angeles basin? Nada.

The view of the San Gabriels from Los Angeles was like Switzerland, a dusting of snow reaching farther down the crags and mountains than in anyone's memory. Vast numbers of employees called in sick with the "flu", but fooled no-one; pristine powder beckoned like a drug addiction relapse for the first time in years. And it cheered the rest of the population when they realized that all that snow would melt and race toward various parched reservoirs, lakes, and streams. Not enough, of course, but there was some re-consideration of artificial grass and the effort to make cactus look like decorative landscaping.

For months, the L.A. Basin had received barely a spritz. Instead there was raw winds from Alaska, bitter cold with gusts nearing 50 mph, temperatures in the low 40's and less in spots. That was for a couple weeks.

Then the temperature shot up to 80 degrees with either no wind at all or the soft, dry Santa Ana winds drying out the parched landscape even further —- who knew there was that many shades of brown? -- not to mention swelling everyone's sinuses. Wherever there was people, there was sneezing. Even dogs sneezed while being walked in the drier-than-dry heat.

The first fear realized was fire breaking out and holocausting all the parched mountainsides, along with the treasured homes thereon, smoke sooting up the air for miles around; then, the wildly fluctuating air temperatures upon the earth's plates invited earthquakes, and there had been three so far. Minor shakes, but warnings nonetheless.

At last, the rains came down to the L.A. basin — cold, steady, sloppy, and almost instantly flash floods began barging everywhere with mud and debris, because the years-long drought had killed off all the usually thirsty and obliging vegetation barriers. But soon the rain did vivid magic: dun-colored hills and valleys and canyons sprouted a carpet of intense green, decorated with bright yellow wild flowers. Everyone paused at least once a week to look and be dazzled. For once, cellphones snapping photos was warranted, and photos were e-mailed to the folks "back east", who were still battling snow and cold. Previous barren years now forgotten, bragging about California weather once again flourished. Then came the coyote problem. Well, with *drama*, there's always *something*.

Hermie remembered that the Jacarandas were blooming everywhere at the time of that first murder scene, and they like heat so the weather had obliged temporarily. So, he had worn a light jacket for those heated days, including when he searched Lila's apartment and her car. So today's flash of memory came when he put on that same jacket because it was courting 80 degrees again outside while 'wiser' heads predicted 60 degrees and more rain by 9 PM. There was a stiff bump from the right pocket: it was the CD he had found in Lila's car; the only CD that had no case, no label, so he didn't think it was part of her *"Patsy Cline"* or *"Phantom of the Opera"* collection, which was why he had pocketed it. And now he just found it weeks later, thanks to dressing for another day of Los Angeles's weather drama.

"We got something that can play this?" he asked Nell, holding up that blank CD.

She took it, pressed a button on her computer's hard drive and startled Hermie when a tray popped out that neatly fit the CD when Nell dropped it in. "You *know* — oh, that's right, you *don't* — you have a tray in your hard drive, too."

"You're kidding."

Nell gave him a saintly smile of patience, then she turned to her computer screen. Hermie could hear the hard drive making odd buzzing sounds, first softly, then louder. But then nothing. The buzzing stopped, nothing came out of the speakers, nothing appeared on her screen, the tray was silent.

"Nothing there. It's blank." she said, frowning.

Experience made Hermie say, "Oh, it's not blank. Of all the things it could be, or oughtta be, it is definitely *not* Patsy Cline or blank. This I *know*. Jordan Hashemi strikes again."

"Hashemi?"

"I found this in Lila Miller's car, lo these many weeks ago. The only CD that wasn't in a case, that had no label. There's something on it, all right. Something important."

"But it's encrypted."

"Yeah, that's what it is," he took a shot that did not fool her.

She spared him yet another pointed tease, "You need a code to make it play, a password to get into it. Or something like that. These days it's always something new, something more complicated. Only nine year olds can keep up."

"Crap!"

"I'll say. The code, password could be anything, it would take an expert and maybe weeks to get in. Since it's Hashemi."

"CRAP! If I bring yet another impossible problem to Hank O'Dell, he may just shoot me. And I'd loan him my gun to do it. Poor guy."

"You say you found it in Lila's car? Well, you know she wasn't the one who was the computer whiz. What about the hard drives in Hashemi's office? One of them or something else on paper probably would have lists of Hashemi's codes for stuff."

"The FBI has every scrap of everything and anything that was in Hashemi's office, and they can't figure anything out. Even if they did, they break out in a rash when asked to play with others."

"Well, surely they'd let *you* use one of those hard drives to crack the code. Didn't you used to be kinda FBI? Plus, they'd be just as interested in what's on this disc as we are."

"'We' she said. Oh, yeah, I'll keep that in mind."

"*What*?" she demanded.

"I ask for help, I get back on their radar, and that could include ordering me to stop investigating Jordan Hashemi altogether and turn over this CD and "Kevin" to boot."

"But it's *your* murder case. The first done by a serial killer *you're* hunting."

"You're so young."

"I'm flattered, but 'huh'?"

"This is the guv-ment we're dealing with. Some fool taught them how to spell 'national security'." My source says Hashemi was indeed selling something, and he was *not* the arms dealer the guv'ment thought he was. So what was he selling?"

"Information."

"Bingo. And in these uber-cyber times, information is more dangerous than guns, bombs, missiles, drones, and 'stuff'."

She took the CD out of the hard drive tray. "What do you want to do with this, then?"

"Hide it, of course!" He snatched it from her, put it in his jacket pocket.

"Wait," she said, and rummaged in her desk drawer, came up with an empty CD case. "Here, put the disk in this, so it doesn't get damaged, scratched."

"Yeah." He thought for a second as he tucked the CD into the case. "Why wasn't there a case for this in Lila's car? Hashemi would not just hand her a naked CD, would he?"

"No. Does that make the CD case important?"

"How the hell would *I* know!" He showed his frustration. "Come into my cave," he said over his shoulder as he went into his office.

He was running out of wall space, crime scene photos festooned with notes scribbled with bits of information and/or Hermie's thoughts. His stack of Murder Books was too high, it was leaning toward a fall. Nell snatched up a couple, turned one tall, precarious stack into three shorter, solid ones.

"Thanks," he said as he collapsed onto his chair's protesting squeak. "God . . . I'm just not getting it! All that slaughter and I have no goddamn clue. Retirement beckons with a 'come hither' smile."

Not for the first time, Nell saw the anguish inside the man's humor. "You've got a lot of clues, you just need to . . ."

"What? Figure them out? Nell, you did more figuring than I've done. 'They were all happy,' you said, and someone hated them for it."

"Maybe I was wrong. I mean, how can you hate a stranger?"

"Read the papers lately?"

"Yeah. That was stupid of me." Her cheeks went rosy with embarrassment.

'No-no", he reassured her. "You're on the only track that fits, when you look at the M.O. Such violence, a weapon and a method from the Eleventh Century, for godsakes. Long time to hold a grudge, but there you are. People are being killed today all over our world for grudges even older than that."

Both their faces went tight with that brutal knowledge.

Nell walked over to the Hashemi/Lila section of photos. Went past the crime scene and its notes, to the photo of the Safir family: Mom, Dad, Sis. "The sister died in the plane crash, right?"

"Yeah."

"She's traditional to the max, judging from her wardrobe. So she can't work, and since she's alone with her parents in this photo, she's not married. Which means, Hashemi had to take care of her. Financially and otherwise."

"Yeah. So?"

"This photo. How old was she when she died?"

"Teens. Mid- to later."

"This woman is older. Late twenties, late twenties, at least. Are you sure it's his sister?"

"Who else?"

"And this photo? Why isn't Hashemi in it? He was the rest of the family. And the son. This photo should have presented the marriageable daughter and the marriageable son. But the daughter . . . it's off. What was her name?"

Hermie shot out of his chair like a lightning strike. "Holy shit! Sorry!" He snatched up his phone, punched in numbers.

Once again, Selah was not offended by the lack of niceties when Hermie nearly yelled, "What was the name of Hashemi's sister?"

"His sister's name was Ayisha. She perished in the plane crash of his parents, as I told you."

"How old was she then?"

"Nineteen. Why?"

"Then who the hell is this woman?!

"What woman?"

"I have a photo here, from Hashemi's office. Mom, Dad, and I thought Sis. But she's too old. She's late twenties at least. Who the hell is she?"

"It could be a relative of Mom and Dad. A niece. A cousin. Since she is past marriage age, they may have wanted this photo to show her family connections as a marriage inducement. I will inquire. FAX me the photo." Hashemi is not in the photo?"

"No. Isn't that odd?"

"In a way, yes, since he was also a prime marriage target. But if he had disappearing in mind, he would not have wanted a photo taken, especially at that time in his life."

"Yeah, makes sense. In a Hashemi-kinda-way. Any news otherwise?"

"Not as yet. Your friends at the Farm are more intrusive than usual. Large money being waved, risks with unknown sources being taken."

"I'm not surprised. Later, then."

"Then." Selah hung up.

Hermie turned a dejected face to Nell. "His sister was 'Ayisha.' Not in this photo. My source says she may be a niece or cousin being advertised for a late marriage."

"Sorry."

"Forgiven." Hermie went too quiet for a moment. Nell braced herself, but needn't have. "That Rolls," Hermie mused.

"Again? Yeah?"

"That Rolls caused a freak-out by Hashemi. Was he freaked because it was a Rolls Royce? Naw. He freaked because it was *the* Rolls Royce."

"Huh?"

"A Rolls Royce owned by someone he knew. A stalker. *The* stalker. Someone who had a reason that was uber dangerous."

"Huh, again?"

"Someone who killed Lila first because it was the first blow planned for Hashemi. Meant to hurt him to the core, the worst, last pain before he died."

"But what's the connection to the rest of the victims?"

"They were evil."

"In what universe?" Nell protested.

"They were not conforming to his version of Islam. HOLY SHIT! Sorry! RASFANI!

"But Hashemi killed him before all this –"

"Yeah. And he was a saint."

"In what *freaking* universe?!" Nell was now disgusted.

"In Rasfani's universe of freaks. He headed cells, a terrorist planning movement. He had followers. *Lots* of followers, gawd help us all."

"And?"

"And, another fanatic as bad as he was could be avenging Rasfani's death, carrying on his bent beliefs. Maybe part of a job interview –- he wants to take Rasfani's place as the leader of those nut-jobs. He started proving his bones by taking out Hashemi, the murderer, and his 'family'. Then he went on to those innocent young women, proving to the movement that they were *not* innocent. Striking them down in the ancient way, because they were an offense against Rasfani's version of Islam. Striking them down as Rasfani was struck down, in secret."

"And now the newer 'problem'." Nell added to Hermie's frustration. "How the hell can we find him? If anyone knows who he is, it sure isn't law enforcement or the FBI or any of the other good guys. Maybe even the bad guys don't know who he is yet. They could be waiting until he announces himself in some gawd- awful manner, this time out in the open, like on a campus, in a church, or wherever the body count will make him the King of Killers. How can *anyone* find him, much less stop him?"

"'Anyone' doesn't have my source." He snatched up his phone, stabbed keys.

Selah, answered at the first ring, amused, "Again?"

Hermie, embarrassed, "Sorry, sorry. But, who ran with Rasfani? In particular, someone who thought of him as gawd almighty."

And Selah teased, "So to speak, yes?"

"I'm desperate. I'm sure it shows. That's why I'm ignoring the ever-listening ears."

"You are never desperate. You are at this moment, 'paused'."

"Always the optimist. What I'm trying to get at is who would start killing in the ancient way to avenge Rasfani's murder because he wanted the job of Head Loon."

"Ah, I see where you are going. This is, how you say, 'juicy'."

"I'm right?"

"I do not know yet, but it is a good idea I can follow. It will take time, though, my friend. This information will be buried deep."

"Shovel fast as you can."

"It will begin in London."

"London? That's a surprise. I was thinking more 'eastern'."

"Rasfani was born in the slums of London. The area restricted to Middle East immigrants at that time. The hatred began there. The hatred was taught. His father was a radical Imam who was prone to beating Islamic 'truths' into his sons and claiming Allah instructed him."

"Another real peach, huh?"

"Ah, there are bushels of them, in all faiths. I think he is still in an English jail for plotting, financing terrorist crimes against the English. They found extensive blueprints of the Houses of Parliament and Windsor Castle in his mosque."

"I'm getting nauseous. You mentioned 'sons'. With Rasfani phffft, could one of his brothers be a contender?"

"No. There were two brothers, younger. They were the ones who told the police about the hiding place in the mosque."

"You're kidding! His other sons went over to the good side?"

"One was in medical school, working to be a surgeon of the heart. The other had a passion for the laws of the English, their history, their coming of age. He wanted to teach these laws. They did this betrayal for themselves, yes, but also for two sisters who were about to be sold into marriage to wealthy men of Rasfani's organization. The brothers got them and their mother out of the country, with the secret help of the English police. New identities, new country. If you wish, I will find out where."

"No, leave them in peace. I'm after a Rasfani clone."

"Rasfani was the apple from his father's tree. Is that the expression?"

"Close enough. So, he was the firstborn. The 'appointed' one."

"It is to be expected. His death was a great blow, to the father and to the plans of many dangerous others. I will look and see and find."

"I owe ya again."

"It is 'nada'." Selah answered, and hung up.

"Okay," Hermie said to Nell. "I got the uber bloodhound on the trail of Rasfani's fan club."

* * * *

He hadn't even noticed it was almost twilight outside. He had a vague recollection of saying vague 'goodnights' to Claire, Nell and the two patrolmen in turn, but his full attention was on the Murder Books and now he was at the end: Shirin Batawi. At least he hoped to good-God- Almighty it *was* the end. Hermie had long since put the reason for a pause in the killings down to the fact that nearly all the young, successful Muslim women who wore headscarves were now traveling in pairs or with male escorts packing heat.

He was stiff from sitting and his vision was getting blurry from the relatively low light in his office. It was okay by summer, when sunlight streamed in until late in the day, even early evening; but it was a while until full-on summer, so decrepitude announced itself in that low electric light that blurred his vision. He rubbed his eyes and once more contemplated a life wearing glasses. *Hell, I can't keep track of my damn cellphone, how am I gonna keep track of a pair of glasses I don't wanna wear in the first place? I swear I will eat my gun before I wear one of those strings around my neck!*

His phone rang harshly in the stillness. He just had time for a horrible thought: *"Oh, God, no, not another lovely girl,"* when he snatched it up. "Grabfelder!" he nearly yelled.

The voice was warm and aristocratic and familiar, "Oh, good, I've caught you. And I hope it's not too short notice." Judge George Patton Pincus said.

Hermie was delighted. "Your Honor! Good to hear you. I was just going over some files, lost track of time."

"And I can imagine why. Because I can imagine the files you're going over. I do sympathize, my friend. Such an awful, awful case."

"'ppreciate it. How are *you* getting along? What can I do for you?"

"I am nearby, in Torrance, had a meeting with lawyers about my wife's Trust that I thought would end hours ago. And now I'm starving, too hungry to drive home. Are you free for dinner?"

"Very free. *My* stomach's rumbling as well."

"Any suggestions? I haven't tooled around the Torrance-Del Amo dining opportunities in years. Was the traffic always this bad?"

"Not quite. Y'see, before the 'renovations, re-designs and renewals' it was just aggravating. Now it's the fourth dimension of hell."

The Judge chuckled, "Exactly. So, where shall I meet you?"

"I know just the place. You like to eat poetry?"

"I beg your pardon? 'Eat poetry'? You're going to explain that, yes?"

Better than an explanation, Hermie gave him the address and directions to the Madame de Lis.

The entire staff was surprised but pleased that Detective Grabfelder had brought a stranger, a guest, especially since the gentleman was obviously so elegant, so gracious, and whose French was enthusiastic and flawless.

"Don't mean to show off," the Judge explained to Hermie after they were seated and comfortable, "but it's been years since I've had the chance to speak French. The wife and I had a long vacation to Normandy and the wine country, and, of course, Paris. We took a month of French classes beforehand, and a lot of it stuck. Afterward, we rented French language movies, got some French novels, just to keep up." The Judge's face softened with good memories.

"I've been picking up a lot of Korean myself."

"Korean? However do you do that?"

"Cable. There's a channel that runs a lot of Korean and other Asian serials. Family dramas, love stories, cut-throat corporate rivalries, and historical bio-pics. I am addicted. Nobody knows why. A Korean coroner and his grandma humor me."

"I must remember to check that out, see if my cable carries it. Sounds fascinating. American television has gotten so repetitive — same manufactured faces and hair-do's on cop shows, or medical shows. Auteur directors who don't know the difference between lighting for television and lighting for films — constant black screens, faces half-lit, half black, can't even tell who's onscreen half the time. Very annoying. Thank God for England sending us such quality programs. Not enough of them, though."

The Judge urged Hermie to order for them, being as this was obviously a favorite place, the ambience calm and fragrant, the staff friendly and cheerfully efficient. He could tell that Detective Herman Grabfelder was held in an admiring affection here.

At the last second, Hermie remembered that Judge Pincus was Jewish and so he didn't order the pork medallions. Instead, he opted for the Michigan memories and ordered the trout. While they were waiting, the Judge asked, "How is your case going?" And Hermie gently told him the Rule: No talking any business until dessert. The Judge approved of the Rule. Especially when he was marveling within the rhapsody of the fragrances and flavors of the savory onion consomme, followed by a hot and cold salad (icy lettuce and tomatoes drizzled with a hot vinegar and olive oil dressing), Trout Almondine gleaming with dark butter and lemon sauce, flaked with sliced almonds, an airy broccoli souffle, and teeny-tiny red potatoes unadorned because they already had their own unique flavor. When dessert came, Hermie was delighted that they once again served the rose petal ice cream and the hot and sugary pie dough cookies.

It was the ice cream that enraptured the Judge. "What *is* this ice cream? It is indeed a 'poem' like you said."

"Would you believe rose petal ice cream? And those cookies? My Grandma and Mom used to make those back home –- pie dough dusted with sugar and cinnamon."

They smiled at each other with the pleasure of it all, pie dough crunching.

It wasn't until they were dreamy with satiety and sipping steaming oh-so-French coffee that Hermie thought he'd better start talking before the two of them fell asleep like lions after that meal.

"As for the case, it's rotten."

Their coffees were discretely refilled three times as Hermie related to the dumbfounded Judge the full narrative of his case.

"Eleventh Century Assassin? And he wears a chador as a disguise? Now I've heard everything!" the Judge shook his head in disbelief.

"I've heard everything, too, and I still haven't a clue," groused Hermie. "And if he hits again —-"

"Now don't borrow trouble, Detective. The word is out, so Muslim ladies are on the alert. They are not the targets they were when this all started."

"Yeah. But now some of them are gonna have to deal with the men in their lives who will revert."

"'Revert'? What do you mean?"

"They will revert to the tribal crap that this is what happens when women go outside the home, unmarried and not pregnant, independent, working, out from the control of fathers, brothers, husbands, uncles. I could tell you stories."

"No need. I've heard about such things. Fathers, brothers actually killing the daughters who disobey."

"And calling it 'Islam'."

"And calling it 'Islam', yes. Such blasphemy."

Since he knew Judge Pincus was a trustworthy man, Hermie said, "Wish I could introduce you to Aida."

"'Aida'?"

"She rescues women from that tribal crap. Arranges escapes, new identities, gives them and their kids all new lives."

"Good God, she sounds like a warrior."

"The exact word."

"You know, I've been wondering what to do with the years I have left. If this Aida or anyone else you know can do with some legal advice or even legal shenanigans, please call on me."

Heremie grinned at this stately man, "The 'shenanigans' would be much appreciated, I'm sure. Especially when I get charged with kidnaping."

"Of "Kevin Costner""? Nonsense. "Kevin Costner" is a fraud."

"Gee, he'll be shocked-*shocked* to hear that."

"No, no, I mean, all the paperwork made out in that name is fraudulent. The boy is a fake in the system. Until and unless the system finds his actual identity, you kidnaped a fraud. You tell your friends at Child Services, and the Harrison's as well, to contact me when and if "Kevin's" real identity is revealed. I'll see to it that Whale Tail does not complicate things. Will the Harrison's want to keep "Kevin"? Adopt?"

"From the looks on their faces and the care they've been giving that boy, he's already their son."

"I look forward to meeting them. I enjoy good people."

Hermie and the Judge saluted with their coffee cups, took another sip of the fragrant brew. Hermie evaluated for a moment, then went for it, but gently: "So . . . how are *you* doing? You said you were working on your wife's Trust?"

"Yes. She wanted certain things done. She inherited quite a bit from her father way back when, shortly after we were married, wise investments over the years have made it very much larger. And she wanted it parceled out to various charities, in particular animal rescue groups in this state and in Africa. Shelters, clinics, no-hunting preserves, breeding and adoption programs, anti-poaching squads. And then there's the bequest to our son."

"As I said before, I can try to find him, if you want. If he's still into drugs, he's undoubtedly been busted now and again, so I could do a search of the whole country."

"I have had that in my mind since you first mentioned it. But . . ."

"You're not ready to know."

A relieved smile at being understood softened those patrician cheekbones, "Precisely. My wife's passing . . . certain thoughts, memories . . . I'm all askew, so to speak."

"That means you're normal. But you're way better than me. When my wife died, overdose, I nosedived into a tank of Stingers and didn't surface until the job and my liver were both almost shot to hell. And I didn't give a rat's patoot."

"Hard to believe that, looking at you, knowing you now."

"Ever hear of Bud's Body Works, the Nazi's friend?"

Un-refined laughter burst out of the Judge. "No, never heard of it. Did the trick, did it?"

"From sweat and threats I emerged sober as a judge -- no offense -- and a slim shadow of my former self. Hated every minute of it. Still do off and on. And a lot of times I'm still absolutely convinced that a Stinger would 'clear my head', I lie to myself, so I could see what I'm missing on this goddamn case. Sorry. But this case has became so personal. Not just its brutality, but because of all the people it damaged. "Kevin", the parents and friends of those wonderful daughters, and the devout Muslims who are haunted by the possibility that one of their own is doing such unholy crimes"

"The political climate certainly isn't helping."

"Do not get me started!"

They both took angry sips of their coffee.

"On an entirely other subject --" the Judge began.

"Which we need. Go for it."

"Should I redecorate?"

Hermie nearly sprayed a few cookie crumbs with surprise. Of all things, he didn't expect *that*. "How's that?" he managed, delicately

The Judge grinned, shyly, "Remarkable, isn't it, the things one thinks of when sleep is out of reach. Well, you once said our house was a reflection of my wife's happiness, so maybe it's sacrilegious to her, in a way, but sometimes I look around and wonder, 'What about a different color here'? Or 'What about shutters instead of drapes there'? Am I losing my mind?"

Hermie grinned, reassuringly. "Absolutely not. Think of it as your creative side stirring. You are . . ." He searched for the right word because he knew it was very important: "You are *emerging.*"

"'Emerging'?" the Judge tested the word, both curious and amused. "Emerging . . . indeed."

"Yeah. You never could think only of yourself for a long time, now you are at the head of the line. So, your neglected self is emerging. And *asking* for stuff, getting interested in things you hadda ignore, or never noticed. I'm kinda surprised it isn't golf or tennis, but --"

"Humph! Golf, tennis, such boring people. Most of them relatives."

Hermie laughed. "Well, redecorating is certainly something different. Maybe even kinda mysterious. Ya never know how it'll turn out. Get an idea, paint a wall, and either it turns out great, or it's just plain awful and you gotta start over. Point is, you *are* starting over. And that's a good thang."

"'Good thang', is it? How did *you* start over? Bud's I know, but, what else?"

"I got picked up by a brassy stray cat I named Eleanor. And a class-full of students and their teacher took over my Crazy Aunt Fern's house and scrubbed and polished and threatened to return with whips if I didn't start paying attention to the care and feeding of my house. And I also met two ladies at a grocery store, Jasmine and Carmen, who taught me the wonderfulness of cooking instead of eating crap for a living. Plus I have two ladies at work who whomp me upside de haid if I get out of line. It all added up to what you see before you — a changed man with a future, thanks to a resurrected liver."

"I am filled with admiration. And somewhat reassured. Although I am surrounded by friends, relatives, kind people who want to help, but . . . they do not know me, understand?"

"Yeah. You've been in disguise for years."

"'Disguised'. That's it," the Judge said through his chuckles, suddenly looking younger.

"By the way, one of the people who helped me along the way could really give you some good advice about decorating. She works in that department store that's now impossible to get to in the renovated-ness of the Del Amo mall. She started out in the Men's Department, now she's in Small Appliances and Bedding, but ignore that — she's been in that store for some years, knows everything, probably get you lots of discounts. Get on over there some day, go a couple floors up, ask for Hetty McDougald. Tell her I sent you. She'll help you out."

And with that, Hermie finished off his coffee, this time lowering his eyes because he was sure the Judge would see that his eyes were dancing with conspiracy.

* * * *

Paperwork, always paperwork. It was too many hours later when his private line rang. It was Gordie.

"Yo, Herms, sorry to interrupt, but...well..."

"When's your surgery date?"

"Yeah. How'd you –? It's day after tomorrow. Seven AM for chrissakes."

"I'll pick you up, say, six-thirty?"

"Really? You'll take me?"

"I"ve been taking you for years."

Gordie's laugh was light with relief. "The Doc says ordinarily I could go home the same day, but he's picky — he wants me to stay overnight to force me to take it easy, go home the next morning. Checkout time is 10 AM."

"Much more reasonable hour. I'll bring coffee and little cakes. Are you okay to stay home alone after that?"

"Oh, hell, yes. I'll be on leave for a couple days, but it's routine, says Homie."

"Sounds good. Tell Homie I said 'Hey'." They were both chuckling when Hermie hung up.

It wasn't thirty seconds later when Hermie made THE CALL: To Sharon Menloe, this time to tell her *ev-vv-er-y-thang*, and tell her that if she hadn't actually decided to dumped that idiot, she should show up at the clinic the day after tomorrow, but wait until Doctor "Homie" Nielsen will have finished the surgery but still be there to answer any questions she had. And since Gordie will be coming out of a drug-induced haze, he'll be helpless enough for her to whomp 'im and whomp 'im good upside de haid for not telling her what the hell was going on from the beginning. And the next day, she can be the one to take Gordie home to continue his recovery and THE RECKONING. Or dump his recuperating ass.

On that day, he got the expected phone call from Gordie: "YOU SONUVABITCHBASTARD! Can't keep a goddamn secret! Who knew?!"

"I didn't decide to save you from your stupidity until the day your surgery was set. 'Swear. I didn't breathe a word till then. Not even when those Bambi eyes saw right through me. She won't trust either of us for many, many *MANY* years. We will be *shamed*, really regular."

"Well....okay. But I can tell you it was quite a shock waking up from the surgery and instead of *you* being there, Sharon was there. Thunder rumbling. I thought I was having a wild reaction to the drugs. Till the lightning struck and she started yelling."

"She whomped ya?"

"Damn near. Patients, doctors, nurses, orderlies, all were wowed."

"Hell. I was hoping she'd womp ya good."

"I know. I deserve it."

"Damn straight, Fool. How are you feeling, by the way? Jewels intact and all? Tinted thought they may be?"

Gordie laughed. "Just fine and color normal. Glad it's over. *So* glad. *Jeez...*".."

"Yeah, I know," empathized Hermie.

"And Homie said the tumor was self-contained, no sign on it or the blood tests that any cells had traveled. But I'll have tests now and then, regular, to stay sure."

"Thank you, God." Hermie couldn't hold it in anymore.

"Amen to that, Bro'. Hermie...well, thanks. Really. Thanks."

"Accepted. Oh, one more thing —"

"Yeah?"

"DON'T YOU EVER, <u>NEVER</u> DO THAT TO ME AGAIN!" Hermie slammed the phone down, sat back, and just *breathed*.

CHAPTER TWENTY-THREE

"There are three things you cannot hide: Love,
Smoke, And a man riding a camel."

Arabian Proverb

"Ya 'forgot' this?" Hank could be nicely sarcastic when the situation presented itself, having been well taught by you-know-who.

"I been busy," Hermie shrugged.

"It was in your pocket all this time. And you still forgot it?" He waved the CD and case, emphasizing its weight and dimensions.

"Let's say we move on. What's on it?"

With a last look of amazement, Hank turned to his computer, slipped the CD into its tray on the hard drive. They both heard the familiar loud buzzing, soft buzzing, then silence. And for the first time, *EVER*, Hank said, "Hmmm..."

Earlier, Hermie had called Hank, opening with: "What are ya doing?"

"Having a fried egg and ham sandwich. Where'd you get this mustard? There's German on the label," said Hank, past a mouthful. "Have-ta go out and get chips, though, since ye-ew forgot," he teased.

Half an hour later, Hermie was knocking not so gently on Hank's door, carrying grocery bags stuffed with every kind of chip made on earth: Italian, Mexican, Middle Eastern, Chinese, Japanese. Along with good old American potato, veggie, bagel, corn (yellow), corn (blue), pretzel and quinoa. Under his arms he hefted two long boxes of ice cold cans of cola, one diet one deadly. He also brought a big box of cookies: chocolate chip, bumpy with pecans.

Hank eagerly ripped an opening in the bagel chips and stuff a cheek, then popped the top off a cold can of the deadly cola, swigged, swallowed, burped loudly, then took the CD and slipped it into his computer's tray. And that's when it happened: Hank said "Hmmmm..."

Now, after some more buzzing and even more silence, Hank peered at the blank computer monitor and admitted: "Well, this is just plain weird!" His long fingers went from tapping to pounding on the beleaguered keyboard. Nada onscreen.

Hermie hovered, glum, "This is Jordan Hashemi. 'Encrypted', right?" Hermie took a wistful pride in using the right word, but it didn't alert Hank.

"Encrypting I get. It can take a while, but it's possible to crack. This is more than encrypting, more than a fire wall. It's a blank disc that *isn't* a blank."

"You got that right. Blank it's not-not-not."

"If someone thought it was blank and tried to record on it, I wonder what would happen," Hank mused.

"Probably a nuclear explosion. Don't dare."

"Wouldn't, because you're right. He's prob'ly got it rigged so it causes a total meltdown of the hard drive it's in, unless it's the hard drive the disc was made specifically *for*. Jeez, I wish I could-a met this Hashemi guy. He's a damn genius."

"'If only he'd use his genius for good instead of ee-vil.'" Hermie crooned.

"What kinda 'evil instead'?"

"Actually, nobody knows. FBI and the rest of the alphabet thought they had him pegged as an international arms dealer. It is to laugh. They were so-o wrong. He was a murderer, but the man he killed was a monster, a terrorist. The damage that monster was planning –- poisoned baby food, for chrissakes."

"What?!" Hank was stunned.

"Don't think about it, it's too puke-worthy." Then Hermie's eyes glowed down to low beam, so Hank removed the CD from the computer, replaced it in its case. Set it where Hermie would see it and remember to take it with him. Worth a try. "What do you think is on this disc?"

"The answers."

"Answers to what? His computer codes?"

"Nothing so mundane. Although they're probably included. I think it contains his motives, his plans, where everything *is*, and especially his character. I think it contains exactly what he was selling and doing, all the poop the FBI and sundry are still lusting after."

"Wasn't Hashemi a terrorist?"

"Absolutely not. That much I know."

"How could ya know?"

"Because of the two people he loved and who loved him. Because of the impression he made on a no-nonsense lady condo board president, and a salt-of-the-earth owner of an Italian restaurant. And because a terrorist stalked him and killed him, because of his value. Has Roland been calling?"

The sudden switch in subjects jarred Hank. "No, no, he's cool. Actually, I've been calling him, keeping him posted, letting him know I am almost finished with those 'damn depositions'. Volunteered some Overtime, free, whenever."

"Heckuva guy, Roland. I've said so before."

Hank was in mid-munch and swig when Hermie suddenly turned those blue lasers back to him and pounced: "This might be a colossal waste of your time, fields having been control-burned and tilled by uber-experts and all, but how would you feel about trying to best an FBI, CIA, NSA, DIA, and Homeland Whatever, etcetera search?"

Hank grinnned, "Stoked! What and where and when?"

"Now. Immigration records. An idea Nell had. Any port in-a storm."

"Lay it on me," Hank grinned. "I take it you want to look for Jordan Hashemi?"

"Nope. I want to look for his beginnings. Winston Delano Safir."

"'Winston Delano'? What-a guy!" And Hank's fingers began their fluttering and pounding. But seconds later, his long bones curved in that familiar slump of frustration. "Crap," he said softly to the monitor screen's disappointment.

"Yeah," answered Hermie. "I may have that printed on t-shirts for us all." Hermie sipped, winced at the odd taste of diet cola, his thoughts drifting in.

Hank swigged the deadly sugar-loaded cola, drained the can, opened another with a pop! and a pssshhh!, and took a swig. Reached for one of the cookies in the box, took a large bite, munched, then, "Are you sure these are sugarless?"

"As God is my witness. Can't tell a-tall, can ya?"

"Who knew?" Hank answered, crunching, swigging. Then Hank apparently got an idea, partial cookie stayed in his teeth when he swung back to his computer and fingers flew over the keyboard.

Hermie was so discouraged, he only paid half an attention. "What?" he asked, cookies crumbs scattering from his gloom.

"London," Hank answered, typing, chewing.

"Hashemi wiped London clean of all records. The FBI and the other fraternity brothers went down those country roads long ago."

"I'm sure they did. Clever dudes. But there's more than one way..." Hank, paused, swallowed. "Uh...legally speaking..."

"How many times do I have to tell ya?"

Hank grinned, "O-oh-ka-ay..." His fingers flew again and Hermie watched the monitor screen flash with various printing, too fast to follow, and besides why bother. Discouragement was now chronic and wearing away at his interest.

"Well-well-well," Hank read the screen. "Winston Delano Safir, born September 2, 1974, 6 AM. In Leeds. Not London."

Hermie perked up. "You're kidding!"

"Ayisha Safir, born January 21, 1977, 4 PM. Also in Leeds. A preemie — premature birth. But released from the hospital at normal weight, 'thriving'."

Hermie was now awed, stood up to hover near Hank's shoulder, tried to read the computer screen, but Hank was typing so fast the screen kept changing. "How the hell did you —?"

"Birth records, but away from London city." He resumed typing. "Ah, here's the official report on that plane crash, 1996. Investigation . . . final conclusion it was not aircraft failure . . . 'pilot error' . . . he was not qualified 'sufficiently' to judge and fly in 'inclement' weather. That's the British way of saying he made a foolish, ego mistake. Poor guy. And the rest of them. That's probably why the *real* record wasn't in the 'Official' place such records usually are. To spare survivors — in this case the pilot's family as well as Winston Safir — the awful truth. That's why I went into 'Classified'. Don't ask. I have a buddy who's a pilot. If it's even a slight shpritz, he does not go up. 'Weather can kill ya', he always says."

"And that's where the records peter out. Winston Delano Safir was left behind. And then he vanished. Into Jordan Hashemi. Who does not exist."

Hank was still trying, "Damn, it's all in Arabic. Back then they didn't bother to translate."

"What?"

"Winston and family were Muslims, right? I was trying to find records or registrations at mosques in and around Leeds or London. Families would be recorded. I assume births and deaths and marriages are registered in mosques, just like in churches?"

"Damned if I know. But there's someone we can ask."

Hermie snatched up the wall phone, punched numbers. "Shakey? Grabfelder. I gotta problem."

Shakey had followed instructions and so had hefted over jugs of green tea and a box of green tea bags. Sometime later the three guys were shoulder to shoulder in front of the computer monitor, watching an endless stream of beautiful Arabic or crisp English type drift down, drift up, drift to the side; Hermie and Hank tinkling glasses of iced green tea.

"Crap?" asked Hermie delicately, taking another gulp of disappointment.

"Yeah," said Shakey, who was the odd man: his tea steamed in a cup, which he blew on and sipped. "The Arabic I can translate for ya, but the other problem is a good thing, actually, dozens of mosques all over England these days. Back in the day . . ."

"'Back in the day', that's it!" Hank said, his enthusiasm refreshed by meeting Shakey. Obedient to his flying, clacking fingers, the computer screen emptied and filled. "Winston was born in 1974 . . ."

"We *think!*" Hermie snorted.

"Okay, back in *that* day there were very few mosques in England. Or anywhere in Europe," said Shakey.

"He was born in Leeds. This is Leeds." said Hank.

Shakey peered at the screen, "Nothing in Leeds. What about nearby? What is nearby, by the way?"

Hank typed, they all looked. "Don't know. I'm just Googling mosques without locations." A small number of lines slipped onto the screen.

"Only two?" Shakey marveled. "Times sure have been a-changing."

"They're both just outside London."

"That would make sense. Immigration headed to the big city –- for jobs, housing, schools. But it took awhile before mosques were built. Or allowed."

Hank, being thoughtful with a stranger, especially a stranger with an Islamic persuasion, "Uh, I'm going into their private records, marriages, births, deaths, names in the congregation. If 'congregation' is the right word for a mosque."

Shakey, being generous with a stranger, especially with a non-Islamic persuasion, smiled reassuringly and said, "Hey, we're trying to find a murderer of Muslim daughters. Whatever works. It might be under 'community'."

Hank nodded, typed. "Here's the first one –- mosque, names are in Arabic."

Shakey peered closer at the screen, "The mosque: Mar-Hab-bee-kum, that basically means 'welcome'."

"Here's the congregation list."

Shakey turned to Hermie, "I'm looking for 'Safir', right?"

"Right."

Arabic flowed by. "Nope."

"Should I try birth records?"

"Yeah," said Shakey. "Maybe the Safir folks weren't observant, but they wanted their kids' births recorded. That's a common thing, casual-Muslim-wise."

Hank typed, Shakey peered. Then Shakey stepped back. "Nada, Herms. Sorry."

Hank typed, "Let's try the other mosque."

In seconds, Shakey saw and whooped, "'Safir'! Winston Delano Safir! Keep going . . . 'Safir'! Ayisha Safir! Parents Farbod and Hannah Safir! In 1974 and 1977. This was the mosque they went to, either to worship or to touch base. Whoop-dee-do! That's Arabic for 'at last, *something*'!"

"So, they must have lived nearby," said Hermie hopefully. "But the FBI, CIA, all those other clowns never got an address in England for Hashemi. Or Winston Safir either. Hermie paused, then said, "Anything on burials? I hadda ask." Hermie said.

Hank typed, Shakey read.

"Yes, there they are," Shakey read: "1996, the burials of mom, Hannah, dad, Farbod, and daughter Ayisha Safir. This is where the family of Winston Safir ended." Shakey's eyes closed for the briefest moment, lips moving in what Hertmie knew was a kind prayer. Shakey was known to pray often, even for strangers.

Hank leaned back in his chair, Hermie and Shakey sat and leaned in other chairs. All three reached for the box of cookies, it was empty. "Damn," said Shakey softly with disappointment. "And they were sugarless? From Ralphs? Swear?"

"'Swear," said Hermie. But his mind was elsewhere.

Shakey recognized that faraway look when Hermie's blue-fire eyes turned down to low. "What up, Herms?"

Hermie looked up at Shakey and knew he could ask anything of him; even if he asked in the wrong way, Shakey would not take offense. "I got a Eleventh Century Assassin slaughtering here. Now, obviously he's not a ghost, and chances of a copycat are pretty slim, given the perfection of the M.O . . . so . . ."

"So he could be a descendant. Who got the training." Shakey said confidently.

"Is that possible? After all this time? Could there be actual descendants of -- what's his name?"

"Ismailian Hassan-I Sabbah, the inventor of Assassins. In Shiite Muslim history, he's a blessed hero. Pride would keep track of that lineage, generation after generation, through the male line, of course. Females would still carry the historic name when they married -- they'd hyphen it onto the husband's name just to let his family know what a prize they got."

"How do you spell it?" asked Hank, fingers hovering over keys. He typed as Shakey spelled.

"Ismailian -- I-s-m-a-i-l-ian, Hassan-I -- two s's and a dash-I -- and Sabbah -- s-a-bb-ah."

They all peered at the screen. Hank hunted, "Let me just Google around everywhere, anywhere in Europe," Hank mused. Then: "Ah, here's mention of a documentary that ran on TV, *'Ancient Assassins'* . . . some history books have a mention . . . Wikipedia, for what that's worth . . ."

"Go back to the first mosques in England, 'back in the day'."

Hanks' flying fingers did, while Shakey zeroed in on the screen.

"Nope," Shakey said. "No 'Hassan-I Sabbah', not even 'Ismailian Hassan'. Any mosque would have been pleased as punch to have that name in its roster. Unless the mosques at that time were all Sunni. It's possible. 'Sunni' means 'community', so it's possible that it was the Sunni's who first branched out into Europe, England. Shiites followed later, maybe. I'd have to look that up, I'm embarrassed to say."

"Wait," Hank said and Hermie wondered why smoke didn't billow out of the keyboard under Hank's pounding fingers. "Let's start with the year Muslim births were first recorded in England, then go backwards . . . Nope . . . nope . . . this is gonna take a while."

"Where are you hunting?" Hermie asked.

"Immigration records. Looking for the if and when date the Sabbahs arrived in England, first. If no-go, I'll try the rest of Europe."

"You're assuming the family would have left Iran," interjected Shakey.

"Didn't everyone?"

"This family would have been rich, well-connected, untouchable from the upheavals of that time."

"Wouldn't they also have been a threat? To Sunnis? With their fame, money, couldn't they have rallied people — Shiites — to a cause, their own cause? And if it didn't match whoever was causing 'current events' of that time . . ." Hermie asked.

"You're right," Shakey said. 'History and money is a whacking good threat against status quo power."

Hank suddenly grinned at the computer screen, "The Sabbah family arrived in Southhampton on March 2, 1994. Mom, Dad and six kids."

"I'll be damned," Hermie said.

Shakey peered at the screen. "This is odd," he said.

"Oh, hell, what!" Hermie, dreading the balloon being punctured yet again.

"Six kids. All girls. Ages 14, 12, 10, 8, 6, 5 and 3. Poor Mrs. Sabbah, she was living on borrowed time, with no sons produced after six tries. It's always the woman's fault, y'see; don't get me started. Had they not been busy fleeing the 'current events' of Iran, there'd be another wife in tow. However, at least two daughters were of marriageable age, there's that future investment."

"Where did they go, where did they live?" The look on Hermie's face was familiar to them both: Hermie was onto something.

"That would be a problem — they'd probably bunk with relatives at first, until Dad got a job, the kids got into school. And the female relatives would educate the wife as to shopping, food, money, some language, that kind of thing," Shakey said.

"What was Dad's occupation?" The hopeful note still in Hermie's voice.

Hank clicked, peered: "According to their Southhampton docs, Mr. Sabbah was a teacher."

"Of what?"

"Secondary school. High school-type."

"Not martial arts?" asked Hermie.

"I see where you're headed. No, Herms, it isn't him," Shakey said, kindly. "Time frame, age, location, eliminates him."

"Them that can't, *teach.*" Hermie was reluctant to let go of a thought. An answer.

"Yeah. But in this case, your 'martial arts' idea would have fit, but *he* doesn't. Much too old."

"And too dead," Hank piped up, looking at the screen. "Immigration records were adjusted in 2004: Mr. I Sabbah died of a heart attack that year. Wife wanted to stay put, put on the waiting period list. Along with eight kids."

"Ah, they finally had a son or two or three?" Shakey asked.

"Nope. Two more girls. No mention of another wife."

"There wouldn't be. Polygamy? This is England!" Shakey declared. "Poor Sabbah, the pressure was what killed him in the end. All those girls. He probably thought there wasn't enough husband material in all of England. Europe, even. And it would take beaucoup bucks to import a good catch from Iran."

"I give up." Hermie drained his glass. "Hank, can you print out all the stuff you just found, so I'll have it when I forget something? Which I'm sure to do."

"Sure. No problem.

"Oh, one more thing: those two original mosques in the London area. Can you print out the members list or burial and birth lists. Marriage lists. Or are they in Arabic?"

"Arabic until about — let's look . . ." Shakey and Hank peered at the screen being scrolled. "Ah, they started doing English lists in late 1980's."

"I'll print from there," said Hank, clicking, clicking. The printer gave a shout of mechanics and printed pages started spewing out.

"Sorry I couldn't have been more help," Shakey said, patting Hermie's arm.

"Oh, no, no, your translations found us some info. Any port in-a storm. We got the assassin's name landing in England. That's more than I got after all this time. And – **WAIT!**"

Both Hank and Snakey jumped, startled.

"**WHAT?!**" Hank yelled back.

"The dates. The date that family landed in Southhampton –- the year -- where was Hashemi -- Winston Safir around that date?"

Hank nodded as if he understood where Hermie was going. Fingers flew, computer screen flipped out. "1994 . . . Winston Safir was . . . was 20 years old."

"He'd be in college yet," offered Shakey helpfully. "His parents were well-to-do enough, so check the elite, famous Universities: Harrow, Oxford . . ."

"Yeah, doin' it . . ." After an interval of clicking that lasted long minutes. Hank sat back. "Not finding him. Maybe he didn't go to an elite?"

"Or that's when he started destroying his existence." Hermie. said. "His family was killed not long after, right? That's when he left the planet, records-wise."

"And not married? Very odd. He was the only son." said Shakey.

"Nell said the same thing. Culture-wise. She's my boss at my stationette. One of them. I have two. One black, one white, so there's no escape." He ignored the curious stares of Hank and Shakey. "So . . . he disappeared when he was in his twenties, give or take."

"When he was single and rich, apparently," remarked Shakey.

"And gettin' busy. If he was a genius, which he sure was, he was born one. So he was planning, plotting long before his twenties. He definitely gave himself a head start."

"I think he lingered because of his parents and sister," Shakey said. "He was an only son, he was responsible for their future. He would have made sure his parents were 'settled' -– we can assume their ages had them thinking of retirement from performing, traveling for gigs. And his sister? How old was she when they were all killed?"

"Not even twenty."

"It was his duty to see her safely married. Before she was killed, I have no doubt he'd have found someone suitable and was vetting him to the max." Shakey said.

"I wonder who he was," Hermie sounded almost wistful.

"That would be impossible to discover. At that stage, only the fathers met, talked. Bargaining had not yet begun because they needed time for some serious financial and social background vetting."

"There was a picture in Hashemi's desk. Mom, Dad, and maybe a prime candidate, cousin or niece being advertised. Like, on approval. You wouldn't say she was anybody's Dream Girl, looks-wise."

"Was Hashemi in the picture?"

"No."

"That's odd."

"Maybe he took the picture?"

"Maybe. But that's still odd, that he wasn't with them. He was much more of a catch than she was, so Mom and Dad would have wanted to show him off, too."

"Maybe they didn't get the chance. Maybe the picture was taken just before they were killed."

"True. Sad."

"Or, more likely, Hashemi's plotting of his escape did not include having his picture taken for everyone to know what he looked like." Hermie stood up, stretched, gathered up glasses, cup and saucer, empty cookie box, put everything where it belonged, sponged up cookie crumbs.

Hank's printer kept up its rhythmic clicking and shuffling. When the printing stopped, Hank gathered up the sheets and divided them into what he thought was overall subjects and stapled these sections, put everything in a sturdy folder, handed it to Hermie.

"Ah, nighttime reading when there's nothing on the TV machine. Thanks, Hank . . . Shakey. I owe you both big time."

"Wish I could have been of more help," said Shakey. "If you think of anything else . . ."

"I will tingle. Hank, go back to work. You're *real* work, so Roland can sleep nights."

"Yeah. Keep me posted about "Kevin"."

"Always. Did you read that report in the Times about the conditions at Juvenile Hall? Kidnaping him outta there was a damn good idea."

"*Your* good idea." Hank said.

"Oh, I get them now and then, here and there." He grinned and turned to leave. And offered a parting shot as evidence of his frustration: "Just not lately!"

* * * *

Nell greeted him back at the stationette, after a quick check at the level of flames in his eyes to judge how the session with Hank went. "Anything?" she smiled encouragement.

Hermie held up a sheaf of Hank's computer printouts. "Lots and lots. But who the hell knows?" He was about to go into his office when he heard the stationette's door open, and he was surprised to see Millie Harrison come in. If she hadn't been smiling he'd have felt the familiar flutter of fear. "'Kevin'?" he hadda ask anyway, it being automatic.

Millie was quick to reassure, having learned herself how to read those blue flames. "Yes. But he's done something — well, I think it's real important."

To start breathing regular again, Hermie made calm introductions, "Mrs. Harrison, this is my assistant, Nell Barlow. Nell, this is 'Kevin's' Mom." The word just slipped out naturally, but Millie caught it and beamed.

"So nice too meeet you at last, Mrs. Harrison. Hermie, you can meet in your office."

"We can?" Hermie sounded kinda surprised. A quick look inside revealed the guest chair had been cleared, his desk top neat as a pin. "You bulldozed?"

"Yet again."

"Men," smiled Mrs. Harrison.

"Men," nodded Nell. "How about some coffee? Or hot chocolate?"

"Oh, no, I can't stay long. Frank and 'Kevin' are — Well, I shouldn't stay too long."

"Come in, come in. Sit down, be comfortable," Hermie ushered her in and onto the guest chair. A sudden panic when he realized the horror festooning the walls smack in Millie's sight line. And she *saw*. "Oh, God, Millie! I forgot — you shouldn't see —!"

The memory flickered pain only briefly in her hazel eyes. Then, "I'm alright, now. Such awful, awful... But they aren't our boy. Is that a heartless thing to say?"

"No, no, I understand. But here —" he hauled her up and guided her to his desk chair, where the wall she now faced was colorful with elephant, cheetah and baboon mothers cuddling their children. Millie looked them over, smiling. "How wonderful. We're all alike, aren't we? Us Moms." Her smile was less, but calm, accepting. Then she rummaged in her large purse, took out a file folder. Paused to say, "We been readin' up, Frank and I, on the kinds of therapies they do for kids who are — well, like our 'Kevin'."

Our 'Kevin'. Hermie's eyes warmed with what would be tears if not for the usual concealed effort. "That's a good idea. Should help."

"It did. One thing we read about was giving kids stuff so they could draw, or a coloring book. So Frank went down to that art supply place in that mini-mall down-by Carson. Picture it — Frank in-a art supply store," she twinkled.

Hermie chuckled, "I'm sure that was an experience for one and all."

"That's for sure. They prob'ly thought he was some kind-a Grandpa Moses, he come away with so much 'art' stuff. He come home with a couple-a big-ole drawing tablets and some colored chalk and charcoal and all kinds-a pencils and even a set of paints. Profit went up in that store that day, I'll say. Well, we set everything out on the card table we got."

"How did 'Kevin' react?

"Nothing."

"Oh. I'm sorry."

"It's like he *saw* everything, but didn't know what anything was, y'know?"

"Yeah. I've seen that look. He's too far away, still."

"So-so far, yes. But then I had an idea."

I knew she would, Hermie thought, admiringly.

"From when I was a kid, see? I took out one of those pads of drawing paper, laid it between us on the table, opened it to a blank sheet, grabbed one of those artsy pencils and — don't know why a-tall — but I drew a tic-tac-toe and put an 'X' in it."

Hermie's eyebrows asked.

"Nope. Nuthin'. But I kept going. Put an 'O' in the center. And 'Kevin' *jerked.*"

"'Jerked'?"

"Like he'd been slapped. I reached over to hold his hand, forgot I still had that pencil in it. Figuring I'd brought up an awful memory, I told him, 'It's okay, 'Kevin'. I'm sorry if I scared ya. You're safe, remember? You are *safe.*'" Millie suddenly sat back, as if she couldn't contain a pride that suddenly came over her. "And then, he did it."

Hermie leaned closer, rapt.

"He took the pencil outta my hand."

"Jeezus! You're kidding!"

"He took that pencil and then he looked down at the tic-tac-toe squares and he moved the pencil to the 'O', but it was like that pencil weighed a ton. He hadda hold it with both hands when he did it."

"What-*what*?!"

"With both hands he drew the 'O' on top of the one what I'd already drew. Then he pushed that so-heavy pencil and..." She paused, opened the file folder and took out a large sheet of folded paper, unfolded it carefully, laid it down on the desk, slid it over to Hermie.

He saw that most of the squares had been filled, each with a single letter, and including the 'O' that Millie had written, now over-written to the point of nearly poking through the paper. He struggled to put the letters in an order, until Millie slid another piece of paper over to him, on which she had obviously printed: 'SORAYA'. "It's 'Soraya'. 'Kevin" wrote 'Soraya' on the tic-tac-toe."

"How do you —-?"

"I spoke that name out loud. Just had time to think it was a beautiful name, until --I have never seen such terror fill that boy's — or any child's – eyes. He clapped both hands over his mouth as though he was holdin' it in. So I said to him, "Who is Soraya, 'Kevin'?" But he just shook his head as if he didn't want me to know."

"He was protecting you. Protecting you from 'Soraya'."

Millie could only nod before the tissue she pulled out of her sleeve could reach her suddenly overflowing eyes, tears being caught on top of her cheeks now rounded with a proud smile.

CHAPTER TWENTY-FOUR

"Success is not final; failure is not final;
it is the courage to continue that counts."

Winston Churchill

"WHO THE HELL IS SORAYA?!
Selah realized he needed to get used to the yell instead of a greeting for a time, because this was now a habit caused by the painful, guilty frustration of his remarkable friend. But this time Selah was at a loss: "Are you speaking of history? The wife of the Shah of Iran who was divorced because she was barren? But this was back in the Sixties. That gallant lady died some time ago."

"WHO THE HELL IS SORAYA *NOW?!*"

"I do not understand."

"Soraya killed Lila Miller and Jordan Hashemi! And because of the M.O. I'd bet the farm that bitch killed all those other Muslim girls! Why? I have no goddamn idea!"

"This is not possible! There were the marks of the Assassin. A *woman* wielding that particular dagger? In that way? This is *not* possible."

"It happened! It's happening! 'Kevin' knows! 'Kevin' *saw!* HE SAW! HE NAMED HER! Selah, don't let me down here –- who the hell is Soraya?!"

"I will discover. Calm yourself. But –-"

"Don't 'but' me, Selah! I'm on my last nerve! If she stabs another young girl –-!

"It *cannot* be a woman! This is an Assassin! Using the ancient weapon, the ancient method. This takes training, for *years!* No such training would be given to a woman! A woman is *less*, she is not taught such high things!"

"But 'Kevin' saw her do it!"

"Your idea of a man disguised in a chador is what 'Kevin' saw. A man skilled in the dagger of the Assassin, disguised as a woman so as to get near the victims. It is the only thing that makes sense — because it *cannot* be a woman! No Muslim man would teach a woman the Assassin's skill! And the Assassin must be *taught!*"

Hermie paused to breathe. Then: "Then why the name, 'Soraya?' 'Kevin' wrote her name on a tic-tac-toe!"

"On a *what*?!"

"Someone's been stalking them — Hashemi, Lila, 'Kevin' — stalking them for years, maybe. Then she/he kills his mother and Hashemi, kills young Muslim girls, for what? Why? For *show*? Revenge for Rasfani's death? Okay, maybe. 'Kevin' saw that first kill, and ran. Maybe the second kill, if he didn't get far enough away. Since then, he's been catatonic. But now 'Kevin' finally had a break-through: he wrote a name: 'Soraya' Why that name? Why *only* that name?!"

Now Selah took some time to just breathe. Then: "Perhaps someone in Hashemi's past named Soraya *hired* the killer. And the boy overheard this? Or was told this by Hashemi? If the killer is a relative of Rasfani — a vengeful sister is possible to have hired him. I will discover his sisters' names. This will take time because they are under the protective cover the English set up for them. First, I will have to discover the country of their hiding. However... and I confess that this is a puzzlement: Surely, with all his powers Hashemi would have eliminated a stalker, an enemy. As he has done so many times before. Why not *now*? He would not only know who the stalker was, but that 'Soraya' hired him. Why did he not *stop* them?"

"I'll know why when I know her. Call out the troops, Selah —"

" 'Troops' ?"

"I mean call out everyone and anyone you know to find out who the hell is Soraya."

"Ah, the 'troops'. I will do so. But I urge caution."

"Why *this* time?"

"Jordan Hashemi could not — or would not — stop the Assassin. You are rarely helpless, my dear friend, but this time you may be if you discover the identity of this monster, and the Soraya who hired him."

"A gun beats a dagger every time."

"But did not Jordan Hashemi always carry a gun?"

"Ah."

"Yes, 'Ah'. If I may speak plainly: You have but a single advantage."

"Let me have it. I'm just sayin'."

"This Asssassin must get *close* to kill. Do not permit that. Shoot first before any discussion."

"What if he decides to switch to a gun?"

"This will not happen."

"And just how do you know that, hmmmm?"

Ah, good, his sense of humor returns, to protect his sanity. "The dagger, the blows, the victims, these are his messages. Or *her* messages. The message is all important, as it is for *all* fanatics. This message is the reason for their existence. The message is their *fame.* They will not change it. They will not change from a dagger to a gun. Of this I am certain."

"Hey, that slime is running around in an Arab woman's clothes, so I'm not putting anything past his ass!"

"Good. That will keep you safe. I will 'call out the troops', as you ask, *all* of them. It will take time. I must start in Iran, and information from there is often slow in coming, because the fear is everywhere. For good reasons."

"With you, it's time well spent. Sorry for the yelling and all."

"Nonsense. It was understood."

"Thanks, Selah. Again."

"Do not thank me now. Express the thanks if and when I find out who these monsters are, and they are on the ground, bleeding. And silent."

"Now that's a picture I'll put in my wallet. Till soon."

And Hermie abruptly hung up and Selah knew him well enough to hope that his exhausted friend just got another idea. Another 'scent'.

* * * *

Since he knew he wasn't going to be able to sleep — *again* — Hermie kept on paging through Hank's printouts. He noticed that all the records they unearthed basically stopped shortly after the Sabbah's landed in England. And it was just a few years after this that Winston Delano Safir began erasing his existence and Jordan Hashemi was created. Who did not exist.

Why that particular time? Parents, sister were cruelly taken from him. He was completely alone, independent, he could do it, uninhibited. No family to ask: 'What the hell, Winston?' School friends wouldn't notice — at that age they were kicking off their own lives, no time to keep in touch, especially with Winston. He was undoubtedly a 'fair weather friend', didn't get close, didn't bother keeping in touch with school friends, neighbors, people. He simply...drifted away. Then... vanished.

Why didn't he stay in Europe? Much simpler to vanish over there, isn't it? If what he was diddling on the computer was so...whatever...fewer watchdogs in Europe, back then. Why did he come here, where packs of watchdogs — FBI, CIA, NSA, yada-yadoo — were onto his presence as far back as 1992? You could hide a helluva lot easier over there in those days. But he came here. Why? He'd be a total stranger here, that was to his liking. For whatever he was doing. So that was the first consideration. Or was it? And-and-AND, if it was, why the hell get mixed up with Rasfani the Loon?

He got up and stretched, didn't check his watch because he didn't want to know how late it was. The blur in his vision let him know that. He shook his stiffened legs and feet out as he walked over to the Hashemi section of his wall. The crime scene photos: *That was something you didn't plan on, hey, Hashemi? Even though you and the family were being stalked and you knew it, you didn't put a stop to it in time. You didn't get your family into the super-duper-uber protection disappearance you knew how to do so well. Why? Only reason that's plausible is you knew who it was, so you thought he could be handled. Or bought off. Or shot off. You did carry a gun now and then, here and there. More important, you were a major prize to offer the CIA, FBI and the rest of 'em in exchange for their major protection, if you wanted. Trots hinted at that. But-but-BUT, it didn't happen. Or 'it' did happen, in the most horrible way, taking away the love of your life, in front of your son. And those lovely girls...I have a feeling if you had lived to see that, things would have been much different. You'd have hunted down those two monsters, and all their kith and kin and scrubbed them off the earth..*

It was now way past midnight and Hermie was still reading and paging. He'd started reading without the slightest idea of what he was looking for, so he didn't analyze, categorize, or even search the lines and paragraphs; he just read, like it was a book.

He was thinking again what he had first thought when Shakey had educated him: it's possible that an Eleventh Century name may have been handed down to sons and daughters from generation to generation. He'd even had an amusing thought about what the hell 'Grabfelder' might have been in the Eleventh Century that got whittle down to something almost simple. Well, simple-*er*. 'Grabfeldermachen'?' Or 'Grabundfelderhoffer'?'

He was almost welcoming that distraction when a large yawn made his eyes drift over to that part of the wall that had the Safir family photo. Mom, Dad...niece? Cousin? *Angry eyes. Did they tell you they had found your Mr. Wonderful and you were dreading your future? Where are you now, Cousin? Now, there's a maybe lead... Add that to Selah's list: Find Winston's cousin. Or niece. Did she marry? To whom? Who? Tracing the Safir relatives and friends may be a good place to start. What was her name? What's her story? Why did she look so...like a woman scorned or something.*

Giving in to bone-deep weariness, he neatened up the pages of Hank's printouts in preparation for returning them to their folders when he came upon the pages of documents from Southampton that listed the arrival of the Sabbah family among so many others on those pages, in those days.

Six girls, poor Daddy, six girls to marry off in a strange country, a country where at the time every man-jack, Muslim or not, was dressed like the Beatles, hair with bangs. Or was it the Stones? Punk rock? Yeegods, Bowie? Who remembers. Try too hard to keep track and then you start counting the years...

On impulse, he was about to scan the names of this gaggle of girls, but never got past the first name because of the thunderclap that smacked into his brain and nearly dropped him onto the floor.

The oldest girl. She was fourteen. And her name was Soraya. Soraya Ismailian Hassan-I Sabbah.

CHAPTER TWENTY-FIVE

"I did then what I knew how to do.
Now that I know better, I do better."

Maya Angelou

Hermie lifted the photo in front of Selah and angled it to catch the lamplight so he could see it clearly. "This isn't Mom, Dad, and Sis, or a cousin or a niece, or any other candidate. This is Mom, Dad, and The Wife. This is Mrs. Winston Safir. This is a serial assassin. This is Soraya Ismailian Hassan-I Sabbah Safir, and she was well taught. By her father. Because she *demanded* it. Because she *refused* to be 'less'. You can see all that in her face, in those eyes. I missed it all this time. But now I *know*. Thanks to 'Kevin'. Thanks to that damaged boy, now we *all* know."

Selah is stunned, an amazing thing to see on that particular man's usually impassive face. "It is just not possible." But he wavered, just a little. "I have told you why —-"

"I'm not gonna argue about that. 'Not possible' until an obsession with sons got wa-ay outta hand."

"Explain, please."

"Dear old Dad had six daughters when the family landed in England, fresh off the boat from Iran. We can assume he added mistresses to the mix, since he couldn't take another wife or wives under the laws of "merry ole". He had *nine* daughters by the time he dropped dead. Soraya was the first child, she was fourteen when they came to England."

"She would have been the first to be married off."

"Yup. And since they've been claiming for centuries that they were descendants of that Sabbah guy, they were *rich*. Uber rich. Soraya was a prize. Hashemi —- or Winston at that time —- was *not* so rich. Mom and Dad were gifted, admired, even famous. But if Winston had plans —- and we know now

that he damn well did –- he needed money. Lots. Money to finance whatever
the hell he was doing with computers. Money to finance his vanishing act.
And he was the only son. It was his duty to marry and to financially care
for his folks and his sister, until he married her off. His connection to the
Sabbah name would have helped little Sis as well, marriage-market-wise, had
she lived. Poor kid."

Now it was a soft mutter from Selah. "Not possible. She is a *female*. Not
possible..."

"It wasn't a guy in a chador. My bad for that detour. Hell, it was so
sensible at the time. But it was Soraya. 'Kevin' saw Soraya commit that
Assassin's M.O. on his mother. She used a particular dagger in an ancient way.
Like she was taught. He knew what was coming for Hashemi. And him. So
he ran. But his sanity ran away, too. So Soraya stayed a terrible secret deep
inside his mind. Till now."

Selah rubbed his eyes as if wiping away the thought, tangling up eyelashes
above and below those large, dark pools.

"You wanna hear my take on the motive?"

"Is it an explanation?"

"Oh, yeah. Winston married her for her money and then dumped her
when he went on his chosen way. 'A woman scorned...' I'm not saying he left
her helpless –- financially, he did right by her. She didn't end up on the street
like abandoned traditional women often do in that culture, without a home
or job or support. But he not only left her and left her childless, when she
tracked him down she found out, she *saw* that he'd fallen in love with another
woman and her son. He created a family with them, the family that should
have been hers. So, if she is a descendant of Sabbah –"

"'*If*,'" Selah was grasping at the last straws of history.

"'*If*,' I'll give ya that, too. *If* she is a descendant and *if* she was taught,
she is also just as ruthless in her revenge. It wasn't enough to make Hashemi
and his family pay. She saw those other young women living independent and
successful. They wore hijabs, but that was their lie –- they lived and worked
happily outside the home, alongside men, so how could they be pious? They
were offensive to her. They reminded her of what she was *not*. They were
all living toward a successful future, she was not. They were all the kind of
women Hashemi admired, and she was not. But she could make them pay
for her loss. She could destroy them. Destroy them all. In the ancient way.
Because she was taught."

Selah rubbed his face with tobacco-stained hands, smoothed his silvery
mustache, looked at Hermie with an apology in his eyes. "I have been of so
little help to you, a renewed offer will seem..."

"No-no-no, Selah, you were and are and always will be my go-to guy."

Selah was always helpless before Hermie's unintentional humor. "Your 'go-to-guy'? I had no idea I was so honored. I assumed I was on a long list." "Top of the list, friend. For how many years? Don't count 'em up. We'll both get depressed."

They both suddenly realized they had neglected their cups of chocolate-blended coffee. They each raised their small cups, discovered they needn't blow on them to cool the volcanic brew, both took several sips and felt the scalp-tingling rush of caffeine and familiarity. The weary lateness of the hour lifted.

"How may I help you now?" Selah asked, hopefully.

"This time I gotta put you on Hold for now."

"'On Hold'?" Selah didn't want to interrupt the flow to ask what that phrase meant, kept it in mind for later. Took comfort in the fact that there would be a 'later'.

"This time, I gotta go to a source entirely out of our ballpark. Well, more outta mine than yours. But if I get hung out to dry, I'll be back to see what, if anything you can do to take up the slack."

"I will wait."

When Hermie had gone, Selah picked up the xeroxed photo Hermie had left with him and studied the warning eyes of Soraya Ismailian-I Sabbah Safir. He muttered, "A daughter. A wife. An Assassin. It is just not possible...

* * * *

He waited until he assumed the morning prayers were done before he called. "Yasmina, it's Grabfelder. I really need to see the Imam as soon as possible. When?"

Some hours later he was being loudly peppermint-kissed on the cheeks by the silvery old man, crushing against the 8x10 manila envelope Hermie tried to hold onto.

"Ah, Detective, it is a joy to see you again. And to thank you personally for the Marines and Navy who keep us safe from the ignorance and bigotry. Our children adore them!"

It was only then and only for a brief moment when the old man's eyes lost their keenness and their merriment that Hermie saw the toll outside events were taking on him. "I wish I could apologize for all the yahoos that populate my countrymen. Hopefully, Time and the Law will rein 'em in. Politics aside, of course."

"Ah, yes, politics aside." The Imam sighed deeply. "But do sit — sit."

The Imam gestured to the familiar chair, and as Hermie sat the Imam went to sink into his protesting desk chair.

Some rattling of crockery was heard from outside, Hermie leaped up to open the door to Yasmina and the tea and treats cart. She began to pour and serve, the calming fragrance of the tea warmed the air, and he was glad this normality was going on as he broached the subject of his visit.

"I've come here to ask for your help. And I'll perfectly understand if it's something you'd be too uncomfortable to do. But you're all I've got."

Yasmina assumed this was private and headed for the door.

Hermie stopped her, "Yasmina, I think you should be in on this. It may affect your future as well as your present."

Puzzled, Yasmina went to stand alongside the seated Imam, as if protective of him.

"And I apologize ahead of time if I say or do something that offends." He opened the somewhat bent manilla envelope, pulled out a single sheet from inside. He turned the sheet around and placed it on the Imam's desk in front of them. Yasmina and the Imam leaned forward in unison to get a good look at the color copy of an enlarged photo of a sad-eyed woman accompanied by an older and smiling man and woman. The Imam snatched up a pair of golden wire eyeglasses, the frames slightly bent, the glass patched with fingerprints. He put them on, peered through and down at the photo.

"Who is these?" asked the Imam.

"The couple are Mr. and Mrs. Safir, Farbod and Hannah. They were professional musicians in England and Europe back in the day. Classical stuff, concerts, he was violin, she was piano. They were both killed in a private plane crash in 1999 while on tour. Their daughter was also killed in that plane crash."

"Oh, how tragic." the Imam said sadly, his lips went on in a silent prayer.

"This is their daughter?" asked Yasmina.

"That was one of my big theories. But, no." Hermie took a deep breath and gentled his voice. "The woman is Soraya Ismailian Hassan-I Sabbah. She was married to the Safir's son."

The Imam looked up, recognizing the ancient name.

"Yes, Imam, she is –- or may be -– a descendant of Ismailian Hassan-I Sabbah, the Assassin. She is also the murderer of all the Muslim daughters."

Both the Imam and Yasmina gasped in horror.

"That's not possible!" Yasmina stated. "She is a *woman*, they cannot –-"

"Yes, 'cannot'. But she was well taught. By her father. He had no sons. Nine daughters, but no sons to carry on their sacred name, history, political power and wealth. Soraya was the firstborn. She wanted that legacy. In the worst way."

"My dear Son, this was never, never done — it is forbidden — to teach a woman such ugly skills. Women are Life, not Death." The Imam was gentle, certain, explaining.

"So I've been told, Sir. By a Muslim who knows just about everything. But, Imam, the first murders included a woman, a mother, whose son saw it happen. A son who came out of a mental collapse just long enough to name his Mom's killer. 'Soraya', he said."

"It's a common enough name," Yasmina objected. "Mispronounce it and it could be a man's name...like Shawaz, for one. That man wearing a chador as a disguise, like you thought."

"At the time, that made so much sense. Disguised as a pious woman so he could get close enough to strike. Now it's no disguise. It is a woman, shaming that pious chador. That boy named the killer in such a way — he had to write it, he couldn't speak it because of the terror that name represents. 'Soraya'. She was an abandoned wife. She was too briefly married to Winston Safir, the only son of this couple. He became Jordan Hashemi, who was killed by Soraya, after she made him watch her cut down the woman he loved. It was her revenge."

"But those others, those dear daughters..." The Imam's aqua eyes were now glittering with tears.

"They were happy, successful, loved, enjoying their future. Soraya was not. Soraya took her revenge. She struck down who she could never be."

Yasmina impulsively put her arm around the Imam's shoulders, opened a desk drawer and quickly removed a fresh handkerchief, handed it to the Imam. He blindly reached for it, pressed its pristine fabric against his streaming eyes, cheeks, the top of his frosty beard.

Yasmina was wiping her face with her bare hands, quickly, neatly. "What do you need from us, Detective?"

"Yes," the Imam lifted his face, sniffed, and made an effort to carry on. "Yes, you have only to ask."

"I appreciate that, so much. Here's the thing: How can I contact — *in secret* — every Imam in Southern California? Not do-able, right? Or it would take *weeks*."

Hermie was surprised to see the ancient cheeks lift his beard in a small smile. "Ah . . . you are in the presence of greatness, Detective. Yasmina, now is the time to be boastful."

Yasmina blushed, and for a second couldn't look Hermie in the eye. Then she came back to him, "I designed a computer program. Every Imam in the state, every mosque — 'official' and 'non' — along with all the names of the members. New, current and non-. Except for those few who only show up for the special holy days. A habit Muslims share with Christians and Jews."

"Jeezus! Sorry. Wish you'd done this in Europe. We -- couple guys I know, a computer nerd and a Muslim cop -- for hours we leap-frogged over and through computer records in English and Arabic, 'official and non-'. The most helpful they got was records of when the Sabbah family landed in Southampton as immigrants from Iran. That was the first mention of Soraya. She was fourteen. The first of what would be nine girls."

"No sons?" asked the Imam.

"No. And Dad carried the name 'Ismailian Hassan-I Sabbah, supposedly handed down for generations."

"Since the Eleventh Century? Who knows," acknowledged the Imam with a shrug.

"What do you want us to do with this picture?" Yasmina asked.

"Starting in Southern California, I'd like you to send copies of this photo to every Imam, in every mosque. Ask if he knows her, if she attends his mosque. If at all possible get an address for her. And this must be done and kept in secret. *Total* secrecy. If she gets wind of this, she'll vanish. She had a husband who was an expert at that. She's obviously a good learner."

"My computer program has a security measure. A code only the Imams know will open e-mail for secret messages. The photo will be sent under that security."

"How the hell did you do that? Sorry."

"It took awhile. But whenever we are under threat, or we hear of a homegrown fanatic's plot, the Imams will know where the threat is coming from and how best to respond, and who to inform in law enforcement as well. I -- we -- assume you will keep this knowledge secret. From *everyone*, in law enforcement and out?"

"You have my word. I take it this program is a constant frustration to the snoops in our guv'ment?"

Yasmina smiled, "No offense?"

"None a'tall. Politics sinking to a lower level damn near every day, I not only don't blame you, I salute you."

Yasmina picked up the photo, looked at it closely. "I'll have her photo in every Imam's secret mail box by tomorrow afternoon. They will reply only to me. And I'll call you immediately."

Hermie recalled his last confab with Trots and the listening-in going on. "Don't call me. You don't know it to look at me, but I was once FBI. To this day, none of my lines are secure, and I've also got reporters stalking me twenty-four-seven. They've been known to tap and snoop, till they get caught. Is there any other way?"

"Yes. You will get a postcard that will have a City's sightseeing picture on it. The City is where the mosque is that she goes to. The Imam there will have her home address, hopefully. He will be waiting for your visit."

Hermie came closer to her, trapped her eyes in his look, "Yasmina, you have wonderful future plans for yourself, will this in any way damage you? Pal-ing around with the enemy, so to speak?" He turned to look at the Imam, "Imam, Sir? Am I asking something too much? Stop me, if you think so. I'll understand."

"Let Yasmina answer you."

"You truly don't know, do you?" Her eyes were nearly dancing normally again.

"Know what?"

"Since Amira Farsadi, all anyone in our community has to do is mention 'Grabfelder' and all is understood, all is done for you that needs to be done."

Hermie was helplessly embarrassed. "Oh, that -- that . . . I'm sure that's not . . . I'm just a *cop*, and that's . . ." He gave up, surrendered to another warm embrace and loud cheek kisses from the Imam.

"Blessings upon you, my Boy." said the Imam, wafting peppermint on Hermie's cheeks.

Yasmina gave him a handshake warm and hearty with trust.

When he left the mosque, Shirin Battawi's former protector, Sam Ordway greeted him as he had moments before, rifle cradled in his arm. "Anything wrong with the Old Gentleman?"

"The Imam? No. Thanks to you and your guys."

"Good to hear, good to hear. He's become like everybody's Grandpa."

"I know the feeling," Hermie said.

* * * *

First, he didn't think it would come so soon, having some idea of how many mosques and their Imams that Yasmina had to secretly notify and then wait for the Imams to first open their mail and then secretly send a reply. Second, he was almost as flabbergasted as he was relieved to get a picture postcard from Yasmina with a sunset scene off the coast of the Palos Verdes peninsula, past San Pedro.

A quick Google by Nell pinpointed the mosque nearest that coastal area. A quick visit introduced himself to the Imam, who was startlingly young-looking, a beard hardly there on his handsome dark face. The Imam genuinely regretted that although he recognized the woman, he did not have her home address because she never gave it. Hermie was not surprised, knowing her husband's habits. But the good news was that Soraya Ismailian Hassan-I Sabbah Safir was devout, never failed to show up for evening prayers. She would undoubtedly come.

She will be in sight. She will be here. And I'll get her! Can you hear me, Amira? Sunny? Shirin? Lila? Hashemi? 'Kevin'? **I. WILL. GET. HER.**

CHAPTER TWENTY-SIX

"God created man in his own image.
Man, being a gentleman, returned the favor."

Jean Jacques Rosseau

An unexpected problem threw off his plans for a surveillance of people entering the mosque for evening prayers: there were separate entrances for men and women, and Hermie didn't dare come near the women's entrance. So he grabbed his cellphone and pretended he was on a call while he wandered in the parking lot, searching for an angle where he could watch the women's entrance while not appearing to do so. A call to prayer soared up from a tower on the mosque and men gathered at their entrance in a convivial jumble, and women began to trickle into their entrance in a quieter fashion.

Most of the women were in California casual dresses, although hemlines and sleeves were decidedly longer, modest, and all wore headscarves. A few were in chadors, only faces uncovered. Just as he was thinking, *How the hell can I pick her out?*, he was astonished to see a silver Rolls Royce Phantom pull up into the parking lot, glide to the women's entrance, and stop. *Jeezus! The Stalker's wheels!* He got a glimpse of the damage still there on a front headlight to one side of the front bumper. The chill he felt was magnified when he saw Soraya Ismailian Hassan-I Sabbah Safir got out of the car, opening the back door herself, before a gigantic man in a chauffer's uniform could get out and get around to open the back door for her. *The Incredible Hulk in uniform.*

She was taller than he expected, remembering the small footprints around Lila Miller's body. *Those were prints made by a short man's shoes, we all thought. Little did we know . . .*

What first set her apart from the rest of the women was she was the only one wearing a niqab, the veil that completely covered the head and face, except for a slit that revealed the eyes. What also set her apart was that she was politely greeted by the other women, in Arabic and English, with smiles and nods, but they didn't draw her in, as they did the others. Their groupings slightly fell away from her, a space appeared around her and remained there until all the women entered the mosque.

Hermie stayed where he was until everyone was inside the mosque. Then he walked out of the parking lot, down a block, and to a side street alongside a small, rural-looking post office in this nice neighborhood, were Roberta was parked. He collapsed inside, weeks of tension suddenly snapped. *She was there, within sight, within reach, she was RIGHT THERE: the sonuvabitch Assassin!*

But he couldn't do a damn thing about it because of a little thing called "Probable Cause". He had absolutely no evidence -- no forensics, no eyewitnesses except for a catatonic boy. In other words, *ZIP* that would allow him to arrest her veiled ass, or at least get her down to a station for questioning. Frustration ground his teeth.

* * * *

When he had received the information from the Imam of this mosque, I.d.-ing the woman in the photo as one of his members, the first thing Hermie did was buttonhole Andy Cho Hui in his cluttered office, among strange smells he didn't want to know from what.

"Help me out, here, Andy, you've had weeks and five bodies. But you haven't called. Don't tell me there's no forensics I can use for a Probable."

"Okay, I won't tell you. But --"

"Aw, hell!"

"The footprints in the first scene. You're now saying they weren't a man's shoe? For real?"

"They were from a woman. For *very* real. I have no idea why she wears such shoes. Maybe they were just comfortable. You know, comfort for killing." Hermie sarcasm was now flat-out bitter.

Andy understood. "There was one more thing, but of no help at all. That's why I put off calling."

"If *you* say it wouldn't help! Yeegods!"

"It was on Vic -- wait --" Andy checked his computer, "Here . . . there . . . Sunidhi Askar."

Hermie suddenly went wistful with the memory: "All who loved her called her 'Sunny'. And that was just about everyone who met her. The most beautiful . . ."

"Yeah. My Techs still talk about her. That perfect face." He turned to a sheet in a folder. "Anyway, on her sleeve . . . yeah, here -- 'tangled in the embroidery on her left sleeve . . . a single hair . . . white.'" He turned to Hermie.

"A hair?! Hell, I'll take a hair! We can match a hair!" Then he saw Andy's expression. "We *can't* match a hair?"

"In this case, no."

"Why the hell not? Oh, no root? But you got machines, you don't need no root nowadays. I watch *"Forensic Files"*!"

"No root ain't the iss-ue. The *source* is. We just got the test results yesterday. It was a horse hair. White. See why I didn't call?"

"A hair. From a horse. White."

"I take it she wasn't a rider?"

Hermie recalled the many photographs of the beloved Sunidhi that filled her home and filled her parents' broken hearts. "Sadly, no. If she was, there would have been a photograph. Among all the others. So many others . . ."

So, now Hermie sat in Roberta, down the street from the mosque, waiting for prayers to end and the mosque to disgorge the women. The monster would be in sight again but he was powerless to get at her. He knew even a home visit would yield little other than the personal satisfaction of letting that bitch know he was onto her and it was only a matter of time. And knowing for sure that the killings would stop. *Wouldn't they?*

With no home address in the Imam's records, Hermie would have to follow the Rolls Royce when it left the mosque. So as not to spook the prey at the sight of Roberta, an obviously retired squad car smoking up the air behind them, Hermie had rented a car for the day. He didn't think anything of the fact that the rental car was a fairly new Honda-something, until he nearly plowed into cars in front of him because the Honda's pick-up damn-near picked up off the pavement, and just a tap of the power brakes with his unprepared foot damn-near ruffled the pavement beneath him. Hermie was not used to a car that actually responded as it should, shame on Roberta's years of deterioration.

He couldn't park in front of the mosque or its parking lot to keep watch, as it was soon apparent that half a dozen men were keeping watch around the property. Some in suits, some in the long shirts, skull caps and trousers of traditional male dress, some who obviously had a license to carry or didn't and carried anyway, and these days who can blame them? So, Hermie pulled into a red zone two blocks away and was immediately spotted by an annoyed shop keeper in a bakery alongside who came out of his shop in an apron-flapping tear, so Hermie flashed his badge and rolled down his window to stop the man in his dudgeon. "Sorry. Surveillance. Won't be long. 'Swear."

The thunder immediately cleared off the man's eyebrows as he raised his hands slightly, and said, "Okay, man. Sorry. I got a problem here. Automatic response."

"I hear ya. Have you called Traffic Control or whoever to ask for a threatening sign?"

"Hell, yes!"

"Ah. Vanishing budgets. We may not live long enough for them to get around to it."

"You got that right."

"Sorry. Suggestion? Kinda lot of trouble, though."

"What? I'm open."

"Get a sign made up yourself, looking official: 'Video Cam Watching, 24/7: License plate numbers are being taken of dorks who ignore a red zone.' Or words to that effect."

"I love it! Why didn't I think of that?"

"You don't have my felonious frame of mind."

The man laughed, pumped Hermie's hand. "Thanks, Man. Have a nice day."

"You, too." Hermie wondered for a second if 'nice' would describe his day, afterward.

It was easy to follow the Rolls Royce because the driver kept a slow pace, the twists and turns of the streets that climb the Palos Verdes Peninsula slowed everyone down when driving uphill. *Driving down was another issue entirely,* Hermie thought.

The gates to the property were tall and ornate, vines and flowers climbed in black wrought iron between two stone pillars past ten feet tall. The fencing that branched out on either side was black spear points just as tall and Hermie detected wiring here and there, indicating the whole thing was electrified. He also spotted surveillance cameras strategically place on top of more stone pillars that supported the fencing.

He realized he could not follow the Rolls through the gate as it opened for admittance and immediately closed behind it. It was then he noticed that the massive pillar of stone on the left of the gate was hollowed out in back to make a guard shack. A burly man wearing mirrored sunglasses and also the same dark uniform that he'd glimpsed on the chauffeur stepped out as the Rolls silkily moved past. This guard eyeballed the drive and street behind the Rolls as the gate slowly closed and locked. This guard had a rifle cradled in his arms, plus a jumbo pistol stuffed into a large holster on one hip. *What? Are you expecting an invasion?* Hermie groused, quietly. Then another thought:

"No, not invasion. Just Hashemi. He'd have been enough. Or did he set up this whole shebang in order to keep track of her? It almost worked, Man."

Hermie took a deep breath, put the gear in drive and remembered not to use his usual pressure on the accelerator. The car went conservative and pulled up quietly into the driveway, where Hermie steered to the side in order not to block the driveway, imitating a courteous bastard to make a nice impression.

As he killed the engine, the Guard nearly bolted out of the guard room, as if not used to finding someone there. The rifle was taken off the crook of the arm and embraced by both hands if not actually raised in firing position.

Hermie opened the car door stepped out and forward, holding up his badge in plain view, plainly not impressing the Guard.

"Private property! Private Property! You must leave!" he bellowed, with a strong Middle Eastern accent.

Hermie mimicked him, with the same accent: "Police! Police! I am not leaving!"

This completely flummoxed the guard. He stopped, his mirrored sunglasses began to flash as they jiggled, betraying his tension.

Hermie kept the badge up as he came nearer to the guard, who made an effort to hold his ground. "Police, Poe-leece," Hermie emphasized, American accent this time. "I am a police officer on an investigation. I need to speak to the lady in the house."

"You are not in uniform of police."

"No. I am a Detective. Homicide. Dead people. We only wear uniforms on special occasions. Birthdays, Fourth of July, first day of Spring . . ." His demanding eyes were aimed directly at the twitching mirrored glasses. "I'll say it again: I am the police. I need to speak to the lady in that house."

"She is not home!"

"I just saw her arrive. That was a stupid lie. Very aggravating."

"No, no, understand — she is home not to anyone!"

"One more time only: I am the *police*. If you do not let me in, I will call on my phone and in -- oh, fifteen minutes? -- I will have police squad cars, police motorcycles, the fire department and a SWAT team here using a blow torch on that gate, and you will be in handcuffs, face down on the ground -- unless you have all the legal permits in your pockets for all those guns."

A second or two of doubt, consternation, then the universal passing of the buck: "You will await here. A moment only!"

"I will await here for one -- ONE -- moment. *Only!*"

The Guard turned and nearly galloped to inside the guard house. Hermie heard some kind of a phone being connected, a voice shouting from the connection in a torrent of Arabic. The Guard replied in a louder torrent of

Arabic and the only words Hermie heard in English were "squad cars", "fire department" and "poe-leece".

I should have brought Shakey along as interpreter. Or Yasmina. She'd have cut this dork down to size in a hurry. Hermie smiled at the thought.

Then, apparently the guard hung up the phone. He came out, his sunglasses apparently forgotten so Hermie saw large, light amber eyes in a dark but bland face. Passing the buck worked and he was glad of it. "You go in. But walk. No car."

"Sure. Nice day for it."

A hum announced the gigantic gates were unclocked and swung open. Hermie stepped through and began to walk up the drive, saluting the guard as he passed. "You're doing a heckuva job, if I may say so."

It was a long walk, up a drive that went up and curved right, then went up and curved left. First tall and waving Pepper trees flanked the drive, their fern-like leaves dappling shade here and there, trunks nestled deep in flowering bushes. Further on, greening Jacaranda trees littered the tops of blossoming bushes with their season's worth of cast-off purple blooms. The left curve of the driveway ended at the entrance to an enormous house. It was one story that branched out seemingly endlessly on either side, walls broken up by ceiling-to-floor windows behind iron grillwork. The grillwork and the red tile roof were in a Spanish hacienda style, a throw-back to the past history of the vast Spanish ranch that was once the entire Palos Verdes Peninsula. The stone steps up the entrance led to a massive double door of dark wood festooned with large brass handles. The doors were framed in colorful Spanish tiles, each tile showing a different flower and leaves. An enormous chandelier hung from a thick chain, down to just above the doors. It, too, had graceful ironwork holding the glass panes of the light.

Hermie went up the steps and searched for a doorbell button. Instead, he found a pull handle and chain. He gave it a tug and heard a pleasant sound of tinkling bells within the house.

An instant later, the massive doors swung open easily in spite of being tugged on by a diminutive woman who was past middle age. She had thick and shining gray hair smoothed back into a neat, braided coil at the back of her head and was dressed in an odd navy blue maid's uniform — it had long sleeves and a long skirt, and a long white apron that went from the neck down to the hem. Her eyes looked down. He got the immediate impression that she spent her days being cowed.

So he reassured her: He flashed his badge, but she didn't look up. He gently said, "Hello, Ma'am, I am Detective Grabfelder. May I ask your name?"

She jumped a little startled. *I bet no one asks your name, huh? Hermie thought.* She looked up at him, saw dangerous eyes smiling, calm, nice. "I am Nazreen."

"Pretty name. Nice to meet you, Nazreen. I am with the police. I need to see the lady of the house. Do you understand?"

She relaxed, nearly smiled, nodded and gestured. "Come in, Sir."

He stepped into the house, but went no further as the lady closed the door behind him. He glanced this way and that to see enormous hallways and rooms branching off to the left and right in windowed space. Everywhere were brilliantly colored Persian rugs atop stone-colored tile floors, their room-sized gathering of flowers and arabesques warmed the look of the bland tile in vast rooms.

He followed her in to what he took to be the living room, one wall nearly disappeared around a giant Spanish fireplace and carved stone mantlepiece. The huge room had too few items of furniture to welcome visitors –- two small couches in red silk flanked the fireplace; four small chairs in the same embroidered silk sat near four small tables of gleaming mahogany. Three tables were bare, no knick-knacks or doilies. One table held an enormous blue leather book. Large gold lettering on its cover told Hermie it was a Koran. Spanish iron floor lamps stood alongside the chairs.

He became aware that the lady had opened one of the tall windowed doors on the far side of the room, as if to show him out to the back of the house. He paused in front of her, his look asking a question. She looked up at him once more as if liking his face and gestured to the lawn outside.

"She's outside somewhere?" he asked.

She nodded. "She will come."

"Thank you, Nazreen," he said kindly.

He went through the door and was startled by the vast grounds. *This isn't a yard, this is acreage,* he muttered to himself. And noticed it was yards and yards of lush, clipped green in spite of the drought. Him being a Michigan man, he couldn't resist stepping out onto the deep grass, feet sinking into the cool, rich cushiony feel even through his shoes. A cool breeze lifted up the well-remembered, sweet scent of stepped-on grass and clover blossoms.

He turned to take it all in, saw that no one was around. But when he began walking forward, in seconds a guard materialized behind him, a clone of the gate guard in outfit and firepower. Hermie was beginning to get annoyed, especially when this guard shadowed him as he walked. "Just where is Madame?" Hermie said, not politely.

The guard pointed off to the left and when Hermie went toward there, past a huge Forsythia bush heavy-laden with bright yellow blooms, he was astonished to see what looked like a smaller version of a racetrack: a vast, oval dirt track outlined by a white rail fence.

Suddenly, he heard hoofbeats getting louder as they approached. Hermie just had time to yell "Ach du lieber!" when Soraya Ismailian Hassan-I Sabbah Safir rode up to him at a mad gallop on an enormous horse, that was only pulled up at the last minute before collision. The horse's panting in his enormous chest sounded like wind gusts coming out of a large cave, blasting moist, grain-scented heat into Hermie's face. His bit and harness jangled in glittering silver, sending drool spraying.

She was wearing a headscarf that showed her entire face, familiar but somewhat more dramatic than her photo. Perhaps it was the arrogance that brought out the fine bones in her face. The sweep of her black chador flowed over the horse's flanks and over the loose black trousers that were tucked inside gleaming brown riding boots resting within silver-decorated stirrups. The entire livery of the horse was deep red leather full of carvings of flowers and vines, these carvings echoed in brilliant silver set into here and there.

The horse rumbled a comment, chewed on the silver bit, jiggling a silver medallion resting on his forehead above his large, black, intelligent eyes. An untrimmed mane and tail rippled silkily in the breeze, tossed with his movements. He was a stallion and he was dazzlingly white.

Hermie glanced down at the grass, saw strands of long, white hair here and there. When he went to show his badge, he faked dropping it and when he retrieved it from the grass he took some of those white hairs with it. Tucked it all back into his jacket pocket.

"Sorry to disturb you, Ma'am, but I'm investigating the murders of Muslim women, so I'd like to ask you a few questions, since you are a member of the mosque near San Pedro."

She merely stared at his face, giving no sign that she heard or understood or cared. Arrogance got more blatant and more beautiful.

He used the old ploy -- whipping out a small spiral pad and this time a ballpoint pen that was an homage to *"Frozen"*. And it suddenly was out of ink. She couldn't see that, so he kept on writing as he spoke. "Uh, what is your full name, Ma'am?"

Silence.

"It's whether you talk here or at my police station. You get to pick. For now."

She had the tone of voice that demanded respect, a warning of danger. More family heritage, no doubt. "I am Soraya Ismailian Hassan-I Sabbah Safir."

Are ya now? Good goddamn. He pretended to write: "Soraya Ismailian Hassan-I Sabbah . . . Safir. Hmmm . . . Now, where have I heard that name before?" He looked up at her, up past the horses's fine face with its searching nostrils and large, black and curious eyes, white eyelashes fluttering, snowy mane blowing this way and that. "And this is your place? You are the owner of this house, this lawn, the track? This whole property?"

She nodded.

From someplace else came the plaintive notes of a whinny sailing on the wind. The white horse answered from deep in his beautiful curved neck and danced. It was then that Hermie noticed that his ornate red saddle had an odd fringe: where it rested on the saddle blanket, tiny holes had been punched into the bottom edge and from these holes fluttered narrow, ribbon-like strips of fabric in different, muted colors. The small holes in the saddle had sharp edges; they were *new*.

Hermie could bullshit with the best of them, so he cut loose: "Wow, that is a *beautiful* saddle. Spanish? Or Middle Eastern?" He didn't expect her to answer, so he carried on. "All that carving -- bee-yootiful! And that silver work! Awesome! Spanish, Middle Eastern, could be either. Y'know, I have a friend, name of Gordie Norris, works in the Sheriff's Station, Lomita? Well, he's into horses, riding and all, and he collects saddles. Has a dozen or more, some antiques, Spanish, mostly. Imagine finding room for all those saddles in a two-bedroom apartment. Obviously, he lives alone. What a character!" *Talk, talk, talk,* he circled her, the horse eyeing him suspiciously, dancing feet about to do a turn to follow him. "Oh, I see the saddle is kinda like a chair on top. Must be downright comfortable, especially for a lady." The horse did not like being circled and Hermie blessed him when he stopped following Hermie and began tossing his head, dancing his slim legs and black hooves in place as if getting ready to rear, so her attention was taken with controlling the horse so she didn't notice Hermie was behind her, reaching for one of the ribbons of fabric and yanking hard enough on it so it tore free. He immediately tucked it into his jacket pocket, but not before he noticed that it was stained. *Dye? Saddle soap? Horse sweat? Or . . . ?*

He came back around to face her. "So . . . you live here alone? Just with the servants?"

"This is my house."

He took a shot: "Did Hashemi buy it for you? A place to put you?"

Hermie hadn't often seen hatred on a woman's face, but it was there now: blatant, powerful, erasing all the beauty. She yanked the reins as if to ride away, Hermie grabbed the reins to stop her, the horse got confused as to who to obey, so he tossed his large, beautiful head, mane billowing, hooves dancing forward then back, and neighed his frustration almost musically, but emphatically.

Immediately the guard came into Hermie's side vision, rifle in his hands, sunglasses glittering with business.

"Soraya Ismailian Hassan-I Sabbah Safir, you will have to come to the police station to answer some questions. You are now under surveillance (he hoped his tone lied well), so do not attempt to leave your house, this city, this state, or this country. If you do you will be arrested and your immigration status revoked. You will be forced to stay in jail until your case is resolved. That would be in *Immigration* Jail. Nasty place. Vermin. Flies. Fleas. Screaming, smelly kids. Really crappy food. Dirt-dirt-dirt. Do I make myself clear?"

She glanced down at him, unimpressed.

Hermie couldn't resist patting the horse on his hot, silky shoulder. To the astonishment of all, the horse calmed down, stared at Hermie. "I know, I know, Big Dude," Hermie said to the horse, "We all have lousy days, worse company."

Hermie turned and walked back toward the house. He didn't see the horse take a few steps to follow him before the woman astride yanked on the reins angrily to pull him up. This time his neighing sounded kinda wistful, Hermie heard and thought.

* * * *

He needn't have worried about manpower or the pause for financing what would surely be Overtime to the max. When Hermie made the call to request twenty-four/seven blanket surveillance of a mansion in Palos Verdes and gave the reason, there was instant response. The Chief started to assign personnel, discovered overwhelming numbers of volunteers. Some officers cancelled their vacations, and when given an explanation, most wives did not object; a couple came back early from vacations. Some retirees clocked in, volunteering for free to cover nighttime hours. Other officers volunteered for free Overtime. *FREE OVERTIME!* Won't that piss off the Union, "dangereous precedent" and all that crap.

But it was Grabfelder and everyone knew the horror and heartbreak of his case; some officers who had responded to his crime scenes still couldn't sleep nights after the sight of those lovely daughters slaughtered for no reason that could ever be good enough.

There was neighborhood concern and curiosity when dozens of squad cars and plain clothes cars began crowding up their very upscale streets —- automatic response being 'Was the President coming for a fundraiser dinner?' And every officer obeyed the direction of "Give out NO —- that's NO, GODDAMMIT! —- information to *anyone*! Do not screw up my

Probable Cause!" from Grabfelder. And his threats were added onto by the Prosecutor, i.e., "Screw up our case and I'll have your badge, your pension, your kids, and your dog, goddammit!" The crime scene photos still living in his own nightmares.

Unfortunately, the news media had helicopters circling overhead in a matter of hours. Shooting them down was mulled over half-seriously. But news vans and reporters that drove up or walked up were unceremoniously escorted away –– WA-AY away –– from the scene, barely courteously and without any explanation. Tommy Velasco was having a cow.

So, a noose was around Soraya Ismailian Hassan-I Sabbah Safir. And everyone waited for Grabfelder to tighten it. And where the hell was he, anyway?

Only a few surmised that he was again begging for a Probable Cause in the office of forensic guru Andy Cho Hui, who had peered at the ribbon of fabric that Hermie pulled out of his pocket and tried to break the news kindly to the frantic detective: "Hermie-baby, *your* DNA will be all over this."

"I know, I know! This isn't for court, this is for an arrest warrant. That's all I'm asking!"

Andy next turned to the clump of white hairs Hermie had pulled from another pocket. "Well, that's familiar –– horse hair."

"Yes. *Her* horse."

"That won't be enough. We found only a single hair on one victim, a Defense lawyer would laugh out loud."

"Stop thinking 'court'! Think 'first things first'! I've got to get her off the streets, get her in for questioning. That's all I'm asking."

Andy used a long set of tweezers to pick up the fabric. Held it up to the light and peered at it. "It's dirty. Stained."

"It's blood, isn't it?"

"Could be."

"I *know* it is.

"How?"

"A hand-made saddle that costs thousands and she punches holes in it to decorate it with dozens of ribbons of –– what?"

"Polyester . . . rayon or something . . . nothing expensive."

"I'm gonna ask the impossible, Andy."

His tone made Andy look at him and see the grim rage barely held in check, his eyes blazing blue fire just this side of madness. "You want a DNA test. Like, *now*."

"How long will it take?"

"With our backlog? No shekels for extras? Weeks."

"I'm not giving her weeks. Can you go private?"

"If I do, it breaks the chain of evidence. A defense lawyer . . . sorry. Won't happen again."

"If I can haul her in for a chat, even with inadmissable evidence, I can still have every inch of her house, property and car searched. It's a Rolls Royce, a silver Phantom. How's that for irony? That'll thrill your Techs. Court-worthy evidence will be found, I'm sure. Including all those other strips. Help me out here, Andy."

Andy delicately tucked the fabric ribbon into a paper envelope, labeled it "Grabfelder". He picked up his phone, dialed and to Hermie's surprise spoke in a rush of rapid Korean. 'Grabfelder' with a Korean accent appeared here and there. Then Hermie recognized the pleading, "Chom, chom! Chebal!" two Korean versions of "Please!" before Andy yelled, "Dude! I love ya! Kamsahamnida!" the Korean phrase for 'thank you' being gushed, and hung up.

He turned to Hermie, "A cousin. Works in one of those labs that do DNA for people tracing ancestors. Oy, you should see their equipment! Anyway, he'll do the testing right now. I'm going down there. I don't know how long it will take. At least lotta hours. Maybe a day?"

"Find me." Hermie started to leave, Andy walked out with him.

"You're gonna get a confession? Are you sure?" Andy asked.

"Damn sure."

"How so?"

"Because I know why she did it."

"Motive? What could possibly make a woman do such a thing to other women? 'Women' -- they were still young girls."

"Because she thought she had the right. And because a man, a father of girls, taught her how."

"Wait! *Her* father?!" Why the hell –?"

"He thought he had a unique daughter. A daughter as good as a son. So he trained her. Into a monster."

CHAPTER TWENTY-SEVEN

"Moral indignation is in most cases two percent moral, forty-eight percent indignation, and fifty percent envy."

Vittorio DeSica, Italian Film Director

He paced. First at home, instead of sleep, to the great annoyance of Eleanor, who only stopped grousing when he put her onto his shoulder so she could ride along. Then at Bud's Body Works, angry feet pounding the treadmill for who knows how long until Bud put a stop to him, fearing a stress-induced heart attack. Then in his office, causing partitions to shudder, windows to rattle. The two patrolmen decamped in a hurry to get out of the way. Claire and Nell knew him well enough to also stay out of his way. Every time the phone rang, they all jumped, but nothing went to Hermie's private line. Nell racked up messages, putting no one through to him, knowing nothing was important except for the call Hermie was waiting for. A call from Andy, he'd said. How long ago?

It was dawn the next day and Hermie was still in his office, but the throbbing in his feet and legs no longer kept him awake — he was dozing, deep and dreamless with exhaustion, draped over his chair. His private phone rang and his sleep had been so deep, he jerked awake and didn't know where he was or how he got here. Then the phone's ring penetrated and he snatched up the phone. "WHAT?!" he bellowed.

It was Andy. "Tried your house, figured there was only one other place you'd be. Was gonna try your cell next, fruitless though that usually is."

Andy sounded cheerful. Was that a good sign? No, Andy was always cheerful, even when wearing latex gloves dripping blood. It was annoying and endearing at the same time. "What?" was all that could be managed on such tenterhooks as Hermie hung from.

"Hermie, we owe my cousin big time. Actually, we owe his whole staff — everyone pitched in, once they heard."

"And?" He'd thank them later, when he *knew*.

"The fabric, polyester and nylon mix, nothing unusual. But the stains — blood, human blood. And . . . brace yourself, Hermie, you've been sent a gift."

"What?"

"That blood, it was Amira Farsadi's blood."

And Andy was stunned to hear Homicide Detective Herman Grabfelder burst into tears, loud and gasping: "Oh . . . Amira . . . Amira, Honey . . ."

* * * *

Something told him to keep her waiting, wondering, give her time to make things up. So Hermie interviewed the chauffeur first, man-to-man, guy-to-guy, cop to lowly and foreign employee, for whom deportation back to the hell he came from was a looming threat.

He loomed six feet, maybe another six inches over that, and Hermie was beginning to wonder if he slept in that uniform, since every sight he'd had was of him in that chauffeur's uniform, deep navy, no embroidery around the cuffs, no gold buttons, the cap undistinguished. Like Pierre had once described the guy who flashed those fake body pick-up documents.

An overstuffed folder was in front of Hermie and he fished out the papers the chauffeur had filled out earlier. Guy-to-guy, Hermie opened with: "I'm Detective Grabfelder," he deliberately fumbled with the withdrawing and flashing of his badge, then had to look wa-ay up to nail the guy's eyes with the zinger: "Homicide Investigator."

It worked. Hermie saw a twitch of eyelids heavy-laden with straight and long black eyelashes. His skin tone said Spanish or Samoan or mixed race black, but in this case he knew it was Middle Eastern. Once upon a history, Persian; now Iranian.

"Sorry to keep you waiting. I have just a couple questions, mostly about your employer. "So — hey —" Hermie pretended to look around, "Didn't anyone offer you something to drink? Coffee? Coke? Bottled water? I need something cold, how about you?"

The eyelashes lifted and he looked Hermie over before nodding.

Good, the ass-wipe speaks English, Hermie thought. "Back in a second," and Hermie slid his chair back, got up, and went out the door, taking the folder with him, closing and loudly locking behind him. Seconds later, he was watching the viewing screen and saw the chauffer lean his mass over to rest his forehead on the table for as long as it took him to moan miserably, before he snapped up as if aware of being watched, rubbed his face with gigantic hands that were shackled at the wrist. He then looked at the handcuffs as if he couldn't believe what he was seeing. Another miserable moan.

Moments later, after unlocking the door just as loudly, Hermie re-entered the room, the folder tucked under one arm, hands carrying two icy bottles of water by the necks, and a small plastic bowl of almond-stuffed dates he'd bought on the way in, after calling Aida and asking her what was her biggest seller in snacks from the Middle East.

He set the bowl down, grinned, "Almond-stuffed dates; my personal favorite," and then opened both bottles of water with loud SNAPS! of plastic letting go, put one of the bottles in front of the chauffeur. "It's really cold," he said before he took a slug from his own bottle, swallowed, "Ah! Hits the spot."

The chauffeur hesitated, then picked up his own bottle, took a sip, and then a compulsion made him gulp down several swallows.

He's thirsty. Really thirsty. Must be what he had for lunch. Or he's got panic thirst. Hermie snapped open his folder, shuffled the papers inside. "You speak English, don't you, Sir?" The 'Sir' to impress him, and it worked.

"Yes."

"You were read your rights when you got arrested. Did you understand those rights? I can say them again, here, in case you didn't. Or I can have someone come in to recite them in your own language."

"Yes."

"Yes, what? You need me to say them again? Or what?" *Oh, crap!*

"I understand my rights."

WHEW! The prosecutor's office will be SO pleased! "Good. Your name is . . . ? I need you to say it to make you 'official'." It was right in front of him, inside the folder, but Hermie had to make sure.

"Reza Sabbah Hussein."

He knew, but he firmed up the bait, his voice easy, non-threatening: "And Soraya Ismailian Hassan-I Sabbah Safir is your . . . wife? Sister?"

"No. Cousin only."

"'Only'? Isn't she also your employer? Your boss?"

He flinched at that word, eyes snapping with annoyance.

"How did that happen? Her being a mere woman and all." Hermie mined the moment just right.

"Her father."

"Come again? I mean, say again and explain."

"Her father. Favored her."

"Well . . . that just isn't right. She's a mere woman. Fathers should favor their sons, in all things."

It was the slightest sneer, but it spoke volumes, "Her father had no sons. Nine daughters only."

"*Nine* daughters? *Only?*" Hermie pretended to laugh heartily and the chauffeur couldn't help but join in, albeit in a lower key.

They both wiped eyes, relaxed, sipped.

"How did he favor her? Exactly."

The chauffer froze for an instant, unsure.

"He *taught* her." Hermie said for him, flatly.

The Chauffeur started to reach for his water bottle, but he saw that his hands were trembling, handcuffs clickety-clicking. He pulled them in toward himself, tucked them under the table, silencing them.

"Why her? He could have had women until he got a son."

"She was better than a son."

"How so?"

"A son was 'expected'. A daughter, never. That is true, is it not?"

"I don't understand."

"A son has duties, obligations to the father, what the father plans, and to carry his name, forward. A daughter has only one: to make a good marriage, one that profits her father. This father had only daughters. In Iran, one wife, three mistresses, and only daughters. Six daughters at home, three more daughters outside. His name was not sent forward. He was cursed by Allah, surely."

"I know some fathers who considered their daughters to be the highest blessing," Hermie said gently, remembering.

"They must be Americans."

"Only incidentally."

The word puzzled him. "I do not understand."

"Not important. So, Mr. Sabbah had no son. Why was he so obsessed when obviously he wasn't gonna have any? Was it because he was a descendant of Ismailian Hassan-I Sabbah?"

Surprise was obvious on the Chauffer's face. "How do you know such things?"

"I'm clever. When the family landed in England, he claimed he was a teacher."

"This is true. He was professor. He taught history at the University in Iran. Because of his name, many came to his classes. Shiite, many, of course. But Sunni as well. It was not approved, but he did teach of the Assassin. He had the dagger."

"'The' dagger?"

"He had the dagger that belonged to Ismailian Hassan-I Sabbah, and was handed down, for many years."

"Is that really possible?"

A familiar shrug, "Mostly believed this. Shiites, of course. But with that history, the desperation for a son . . ." He shrugged again.

"Grandsons won't hack it."

"I don't --"

"No son, no *direct* descendant. Grandsons not direct enough, blood-wise."

"That is so."

"So his first daughter stepped up to the plate."

"She stole the dagger. Hid it. Would not return it unless her father taught her. He beat her, her mother beat her, she was cast out, but she would not tell where she'd hidden the dagger. Unless she was taught. The father had no choice."

"So, he taught her."

"In secret, so no one would know, not even the sisters. The mother was not told, but she guessed when Soraya's body changed."

"How so?"

"Muscles came in her arms, legs. More when she began to ride. The father taught and was amazed at the strength, the skills, the courage of this daughter. She was what he had prayed for in a son. But he could tell no one. It would have been the horrible shame if anyone knew a female -- his own daughter -- was taught the skills, the glory of Ismailian Hassan-I Sabbah, may Allah continue to enfold him."

"Why did she want this?"

"To love her father. She did not want to be . . . to be . . . *less* in his eyes. She wanted to be his longings fulfilled."

"He wanted a murderer in the family and by God he got one."

"This was not his intent. He had no need of an Assassin, his *name* was his power. The Assassin came after."

"'After'?"

"After her marriage."

"To Jordan Hashemi. No -- to Winston Safir."

"Yes. The father Safir met the father Sabbah at a concert he and his wife gave at the University, where Winston was a famous student. He was amazing his teachers -- he was brilliant, especially in the mathematics and the new computers. He was building his own computers when everyone else was just learning how to use them."

"So . . . one family had a brilliant son, the other family a brilliant daughter."

"Yes. They were introduced. Both resisted, refused, even. But then the finances were arranged. The Sabbah family was very, very rich. Riches in spite of being Shiite, because of history. Money from influence of government departments, the military, the special favors granted for import/export of goods. Most secret, money came from the Sunnis, clerics in power. Who feared Shiites. Paid them to keep their place. The father, Sabbah, was most famous Shiite, could control any movement toward more power, so he was courted. Courting that came with cash. And, of course, all those daughters would bring another source of cash, when to marry."

"No wonder capitalism never quite caught on over there."

"I don't —" Confusion in his eyes, embarrassment hovering near.

"Skip it. Uh, never mind. So, since it wasn't money, what was the attraction of Winston Safir?"

"The future his mind would create."

"Come again? Uh, explain that."

"The father Sabbah had him investigated, of course, and the reports of his mind, his work with computers, mathematics, amazed everyone. Computers were the future, for making much money, for getting much power, Sabbah knew this. The son Safir would bring all this into the Sabbahs, to the Shiites. And he was handsome, kind, respectful. In truth, he was the son Sabbah had longed for, for so long. After much persuasion by the parents, it was arranged."

"So they were married. What then?"

"Not many months later, the plane crash. Then Winston Safir took money and disappeared. Money remained to support Soraya, money to flow to her from secret sources she was not able to find. She was also not able to find her husband. He vanished. She went mad with grief and hate at first. Then she remembered she was smart."

"And she tracked down Winston/Jordan."

"Yes."

"How?"

"The car."

"The Rolls Royce?"

"Yes. It belonged to Safir. The only thing that was not auctioned off before he vanished. It was hidden, stored. Later, she went to look for it and it was gone. She knew he had taken it or had it sent somewhere. She was a very rich woman. She spent much money in bribes and investigate and they found he had it shipped to America, to the California. She came here, found the car's shipment records to the Long Beach. And then to the Century City. But there was no Safir in the Century City. No records. But still she watched, searched the garage at days and at nights, for weeks and weeks. One day, she found the car, parked in its special place. She waited here. For hours. Days. Until, at this place, she showed her presence to him."

"Hoo-boy, to be a fly on the wall for that conversation."

"A 'fly on the wall'?" He was worried he'd missed something important.

"Not important. Go on."

"She was his wife. Never mind the years ago. He must care for her. He must give her children. His answer was to give her the keys to the Rolls Royce and tell her they were divorced. He had said 'I divorce thee' three times back in London, but she knew this was not the law. She was still the wife. The only wife. So, she bought the house here, and then she began."

"'Began' . . . ?"

"She hoped to persuade him of his obligations to her, how he could not escape these things. But then he vanished again. She hired detectives again. Many. For months and months. They could not find him. Could not find any records of him. Then, one day, there he was."

"How?"

"We were driving the Crenshaw Boulevard in Torrance, to home to Palos Verdes, when there was a traffic stop. A bad accident had closed the street, everyone turned aside to the many streets in Torrance that would lead past where the accident was, and then turn back to the Crenshaw. We were driving on a side street when *there* Safir was, standing by a car, in front of an apartment building, helping a woman and a boy to get into this car. He did not see us, praise be to Allah. If he had, I am certain he would have killed us. But Soraya, she screamed all the way to her house. She lost her mind, truly."

"Is this when the stalking began?"

"Yes. We were only sometimes successful, because Safir never drove the same car, surrounded them with invisible computer guards that disappeared any records. The apartment building had locks and cameras and did not have his name anywhere on the building or in any records of an owner. We were looking for Safir. We did not know he was now 'Jordan Hashemi'. Most days, nights, she watched and waited and tried to follow. But they would vanish into strange cars, traffic, streets, freeways. I know Safir saw us often, he is that kind of man."

"'Was', anyway."

"'Was'?"

"He no longer 'is'."

"Ah. Yes."

"Nor is the woman and the boy."

The chauffeur bowed his head. Twisted his hands as the cuffs rattled.

"Don't be shy. I'm sure the D.A. will dangle an offer at you for your testimony against her. Instead of life, *alone*, in a cell. Or the death penalty. Or, of course, deportation. Back where you came from. What fun."

His tan skin blanched, yellowed. He grabbed up the water bottle, gulped a couple swallows, his large Adam's Apple bobbing.

"How did she find them that day?"

"Weeks before, one of her detectives who was off duty saw them in a restaurant, in a night.

"Poco Paesano."

He couldn't hide his shock. "You *know* this? Yes. The detective and his friend were having dinner and walked in Safir, the woman and the boy. The detective noticed how Safir kept stepping out to check the streets. When it was the next day, the detective returned and found all the guarding cameras. And the garage in back. He spent a month waiting until he saw Safir return and drive into that garage, in a different car, with the woman and the boy. He reported to us. Soraya was too eager, we drove there that night and nearly could not get out of the small parking lot."

"That's when Hashemi spotted the Rolls Royce. And knew. Should-a taken a Hertz."

The large man's dark eyes once more betrayed confusion.

"I do not understand."

"Skip it. Uh, never mind."

"A decision was made to wait on a nearby side street, days, nights. We would wait for them, to follow. The one afternoon they came, for to have the dinner. We waited, unseen."

"On Mother's Day. And you followed them. On and off the freeway."

"Yes."

"Did you know what she was going to do?"

"When she ordered me to bump them off the freeway, I thought she was going to confront Safir again, threaten a public, legal divorce in this country, in this state. He would not be able to remain vanished. Whatever business he was doing in America, this was a threat to that."

"Hardly."

"When we left the freeway and stopped, she ordered me to tie Safir to the steering wheel of his car. I was shocked –- she had brought a tying-up-strip within her chador. I did as I was told."

"Did you see the murder?"

""Not this one. I was tying up Safir, taking his gun, he was cursing at her when she yanked the woman out of the car by her hair, forced her up toward the freeway. The woman clutched a small flowers. I only saw the woman fall in a spray of blood. The boy screamed and ran to the woman, kissed her face. Soraya raised the dagger behind him and Safir yelled very loud, 'Run, boy! Run! Now!' And he did."

"Soraya returned to Safir's car, sat in back, screaming: 'You think I cannot find that boy? I found *you*! I found *her*! I will find *him*! I will send him to the same hell as his whore mother! And *you*!' She threw the flowers at him. I was ordered to the passenger seat, Safir was ordered to drive away, but a few blocks. She was screaming at him, still: 'You will not die alongside her! You will not be with your whore at the last, at forever!' When we stopped, one of his hands was free. Soraya and I left the car, she came around to the driver's side door. Safir was struggling to get out of the car, one hand still bound. He had time to slap her, once only. And very hard. It was not enough."

He drained the water from the bottle. "I had only heard about that dagger blow that was taught by Ismailian Hassan-I Sabbah, the mark of the Assassin. To see it happen, to see someone actually *do* it . . . Safir fell backwards, half in the car, blood sprayed like from a fountain. She wiped the dagger with one of his pants cuffs, the only thing left that was dry. We walked back to the Rolls Royce. It was only then that I saw the woman's purse sticking out of the pocket of her chador. We drove away in silence."

"But she made you stop so you could drive over the violets she threw out of the car."

His eyes were wide with shock: "You know of that? How —-?"

"Did you help her stalk those girls?""

"No-no! Upon Allah's name I swear I did not! I bless Allah that she did not trust me. So I saw no more."

Hermie was having none of it, and it showed. The chauffer looked away, guiltily, trapped, forced himself to go on.

"She rented a small car, leave the house most all days, without me. And she came back stained with blood, a bloody headscarf stuffed in the pocket of her chador. But...she was happy." He swallowed, painfully. "And then I saw...I saw the news on the television. And I...I knew."

"The saddle?"

"One day she started working on that saddle. When she went to get a more tea, I close looked. She was carving holes into the bottom of the saddle, using a pointed metal. More bloody headscarves were nearby. Later, I saw strips from those headscarves tied into the holes."

"And you told no one?"

"Who could I tell? *What* could I tell? I was not a witness!"

"But you *knew*! And you did nothing to stop her. *Nothing!*"

"I could not!"

"Why the hell not?!"

He paused, shame blatant on his face, in hunched masses of shoulders. "Her father put me in charge of her protection. He gave my family money in exchange for my protection when she left England and came here."

"If you squealed, the money would stop."

"In my family are eleven children and me, the oldest son. There is a new baby almost every year. My father has pains, he cannot work!"

"I'll just bet he can't. Why did you try to claim Hashemi's body?"

He looked as though he'd been caught again. "Soraya wanted it."

"Why?"

"She was going to burn him. A final insult. When I failed . . ." Embarrassment reddened his face.

"She beat you?"

"Yes."

"With what?"

"She has a whip. For the horses."

"And you took it?"

"Yes. For my family."

Before a kind of pity could drift into his mind, one by one, from the folder, Hermie pulled out the full color photos from the murder scenes, and spoke their precious names: "Amira Farsadi . . . she was just past nineteen, a brilliant student, loved by her teachers and classmates, defender of her abused mother, against her own father and brother. Sunidhi Askar . . . she was a very pious daughter of Islam, studying to be a lawyer, so loving and so loved, everyone who met her called her 'Sunny'. Shirin Batawi . . . shy but brave, she just got a wonderful job with a great future, and had a neighbor who treated her like a daughter. All innocent, all slaughtered. Because your father has 'pains'. Because you didn't want to stop the money."

Hermie stood up, "Reza Sabbah Hussein, you are under arrest, for multiple counts of conspiracy to commit murder, before and after the fact. And that's just the start of your troubles."

For a second or two, Reza was transfixed by the horror in the photographs. Then he burst into howling tears as Hermie retrieved the photos, files, and left the room.

Outside, a tall and lanky police officer was waiting. Hermie became aware that other officers' eyes were all around, looking out various office doors, watching as if bearing witness. "Lock him up," Hermie said to the tall officer. "Don't call the D.A. just yet. I'll let you know."

"Okay, Sir."

"Make sure a large box of tissues are in his cell. It's the least we can do for the sorry sonuvabitch."

The officer recognized sarcasm, but never accompanied by this much rage.

* * * * * *

Strategy. In this case it had to be uber careful, uber clever, and *very* uber relentless. Because he wanted the death penalty. *Bad*. Really, really *BAD*.

His first step was to be accompanied by a female interpreter who spoke every version of Middle Eastern languages there is. Luckily, there was a Jordanian cop who fit the bill, working out of the Inglewood Station, of all places. But she strongly and profanely objected to wearing a full-blown chador and hijab, until Hermie explained why. Then she blinked away a sudden rush of tears because she knew the case, and solemnly shook Hermie's hand as she said, "Okay. I'm in."

Hermie double-checked to see that all the microphones and videocams were on and recording before he opened the door to the interrogation room and stepped aside to let his interpreter, Belinda "Bunnie" Hussein in first. A shiny policeman's badge was defiantly pinned onto the front of the chador she wore. He noted that his instructions had been followed: A cold bottle of water and a bowl of almond-stuffed dates were in front of the silent Soraya Ismailian Hassan-I Sabbah Safir. He did a quick count and noted that two of the dates had been eaten, the water bottle was opened, and a third of the water had been drunk. *Good. She's hungry and thirsty.*

She was wearing a chador, gloves, and the niqab, the veil that covered her face except for a slit to reveal her eyes. All were in a gray so deep, so dark, at first glance it was black.

Hermie had already been told how Soraya had objected strongly --- to the point of a physical, screaming struggle --- to being forced to remove her gloves for fingerprinting, and remove the niqab for the booking photo. However, her objections fell on deaf ears --- *female* ears, because Hermie's orders had been followed: only female cops dealt with her or touched her. And a couple --- Christians --- volunteered to wear a chador, also just for spite.

At his first encounter with her in her backyard, Hermie had been so intent he had failed to take much notice of her face, other than to note the imperious arrogance on the fine bones. Now, the slit in the niqab revealed Soraya's eyes were a very dark blue, made darker by a thick hedge of blacker than black eyelashes that shadowed them. Perfectly trimmed eyebrows could be glimpsed curving up and around her eye sockets. Hermie heard that the female cops had discussions as to how they got so perfectly trimmed --- "Did she pluck them or get them threaded?" Hermie was not about to ask what the hell they were talking about.

What first struck Hermie --- and only he would know --- was that there was no scent at all coming from this woman. No flowery cosmetics, no fruity shampoo, or creamy-sweet soap, not even the ever-present scent that differed a woman's skin from a man's: the warm, inviting, hormonal,'this is a female' scent that Hermie always detected beneath the usual array of scents women used. *No scent at all; she doesn't exist,* thought Hermie with irony.

Hermie and Bunnie sat squarely across from her, Hermie setting the now closed folder in front of them. "As you know, I am Homicide Detective Herman Grabfelder, and this is my interpreter, Ms. Hussein. You may speak in English or your own language, whatever that may be. All is being recorded and filmed. You were read your rights when you were arrested, however, they were spoken in English. Would you prefer to have your rights spoken to you again, in your language?"

"Yes. Farsi."

"Egyptian or Iranian or Jordanian?" Bunnie piped up.

It startled Soraya. "You know the difference?"

"I do. Which do you prefer?"

"Iranian."

Bunnie rattled off the rights in staccato Iranian Farsi while Hermie pretended he knew what she was saying. Afterward, he said, "Do you understand those rights?"

"Yes."

"All right. If ever, in this conversation, you wish Ms. Hussein to translate my words from English to Farsi, or your Farsi words into English, you have only to ask and we will do this for you."

It worked. She thinks she is respected. So calling a lawyer was far from her mind. Yet. Bitch! Smile, Herms, so you don't go for her throat.

"Thank you," she said with a slight, noble nod of her head.

Now, shock value: he opened the file folder and took out the bloody photos of the murder victims and laid them down in front of her, one by one: "Amira Farsadi, Sunidhi Askar, Shirin Batawi. Why did you kill these girls?"

No denial at all. Just calm conviction. "They were whores. An abomination against Islam." she said, so matter-of-factly Hermie thought he hadn't heard her correctly. Then she said it in Iranian Farsi.

Under restraint, Bunnie turned to Hermie and translated: "They were whores, an abomination against Islam."

"Why do you say they were whores? Did you know them?"

"I do not know whores." This in perfect English.

"So you killed women you did not know. How'd you manage that? Your father teach you that? Yes, we know his ancestry. You were taught by him. You learned well. The one daughter who wanted to be the son among all those sisters. We found the dagger in your house. You didn't clean it. It's dosed in DNA. I think you liked to see the blood the dagger had taken up when it struck."

Her eyes were absolutely still, the bottom of her niqab flowed forward and back with her calm breathing.

Hermie tapped the photo of Amira Farsadi. "Amira Farsadi. She was only nineteen, going to school, a brilliant student. How was she a whore?"

"She went to that school with boys! Why for was she in school? She should have been a good Muslim wife, at home, with babies! She was in school to be with the boys! Whore!"

Hermie tapped the next photo: "Sunidhi Askar. She was called "Sunny" because of her nature. She graduated with honors. She was still studying and working because she wished to be a lawyer."

"Whore! She worked with men! She walked with men on the streets, she ate in restaurants with men! Where is a Muslim husband to control her?"

"Well, actually, she had asked her Mom and Dad to find her a nice Muslim husband. She was very devout."

"A whore cannot be devout! She is a lie! She is damned!"

Hermie tapped the photo of Shirin Batawi. "She had just started a new job at a store where she was doing very well. A lot of women around her there, working to help support their families. She had made friends of her new neighbors."

"I saw her 'friend'! She walks the streets with an old white man!"

"He was her bodyguard. A former Marine, a soldier."

Trapped within the niqab, her eyes widened, startled.

"In their neighborhood, because she also was devout, he felt she was not safe. He thought of her as a daughter that needed protecting. Now, he and his friends guard a mosque. They are all retired soldiers. None of them are Muslim, but they are defending Muslims."

Now her eyes narrowed with contempt. "You lie," she hissed.

Then Hermie pulled out the last of the photos, of Lila Miller and Jordan Hashemi.

The blazing hate that came out of the niqab's slits was accompanied by a hiss of rage.

"This is where it all started. You killed your ex-husband and his lady friend. Jealousy?"

"He marry *me!* He took the dowry, then he turned away! I was good Muslim wife! He gave me no love! No children! I was good Muslim wife and he say, 'I divorce thee'! Why for? Why for he left me?! Where did he go? *Why* did he go?"

"Apparently he left you well provided for. Money, a home."

"He belonged in *our* home! With *me!* To give me children, *sons*, so I have a place! A place for *me!*"

"How did you find him? No one else was able to find him."

She sat back, as if pleased, challenging.

Hermie didn't take the bait. "Doesn't matter. What matters is that you started off with these two murders and you left a witness. Their son."

"He is not a son! He belongs to that whore! How does he take care of a whore's son but give no son for *me*!"

"Who can figure out feelings? He met Lila — her real name is Ashwari, by the way, she was a Muslim, back in the day. Her parents were from Iran. She escaped a father who basically sold her to the highest bidder, a husband who beat the crap outta her until she got pregnant, and then started taking a swing at the little boy — his own son. When her father discovered what the husband had done — by the way, he didn't find out until Ashwari ended up in the hospital, so beaten up police were called. So, he killed that husband, but it was too late to make it up to Ashwari. She took her six year old son and ran. Started important work, dangerous work, for the FBI. She was very brave. It wasn't until years later that she met Hashemi."

"And became his whore! 'Jordan Hashemi'! she hissed, spit, "Where he find that name? He is Winston Safir. He is *MY* Winston Safir!"

"Now he's nobody's anything. Except to a young boy who he loved as his own. The young boy who saw you murder his mother and his 'father', his parents. He will be a witness against you. He will put you on death row. Where you belong."

"Allah will not permit this!" She suddenly broke into a storm of Arabic that Bunnie calmy translated into English: "Allah knows I am in the right! Islam puts me in the right! I avenge! I avenge! Against whores and their spawn. Allah sees all sin, Allah knows I stopped the sin! I am warrior for Allah!" She stopped for breath.

He turned to Bunnie and Bunnie saw he was about to lose it. "Tell her in whatever language she understands: Tell her Allah and Islam command *against* the harm or murder of innocents. These were innocents: precious daughters living blameless lives, and three people who formed a loving family against all the odds, known and unknown. You did *NOT* 'avenge'. You *murdered*. You are *NOT* a warrior. You are a *murderer*. You are damned by the law, you are damned by Islam, you are damned by Allah."

While Bunnie was still gushing his words in Farsi, Hermie started to slide all the murder photos back into the folder and abruptly got up. Amira Farsadi's photo was left. He held it up to Soraya. "See her? She was . . . she was . . ." his throat closed, he coughed. "Her father tried to sell her once, when she was just eleven years old. He did not allow her to be loved. But in secret she was dearly loved -- by her mother, by her classmates, by her teachers. By *me*. She's the one who caught you. I stole one of those ribbons off that fancy saddle of yours. You should have scrubbed all those hijabs you stole from those girls. Their blood was on them. *Her* blood was on that strip I stole. *She* caught you. Amira's innocent blood condemned you. Amira, Sunidhi, Shirin, Ashwari, and Jordan. You think you killed them? They all live on, they are loved-loved-*loved* in so many memories in so many hearts. Tell me, Soraya, who will remember *you*?"

He turned and left the room, Bunnie hurrying after him.

* * * *

Hours later, when he came back to the stationette after endless meetings with the Prosecutor, the Chief and a gaggle of Attorneys, both defense and prosecution and Union, his eyes were red, his walk was infirm, his clothes rumpled, his insulin levels ran riot, until someone brought him some nuts at his request and explanation at one of those interminable meetings.

For maybe five seconds, Nell and Claire thought he'd fallen off the wagon, big time. The news stories were still blaring from Nell's computer, the "Mother's Day Daughter Killer" was finally caught. And it was a *woman*, a female serial killer, a Muslim killer killing Muslim daughters. Did he celebrate the arrest? Wouldn't blame him if he had. But . . .

But they knew him so well, loved him so thoroughly, whether he deserved it or not, so they realized that it wasn't booze that had struck him almost down, that it wasn't Stingers that had shook him so to the core that he could barely walk, struggled to remain standing.

They froze where they were and waited for it. He could barely get it out, but they thanked all the gods that he did get it out because it was a poison, it was an affliction, it was a curse he needed to get out of his being or he'd be lost to himself and to them for all time.

"She killed them. She killed them all." He gave Nell a smile that was wreathed in pain. "And you were right: she killed them because they were happy. And she hated them for that."

They rushed at him intending a group hug of sympathy and empathy, but it was more like holding him up. And for once, he let them do it.

CHAPTER TWENTY-EIGHT

"Here I understand what they call glory: the right to love without limits."

Albert Camus

He lied like a rug.

He swore up and down and sideways that he would go straight home and go to bed until further notice, "Honest t'God."

Claire went so far as to declare him on an official leave of absence, so if he showed up at their stationette in less than a week, she'd "Whomp you upside de haid. I'm damn serious, Hermie, you take a whole week off or I'll tear your pension to shreds, honest t'God."

Nell promised she'd handle his phone calls, put off any that weren't urgent or were reporters in disguise, and swore she'd call him with messages she knew he'd want to know about, "Honest t'God."

As he was walking out, both cheeks still having wet spots from their fond kisses and tears, he checked his watch to no avail –- his exhausted eyes were in a nearly total blur-out and he couldn't see what time it was. And he'd be damned if he'd ask those women, because then they'd *know*. To his relief, when he got into Roberta and switched on her headlights, he could see well enough to drive.

He knew it was late, really late, but he had to go there, just had to. As he drove, slowly, like a good boy with diminished vision, he made up his mind that if the house wasn't lit up inside, he wouldn't disturb them; he'd come back tomorrow at a decent hour. *What's one more day, especially now. Especially now.*

What's one more day, especially now, was that he wouldn't be able to let it all go until and unless he told him.

When he pulled up in front of the Harrison's, he was relieved to see the lights were on inside, but still hesitated because he didn't trust his vision. *Maybe it was wishful thinking. Maybe they were all night-lights.*

He got out of Roberta to make sure and was startled to see Frank and Millie rise up from the front stoop, where they'd been sitting, waiting.

"I'm sorry. It's so late, I was afraid you all would be in bed. I was gonna come back tomorrow."

"We knew you'd-a come," said Millie, before she wrapped her arms around him, seeing his condition and knowing the cost.

Frank grabbed his hand, "Been watchin' the news. Ya did it. So glad for ya. For the families. It don't change nothing, we know about that, but it's still *something*, y'know? 'Specially for our 'Kevin'."

'Our Kevin'. So, it was complete. He was really theirs, really home. Except for the miles of paperwork and batches of court appearances to come.

They assured him that "Kevin" hadn't gone to bed yet. He was out back, in the porch swing.

"Prob-ly listenin' to that hootie-owl. It's courtin' time, y'know. We got this one comes 'round every night, tryin' to get a date, hootin' and hootin'. 'Kevin' . . . well . . . he . . ." and Frank suddenly choked up.

"He's aware," said Millie proudly, "He's actually *aware*. Even talks some. Not much, yet, but some. He's *starting*."

To his surprise and instant relief, "Kevin" heard him and turned to look up at him from the slowly moving porch swing. The lights from the back windows of the house were enough to show that "Kevin's" eyes were seeing, aware, he knew who Hermie was.

Hermie suddenly realized that Kevin had been *waiting. Did he hear the news on the TV?*

"Hey, 'Kevin'. Up late, huh? Me, too. Good to see ya."

Hermie carefully came over and sat beside him on the swing. "Kevin's" eyes followed him, waiting.

The hootie-owl picked that moment for another attempt, but it was soft, magical in the blackness and flowery fragrances of the night. Apparently, "Kevin" didn't hear him this time.

"I'm glad you're still up because I have some news. *Good* news." Hermie said.

The swing stopped moving. "Kevin" looked away. His hands came up into his lap and clutched together as if he were hanging on for dear life.

Hermie took a chance: he reached over and put his large, calming hand onto "Kevin's" cold, clenched fingers. "You don't have to hang on anymore,

'Kevin'. I got her. *I. GOT. HER.* She's in jail, locked up, and she'll stay there forever. She's done-done-done. Soraya is caught. Soraya is *stopped.*"

"Kevin" turned to him and Hermie could actually see something lift away from the boy's face, his eyes, his entire body. His clutched hands warmed, suddenly grabbed onto Hermie's hand. And he spoke: "Soraya . . . she's gone?"

"So-o gone. She is over with. You're free, 'Kevin'. We all are."

To the end of his days, Hermie would remember what he saw in that instant: A child's eyes empty themselves of fear.

They weren't concerned, exactly, because they didn't hear anything unusual coming from out back, except for when the normal soft squeak of the porch swing had stopped. But it was almost an hour, now, and neither "Kevin" nor the detective could be heard anymore.

So they very quietly went to the back door to see what was going on. And they both wept at the sight: They were slumped on the porch swing in a tight embrace, the boy who once feared touch and the man who had once lost touch. The detective's massive arms were wrapped completely around their slender boy, and the boy's thin arms were wrapped around the detective as far as they could go. And both were deeply asleep, snoring with the peaceful sound that comes from those who have finally set their burdens down.

CHAPTER TWENTY-NINE

"All things lead me to thee."

Jordan Hashemi

Trots waited for a decent interval after the news made headlines all over the place, even in Quantico, because he knew solving the case — especially *this* god-awful case -- was a great relief to one and all, considering the politics. But then came the follow-up he'd be stuck with: paperwork, depositions, meeting with troops of lawyers, meetings with the Chief, the Union, etcetera and endlessly etcetera. And, because it was Hermie, there was also the Invasion of the Reporters. Some were new or out-of-towners so they didn't believe his threats; he *educated* them. The veterans, led by the ever-crusading Tommy Velasco, knew enough to back off of Detective Herman Grabfelder and spend their time going after people on the perimeter of the case, whose comments weren't all that illuminating, but enough to embellish into what looked like newsworthy stories.

The families of the murdered daughters acted as one and released to the press a single statement of gratitude to the LAPD "investigator" (knowing Hermie would be craving anonymity about now, he was that kinda modest guy), and all the "officers", and summing up with a request for privacy. The statement was read for the TV cameras by a lawyer who was known to sue reporters and their bosses who didn't take seriously a 'request for Privacy'. Freedom of the Press being as sacrosanct as it was, the lawsuits didn't win but they were expensive, *very* expensive to fight. So, the families were left alone to dread when they'd have to attend the trial of the monstrous woman who had broken their lives.

The Prosecutor was valiantly pressing for a just punishment to avoid that trial. He threatened the death penalty, but no one knew when, if ever, California would crank up its moribund (so to speak) death row, so it was not the threat it used to be, which was why voters had recently voted a "need for speed". His only other offer was a choice: Plead insanity and agree to be locked up in Psychiatric until whenever; or simply plead guilty to everything and be jailed for life, and when the time came she would be sent back to England to be buried alongside her father's grave, in full accordance with Islamic dictates.

Soraya had refused to hire a lawyer and went snarling or mute in front of several court-appointed attorneys. So four of her eight sisters arrived from Iran, hiding inside full hijabs and niqabs, begging her to take the 'guilty' deal in hopes that this horror would all die down and their shame would get the chance to leave the headlines, not to mention the marriage market gossip.

So, Trots waited a month and then some before he called Hermie's home land-line.

"Snoopy? Congratulations! Well done, buddy!"

"Yeah. It's a relief to stop puking."

"A *woman* serial? I mean, I know it's Los Angeles, but that is beyond the beyond."

"As always, we lead the nation. Even in Persian."

"I'll say! But why I'm calling is I got clearance to tell you something that's rocked our world. And it's not tangled in your case, like I said, but somewhat peripherally. Maybe. But, it's only fair to share."

"I love presents."

Trots chuckled, then: "It's about Jordan Hashemi."

"You cracked his code? Or is it code-sss?"

"What it is, is a glimpse."

"Huh?"

"Hermie, nobody's seen anything like it and we wish to great Gawd almighty we could resurrect that guy because he could change everything."

"Details, details."

"We can't crack his codes. Yet. But we know what they *do*. Just not *how* they do it."

"I'll say it again: Huh?"

"Since you are still cyber challenged, I'll keep it simple. You know how Isis and all those other fanatics go online and recruit the loser gullibles, or go on websites and show executions or blowing up historical sites, or broadcast propaganda after they bomb innocent people."

"Yeah. They jest lu-uv being famous. Sonsabitches. They've turned the Internet into the devil's underpants. You will recall that I did warn everyone about computers at the start. Now they're unstoppable."

"Hashemi can stop them. Or could have."

"What?"

"Hermie, he created a cyberspace program that is like an internet drone."

"Seriously?"

"We're calling it the "Boomerang". Every time Isis or El Qaida or Boko Haram or any of those assholes go anywhere online, Hashemi's program seeks them out like a guided missile or drone and destroys their computer and the network connection they're using. Melts it down. Blows it up. Stomps it all to hell. And, most importantly, it reports the location of these clowns, a headquarters, so one of our drones can drop a load on them as an added bonus, while they're trying to figure out what the hell is going on."

"Jeezus. So, he *was* going to use his genius for good instead of ee-vil."

"Unless-*unless* he was fixing to sell it to the highest bidder. If not a terrorist group, think about those cyber hackers attacking our computer systems and others worldwide. Nobody is safe. Hashemi could not only stop them, but destroy their systems. And they knew it. So, they'd all pay larger than large for protection. So, what if he threw in with them instead of us good guys? That's newest nightmare."

"I don't think he would have done that."

"How the hell would *you* know? How the hell does *anyone* know, thanks to that . . . that . . ."

"I know. We gotta invent a new word for her. 'Evil Spawn' doesn't quite hack it. The only thing that would have prevented her was birth control. Made of kryptonite."

"Hmmm. Well, I'm glad you got her. Those poor families . . ."

"Yeah. If only I'd gotten her sooner."

"Shoulda-woulda-coulda –– you do your best and hope. Nobody coulda done more, Snoopy. Let it go."

"Tryin'."

Trots heard that tone, knew what it meant: *Change the subject!* "Speaking of, what are you doing home on a work day? You been promoted to "Work at Home"? Eleanor must be either thrilled or pissed off you've interrupted her card games."

"I've been ordered to take some time off. Claire used the threats made famous by her people."

"Smart woman."

"Speaking of, now that the bouncy Brenda knows I'm free here, expect her to vanish with a packed suitcase, heading West."

"Not gonna happen. I've sent her to Bermuda with her Mom and the kids. I'm flying there tonight. Just wanted to tie up the Hashemi thing –– not that any of us can ever –– *EVER!* –– tie up anything about that man. We called in every cyber expert on the planet, then we called in every hacker on our radar –– including scary-precocious nine-year-old boys and teenagers fooling around in our computer neighborhood –– offered large money and no prosecution for life, plus free lifetime passes to Disneyland or NASA's Space Camp. Then we called in Apple, Sanyo, Verizon, AT&T -– and so on and so forth –- reminded them of their patriotic duty, yada-yadoo -- and had them *all* take a look at Hashemi's toys. Everybody sees it work but nobody knows *how* he does -– did -– it. By the way, I had another thought."

"Aw, Jeez, not another one!"

"Mirth-mirth. Hashemi's boy. How's he doing?"

"He's doing. Coming back, slow but sure. It's something great to see, considering where he's been, what he's seen."

"My thought was, do you think Hashemi taught him anything, computer-wise?"

"Coulda. I first met Kevin at a computer store. Intro'd by a computer geek friend who helps me out. Hank O'Dell, you've seen his work and strongly objected on more than one occasion. He should take a look at Hashemi's stuff. Maybe he can figure it out. I'll have him give you a tingle."

"Do you think –-?"

"Goddammit! Don't you dare think of "Kevin"!"

"I knew that's what you'd say."

"That boy's mind was nearly destroyed. I won't have *anyone* coming near him for any 'national security' crap! He's going to be a safe, loved, protected, and normal boy. When he grows up, gets wise, he can decide for himself if he knows anything, and if he wants to share. Until then, I swear to God if any guv'ment geek gets near him, or even starts watching him –-!"

"Yeah, yeah, I get the message. And you're right. Really right. If anyone here suggests anything, I'll head them off at the pass and give you a heads up so you can get him into Uber Wit-Pro-. I'll help with that, so even the Feds can't find him."

"I'm trusting you, Pal."

"You have my word. Well . . . Bermuda calls."

"She's headed *West*, I keep telling you. And she won't be bringing Mom or the kids. She's always such a free spirit with me. You understand -– it's the magic of my charm."

Trots laughed loudly. "Did you say 'charm'? Oh, Lord, that's SO-O not the word! I'll keep you posted on Hashemi-mania. Congratulations again. Rest, eat, walk the cat. Do people walk cats? Take care of your little self, Snoopy."

"You, too, Red. Gray. White?"

"Up yours!"

He hung up and Hermie hung up as they both laughed.

Hermie sat there for a moment, feeling better. *How long's it been since I been to Quantico? Might make a nice reunion trip. See all the new furniture, try to dissuade the new crop of fresh-faced lads. And lasses.*

Hermie had turned the sound off on the TV when the phone rang, the screen was now showing a commercial because Hermie had been channel surfing, flipping past his favorite Turner Classic Movie Channel because it was showing *"The Million Dollar Mermaid"* yet again and he wasn't having it. Unfortunately, that left him on a commercial channel showing a chat show peopled by women with voices screeching in several decibels. He was about to, "Daytime TV sucks!" and turn it off when the phone had rung with Trots, startling him just enough that he hit the "MUTE" instead of the "ON/OFF" button.

His house smelled of Lilacs from the latest going-over by Maya and her students doing their version of Fall cleaning, which Hermie knew was more like checking up on his housekeeping skills than actual cleaning. But it was a lucky break because the students spotted a termite entrance just outside a kitchen window. So, they attacked likely nest sites inside with non-toxic repellants and outside for piles of rotting leaves and old dirt that beckoned termites to use as a jumping off place to the house. They had declared the house "invasion-free" yesterday.

Now the house's utter silence was only broken by Eleanor's rumbling purr on his shoulder, so he hesitated with the TV remote, reluctantly switching the audio back on, as the screen showed the screeching women were still there.

Suddenly, the TV screen switched to a long commercial for a collection of "Your favorite Oldies from the Seventies and Eighties, the original artists now available on re-mastered CD's for the perfect sound on today's audio devices."

An artistic display of CD's came on and Hermie's memory took a jump: he remembered the CD that he'd put into his coat pocket *Hell, how long ago?* Taken from Lila's car, and even Hank O'Dell's eerie talent had failed to get it to play. The CD that declared itself blank but they all knew it wasn't blank. Hashemi would not have left behind a blank CD. Especially not one he'd given to Lila.

All his Murder Books and notes on the case were either in his office or in the Prosecutor's office, so Pepsi's phone number was temporarily lost to him. So he gently gathered up Eleanor, who eyed him sleepily as he set her onto his bed, snug against his pillow, then he went to his closet.

He couldn't remember which jacket, so he checked three before he found the one with the pocketful of CD. Then he went out of the house, locked up, then fired up Roberta.

When he parked outside the condo building, he vaguely recalled Pepsi Potter mentioning her appointments at Curves and wondered whether he'd catch her at home. If she wasn't at Curves, she might be elsewhere, Pepsi being that kinda active gal.

The Jacaranda trees were blossom-less now, summer having snuck past; but their green shade still dappled him as he went up the walkway, past the still-blooming bushes, and scanned the directory tucked in a nook on the wall alongside the door. "Pepsi Potter, HOA President" was the first name on the list. And Hermie noticed that neither Lila's name nor her apartment number was on the listing, as before. She still didn't exist. He idly wondered what kind of a discussion Hashemi or even Lila had with Pepsi in order to get her to not have Lila's existence on that list.

He pressed the button alongside "Pepsi Potter, HOA President" and waited. After an unpleasant crackle her voice came through, too loud, as if she didn't trust the device: "Hell-OH-oh?"

"Miz Potter, it's Detective Grabfelder." It was catching, he found himself shouting in kind.

"WHO-O?"

Another yell, "It's Grabfelder!"

"Oh –– OH! HI! I'm buzzing! Push the door!"

A loud BUZZZZ! seemed to come from all sides, Hermie pushed the heavy door open.

Pepsi was waiting for him in the hall outside her door. Her perfect, tiny frame did justice to a fuscia T-shirt and pink Bermuda shorts. On her feet were fuzzy pink bedsocks.

"Detective! I just knew you'd be psychic!"

"Pardon?" he was thrown off point right off the bat.

"When it hit the news –– about your solving the case, I wanted to call you to tell you 'Congratulations' and that the boy needn't worry."

The boy' –– she's talking about "Kevin". "Oh. Lila's son."

"Yes. Come in, come in ––" She ushered him into the cool Japanese enclave of her apartment, the fragrant tea leaves scent still there like before.

Since it would be faster not to resist her, he let himself be sat down on the not-so-comfortable cushions of the couch and sipped the lemonade of before with pleasure. Then he got back on point: "Why should the boy not worry?"

"Oh –– wait –– she got up and went to a large, plastic shopping bag set in the kitchen, brought it over. "Here is Lila's mail –– it's junk mostly, isn't even addressed to her by name, but *he* should judge, not me. And apparently her utility bills are paid by direct deposit, as she got no bills, just receipts. I checked, just in case, wouldn't want her power or water turned off, you know. As for her car, it can stay there as long as her unit is in her name and the maintenance is paid for. I take it the boy inherits, so we will wait to see what he decides. If he moves in or puts it up for sale. Normally, we wouldn't allow someone so young to be in charge of a Unit, but I know that boy, we're willing to give him a trial run if he decides to move in."

"I have no idea what he'll do at this point. He's been seriously ill, but is recovering very well. And he's now living with . . . with family and is very happy there. So . . ."

"So, tell him not to worry. His condo and car will be here for him, if and whenever."

"The car —" Hermie started.

"Oh! The car!" She jumped up, went to the kitchen, yanked open a drawer. "When your forensics team returned it, they gave me the keys." She rummaged, came up with a set of car keys, brought them to Hermie.

He told a white lie, hoping it would keep her from following him. "Speaking of the car, that's why I'm here. I thought I'd start it up, re-charge the battery, just in case. "Kevin's" getting close to driver's license age, he may want the car to drive to school."

"Oh, of course. The garage door clicker is still clipped to one of the windshield shades, in case you want to take it out for a spin."

"I'll do that." He got up, noticed that Pepsi was disappointed.

"Is that all?" she asked, wistfully.

"For now. The boy may need some things from the apartment. I'll bring him by, whenever."

"Any time."

"Oh, I'll need your phone number again. My Murder Books are all with the Prosecutor."

"Ooh! 'Murder Books'!" she shivered.

"My notes, the phone numbers of people I talked to, 'stuff'."

Pepsi popped up again and went to the kitchen, to a small crystal swan bowl on a counter-top that held business cards. Brought a couple over to Hermie. "I just had these printed up."

He read a beautifully embossed card, "Pepsi Potter, Sea Breeze Condominium Apartments, HOA President", with the address and phone number. The card also had a Japanese-style delicate water color of a flying crane. "Oh, these are very classy," Hermie remarked.

"Thank you. I was thinking of going into business designing business cards, stationery."

"You should, you obviously have an eye."

"Problem is, everybody does everything by computer these days."

"Don't ya just hate that?" he confessed.

"Oh, I do! Dealing with machines instead of people, sitting in front of that computer screen. So little done on elegant paper, I doubt there's a market for me anymore."

It was an instant inspiration inspired by this energetic woman and by the serenity surrounding him. "Seems to me you've got a book in you."

"I beg your pardon?"

"You told me you and your husband lived in Japan for some years and you fell in love with the country, the people. Even the food. You could write a book. I'm sure you have tales to tell about adjusting, making mistakes, making friends, that sort of thing. Maybe throw in some of your favorite recipes. That'd be something even *I* might read."

Pepsi Potter blushed and beamed. "Detective Grabfelder, you are an inspiration in so many ways."

"Aw, go on," he teased, and headed for the door, pocketing the cards. "I will keep you posted about Lila's boy. But I can tell you that it will be awhile before he's steady enough on his feet to make any major decisions. He's not up to managing life yet."

"No problem at all. Tell him I'm here to help, whenever."

"I will. Thanks a lot."

And she watched him go down the hall and, not for the first time, she wondered how old he was and if he was, well, "unattached".

* * * *

The motor started up instantly, battery not weak at all, but nauseating exhaust fumes began to billow all around, so Hermie backed up and out of her space and drove out of the garage.

This being a work day he had the choice of driving up and down neighborhoods looking for a parking space that was not due for a street sweeping today; or heading for the unshaded parking in a nearby mall –– dozens of malls being nearby and dismally few shaded by trees, due to contagious "re-designs". He decided to head for the beach. On a work day there was sure to be some parking and the windows open to the ocean's breeze would make up for the dearth of shade trees.

The nearest beach front was Redondo. There was metered parking demanding, but since he was going to stay in the car, screw it.

"Either it's encrypted for a password, or it requires a certain computer or player," Hank had mentioned when he first tried and failed to play the CD.

There was a CD player in Lila's car, he had remembered when seeing all those discs displayed on his TV a couple hours ago. *"Patsy Cline", "The Phantom of the Opera",* some Arab music . . . *And this disc with no case or*

markings. This disc was not blank. It was left for her. He left it for her. Which is
why Hermie did not turn it over to Forensics or one of the attorney's, pro- or
con-.

He turned the motor off but left the power on, slid the disc into the player
slot. Immediately, he heard the disc spin, connect and a light turned on the
radio console, saying "Tracking".

He jumped, startled at the male voice that came over the speakers. A voice
deep, mellow, with the Middle Eastern accent that gentled the English from
England. It could only be Jordan Hashemi who spoke:

*"My dearest Ashwari, I watch you sleep, as always, and bless you with
my heart, my soul. This is the man who did not exist before you came.
This is the man who had no heart, no soul, no hope before you came. This
is the man who did not know anything of love or even friendship until
you came. That you allow me to love you is a constant astonishment.
That you love me is a gift from God, a gift I can never deserve but will
always treasure.*

*For a time, you and I and our boy did not exist. This kept us safe.
But now I know that there is a threat I have not been able to keep from
us. You and our boy have done everything I have asked of you to protect
us, but I fear everything may not be enough. Her hatred grows. This is
why I am giving you this, so that if anything happens to me -- and I pray
God it is only to me -- here is all you shall need to know to protect you
and our dear boy.*

*You will need to write some of these things down, it will be all you
need to access all that is required for your future."*

To Hermie's astonishment, Jordan Hashemi recited all the information
that had been invisible for so many years, all the information about their
"family": he listed whereabouts of Records of Marriage of him and Ashwari,
birth certificates and adoption records for their 'son'; passport information
for all three of them, immigration papers, banking information as to what
banks were paying what bills, for the condo, for his Century City office, even
for the constant rental cars he'd used. He named the banks and their account
numbers. *"They have been well paid to swear that we do not exist, but
these numbers will open our accounts to you."*

He named the bank Hermie had tried to crack: "There is no account here
for Lila Miller," he'd been told with a straight face. *Ha! I wonder how much
money bought that bald-faced lie.*

Jordan went on: *"That account, that bank is most important for you.
It is nearest you, in the event you have to flee. It is a safety deposit boxes
there that it will be of help to you both. Most important, my Dear One,
are my computer programs and codes . . ."*

Hermie jerked upright when Hashemi told her about his computer programs as if he knew someone was trying to figure them out.

"Tell them to look to the skies for the codes. The planets, the stars and the mathematics of their travels; they <u>*know*</u>*, they know how creation and destruction works."* And then he recited dozens of numbers and combinations of numbers and letters. *Jeezus, are they gonna need Stephen Hawking to figure this guy out?!*

Afterward, he went on: *"Presently, this disc can only be played by your car radio, but I have built another computer to play it. It is in our home. It is an old computer, it looks out of date, of no importance. No one shall give it a thought. If they open it for a search they will find our son's computer games and an old word processing program only, an old version of what they call 'Wordperfect'. There is what they once called a "floppy disc" among those of the games. It will show only the games unless you type in this code: 'ASHWARI IS HASHEMI ALWAYS, then the numbers of the letters for 'always': "A" is "1", "L" is "12", and so on. You must also press your thumb on the monitor screen. The machine will read your thumb-print and know that it is you who wants to know. Only you will be able to open this computer and its program of the skies. And only you will teach it to our son later on, if he wills.*

My Dearest One, I have given you all that you and our son shall need. Forgive me for the darkness I have brought around us. My love is so poor to repay you for yours.

Ashwari, I think there shall be a mistake in Islam, a mistake in Christians, a mistake in the Jews and all those other faiths. They all say that Paradise or Heaven will welcome the righteous when they die. But I am the most fortunate, I have Paradise and Heaven and Nirvana and all of them <u>*here*</u>*, in you and with you. And I swear by all the holy things that I will bring a wondrous life to you, to our son, to us.*

In so many nights like this I sit and watch you sleep, and you are such a wonder my tears flow with the joy of you. Remember when we first met and we shared so much of our history of sorrows and were so astonished to realize that none of it mattered, all of it made us possible.

"I kiss you and our son with all my love now and to come. As always, all things lead me to thee. This is from your Jordan Hashemi."

The disc suddenly went silent, then pushed half out of the player. He took it carefully out, tucked it into the plastic case. His eyes were moist, just short of a sniff of emotion. Sleeve, nose quickly got it under control.

"Warrant" crossed his mind, for just an instant, along with the problem of writing down the contents of the disc so he could show it to a judge, to Trots, to the Chief. But first to "Kevin".

That last thought decided it. This disc was "Kevin's" now. Only he had a right to it, the right to decide what to do with it. Even the codes Hashemi created to smash up Isis and the rest of those blood-letting monsters, the weapons Trots and the guv'ment were salivating for, those weapons were "Kevin's" now. He would decide who got them, what would be done with them. The experiences of his life — the good, the horrible — would shape his decisions once he recovered. And recover he will because his experiences included so much love.

Then, curiosity aflame and because he wanted to one-up the bald-faced liar at the bank who'd told him there was no account at all under the name Lila Miller, Hermie wrote down what he would need and went to the bank Hashemi mentioned, the only mention of safety deposit boxes.

His badge and the code convinced the bank's manager (thankfully, "Warrant" didn't cross his mind, or perhaps the code included reassurance that a Warrant was not required, thanks to Hashemi's obsessive planning). Then the oddity — after the Manager brought him an extremely large deposit box onto the table that took up a corner of the room, a clutch of keys jingled in his hand. He asked, "Would you like to see all the others?"

"'The others'? How many are there?"

He held up the bunch of keys: "Forty-two."

"Forty-two!?"

"Yes. We had to expand the room quite a bit. For Mr. Hashemi. But he gladly paid for the renovations. Such an elegant man."

"I see. No, just this one will be enough. For now."

The Manager nodded, relieved, and handed him the clutch of keys. "They are all numbered, should you reconsider. This is 'One'," he pointed to the engraved number on the key. As he left, he gestured to the wall device, "When you're finished or need assistance, just press the buzzer." and he locked the room behind him.

Tomb-like silence descended into the locked room, an instant, claustrophobic uneasiness descended on Hermie. *Take a peek and get the hell outta here.* He quickly shoved the key where it belonged and snapped open the metal box, whose lid squeaked as he lifted it.

LAPD Homicide Detective Herman Grabfelder had never fainted in his life, but he had to grab onto the table before he went flat-out *down*. It was the contents of the box: neat stacks of money, bills large and not-so with bright yellow bands announcing their count. Hermie did a quick shuffle and mental addition: *A million dollars in this one box. There are forty-two boxes. "ACH DU LIEBER!!"*

He was replacing and neatening up the stacks of bills and closing, locking the box when Hermie had a thought: *He must have put a million in every year, a birthday present to himself for them, his joy. And this year, his last year of giving, Jordan Hashemi was forty-two years old.*

CHAPTER THIRTY

"God hugs you."

Saint Hildegarde

Summer had come and gone, it was supposed to be Fall, but this being the climate-changed version of Los Angeles, the windswept day was soft and sunny, friendly-like, nobody thought about the icy blasts from Alaska that were overdue and thus sure to come soon. Only Detective Herman Grabfelder could smell ice on the friendly gusts, so he alone was warned.

High in the intense blue sky, two ravens were waltzing in wing-brushing tandem on thermal winds in and out of filmy clouds, caw-caw-ing with delight. The wind had tipped over several floral displays in the cemetery, splashes of red and orange and pink scattered on the real and healthy green grass. Hermie hoped that sight wasn't upsetting to the boy. "Kevin" had come so far these past months, but Hermie still feared setbacks. A contrast to the Harrisons, who had every confidence that "our boy" had recovered and every day released him further into the world, a world that was no longer fearful.

He had started school and was easily "catching up." Since he had never been to school and couldn't prove he'd been home-schooled, he'd had to take a test beforehand to see what class he was up to. He'd blown away the testers, they were tempted to send him straight into college; but the Harrisons demurred, thought it was best for "Kevin" to be around kids his own age for now, hopefully to make normal boyhood friends. So a compromise was reached -- when the school year started, "Kevin" was put into the Eleventh Grade and given advanced assignments by teachers who knew the gold to be mined from within this quiet, polite teenager. And he was still a star player on Hank O'Dell's baseball teams.

He was also seeing a therapist weekly, a plan the Harrisons "made do" because they feared "Kevin" might hold something back for fear of hurting

MELODY ORTENBURGER SUPPES

their feelings. They wanted him to have a stranger he could freely "unload" to, as Frank said.

On this breezy day, they were all standing close alongside "Kevin", the Harrisons wearing heavier coats than anyone else because they were Midwesterners and knew that when the sun started to tilt down the temperature would also start to go down. Hank O'Dell took up the other side, groomed to the max, having spent some of Hermie's largesse on a decent dress suit that not only fit him perfectly, but made him realize he was actually a grown-up, surprise-surprise. His hand rested on "Kevin's" shoulder, reassuringly.

Hermie stood a little apart, keeping watch, wondering if there'd be a reaction to the photo of Hashemi and Lila that he had purloined from the FBI's files. The photo of them seated at that glittering table, close together, looking at each other in happy conversation, in recognition, seeing so much in each other, seeing *All*. He had given it to 'Kevin' after taking him to a visit with Pierre Bonay, who still had Lila and Hashemi in his protective keeping. "Kevin" had chosen not to view them, saying, "I don't want to see them dead. Ever. I don't want them to be . . . that much gone." But he asked that a nosegay of violets be placed in both their hands, in memory of that last Mother's Day.

Now that photo of them, alive, happy, and so beautiful, was set into their tombstone. "Kevin" had asked if the photo could be set into the tombstone when Hermie brought him to Aristotle's stoneworks to create one. Aristotle shook his hand with a warm sympathy upon hearing that this frail-looking boy had to bury his parents. Pierre and Hermie had found these two side-by-side plots, near a tall, graceful pepper tree whose fern-like branches dappled shade down on the graves. On the other side, Hermie realized that another large tree was a Jacaranda. Green now, but after months to come it would be dressed in spectacular purple, not quite as purple as the two nosegays of violets being buried now, nor the two nosegays "Kevin" had in his hand.

He was very still for a moment, then he came close to carefully place violets on both sides of the tombstone. "Kevin" loved his parents so well, he knew how they wished to be remembered, with the names of their happiness: *"Ashwari Hashemi, Jordan Hashemi."* A delicate carving of flowers and leaves encircled their names and their photo. And below that was an inscription. When Hermie had heard it on the CD, he remembered reading it on a fragment of a card attached to violets that were crushed beneath jealousy and rage and a tire in the street. But "Kevin" remembered it because of Hashemi's making sure it was written on the card attached to that Mother's Day bouquet. So he asked for the inscription: *"All things lead me to thee."*

* * * *

Later, they were in the Harrison's car and everyone had just agreed to Frank's assessment that an ice cream cone would hit the spot right now. Hermie was up front in the passenger seat, Millie and Hank in back, sitting close on either side of "Kevin".

To see "Kevin" actually grin, with eyes seeing all the world unafraid and beaming, gave Millie the instinct that the time was right. She took his hand and said to everyone, "'Kevin' has a little surprise for you all."

Frank froze, stared, unsure, "Oh?" he said. And he couldn't help it -- he pulled the car over to the first empty spot on the curb, smack in front of a fire hydrant he didn't notice. "Oh?" he said again. "Is that right, now?" he added, being a Midwesterner. He was clearly braced, waiting and wondering whether to dread it.

"For real?" Without typing it, Hank lacked sufficient expressions.

Hermie turned in his seat in time to see "Kevin's" face pull on a resolve, almost like a courage. He, too, braced himself a little.

Millie's voice was so warm, so loving, so *sure*:, "'Kevin', what's your real name?"

Hermie flashed on the mention of adoption papers on that CD, Hashemi making Kevin his own son. And he knew now that the Harrison's had just recently started to wade through the endless paperwork and hearings required to adopt "Kevin".

"Kevin" took a breath and said quite calmly and quite freely: "My name is Jordan Ashwari . . . Harrison."

"Good for you, Jordie," Millie said, smacking a kiss on his cheek that made him blush with fun.

"That's a stand-up name, my boy," Frank said, emotionally, turned away to wipe his eyes, then realized: "For crying out loud -- a dad-blamed fire hydrant! Where the Sam Hill did *that* come from?" And he jammed the car in gear and drove on.

Hermie took a last look at "Kevin". *Of course, he was Jordan Ashwari Harrison. He was All of them. Now and forever.* To give his eyes a chance to dry, he turned away and said cheerfully, "I hope this place has butter pecan."

Jordie piped up, "I'm hoping for strawberry."

"Sounds good to me, if there's nuts on top." Millie said.

"I'm hoping for green tea," Hank sounded a little emotional himself, until Jordie lightly punched him in the shoulder and said, "You would!"

And Homicide Detective Herman Grabfelder looked out the window and rolled it all the way down. And only he caught the scent of 'happy" on the soft wind.

EPILOGUE

It came tucked inside an envelope from Aida: a smaller envelope with no return address, made out to "The Grabfelder" in pencil, in penmanship laborious. Inside there were some words that had been erased and then written over the erasures with extra care:

Dear The Grabfelder,

It is Lela, the mother of Amira who writes. Some mistakes because I am only learning more from when my Amira taught me.

I have the picture you made of the stone on her grave. With our happy picture on it. Aida sent me it. And Aida show me you have made a special place for me, beside my daughter when Allah calls me to her. I am most thankful to you!

And me, I go to school now, I can read every book I find almost! I write not so good, but I try again all the time.

My Amira now can see I am free, I am happy, I am much loved here. She is with me all the time, I feel her happy too.

We bless your name every day, Grabfelder, every day with much love. Many, many thank you.

We send our hearts,
Your Sisters Lela and Amira

He folded it carefully, making time for his rush of tears to calm. Then he tucked it into his wallet where he would see it, often, for all time.

THE END

Printed in the United States
By Bookmasters

Printed in the United States
By Bookmasters